IR

FORSAKEN DUTY

THE RED TEAM, BOOK 12

ELAINE LEVINE

This book is a work of fiction. Names, characters, businesses, places, events, and incidents are either the products of the author's imagination or used in a fictitious manner. Any resemblance to actual persons, living or dead, or actual events is purely coincidental.

Published by Elaine Levine
Copyright © 2017 Elaine Levine
Last Updated: February 12, 2018
Cover art by The Killion Group, Inc.
Cover image featuring Chase Ketron © Golden Czermak @ Furious Fotog
Editing by Arran McNicol @ editing720
Proofing by Carol Agnew @ Attention to Detail Proofreading

Print ISBNs:
ISBN-13: 978-1981222681
ISBN-10: 1981222685

FORSAKEN DUTY BLURB

THE RED TEAM, BOOK 12

The only truth Owen Tremaine's certain of is that everything in his life has been a lie. Not only is his former fiancée alive, but so is their son…a child he never knew existed. Raised as a fighter in the resistance against a violent and secretive cult, Owen abandons his team, his family, everything to extract the woman he once loved and the son he's never met from the clutches of his enemy.

Adelaide Jacobs has only loved one man…Owen Tremaine. She grew up in the long shadow he and her brother cast, toddling after them as much as her brother tolerated. Owen's visits were the best memories of her childhood…until the day he saw her as a woman. They had one night together before hell took over her life in a war that's framed her world ever since.

Now she's a fighter too, battling an unknown disease that consumes a little more of her each day. She'll never forgive her brother for bringing Owen into her hell. Is there enough time to find the cure so they can have the future they both thought they'd never have?

Or is now—this very moment—all the time they'll have?

~

Length: Approximately 450 pages
Ages: 18 & up (story contains sex, profanity, and violence)

Forsaken Duty (The Red Team, Book 12) is part of a serialized story that includes nine full-length novels and nine wedding novellas. This series is best read in order, starting with The Edge of Courage.

Join the conversation on Facebook: Visit Elaine Levine's War Room - http://geni.us/hxFk to talk about this book and all of her suspenseful stories!

OTHER BOOKS BY ELAINE LEVINE

O-MEN: LIEGE'S LEGION

LIEGE

RED TEAM SERIES

(This series must be read in order.)

1 The Edge of Courage

2 SHATTERED VALOR

3 HONOR UNRAVELED

4 KIT & IVY: A RED TEAM WEDDING NOVELLA

5 TWISTED MERCY

6 TY & EDEN: A RED TEAM WEDDING NOVELLA

7 ASSASSIN'S PROMISE

8 WAR BRINGER

9 ROCCO & MANDY: A RED TEAM WEDDING NOVELLA

10 RAZED GLORY

11 DEADLY CREED

12 FORSAKEN DUTY

13 MAX & HOPE: A RED TEAM WEDDING NOVELLA

14 OWEN & ADDY: A RED TEAM WEDDING NOVELLA

SLEEPER SEALS

11 FREEDOM CODE

MEN OF DEFIANCE SERIES

(This series may be read in any order.)

DEDICATION

It's not easy being married to an author. I couldn't do it, but somehow my husband makes it look like a breeze. He knows from my fits of paranoia just where I am in the story creation process. He remembers all the arcane facts about my characters that I tell him. I'm still trying to figure out what sandwiches have to do with the fictional love scenes I write, but whatever it is, he deserves them!

Barry, you're a one and only, forever kind of guy. I think I'll keep you.

A NOTE FROM THE AUTHOR

We begin *Forsaken Duty* at the point where *Deadly Creed* left off. To maximize your enjoyment of this serialized story, I highly recommend reading the series in order, starting with *The Edge of Courage* and including the Red Team wedding novellas, before beginning this book!

And make sure you never miss a book from me by signing up for my new release announcements at http://geni.us/GAlUjx.

—Elaine

WHEN WE LAST VISITED THE RED TEAM...

Here's a refresher for those of you who have read the previous Red Team books (skip this and go read them if you haven't yet!). This is where we left our heroes...

* * * * * Spoilers! * * * * *

- It's November, and the team is in their sixth month of investigation.
- The team's getting ever closer to discovering who King is.
- Owen has mysteriously gone AWOL with Jax.
- Jason Parker—Val's dad—announced everything that was happening was part of a game.
- While being held by Jafaar Majid, Wynn Ratcliff may have spotted the parents she thought had died long ago.
- Lion and his pride of watchers have been found, but Mr. Edwards has taken Owen's son.
- Yusef Sayed is still acting as the team's eyes and ears from his motel in Cheyenne, WY.

- Jafaar has outed Rocco (aka Khalid) as a Fed.
- Deputy Jerry is Jafaar's spy.
- Mandy and Ivy are pregnant.
- Casey still has a crush on Lion.

And now, we continue with **_Forsaken Duty_**…

1

Owen Tremaine hoped he'd survive the next punch. He kept his eyes closed, but couldn't shut out the pain. Life's bitter ironies. Addy Jacobs was alive...but he was going to die here, before he could see her again if he couldn't end Mr. Edwards' interrogation. Life fucking sucked. He laughed at his own morose thoughts. Wasn't like him to feel sorry for himself. This wasn't so bad. Not like the day she was taken from him. This was just physical, not a soul injury like that had been.

He'd gotten through that; he could get through this. For her.

He'd been some meathead's punching bag for what, a day? A week? How long had it been? What was it they were after? He tried to think through the pain. He could hear Jax's muffled shouts in another room. How far away was he? How many men were with Edwards?

He cracked his eyes open, trying to figure out where he was and how he got there. Oh yeah, the accident. Jax's car had been broadsided on a country road outside of Denver. They'd exchanged gunfire before a flashbang had been tossed under their SUV, knocking them down long enough for the others to take them. After that, he woke up in this hellhole, tied to a rusty steel chair in the middle of what looked like an old jail cell in some long-abandoned piece-of-shit property, if he were to judge by the peeling paint and the persistent sound of dripping water. He wondered if he was in the tunnels somewhere.

He slowly straightened in his seat. Who knew how long of a break he'd have before they came back to him? If he was going to act, now was the time. He tugged against the ropes on his right ankle, once again maneuvering his foot to the support bar connecting the front to the back of the chair. Wedging his boot in the weakened corner, he used his other foot to push the chair and himself up a few inches, then slammed down on the one leg. The rope felt like a garrote around his ankle. Didn't matter. He had to get free. Had to get to Jax. He did it again and again until the chair's decaying support bar gave way. He repeated the motion with his other foot, breaking that bar too.

He sat for a minute, letting the pain wash through him, listening to hear if the bastards who'd been torturing them were coming back. When he didn't hear them, he leaned the chair off one leg and wiggled his tied ankle free, then did the same with his

2

other leg. That was all he could manage before he heard them coming his way.

He tucked his ankles close to the chair legs so no one would notice he'd gotten them free. The meatheads came back in, followed this time by a trim, middle-aged man with blond hair and blue eyes. His nose was too small for his face. His skin was weathered. Bastard apparently liked the sight of a man beaten to jelly, for he smiled at Owen.

"I see you're awake again. Wonderful. Shall we start over?"

Edwards was the man who'd carved up Wynn's hand. The man who'd strung up Ace. Probably one of the costumed observers to Fiona's attempted initiation. He was the devil himself, and he had a blood price on his head among Owen's team.

Owen would be quite pleased to collect it.

He closed his eyes, knowing the bastard fed on negative emotion—fear, anger, hopelessness. He stuffed those emotions away, starving Edwards of his jollies. "You go ahead. I can't remember what we were talking about."

The edge in Edwards' voice was the only indication Owen had hit his mark. "Who's funding you?"

"I already answered that. Pay attention, man."

Edwards nodded toward one of his paid fists. Owen took a hit in the jaw. He looked up at the guy, visualizing a steel chair leg going through his chest.

"Answer it again," Edwards said through clenched teeth.

"Family money."

"What family?" Edwards asked.

"What does it fucking matter?" Owen's hands were almost free from the rope binding them behind him. He wasn't about to sell out his investors. Val was a minority shareholder. He could take care of himself, but Senator Jacobs, who'd provided the other minority stake in angel funds, couldn't. Beyond that, the government had footed the bill for this lucrative contract from their dark ops budget.

Before the goon standing near him could throw another punch, Owen said, "Uncle Sam's family. It's classified. Don't you have friends in high places? Go ask them. By the way, while I have your attention, where's my boy?"

"How would I know?"

"You took him from Addy."

Edwards went absolutely still. "She still has her boy. For now."

So it was true; Addy had had a son. "Word on the street is you put him with the watchers."

"What makes you think he's yours?"

"Good intel. Where is he?"

Edwards nodded toward his hired muscle. "I'm done here. Finish him. He's got no info for me."

Owen leaned back and braced himself by gripping the bars of the seatback so he could kick out. He hit the man's chest with his heels, knocking him back several steps. The other guy rushed forward. Owen twirled to his feet, slamming him with the steel chair.

In the seconds that opened for him, Owen finished freeing his hands, then kicked in the other side of the broken bottom rung, separating it from the chair. He grabbed it in time to shove it upward into the guy's chest cavity, using his own forward momentum to impale him. Owen shoved his body into the second guy, then ran after Edwards, but he was too late.

Edwards had already rushed out of the jail cell, leaving the door locked behind him. The second guy charged toward Owen. He ducked. The guy's fist hit the steelwork of the front wall, shaking it loose. Owen punched him in the gut then double-fisted the back of his head when he bent over. He slumped down, exposing the knife in his holster. Owen grabbed it and, fisting the guy's hair, lifted his head and sliced his neck.

Shoving him aside, Owen looked around the room, assessing his situation.

The door was locked, and he had no key. Neither man had the door key or wallets, but one had car keys. He pocketed them then gave the cell bars a tug. Flakes of rusted metal and paint fell away. Two bars were loose. Owen looked around the room again. His gaze fell on the busted chair. He broke off the other support he'd loosened, then used it to pry the compromised cell bars free, giving him enough room to climb up and squeeze through.

He rushed toward the area where he'd heard Jax, finding him three cells down. Owen had to move fast —he didn't know where Edwards had gone or if he was coming back with reinforcements. Jax was slumped over in the chair he was tied to. The door to his cell was locked, too. Owen used the knife he'd taken to fish around in the big skeleton keyhole. It worked. The gate came loose.

He hurried over to check his friend, who looked as mangled as Owen felt. At least he had a pulse. Owen cut the ropes binding him. Jax was in a fist-induced stupor. Owen wasn't certain, in the state he was in himself, if he'd be able to carry Jax out...or even drag him.

He knelt in front of Jax and gently lifted his head. "Hey...you in there? Anything broken? Can you move?" They had to get out before Edwards came back.

Jax instantly came alert, ready to fight.

"Whoa. Whoa," Owen said. "Just me. We need to move out. Can you walk?"

"Owen?"

"Yeah."

"Edwards..."

"Is gone. For now. We gotta go." He pulled Jax's arm over his shoulder and hoisted him up from his chair. They moved as fast as they could down the hall to a flight of stairs. Up was the only direction to go. It was dark in that part of the building—no windows anywhere and no lights on. Owen had no idea what time of day it was, where they were, or what the hell they were going to do next.

They made it to an exit. A chain had been cut and

now draped from one of the push bars on the industrial door. It was night outside. The climb out of the hellhole had let Owen's eyes adjust to dark. They were nowhere. Absolutely fucking nowhere. The building was in the middle of wide-open prairie, inside a tall, walled space. No lights shone anywhere around them, not even on the outside of the building.

A single SUV sat in front on the overgrown driveway. Owen used the key fob to see if it belonged to the guy below. The lights came on. He ran with an arm around Jax to the vehicle and managed to get him inside, laying him across the backseat. Owen jumped into the driver's seat and started the SUV up. The building they'd just left was lit up in the headlights. It was a stately brick monolith with gothic arches over the front and side doors. The headlights illuminated a sign over the grand front door: Hawthorne Sanitarium, est. 1878. Jesus. The guards could have just left them there to die and no one would ever know before they were a pile of bones.

"Hang on, bud," Owen said as he got them the hell out of there…wherever *there* was.

WHEN THE SUN CAME UP, Owen changed directions, heading west. He knew the moment Jax woke up from the string of foul words he growled. They were so far east that there wasn't a hint of the mountains, only miles and miles of parched prairie grass and dirt road in the predawn light.

Owen looked over his shoulder. "How you feeling?"

"I need to take a piss. And I could use a gallon of water."

Owen stopped the SUV. "The piss we can do. Water, not so much."

"Where are we?"

"No fucking clue. I'm gonna need gas soon. I got no cash, no cards, and no ID to get cash. How about you?"

"Yeah. I got my wallet. They didn't take it."

Owen pulled over. They both got out and relieved themselves in the dust on the side of the road. The sound of their streams made Owen's thirst even worse. Afterward, he looked in the SUV's back hatch, searching for bottled water. The trunk was empty. He slammed the door then glared at Jax. "What the fuck happened? How did Edwards know where we were?"

"No idea."

Something about Jax's quick answer made Owen question everything about him. If Jax weren't in as bad a shape as Owen, it would have been easy to believe his old friend was in with the Omnis. Owen also found it hard to believe that Edwards didn't know where his funding came from. Sure, it was funneled through a couple of dummy corporations, but not so deeply hidden that a patient and persistent investigator couldn't figure out Jax's dad and Val were his partners—especially an investigator with deep Omni pockets and plenty of time.

At Owen's continued stare, Jax's eyes narrowed. "You think I had something to do with it? Like I *like* getting pulverized?"

Owen sighed. Fuck. Edwards was sneaky as hell. The Omnis probably had someone watching Winchester's, since it was a popular hangout with Owen's crew. They were likely tracked leaving the bar that night.

"You hear that?" Jax asked.

Owen tried, but couldn't hear anything. "No. My ears are still ringing."

"It's a highway. Or at least a paved road."

"Where?"

Jax listened for a minute then pointed in the direction they were headed. "Let's stay headed west."

They got back into the SUV. Owen didn't press Jax for answers. He needed to rehydrate, sleep, and eat something before anything Jax said would make sense. They found the road Jax had heard. It wasn't a highway, just a two-lane country road. But there was heavy truck traffic, which made Owen fairly certain at one end or the other they'd hit a gas station. Eventually, they pulled into a little town that didn't have a single traffic light but did have a gas station.

Owen used Jax's cash to get them some food and water while he filled up. The girl behind the counter stared at him in horror.

"You want me to call an ambulance, mister?" she asked.

"No." He managed a laugh. "My buddy and I were off-roading at a friend's place. Guess helmets shouldn't have been optional."

An older lady joined the convo, eyeing Owen like he was trouble. "Little old to be learning that, doncha think?"

Owen laughed again as he set the money on the counter. "Was a helluva weekend."

"It's Thursday." The clerk punched in his purchase and gave him change.

Fucking Thursday. They'd been questioned for four days. He took his case of water and sandwiches and returned to the SUV.

"It's Thursday," he said to Jax as he handed him a water bottle.

"Yeah, I saw the date on the pump." They guzzled down a bottle each, then took a couple more before heading back down the road. This time, Jax was driving. He turned south out of town.

"Where are we going?" Owen asked.

"I know where we are now. I got a place we can lay low for a bit."

"I don't want to lay low. I want to see Addy."

"In time."

"No. Now."

"You go see her like you are right now, you'll scare the shit out of her. She's safe, but we aren't. I need to dump this vehicle, get a phone, and sleep for about a week."

"A night. Not a week. We've already lost four days."

"I'll take it."

Owen dozed off. The day was well into the afternoon when he woke again. They made another pit stop, then ate the sandwiches he'd bought at the last gas station.

"So where are we headed?" Owen asked when they got back in the SUV.

"I have a place an hour west of Denver."

"What's your status with the Red Team?" Owen asked.

"I'm on a special assignment for the senator."

"You were Ace's handler."

Jax nodded.

"You gave her Adelaide's picture."

Jax neither confirmed nor denied that statement.

"What happened to the boys Ace recovered? The watcher groups."

"I'll show you soon."

"Why did you direct Ace to find them?"

"Because King was using them as his private lab rats. I had to get them away from him. That's why I got Lion's group vaccinated. And it's why the Friends kids and others from his various cults were targeted with the smallpox; King had no one else to test it on."

Owen's eyes narrowed. Jax had sent Ace to Wolf Creek Bend well after he'd already found Lion's pride himself. He'd had them inoculated at least a month before she got there. "You already knew about Lion before Ace got to town. You didn't send her there because of the watchers."

Jax looked Owen in the eye. "So I passed one of my operatives off to you. What of it?"

"Why?"

"You were close to finding the tunnels. She needed justice. It was all coming to a head." Jax shrugged. "It was time."

Owen doubted that line of reasoning, but let it go for now. "Is it true that I have a son?"

"It's true."

"Where is he?"

"He was with Lion's watchers. I don't know where he is now—I don't know where Lion's pride is now. They were moved before I could get them out."

"What's his name in the pride?"

"Beetle."

"You're sure he's mine?"

"The DNA said so."

Owen looked out the window. Every part of his body hurt. His head wasn't on straight. He needed a good night's sleep, more food and water, and a long, hot shower. If pushed hard now, he'd make a mistake, compromise himself.

He still wasn't sure which side Jax was on, but if they weren't on the same one, then he'd gone through hell just to make it look like they were.

A few hours later, they made several turns onto

dirt roads in the foothills northwest of Denver before going down a long drive in the middle of a patch of evergreens. Their headlights showed an old, nondescript, one-story farmhouse, like so many others up and down the Front Range. There was a black Expedition parked out front. No lights were on in the place.

Owen checked Jax, wondering if he was expecting anyone. He looked as tired as Owen but showed no signs of tension. The door unlocked when Jax reached for the knob. Lights came on inside. Owen didn't have to look around to know there were cameras monitoring them and that access had been remotely granted.

Inside, the little farmhouse had been fully renovated. New kitchen, small dining area, new living room with a wall of bookshelves and a TV. Beyond that, there were two bedrooms, both with their own en suites. Simple, clean, and complete with two dinners sitting under warming caps. Owen lifted a brow at Jax.

"I called ahead while you were in the bathroom at our last stop. You'll find clothes in your room too." Jax shrugged. "What? Surprised I have my own crew?"

"No. I don't know you at all anymore."

"Fine. You can eat, shower, sleep, whatever the hell you want. I'm gonna clean up. You need a doctor?"

"No. You?"

"No. We'll talk in the morning. I gotta crash."

Owen went into the second bedroom. A phone and a change of clothes were on the bed—a pair of jeans, black boxer briefs, and a white T-shirt. He and Jax were about the same size. Good thing, because Owen hadn't packed for a trip. Toiletries were in the bathroom. Probably wouldn't be shaving for a few days. His face was filled with cuts and bruises. His mouth and jaw were swollen. He looked like road kill. Maybe Jax was right about giving themselves a few days before going to see Addy.

No, fuck that. Owen wasn't waiting. Not a goddamned minute more than he had to.

He ate his dinner, beef and broccoli on rice. Nothing too hard to chew for his sore jaw. He didn't have an appetite, in part from the beating he'd taken, but also because they hadn't been fed the four days they were being questioned—his body had gotten used to having no food. Owen looked at the phone, considering checking in with his team. He knew the phone Jax had given him was keyed in to whatever system he had rigged up. Owen didn't know what his team might reveal on the other end. And truthfully, he didn't want them involved; if he was walking into a trap, they couldn't be anywhere near him.

After dinner, Owen had to decide between sleep or a shower. The bed, with its clean sheets, looked like heaven, but he needed that shower first. The hot water was soothing. He let it spill over him, wash the past few days away.

When he got out, he dressed. Who the hell knew

what fun new torture would come as soon as he let his guard down; he didn't want to face it naked.

He got into bed. His body was screaming. He wondered if he had a broken rib. Addy slipped into his mind. He thought of their childhood together, remembered watching her mature, feeling an unholy hunger for her, wondering if she'd like him when she was a woman.

She was fifteen when he and Jax graduated from West Point and took their commissions in the Army. She'd been eighteen when he and Jax came to her high school graduation party. Twenty-one when she got her college degree.

Twenty-one the day their lives started and ended.

Owen thought back through the small bit of info Jax had told him about her. Not once had he actually said Addy was still alive. For all Owen knew, Jax was taking him to see Addy's grave.

That thought caused him worse pain than Edwards' goons had.

He'd lived so long without a heart that it hurt to think of having one once again...and it would be worse to learn his fresh hopes were just smoke and mirrors.

He threw the covers off and stormed into Jax's room. It was dark. "Wake up, you son of a bitch." He gripped Jax's throat and squeezed, lifting him from his mattress.

Jax didn't fight back.

"Tell me she's alive."

Jax broke free of Owen's grip. He stared at Owen, then scooted himself up to lean back on his pillows.

The delay was all the answer Owen needed. A tear spilled down his swollen cheek. Jesus fucking Christ. He was glad his team wasn't here to see him break. Addy was the perfect way to torture him. He'd give his soul away to have her back in his life.

His shoulders slumped as he sat there on the edge of Jax's bed. So many people he'd thought dead had emerged from the shadows of the Omni World Order that it had been a short jump to believe that Addy would, too.

"She is alive, O. But different."

"How so?"

"We had four days of tender focus from the Omnis. She had years."

"What happened to her?"

Jax shook his head. "I can't… I gotta leave that to her to say or not."

"But she's alive?"

He nodded. "She doesn't want to see you. When I finally found her, after everything she'd gone through, I couldn't violate that trust."

Owen left Jax's room and went back to his. She was alive. It wasn't much to go on…and it was everything. He'd take it.

2

Twenty-five Years Ago
Fairfax, Virginia

Owen looked out the window from the senator's gym. His and Jax's mixed martial arts class wasn't due to start for another half-hour, which suited him fine. The two of them had been practicing the whole week in preparation... and Owen had the bruises to show for it.

Jax's sister was outside on the playground. Alone. The hairs lifted on Owen's neck in a way he'd long ago learned was an alert to danger. He walked outside and went straight to the playground where she was halfheartedly swinging. He looked around for her nanny and found her relaxing in the shade at a table about a hundred feet away, too far away to get to Addy if trouble came.

Owen slipped into the swing next to Adelaide. "What's shakin', short stack?"

She gave him a baleful glare. Without straightening out of her slump, she spread her arms wide, indicating the gossamer costume she wore. Her nanny must have been letting her watch princess and knight fairytales again.

"I'm a princess, Owen, not a pancake."

He grinned at her. "Why the long face? It's a beautiful day."

"Wendelly's friends are coming in for the class and they didn't bring their families. I have no one to play with. I can't be a princess without a prince."

"Oh. Well, I'll be your prince."

"You can't be my prince. You can only be my knight."

"Why's that?"

"Because Bruce Williamson is my prince."

Bruce was the younger brother of one of their MMA classmates. "Ohhh. You sweet on him?"

All kinds of color flooded her face. She looked away, hiding her unsuccessful attempt not to smile.

"Never mind. I'll be your knight, Addy."

She frowned at him, the glow she'd had seconds ago quickly receding. "I don't like that name. Everyone calls me that."

"It's just a nickname."

"I want you to call me something else."

"But 'Addy' comes from Adelaide."

"So does 'Laidy.'"

Owen laughed. It was easy to slip into her make-believe world—its rules were so clear to her that he had only to follow her lead. He got off the swing and went to stand in front of her, where he gave her a low bow. "Tell me, my Laidy, how I may serve you today?"

She straightened in her seat and beamed at him. "There's a dragon attacking the kingdom. You must go kill it."

"Must I? Even dragons have a right to live."

She waved her hand as she glared at him. "That's not how this works, Owen. You have to do what I say. I'm the princess."

"Oh. Right. And that's Sir Knight to you, my Laidy."

"The dragon is blowing fire and burning people. You must stop it."

He bowed again. "As you wish, my Laidy. But I have no weapon."

"It's there." She pointed to a cardboard box with props from all of her make-believe worlds: costumes, plastic guns, swords, lightsabers, stuffed animals, dolls.

He grabbed a sword then faced her again. "Where's the dragon?" God help him if he started slashing at the air when she thought the dragon was someplace else. He looked where she pointed; Jax was closing in on them. Owen glanced back at Addy. "Is Wendell your dragon?"

She nodded vigorously.

"That would have been nice to know ahead of time," he muttered as he waited for Jax to join them.

He didn't have to wait long.

"What are you doing?" Jax asked, stopping only when he was nose to nose with Owen. Though they were born the same year, Jax had almost eight months on him. It showed in his size and dexterity. Owen's dad said what Owen lacked in size and strength against Jax, he made up for in wits. Owen never was sure what that meant, but he'd gladly take any advantage he could muster at the moment, facing Jax with Addy's plastic sword.

"Shut up and play along," Owen growled between clenched teeth. Everything with Jax was a competition. He judged everything based on physical strength.

"Why would I? Why would you?" He gave Owen a disgusted look. "We aren't babies."

"I never said you were a baby."

"Well, I'm saying you are."

Owen laughed and pushed Jax back. "Prepare to be skewered, dragon."

Jax's eyes narrowed. He stepped back, out of the way of Owen's wicked sword thrusts. At the prop box, he grabbed a lightsaber and began fighting back. Owen laughed. They both got good swings in.

Off in the distance, Owen could hear the sounds of their sensei and some other adults coming out of the dojo. The kids' class was about to start. He supposed that Jax heard it too, for the tenor of their play changed. Jax knocked Owen's sword out of his hand then gave him an evil grin as he thrust forward. Owen twisted so the lightsaber slipped between his arm and body, then began to dramatically fall to his death.

Addy screamed and rushed over to him. She threw herself across his body and wept. "Get up! Get up, Sir Knight! Get up!" She yanked on his clothes, but when Owen didn't stir, she looked over her shoulder and shouted at Jax, "I hate you!"

Owen sat up, holding her close. "Whoa, my Laidy. You can't hate him. He's no dragon. He's just your brother."

She looked up at him with tears sticking to her eyelashes. "He killed you."

Owen smiled. "Not yet, he hasn't."

Her chin trembled. She threw her arms around his neck and squeezed tight. "Owen!"

He rubbed her little back, holding her until her gasps settled out. "You're all right. I'll live to fight your dragons another day, my Laidy."

3

Owen's room was bright with sunlight when he woke next. The house was silent. The smell of bacon was probably what had roused him. He looked at the phone Jax had given him. It was almost 9:30 a.m. He woke fast, realizing he'd almost slept through the entire morning.

He jumped out of bed, ignoring the pain that caused his body. He went to the bathroom, then washed his hands and held his burning face in the cold water pooled in his hands. He looked worse today than he had last night, not that he gave a fuck about his appearance. It was just that this was the face Addy was going to see for the first time in a decade.

He walked barefoot into the living room. The house was cold. Apparently, heat was optional here. Someone had cooked breakfast—a plate was left on the counter with plastic wrap over it. Eggs, home fries and bacon. A pot of coffee was still hot in the coffee maker. Owen's stomach growled. He poured a cup of coffee.

He looked around and saw packed go bag, with a black puffer jacket lying on it, sitting on the dining room table. Next to it was a SIG Sauer 9mm and a couple full mags. A folded outfit that included a gray cashmere sweater, jeans, underclothes, and hiker boots was also there, next to a note that read, "Helo arrives at 1000." Under the note were five one-hundred dollar bills.

Helo to where? Addy's? He bellowed out Jax's name, but received no answer. He checked his room and other places around the little cabin. No Jax. Checking the clock on the stove he, saw it was half past 9. He nuked his breakfast and scarfed it down, then changed into the clothes that had been laid out on the table.

Right at 1000, the helo came in somewhere behind the house. The SUV he and Jax had taken from the sanitarium was gone. So was the Expedition that had been parked out front last night. Jax's crew had been busy.

Owen went around back and walked up to the chopper. He tossed his bag in the back and climbed in next to the pilot. Once he was buckled in, they took off. "Where are we headed?"

"Winstead Castle, up on Saddle Notch Ridge in Wyoming, sir."

The flight took less than two hours. They set down on a helipad in the middle of a bare pasture a little distance from a huge stone mansion perched on the top of a mountain. While they were in the air, he'd seen that it was a V-shaped building with two wings and a massive conservatory in the middle. At the ends of both wings, and at the point where they connected, were tall towers. The front tower was about double the size of the other two. Not the sort of a building Owen would have expected to see at the top of a jagged ridge line in this remote wilderness.

The helo took off when Owen was halfway to the house. Great. What if Addy wasn't home? What if she completely booted him off her property. He had no idea what his reception was going to be. The road down from the helipad ended in a wide gravel circle with an island of skeletal lilacs and other shrubs in the middle.

And wouldn't you know, Jax was sitting in the middle of the wide front stairs leading to the huge double front doors.

"Didn't feel like flying in together?" Owen asked.

"I wanted to come ahead so I could let Addy know you were on your way," Jax said.

"What is this place?" Owen asked.

"Winstead Castle. A nineteenth-century industrialist built it as some kind of retreat. Something to do with the springs nearby and big game hunting. The Omnis bought it after the Second World War and restored it. Addy got it in her divorce settlement."

That caught Owen's attention. "Who did she marry?"

"You'll have to ask her that. And everything else you want to know. It's her story to tell. I'll wait here."

"Why?"

"I told you. It's time for me to bow out. Go talk to her."

ADDY WAS ALERTED about her visitor by a phone call from the butler. He was here. Owen Tremaine. Her brother had brought him despite her wishes. Despite everything Owen had done to her.

Jax only this morning said he trusted Owen, but Addy still didn't.

She wasn't a fool—she'd known it would be only a matter of time before he'd come to gloat. She'd had years to prepare for this, and still she was unready. She changed her clothes, put some jewelry on, and pulled on the wig that best represented what her hair had looked like before it all fell out. She was presentable, but nowhere near ready. She went down her wing and out to the grand entryway that took up two floors and an entire tower of the mansion.

She saw Owen. He was tall and blond, looking at the paintings that filled the formal entryway like a gallery, paintings she no longer even noticed. He must have heard her, for he looked up. She almost ran back to her room. His face was battered. Who would dare to do that?

What had changed in the Omni world that brought him here?

She regained her composure quickly and continued down the marble stairs. She stepped off the bottom stair and paused, studying him, wondering what his presence meant. She felt outside of herself. He was here. *Owen.* The boy she'd worshiped as a girl, the guy she'd fantasized about as a teenager, the man she'd known as a woman, the monster she now hated. He was here, following her from the foyer into the blue salon.

Standing in the middle of the room, she faced him. For a moment, they just glared at each other. His eyes were still the pale blue she remembered—colder maybe. She squared her shoulders.

He lifted his hand, letting his palm touch her face. She waited for the pain, waited for him to dig his fingers into her skin, waited for him to bare his teeth as he spewed vile words. The threats. The—

"Laidy." His voice broke on the nickname he'd given her decades ago, a play on her name that he'd used when he'd pretended to be her knight in shining armor. He caught her face in both hands. His nostrils flared. "My Laidy." His voice was a hoarse whisper.

Tears filled her eyes. Her fingers wrapped around his wrists, at first to keep him from ripping at her face, then to feel his hands, remember for an instant the man she'd thought he was. How she wished things were different.

He dropped his hands and wavered on his feet,

then pivoted and walked out of the salon, out of the foyer, letting the big front door slam behind him.

All the air she hadn't dared breathe left her in a rush. She stood there, frozen... Too soon, he came back in.

"Your brother's leaving," Owen said.

"Wendell comes and goes as he pleases." Apparently, Owen was staying.

She stepped away, dragging two fingers across the back of the sofa, grounding herself as she strolled around the outer rim of the room toward a credenza with a tray of glasses and a couple of cut crystal decanters. The sofa wasn't much protection, but it was something between her and him, something more than a few feet of air.

She'd kept Balcones on hand ever since her brother had begun staying here off and on. Not because he liked it, but because he'd said Owen did. She was, as always, torn between yearning for the boy she'd worshiped and the thing he'd become.

"Care for a glass of whiskey?" she asked.

Owen stood in the middle of the room, watching her. "You have Balcones?"

"I do. Wendell prefers it."

Addy kept her back to Owen, using it as a shield to hide the fact that her hands shook as she poured out two fingers into a small whiskey glass. She took a couple of fortifying breaths, to steady herself before delivering his glass. He didn't know that she knew all about him. Sometimes words were the only shield a person had. Not space or time or the bliss of a forgetful memory; no, words were all that could keep a person sane.

She gestured toward a slipcovered white armchair, offering him a seat. She took its mate, thankful for the cherry table separating the two chairs.

Owen did not sit down. He threw back his whiskey, then glared at her as he slammed the glass on the table. He straightened and shook his head. She held her composure together through sheer will and long years of practice.

"Why are you here, Owen?"

The question made his eyes widen. The violence in his gaze hit her like a physical blow. Perhaps she should bow and show him the deference he surely felt he deserved. Her husband had made her do that often enough that it held little meaning for her.

A harsh laugh broke from him. He grabbed his glass and walked over to the credenza to pour himself another. He didn't drink it, though. He just stared into the middle of it.

Why was he angry with her? Hadn't she done everything they'd ever asked of her, ever forced on her? She'd given her husband two sons. Maybe Owen was angry because she drew the line at the Omnis taking her boys. Maybe he was angry because she'd reached out to her father. Interacting with the outside world was strictly forbidden once you were inside the Omnis. Maybe he refused to recognize the settlement

Wendell had brokered for her. Maybe he wanted this property back.

He could have it all. But not her sons. Never her sons.

OWEN STARED into the amber liquid. He'd lost his balance. The woman in this room with him now was no one he knew. She was cold and composed and distant. He'd given up his whole life for her, and she felt nothing for him. Jax had said the Omnis had fucked her over. What she was now was Owen's fault. He should have known the extent of the games the Omnis played, even a decade ago. He'd been raised in their shadow.

He looked at Addy. How the hell did one communicate with someone under these circumstances? He didn't know her, though they shared their childhoods. Part of them, anyway.

Maybe he should just accept that she was a stranger. A dying stranger. Maybe she was like someone who'd suffered a traumatic brain injury and had lost access to her memories. Maybe the brainwashing they'd done on her was the same level as a brain injury.

He went back over to her, tamping his anger down. No matter how this played out, anger—and a general loss of self-control—would not assist him now. He sat on the sofa and faced her. Her features were carefully arranged in a serene mask. Her composure made him feel like a deranged asshole. How many of those had she seen in the last decade that facing one now was routine for her?

Start at the beginning, he supposed, at the point where they lost themselves. "Tell me what you remember about the day you were taken," he said.

Pain flicked through the edges of her eyes. Her gaze slipped to his mouth, then his chin, then the hand that held his whiskey. She shook her head. "No. I have no desire to slip back into those days."

"Tell me about our son."

She gasped. "He's not your son. He's mine."

Owen drew a long breath, centering himself. "He's my flesh and blood too."

"We were together one night, Owen. It's not enough to conceive."

"Once is all it takes. You'll remember the condom I used broke." She waved that away with a flash of her hand, but he persisted. "Jax collected Augie's DNA. I am his father."

Addy's eyes widened. Her nostrils flared on a broken gasp. "Is that why...is that why they took him?"

"I don't know why they took him. It could be."

"Do you know where he is?"

"I believe he's with a group of boys who live inside the Omni world. These boys are called watchers. Their group is a pride. This particular pride is run by a boy named Lion. He's a strong leader. If Augie is in Lion's pride, then he's in as good a place as can be until we retrieve him."

She stared at him, then blinked. Her gaze darted about him, the sofa, the room as if energy was zinging around inside her like a tiger in a cage four sizes too small. "Wendell mentioned his theory that Augie had been taken into one of the watcher groups. I didn't know it had been confirmed." She lifted her crystalline blue eyes to his. "He said they named him Beetle. I wonder why?"

"It seems all the boys in prides get animal or insect names. Perhaps it has to do with a certain trait of theirs or a role the pride needs to have filled." Did she really not know these things…or was she playing a role to throw him off some scent?

"Why did you name your son after me if you didn't know he was mine?" Owen asked.

She lifted a shoulder. "Defiance, perhaps."

Her eyes came back to his. Each time they did, a frisson slipped across his skin and down his spine. It was uncanny, as if, while the shell of her still looked like the woman he knew, the soul of her had been swapped out for someone else's. Who was this woman sitting before him?

"Of course, that was before I understood who you were," she said.

Owen frowned. "Who am I?"

She gave him a cryptic little smile then stood. "Why are you here, Owen?"

She'd make a helluva politician, so expert was her

ability to say nothing. He stood as well, and when she started to move toward the door, he caught her arm at the crook of her elbow. Because he was touching her, he felt her whole body stiffen. He didn't let her go. Instead, he turned her to face him.

"We're not finished."

She didn't speak. Didn't resist. Her face resumed its blank mask as she silently regarded him. Owen had no idea what was happening inside her head...as was no doubt her intention.

"I'm here because of you," he said. The shadows had deepened around her eyes. She looked exhausted.

Her brows lifted. "Oh. Why?"

Why? Fucking *why*? Because she was his life. Though he'd believed she'd been killed a decade ago, she was still his first and last thought every day. She was the meter he'd measured every other woman by. She was why, though he might have accepted a sex partner in his life, he'd never loved anyone again.

She was as much a part of him as he was.

"How long are you staying?"

He studied her eyes, seeing nothing in them he recognized. "I don't know. Until Jax gets back, I guess."

She gave him a polite nod. "Then I'll have a room made up for you." She pulled free and walked out of the room, leaving him empty and confused and angrier than ever.

4

Addy made it out to the foyer and up the stairs, slipping behind a closed set of double doors leading into her wing of the house before collapsing against the moiré-papered wall, overtaken by the shakes. Her hands trembled. She flapped them about, releasing the energy pent up in her.

The Owen she thought she knew, the man she remembered—the real one—was here. Here. In her house. She could almost believe in him again. He'd said he'd come for her. She imagined he was angry at losing her to the world beyond the Omnis. She closed her eyes and huffed a laugh. As if she could ever rejoin the real world. This half existence she lived between the Omnis and the outside world was the closest she could come to freedom.

Maybe she'd never been in the real world at all.

Her little boy poked his head out from one of the doors in her hallway. "Mommy?"

"Troy." She smiled at him.

He ran toward her and wrapped his arms around her waist. "Are you all right?" he asked.

The question cut her to the quick. She was the one who should be worrying about him, not the other way around. She brushed his thick brown hair back from his forehead and smiled into his light brown eyes. "Of course. I'm fine. You needn't worry about me."

His little face was starting to look more like a boy's face and less like a toddler's. He was almost six years old. Close to the age Augie was when they took him. A terrible thought occurred to her: had Owen come for Troy?

"How are your studies going today?" she asked.

He huffed an impatient sigh, his face contorted to show his exasperation. "We were learning to read this morning. I don't like reading."

"That's not true. You like it when I read to you."

"I have to go back to Ms. Denton. We're on math now. Are you going to nap? You look tired."

Again her son was caring for his mother. It wasn't fair at all that this was his life. "I am. We'll play a little when I wake up."

"Okay. I'll see you later. Have a nice sleep."

She watched him head down the hall to his classroom. She missed Bonnie, the nanny and companion they'd had before her divorce. Addy wasn't particularly fond of the tutor her brother had brought in, but she was giving the woman a chance. She was very stern and didn't seem to enjoy children very much. But Troy was making progress with his studies.

Addy wondered if there was any way she could keep Troy and Owen separate while he was staying here. That was probably a waste of energy. It wasn't as if Owen didn't know about her son. He knew everything.

OWEN LOST track of how long he stood in the middle of Addy's blue salon. Long enough, he supposed, for his room to be made up, as he learned from the butler, who introduced himself as Spencer Hudson.

"I'll escort you there now, if you like, sir."

Owen looked at him, wondering if he was a new hire or if he went back to the days of Omni employment. "Thank you." They crossed the foyer and went to the east wing. "This is an unusual home to find in a location like this. Do you know its history?"

"Oh, indeed. Mr. Winstead made his fortune in the 1849 gold rush in California. He became quite the industrialist and decided to build a monument to himself, an elegant place where he could entertain the nation's elite. Being the businessman that he was, he decided to open the castle to wealthy travelers who came to take the waters and gentlemen who wished to hunt. Sadly, he only lived here a decade after it was completed. His heirs formalized this estate into a business, which continued until the Great Depression, when many of its clientele went belly up. Prohibition just about finished it off. It managed to limp along for another couple of decades until the Omnis bought it in the fifties. It was painstakingly restored to its original grandeur in the eighties."

"Have you worked here long?"

"No. I started only a couple of years ago, after Ms. Jacobs' divorce. Mr. Jacobs said you would like to look around. May I give you a tour? Or would you prefer to do a self-guided tour?"

"I'd love a tour." It would be a great chance to dig for some info on what was happening here…and what kind of security Jax had in place. Owen wished he had his own phone so he could test for wireless devices, which he had a strong suspicion were every-where. Jax was no idiot. He said he had his own team. They had to be watching everything, like Owen's crew did at Blade's.

"Very good, sir." They went into one of the bedrooms. "I've taken the liberty of putting your things in your room. If you find you require anything that you forgot to bring, do let me know. Mr. Jacobs has offered you the use of anything in his closet. He's also instructed me to tell you that you are free to explore the house and grounds as you like."

"I appreciate that. What time does Ms. Jacobs have supper?"

"She eats early, sir. At six. She's asked me to serve your meal in your room."

Owen smiled. "That won't be necessary. I'll join her in the dining room."

"As you wish. Shall we meet in the foyer in ten minutes?"

"Sounds good."

THE MANSION, as Owen had observed from the air, was comprised of two wings terminating in round towers and joined at the center by a massive one where the main stairs were. Between the wings, facing south, was a conservatory that spanned two floors. It was original to the house and was still in working condition, with both ornamental and edible plants and a large center fountain.

The restoration had returned the castle to its Victorian elegance—too ostentatious for his tastes, but much more luxurious than other mountain resorts built in the same era. This was no oversized log lodge. This mansion would have been at home anywhere along most of the eastern seaboard.

After a lengthy tour of the first floor, the basement —where the staff housing was—and the attic, which had amazing views of the surrounding terrain, they walked through the upper east wing. Most of the house was closed up, with sheets covering the furniture. It was a big place for just Addy and Jax.

All along the tour, Spencer pointed out art by

famous potters, sculptors, and painters. The collection was probably worth more than the mansion and grounds together were. Owen wondered if it was left over from the time of the Omnis. He was surprised they'd agreed to transfer ownership of it in whatever settlement Jax had negotiated for Addy...which made Owen wonder how fully this property was disconnected from the Omnis. Maybe not at all. Maybe it was only on loan. Maybe they were waiting for something before taking it from Addy...or taking Addy back into their custody. The Omnis never let go of what was theirs.

And that made him wonder again which side of the fight Jax was on.

They stopped at the closed doors to the west wing. "Sir, I feel we should conclude our tour here. The upper west wing contains Ms. Jacobs' private quarters. She usually rests for a while in the afternoon. I would not like to disturb her."

"Of course. Thank you for the tour, Spencer."

Owen returned to his room and contemplated his next move. He thought about contacting his team, but discarded that. When they learned where he was, they wouldn't waste time getting there. There were things he still needed to figure out here, like what kind of illness Addy had and if it was contagious. He couldn't bring himself to say the C-word, but it was there, at the edges of his mind. Was her hair loss due to chemo? What had they tried as far as a medical intervention? This was too damned remote of a place to make full use of all an urban medical center could provide. Jax had said she was dying. Jesus, had they given up the fight already?

How could she die when Owen had only just gotten here, when her son was still lost to her?

Owen folded his arms as he looked outside at the wintry afternoon, deciding if he did nothing else before losing her again, he'd get their son back.

To do that, he needed more time before contacting his team. Addy was in a fragile state and probably shouldn't be exposed to too many outsiders. Even getting her out of there before he had a handle on what she was battling was a bad move.

More info was what he needed. He went up the backstairs in his wing, down the long hall to the grand stairway, then into Addy's forbidden wing. Most of the doors were closed, but one was open. He heard voices. A child and a woman. A boy was asking the woman questions. Owen didn't pay attention to the topic of the conversation. He couldn't. His heart was beating too hard. Was that his son? Was Augie here? Why hadn't anyone told him?

Anger washed through him. He almost ran to the open door of the room where he'd heard them talking. There he was. A little brown-haired boy sitting at a table with a middle-aged woman. Rage washed through Owen, quickly chased by disillusionment. Both gutted him. Was this boy his? He glared at the child, who gasped at him, which caught the woman's attention. She stood and moved between them.

"You aren't supposed to be here in Ms. Jacobs' private quarters," she said. The boy peeked at him from around the woman's hip.

Owen didn't answer her. His gaze dropped to the boy. He looked a little older than Zavi, but not twice his age. Augie would have been bigger. "Who are you?" Owen asked.

"I'm Troy," the boy said. "Who are you?"

"Owen Tremaine."

The woman dragged Troy with her over to a phone mounted on a wall. When she dialed, he slipped away, venturing over to Owen. Troy stared up at him. Owen remembered he had to look pretty scary with all of his bruises and cuts. Even so, the kid took his hand and led him over to a long, padded window bench.

"What are you doing?" Owen asked.

"Taking you to sit down. You look like my mom does just before she faints."

Owen pulled his hand free, but did sit down. "I'm not going to faint."

The boy stood close to him, seemingly unconvinced. He clearly had no sense of personal space, either. "Maybe you should put your head between your knees."

"I'm not going to faint. I never faint." Good grief. Was he really having this convo with this child? "Who are you, Troy? Who are your parents?"

"My mom's just down the hall." Troy's gaze

lowered and shifted to the side. A telltale sign if ever there was one. "My dad's gone."

Owen's brows lowered. It was an expression that made grown men nervous, but not this boy. He seemed more at ease looking at Owen than dredging through his own thoughts.

"Who are your parents?" Troy asked, taking Owen aback.

"My parents are neither here nor there."

"I didn't ask where they were. I asked who they were."

"They were Mr. and Mrs. Tremaine. And 'here nor there' is an expression that means they are not of consequence in this conversation."

"Oh."

"What's your last name, Troy?"

He scrunched up his face. "It was Edwards, but now it's Jacobs. My mom divorced my dad."

Owen's brows lifted as he gasped. Edwards? Fucking Edwards? Addy had been forced into marriage with that bastard? Her parents had to be in on it. Her dad was a senator—he could have gotten her out if he'd wanted to.

Troy crouched on the seat next to Owen and bent over to put his head between his knees. "You do it like this." He ducked his head down, muffling his words. "It doesn't hurt. You should do it. Your face is very white…where it isn't purple."

Owen was tempted. He became aware of the tutor

speaking on a house phone. Her voice had been strident, but evidently whoever was on the other end of the line vouched for him. She sent him an uneasy glance, then hung up. She went into the bathroom and came out with a little glass of water, which she handed to him.

"You do look pale," she said.

He took the water, glad that his hand was steady. "I don't faint." He swallowed half of it then handed it back to her. He stood and held a hand out to Troy. The boy reached for his hand and grinned up at him. "It was very nice meeting you," Owen said.

"Will you be here long?" Troy asked. "We don't get a lot of visitors. My mom doesn't like them. I didn't either, but you seem different from the others." He stood on the bench. He was almost to Owen's shoulders. The boy would grow into a tall man. Interesting that he didn't resemble Edwards in the least. This child was brown-eyed with deep brown hair.

"That'll do, Troy," the woman said. "We don't gossip. Let's cleanup in here so we can go out to play." He jumped off the window seat and gave Owen a short wave.

Owen returned to the hallway. He paused, looking out into the conservatory that filled the space between the two wings, then pressed his forehead against the glass. Addy had two sons. He wondered what his own boy looked like. Had he been blond and blue-eyed like the both of them? He glanced back at the classroom, considering going back to ask Troy questions about his brother. The boy was the only one here freely offering up information. Surely he would remember his brother, though he would only have been a toddler when Augie was taken. But Owen doubted the dragon with him would welcome a second interruption.

Instead, he went down the hall, opening doors, looking for Addy. He needed answers. Time wasn't on their side. Three years had already passed since Augie was taken. Owen needed Addy to start talking if he had a hope of retrieving his boy…before the inevitable happened.

He guessed her room would be the last in the hall, the one with the round tower at the end of the wing. He tried the doorknob. It was unlocked. The suite he stepped into was darkened. The drapes had been drawn. It took his eyes a minute to acclimate. When they did, he saw a huge bed that looked big enough for two couples. Two very tall couples.

Addy was lying in the middle of it, so still and quiet that his heart clenched until he heard a slight sound from her. He pulled up a side chair and sat next to her bed. She was a little too far away for him to easily take her hand. He wished they weren't strangers now. In the ten years they'd been apart, she'd never been out of his mind.

Clearly, it hadn't been that way for her.

He remembered the time they'd been quarantined together at Jax's house. She was four and he was eleven. They both had chickenpox. His father had never had it, so Owen had had to convalesce at the Jacobs'. She had a high fever. She cried for her dad to come, but when he didn't, she cried for her mom. Everyone knew it wasn't Roberta, her stepmom, she was crying for.

Addy had lost her real mom two years earlier, the same year Owen's mom had died. It gutted him that no one went in to comfort her, not even Jax. So Owen did. And that was how he got the chickenpox himself.

Addy had a worse fever with the pox than he did, but he had more spots. Her nanny visited every few hours, but never stayed long. Addy would whimper and cry and scratch at the pox. He told her to come over and get in bed with him, that she could connect his dots and make pictures. He found a marker and gave it to her. She drew all over him. And laughed. And forgot about her sores.

She healed before he did, but she still sneaked away from her nanny to keep him company while he recovered. She couldn't read yet, so she sat there with him, making up stories. Silly things, like the adventures of various rabbits and mice.

To this day, whenever Owen was sick, which wasn't often, he thought about those days they spent together, helping each other get well.

Maybe he could do that again.

His eyes watered. How unfair it was that she was dying.

Addy's hair was short like it had been when they had chickenpox. She'd cried when they cut her hair off so they could tend the sores on her head. He'd told her how cute she was and that every princess had her hair cut when she was sick like they were.

He watched her sleep for a while. How much time did they have left? Troy said she fainted a lot. Owen had seen the shadows under her eyes deepen when she'd confronted him earlier. And now she was lost to this exhausted sleep. Stress seemed something to avoid.

Thinking of a way to cheer her up, he went back to the little schoolroom. It was empty now, thankfully. He dug around until he found a piece of paper and a black marker. He drew the shape of a person, then frowned at how much it resembled a crime scene murder victim's outline. He made little dots on it, then connected a few of them, like the haphazard lines she'd drawn on him. Below the figure, he wrote, *Do you remember?*

He left that drawing on Addy's nightstand, then let himself out of her room.

5

Thirteen Years Ago
Fairfax, Virginia

Owen should have been tired after the red-eye cargo transport he and Jax had taken. It was already midmorning by the time they reached the Jacobs' home in Fairfax, Virginia. The humid air was thick. Crickets and cicadas were making a loud buzz. The day promised to be a hot one.

They hadn't been certain what time their transport flight would leave—they'd been on standby for several hours, so they hadn't made it home in time for the actual graduation ceremony, which was where everyone was. The house was anything but quiet. The staff were hurrying about, doing the bidding of the party planner who'd been hired to oversee Addy's graduation celebration. It was going to be a big shindig, with the wealthy parents of her friends, their families, and the Jacobs' neighbors. Doubtless a fine time to do some fundraising for the senator's upcoming run.

Owen stopped on the stairs before going up to the rooms he and Jax had been assigned. From his vantage point, he could see the house seemed ready for something much bigger than a high school graduation celebration. Big vases of hand-blown glass and cut crystal were overflowing with bouquets of white roses and pink peonies. Every surface, from the tops of bookshelves to the wide plank pecan floors, had been dusted and spit-shined. New slouchy white covers had been pulled over the sofas and love seats in the family's informal living room. A feast was being set out on the long dining room table. Hors d'oeuvres were artfully arranged on various side tables.

Outside, several round tables were being set with white linen tablecloths. The folding chairs were covered with natural linen covers. All of it put Owen in mind of a big wedding celebration.

"You comin'?" Jax asked.

"Yeah." Owen followed him up the stairs. "I'm gonna marry your sister."

"I figured."

Owen grinned at Jax as they hit the landing and turned for the second half of the stairs to the second floor. "What, you're not gonna beat me up for that announcement?"

"I will if you think to make it public this weekend." They'd turned down a hallway that led to the guest rooms where they'd be staying. "This is Addy's weekend. Let her have it unencumbered."

Owen held up his right hand—the only hand that was free. "I will. She's too young anyway. And she has no idea how I feel. I'm just telling you how it's gonna go."

"Right. She's still a baby. You keep your dirty hands off her. Let her finish college before you make a move on her."

"Not sure I can wait that long. But don't worry; any moves I make this weekend will all be innocent. I just don't want her to forget about me this summer."

Jax leaned back, frowning as he looked at Owen. "Forget about you? Are you fucking with me? My sister worships you. If you told her to jump off a bridge, she would, just to make you happy."

Owen chuckled. Jax sounded jealous of the friendship Owen had with Addy. He always had been. "That's ridiculous. She's stubborn and opinionated. She's no pushover."

"Well, I know just the bridge. Ask her to jump."

The humor slowly slipped away from Owen. "Says the brother who claims to protect her."

"I am protecting her."

"From me? You really think you need to protect her from me?" He dropped his duffel bag and spread his hands.

"Look. Forget it. I hate these family things. We got a mission on Monday. We have to head out early

Sunday. Let's just drop it and enjoy the next day and a half."

"Sounds good to me." Owen rocked back on his heels. Family had always made Jax nervous. Owen had never understood why. Sure, Jax's stepmom was a piece of work. Owen would have given everything to have his own family back. But they were gone. Long gone. The Jacobs and Val were all the family he had now. As far as he was concerned, no one was going to be jumping off bridges or burning bridges or fucking anything up during Addy's graduation weekend.

Owen followed Jax down the hall to their assigned rooms. He hung up his clothes and got settled, then wandered downstairs toward the kitchen, hoping the staff had some food he could help himself to before everyone came back from the graduation ceremony.

He made it as far as the bar in the family room when the front door opened and noise filled the foyer, spilling outward to all the rooms connected to it. Giggling, happy girls and boys, chattering adults. Owen turned to see everyone, shocked how much of an outsider he felt like. No one had celebrated his graduations—from high school or West Point. He'd been homeschooled at Val's. Even Val's sisters had long since moved away. Well, that wasn't entirely true about not celebrating his high school graduation. He and Val had had a long and decadent night with Val's friend, Debbie.

"Owen!" A girl's voice cut into his thoughts. *Addy.* She ran across the room, her arms open. He caught her, hugging her tightly as he lifted her up off her feet. She laughed in that way of hers that sounded like little bells. His arms tightened a little. How he'd missed her. She was as slight as ever, but curvy in all the right places. He eased her back to her feet and smiled down at her. She rubbed her hands over his upper arms.

"Laidy." He smiled at her.

"I can't believe you still call me that."

He leaned close and whispered, "You ordered me to, remember? You wanted a nickname all your own, as I recall." His gaze swept across her face, which was absolutely glowing. "You look beautiful."

"How can you tell with me covered head to toe in this?" She quickly unzipped her graduation gown, peeling it off to reveal the white sundress she wore underneath.

It was just a nylon robe she'd removed, he told himself. And she was fully dressed underneath it, but he still felt himself hardening. He nodded. "Yeah. What I said."

She laughed as she draped the black gown over the bar and looped her arm through his. "Come meet my friends."

He stiffened, catching himself before telling her he didn't want to meet them, that he wanted her to himself for the next twenty-four hours, but already she was drawing him out into the foyer, where her friends were gathered.

A pile of discarded graduation robes was

mounded on the entrance table. Others were tossed over the sectional sofa in the living room. Caps were dumped everywhere. It looked like Addy's entire class had come home with her for the party. They were laughing and talking in endless loops, rehashing memories from the day and from their years together in school. It was a mix of several different ages, younger than Addy, older than her, and far more boys than Owen would have liked.

Addy dragged him over to a group of girls. Their circle went silent when they saw him. He shook their hands as he read their faces, looking for micro-expressions that might indicate if they were friend or foe. Foolish thing to do with these kids, but he liked to practice his craft. He'd long ago learned there were plenty of the latter and too few of the former. He must have seemed like a growling dog to them, for they all stepped back after meeting him, giving him a wide berth.

Addy laughed nervously and pushed him over to the next group, with the same results. Owen was wondering if all these guests had been vetted and cleared, when a boy came over to them. Addy pulled free from Owen and looped her arm through the boy's. Never had Owen felt a separation so keenly.

"Jake, this is my very dear friend, Owen Tremaine. Owen, my boyfriend, Jake."

All humor, all warmth, all fucking humanity drained from Owen. The boy's eyes widened, then jumped about, moving from Owen to Addy to the furniture near them, back to Owen. He tilted his head, fighting the persistent desire to pick the boy up by his neck and escort him outside for a little chat.

Jax joined them then. He slapped Jake on the back, congratulating him, then hugged Addy. Somehow Owen became the focus of the group again. He forced a grin, which had to be one of his most terrible ever. Jax laughed and dragged him away for a beer.

"She has a boyfriend," Owen said.

"Of course she does. She's eighteen."

"You could have told me."

"What difference would it make? It's her life to live. You don't get to live it for her. You're never even here."

Owen closed his eyes. "Does she love him?"

"Fuck no. Who does at eighteen? Pull it together, O. This is what I meant when I said this was her weekend. You looked like you were going to kill the kid."

"I thought about it. Good thing I'm out of uniform." He grinned.

"Shit." Jax lifted his beer and drained the bottle. "Good thing I'm here to ride your ass."

Owen turned to face the room. "Yeah, thanks but no thanks. Don't want you anywhere near my ass."

Jax choked on a laugh, which made Owen feel better.

Senator Jacobs came over with his wife, Roberta. She was a middle-aged bottle blonde, with sharp eyes, a sharp tongue, and razors for nails. Owen had never liked her. Nor had Jax and Addy. She'd married the senator when Addy was four, bringing with her the dragon nanny, who was probably still around here somewhere. She was the only mother Addy ever really known, though in her case, Owen used that term lightly; she'd never been much of a mom to Addy or Jax.

Owen shook hands with both of them. "Senator. Mrs. Jacobs."

"Oh please," she said, "you're old enough to call me Roberta." She accepted a glass of champagne from a silver tray a waiter brought over. Sipping it, she looked over the room. "Our little Addy is an adult now, about to go off to college." She looked at the senator. "How fast the time went. We're going to be empty nesters in only a few months."

The senator gave Owen a pained look. "I have only a few more months to be her father."

"You'll always be her father, senator," Owen said.

"But she won't need me anymore."

"You mean home to her. She's going to need that grounding more than ever when she moves out."

The senator gave him a long look, then nodded.

"Don't torture yourself, dear," Roberta said. "We'll finally get to take that trip we've been planning —the honeymoon we never had."

Owen sipped his beer. "When are you doing that?"

"We haven't set a date yet," the senator said. "It

won't be before Addy's off to school. And then I'll need to check with the Senate schedule to—"

"Always with the excuses," Roberta complained. "You promised me this trip." She smiled. "Dear, I do believe I've earned it."

Fear washed over the senator's features, quickly followed by a placating smile. He reached down and squeezed her hand. "You've more than earned it, my love. We should just set a date and make it happen."

Addy came over to their small group. The senator pulled her close for a hug, which she gleefully returned. "I'm proud of you, little girl."

"Thanks, Daddy. Roberta, this is an amazing party. Thank you for putting it together and letting all my friends come."

"Of course, darling. It serves two purposes—you get the kids and we get the parents." Her smile was ice cold.

Owen looked at Addy to see if she'd caught her stepmother's hatred. How could someone as kind and thoughtful and cheerful as Addy inspire such contempt?

She reached across the group to grab his hand, which he didn't resist, and pointed a finger at her brother. "Wendelly, it's time for the pool. Go get your suit on."

Jax didn't move. "Addy, I'm too old for your girl-friends. Hell, half of them don't even look legal."

"I know. And some of them aren't. But they're crushing on both of you. I know that I can count on

54

both of you to be gentlemen around them. Please don't be curmudgeons and ruin my fun."

Owen grinned at him as she pulled him away. "We've survived worse missions..." *And will again on Monday.*

Jax huffed a loud sigh and followed them upstairs. The wide staircase let Owen and Addy ascend side by side. She'd stopped holding his hand, which Owen regretted. In their hallway, he and Jax disappeared into their rooms. Didn't take long for Owen to strip and pull his Speedo on. When he opened his door, Addy was coming down the hall, carrying three beach towels. At first glance, she looked naked, but then Owen realized she'd changed into her suit as well. Her blond hair spilled about her shoulders, covering the straps of her suit. Her hair was a rich blond color with darker undertones and almost bright white highlights.

She looked at his bare legs, then her gaze parked at his crotch, which grew beneath her heated stare. He smiled at her, then took the towels she clutched to herself and set them on a nearby side table. If his body was fair game, then so was hers. She didn't try to cover herself up, but it seemed she wanted to. Her blue eyes went big as she held his gaze.

He gave himself the gift of slowly enjoying her nearly naked body, but then a darker thought slipped into his mind. He stepped forward, forcing her to either let him come into her space or back her to the wall. "You can't go downstairs like that. I'm not the only male here."

The tip of her tongue slipped between her lips, moistening them. "It's a bathing suit. There's more of me covered than there is of you."

Owen braced his arms on the wall behind her. Though perhaps of average height, she was still little compared to him. She'd always been small. He leaned in, bending close to her lips, hungry for a taste of her as he'd never been for anything in his life. His mouth hovered above hers. Her lips parted. Her breath was warm.

And then he remembered she wasn't single…or old enough yet.

"Addy…" His voice was gruff. A sure tell, if she were paying attention to such things. He hated being so obvious, but when it came to her, he couldn't help it. "When you're finished toying with little boys, call me."

Her hands flattened against his ribs. Her fingers were cold and he was hot. He sucked in a sharp breath. She smiled up at him. "I didn't think you saw me like this. Like a woman."

"I didn't want to. Yet. But the truth is, you've always been mine. I've waited a long time for you."

Sorrow, regret, and something else, washed through her eyes. "You tell me this now… I'm going to college. You're always off on assignments. It would never work."

Owen closed his eyes and bent his face down to

the crook of her neck, stopping just short of burying his face in her skin. It was easier than looking at her in that moment, and he was a fucking coward. He sucked in the warm air haloing her skin. Gooseflesh rose along her shoulder. When he got to her ear, he whispered, "Wait for me. Please, Addy. When you finish college, we'll be together. I swear it."

She slipped her arms over his shoulders, hooking them behind his neck. "Will you wait for me?"

"Yes. I will wait for you forever."

A tear slipped down her cheek. He brushed it away with his thumb. "I'm going to miss you. We can write to each other," she whispered.

He gave her a half-smile. "Like we promised to be pen pals when I went to West Point? Or when I went into the Army?"

She shook her head. "I was little then."

"Yeah, you were. You still are."

"I will write this time. Will you?"

"Yes." But he knew they wouldn't.

Owen heard sounds coming from Jax's room. He wondered if the bastard had been eavesdropping. He straightened, putting a little distance between him and Addy, though nothing short of an EMP could neutralize the charged air surrounding them.

Jax came into the hall, sending a look from his sister to Owen. Addy grabbed the towels, kissed her brother, and told them both to hurry down. When she was gone, Jax gave him a dark look and waved at his Speedo.

"Jesus, O. Point that somewhere else."

Owen sighed. "I hope the water's cold, though it may not matter if your sister is anywhere within sight."

"You must be very proud."

Owen laughed. "If I were proud, I'd swim nude. I'm more concerned about keeping my suit on, unlike you. Don't the girls call those baggy things you're wearing culottes?"

"How the fuck would I know?"

Owen sent a look down at himself, glad Addy had gone on ahead of them so he could cool down. He went into his room and grabbed the shirt he'd been wearing before, a white Oxford. He had no doubt his body would keep reacting the way it did every time he saw Addy; the shirt would at least give him some coverage.

6

Addy slowly came awake. She felt as if she'd slept a day and a half. The thought made her frown. She was worried she'd missed her playtime with Troy. She leaned up to look at the clock. It read 3:30 p.m. She'd slept for nearly two and a half hours. Something on her nightstand caught her attention. A folded piece of paper. She smiled, thinking her son had drawn her a picture...but what she saw was horrifying. The outline of a body. A chill slipped down her spine. Was it a threat? She sat up, then noticed the side chair had been moved closer to her bed. She gasped and sent a look around the shadows of her room. Was someone here?

She ran barefoot over to the drapes and threw them open, then frowned down at the paper. There was more than just the body outline...there were dots on it. And lines drawn between the dots. The writing said, *Do you remember?*

No. She did not remember. Remember what? What did this mean? Had Owen taken Troy? Were these wounds he was going to inflict on Troy or her?

She ran down the hall to Troy's class. It was empty. She hurried down to the kitchen. No one there had seen him. She never let her son be alone in the house. Never. He knew he was supposed to come to her room if Ms. Denton had to do something. But then, Addy rarely slept so late in the afternoon. Maybe he'd gone out to the playground.

She ran outside without shoes or a coat. She didn't even feel the cold. She called for Troy as she rounded the corner. She called again and again until she came to an abrupt halt. He was on the playground...with Owen. Ms. Denton stood off to the side.

Hot relief chased away the icy fear in Addy's veins, leaving her angry and shaken. She marched over to the hand-over-hand module where Troy was showing off to Owen. She stubbed her toe on its metal base, but didn't even pause in her rush to get her son away from the threat.

Owen saw her before Troy did. He straightened and faced her. She glared at him, her eyes narrowing in fury before she reached up to pluck her son from the bars. Owen noticed the trail of blood she was leaving behind her as she hurried back to the house.

"Hey," he said in a lame attempt to stop her. The

woman was furious; he was going to have to do more than that to get through to her. He reached out and caught her wrist so she would turn around and face him.

Her face went pale as she looked down to where he was holding her.

"Addy."

She didn't look up at him. When he reached for Troy so he could set him down, she began to fight against him. Troy looked terrified. Owen finally got him free and set him on his feet. When the nanny came forward to take him, Addy screamed and pulled her son behind her. A pool of blood was spreading around her foot on the concrete sidewalk.

Owen bent close and caught her face in his hands. "Whoa. Easy, Addy. It's all good. Troy's fine. No one's hurt. Except you. Your foot's bleeding. Let me help you, all right? Troy's not going anywhere. He's going to stand right here next to you. Yeah?" Owen nodded to the tutor.

Addy reached down and gripped a fistful of her son's fleece pullover. She released a ragged breath that immediately condensed in the air between them.

Owen pulled his jacket over her shoulders. The sidewalk was red under her foot. He was ticked that she'd run outside in this cold weather barefoot. A cut like that needed stitches. Maybe a tetanus shot. And they were a long way from a clinic. She didn't let go of Troy. Owen reached over and pushed one of her hands through a sleeve of his jacket.

"Honey, you'll have to let go of Troy so I can get this on you before you get a chill," Owen said. Her eyes met his and her jaw clenched. "Please?"

He thought about promising that he'd never hurt her son, but he didn't. He'd learned the hard way that even if he didn't cause the boy harm, his being here might be its own kind of harm. Owen caught her hand and pulled it away from Troy then slipped it through its sleeve.

When she was covered, he swung her up into his arms. Again she fought, pounding at him, kicking to be freed. Owen brought her close in a tight hold. "Stop. Addy, look at your foot. You can't walk back to the house."

She did look at her foot then. Her face went pale, as if it was the first she'd been aware that she'd hurt herself. "I can walk."

"Not barefoot. And my boots won't fit you. I'll carry your boy, too, if I have to. Or he could just walk ahead of us so you can see him."

She appeared to relent, so he readjusted her weight. "Put your arm around me."

"I'm too heavy. Really, I'll be fine walking."

"You aren't even half as heavy as some of the guys I've had to carry out of battles."

She put her arm around his neck. He had to stifle his body's heated response to that. "You probably fireman-carried them out, not held them out in front of you."

He grinned at her. "I could fireman-carry you. In

fact, I could put you over my shoulders and race Troy back to the house."

Troy laughed and clapped. "Do it, Mommy!"

Owen laughed, then made the mistake of looking down at her. Her serious eyes were watching him. He got lost in them for a few seconds, and found himself at a complete loss for words. The only thing he knew for a fact was that he had her in his life once more and wasn't about to let her go.

That...and a smart man never got between a mama and her kid.

She lowered her gaze. "I couldn't find Troy. I thought you took him."

"I would never do that."

"You took Augie."

"I did not."

"Then you ordered him taken."

Owen shook his head, trying to understand how she could be so mistaken about him. Just the talk of her boys made the shadows around her eyes darken again. She wasn't handling stress well. She never fully relaxed against him, but at least she'd stopped fighting him. He'd been her hero since she was two, but now she hated him. He looked away from her. They were nearing her house. Troy held the front door open for them.

"I'll take Troy upstairs," the nanny said.

"No," Owen said. "I want him with us. Why don't you take a break? I'll come get you if you're needed."

She disappeared down the hallway leading to the

kitchen. "Where's the nearest bathroom?" Owen asked Troy. He pointed to a short hallway off the foyer. Owen carried her in there and set her on the large vanity, then began looking through the cabinets and nooks for a first-aid kit.

"I know where the medicine is," Troy offered.

Owen nodded. "Go get me some disinfectant and some bandages. Be quick about it." The boy ran out.

"I can do this myself," Addy protested.

"I'm sure you can."

"Then leave me to it."

"But why should you do it alone when you have help?"

"If it weren't for you, none of this would have happened in the first place."

Owen absorbed that volley without blinking. "True. I can't undo what's been done. But I can change things from here on out."

"No. I made an agreement with the Omnis. I'm out of their organization. So are my children. You aren't welcome here."

Okay, that hurt, but he didn't have time to pick it apart. A lot of what she said just didn't make sense. "I'm not going anywhere until we get Augie back… and until I know Troy is safe."

She scoffed. "Troy is not your concern. I don't want you talking to him or interacting with him in any way."

Owen helped her turn so that she could get her

foot under the tap. "That's a little dramatic, don't you think?"

She straightened and glared at him. If her eyes were lasers, he'd be fried.

"No, I don't. And I don't need you to talk down to me. I'm Troy's mother. I have sole custody over him. And after having one son taken, I'm not going to run risks with my other one."

"Who's trying to take him, Addy?"

"As if you don't know."

"I don't."

She poked his chest. "You can't have him. And you can't have me."

Owen met her hard look. "I can have you. And he comes with you, so I can have him too."

Her eyes went wide. He felt her pull away from him, though he still held her foot under the cold stream of water. He didn't press his point. Instead, he focused on washing her foot and injured toe. Troy came back with the requested supplies.

Owen glanced at the boy's anxious face. Deciding it was better to include him and calm his fears rather than send him away, Owen moved to one side so that Troy could stand on the toilet and watch what he was doing.

"Mommy"—Troy pointed to his head and then to hers—"your head's uncovered."

Her hands flew to her head as her face paled. She gave Owen a resigned look as she lowered her hands to fuss with the scarf draped around her neck. "It's fine. No biggie, honey."

Owen tucked that away for future consideration. Her hair was short, still very blond, and had the slight curl that he remembered. It was beautiful. She didn't need the wig she'd been wearing.

"Hand me that." He nodded to a linen hand towel hanging on the bar near Troy.

"Does it hurt, Mommy?"

She smiled at her son. "A little. Nothing too bad. You've had a skinned knee before. It's no worse than that."

"I cried when that happened. You aren't crying."

She smiled. "I cry at other things."

He nodded. "I know. You cry a lot."

Owen frowned at her, wondering what made her cry. He made short work of drying off her toe and getting the first butterfly bandage on it. He put a second one on, then covered the toe with gauze and tape. "One more errand, Troy. Your mom needs slippers."

She told him which ones to fetch, and he ran off without argument. Owen helped her to her feet, but kept her between him and the vanity. "Why do you cry?"

"I miss Augie."

Owen held her gaze a long moment before nodding. "We'll get him back."

Again, that caustic laugh of hers. "You could snap

your fingers and have him here in an instant. But you don't, so I don't believe your words."

"I'm no magician."

"Give him back to me." Her face hardened. She caught a fistful of his cashmere pullover and twisted it as she drew him close. "I will kill you if anything happens to him." She gave a little shake of her head. "In fact, I'll likely kill you anyway for taking him."

Owen braced a fist against the wall behind her to keep himself from touching her. "I didn't take him."

"Of course not. Your minions did. Same difference."

Owen stared into her steely eyes. They were the same eyes she had when she was two and he'd first met her. They were the same eyes she had when she was six and had asked him to be her dragon slayer. They were the same eyes she had when she was eleven and had cried over the braces she'd just gotten. They were the same as ever…and yet different. Filled with hate and fear, things he'd never thought to see in them.

He switched his gaze from her eyes to her cheek, which looked soft and young. She smelled sweet, like a field of daisies heated by the sun.

He met her eyes again. "I don't have minions, Laidy. I've only ever been your minion," he whispered.

"Such an expert manipulator. I could almost believe you…if I didn't know better."

"If you must hate me, then hate me for the right

reason. I didn't take Augie from you, but I wasn't here to stop him from being taken. Hate me for that. I do."

Troy was taking a while fetching her slippers. Owen was glad for the time it gave him with her; they needed to have this convo. "And as for killing me, give me the chance to bring Augie back and secure Troy. Once that is done, I will stand in your firing line." He leaned in close, bringing his face near hers, as close as he could without touching her, while he whispered, "But you alone must pull the trigger." He leaned back so he could watch her reaction to his words. He saw the sorrow that passed through her expression before she released him and straightened.

"You were in my room."

"I was."

"Why?"

"I was worried about you."

"*Now* you worry about me."

"I didn't worry about you before because I thought you were dead," he said. Her eyes widened. "But there hasn't been a day that passed that I didn't think about the accident. It changed my life, Laidy, losing you. It cut a piece out of me that never healed over. That piece, this past decade, it's just gone."

Her face hardened. "I lived it. You missed it. But it's you who are the victim. That's just great, Owen. Really great."

She was angry. Understandably so…and yet he still didn't understand. He probably wouldn't until she opened up to him. Jax certainly wasn't going to fill in the blanks. The coward had already taken off.

"What was the meaning of that picture?" she asked.

"You don't remember?"

"No."

Owen drew back. He stared at her. They'd spent a week together with the chickenpox, both of them feverish and miserable, and she didn't remember. Clearly his stupid drawing had sucked. He tried to focus on that rather than dwell on the fact that he remembered everything about her...everything, while she'd forgotten everything about him.

He shook his head. "Don't worry about it. It was nothing." Troy was coming down the hallway, sparing both of them further torture.

7

O wen went downstairs for dinner. He'd borrowed a suit from Jax's wardrobe. They were still the same size, though Jax's taste in clothes was different from Owen's. At least he suits in his closet. Owen thought about how casual things were at Blade's. The only thing the team dressed for was missions.

The house was quiet, but then, he was about a half-hour early for supper. He wandered into the dining room. There were only two place settings on the table. Wasn't hard to guess who was the unwelcome party. Owen bellowed for the butler. He came out of the kitchen wearing a starched white apron over his suit.

"Mr. Tremaine. How may I help you?"

"There seems to be a place setting missing."

Spencer looked at the table. A faint wash of color tinted his face. "There is not a place setting missing.

Ms. Jacobs insisted you would be taking your supper in your room."

"No. I will be joining her and Troy."

"I see. Then I'll add a place for you."

"Thank you." Owen wandered into the parlor to pour himself a glass of Balcones. At six, Owen heard Addy and Troy come down the stairs. They were having a cheerful conversation about several sets of mathematical equations, which stopped when Addy saw him. He gave a slight nod to her. She wore her wig again. Why? Why hide herself from him or anyone?

"You," she hissed.

"Yes, me." He stood and set his glass down. "May I walk you in to supper?"

"No. I made it clear to Spencer that you won't be dining with us."

He gave her a frosty smile. "Then you've made an error, for this is exactly where I need to be."

Had he not been watching her so closely, he might have missed the shiver that passed through her. There was a time she screamed to see him, but with joy, not fury. Troy's eyes widened as he glanced back and forth between them. He put his hand in his mother's.

Owen gestured toward the dining room. "Shall we?"

They stood there as if frozen in place. It gave Owen a chance to take in everything about her. Her silky shirt. Her earrings. Her slacks. Her strappy heels. And the small bandage on her toe. He frowned at it.

How was that possible? At the time he'd cleaned her wound, he'd thought they really should go to a hospital for stitches. He'd managed to seal the wound, but had still been worried at leaving it that way. Now all the wound needed was a regular bandage. It didn't even look swollen or bruised.

He let it go for the moment. Later, when Troy wasn't there, he'd ask her about it.

Addy seemed locked in place.

Owen frowned.

"Mommy?" Troy whispered when they didn't go into the dining room. He tugged on her hand.

Her smile looked forced. "I'm sorry, honey. I'm suddenly not feeling well. I think we'll have to eat upstairs." She pulled Troy with her out of the living room.

Her son frowned and looked behind them. "But Mr. Tremaine's here."

"He's a grownup. He can fend for himself."

"But…"

ADDY RUSHED her son into the foyer and up the stairs. She tried to keep her hand steady, though her whole body was shaking. Echoes of all the times her husband had brought unwanted guests to their house kept ripping through her. All those years. Night after night of hell. Day after day of forced smiles, despite the bruises, despite the threats to Augie, and then

Troy. The years since her divorce weren't enough time to make her forget. A lifetime wouldn't be enough time.

A cold sweat broke out all over her body. There was no way she could have sat at the same table with Owen, knowing what she now did. None of her life was the same as before her divorce—the staff were different; she was different. Stronger, maybe. She'd promised herself she would never again have to suffer through unwanted visitors, and yet one—the worst one of all—was being foisted on her.

"Mommy?" Troy whispered as he jogged up the stairs beside her. "Mr. Tremaine's a nice man. He was playing with me this afternoon."

"I'd like you to stay away from him. We don't know his intentions. I'm not ready to trust him."

She thought about her escape plan, the one she'd put in place after Augie was taken. Bonnie, her former companion and the boys' nanny, had helped her set it up through her friend Santo. When Wendell fired Bonnie, she'd left Addy a note that the escape route was still safe, if she ever wanted to use it.

Should she go now? She shut her eyes, remembering she'd had the same misgivings about leaving before…and then it was too late. Augie had been taken.

Three Years Ago

Saddle Notch Ridge, Wyoming

I CAN HELP YOU. Hope started with those simple words that Bonnie had written on a note and handed to Addy on her breakfast tray, hidden beneath her coffee cup. *Come outside so we can talk.* Addy looked at the nanny. She'd been with Addy since the day Augie was born. Unfailingly kind and always sympathetic, Bonnie had been a lifeline. Addy jumped at the thought of getting out of her hell, until reality sank back in. She'd tried to run before. It hadn't ended well.

Before Addy could ask questions, Bonnie cut her off. "I'm going to take the boys for a walk. They'd love you to join us."

Addy met Bonnie's intense look. A little flutter of hope blossomed in her chest.

"Just go dress."

Addy showered, lingering a little too long in the hot water. It made her bruises ache a little less. Maybe it also washed off a little of the ugliness of her marriage. It took her an hour to shower, dry her hair, put her makeup on, then slip into a proper outfit. She couldn't just throw on some slouchy comfort clothes. Cecil didn't like them. He wanted her to dress as befitted his wife. All couture, all the time.

Even when it hurt, as it did now.

She slipped on a pair of Burberry ankle boots, then rushed outside, hoping Bonnie was still waiting. She was. Sitting on a bench while the boys played a game of chase around the large playground Cecil had put in for them.

Occasionally, visitors brought their children, but that was rare. Her boys were growing up with only themselves as companions. Echoes of Addy's own lonely childhood slipped in through the cracks in her wall. She'd rarely had playmates either. Only Owen, when he would visit Wendell.

Anger washed the warmth of that memory away, as it always did. She'd believed the lie her father, Wendell, and Owen had convinced her of, that her future was bright and full of delightful dreams.

That had never been her fate.

Bonnie came over. Her kind eyes read too much in Addy's. Addy had to look away. "I have money I've been saving. I want to give it to you."

"No," Addy said. "They would know."

Bonnie shook her head. "I've been setting it aside from each paycheck. I don't need it. I receive food and boarding here. I have little need. And I still have my official savings that they could track."

Addy looked around, wondering if this conversation was being listened to, even though they were outdoors...which made her wonder how much of what was said indoors had been heard. "They listen to us inside, don't they?"

"I think so. Maybe they watch us, too. We have to be very, very careful."

Addy closed her eyes. She'd been in this hell for seven years. How had the time gone so fast? When this nightmare started, she'd woken up to find herself in a hospital, her mind twisted with memories and visions that haunted her still. Her stepmother told her the truth then. About Owen. How he'd rigged her death, killing an innocent girl so he could steal Addy away. Roberta had told her she'd been married to protect her from Owen. She reminded Addy that she and her dad had never liked Owen, had always feared it would come to some terrible end. Like it had.

Addy had had a hard time putting the pieces together. She'd stayed in the hospital for weeks. A shrink was brought in to work with her. She'd never seen the side of Owen her parents and the doctors talked about, but she must have been blind, because she was living proof of what they were saying.

The depression she went into was severe. And then came the day that her husband came to take her home.

The first time she met Cecil, she felt sick. He was older than her, by maybe thirty years. And though his voice was soft, his eyes were hard. She couldn't remember marrying him. She wanted out of the marriage, but her father said doing so would harm his career. She would be taken care of in a style befitting a princess. Like she cared for that. Like she cared for anything since Owen had turned on her so terribly.

She didn't see Wendell in those days. Her dad said he was not happy with her marriage and was crushed by Owen's actions. He said Wendell would come around eventually, but it took him years to do that.

That first year was a fog, most of it spent under Cecil's harsh focus and brutal intimacy, until her pregnancy was far enough along for all to see. After that, he was never around. She'd gotten more than a year of peace following Augie's birth. She began to heal a little, find a new norm. Her parents visited. Cecil came home when Augie was a year old. That was when her hell really began. There were times she'd attempted to get out, but they all worsened her situation.

What made her think this attempt would be any different? "It won't work," she told Bonnie.

"I have a little house. They don't know I own it. I bought it before I started here. I gave my friend the money to buy it for me."

Addy frowned. Bonnie had been preparing this for a while…and not for Addy's benefit. How terrible this world was that her own nanny was trying to sneak out of it.

"It's for my retirement. It's safe. You can go there. The money I've been stashing is there. You can use it to get food and supplies so they can't track you."

"Why would you do this? It's a risk for you as much as for me. It's your retirement. And if they find out you helped me…"

Bonnie turned to watch the boys. "I can't have children. You and your boys are the closest I'll ever be to a family of my own. I can't stand by and do nothing when I could help you."

Addy's heart beat hard. It could work. Cecil

wasn't home. He was usually gone for weeks after one of his attacks.

But then she remembered why it wouldn't work. "The guards search your car when you leave."

"The drive is a couple miles long. I could let you out before I get to the guard station, then meet you on the other side. It's rough terrain, but if you're careful, you and the boys can make it."

"You've given this some thought."

"I have. His attacks on you are getting more frequent and more violent. He's going to kill you one day. And then what will happen to your boys?"

Addy closed her eyes. She had only to inventory her aches and pains to know her window of opportunity to get out was closing fast. "How will we do it?"

"I go shopping every Tuesday at about this time. We'll go today."

"I can't get in your car. If they're watching us, they'll see that."

"Then take the boys for a walk in the woods. When you're out of sight from the house, head southwest, straight for the road. It's a long walk for the boys. And you'll have to move fast. That will bring you to the road far enough from the guard station that no one will see you getting into my car."

"Bonnie, you can't come back either. He'll kill you for this."

"I know. I'll stay with you at my house. The search will die down in a little while."

God, the search. She hadn't even thought of that.

Cecil would have his men out looking for them, telling the media lies, getting the cops involved. He'd say Addy kidnapped her own boys.

Before she could let her panic explode, she reminded herself that she had to take it one step at a time. Get out. Then make a plan. She would be completely on her own, though. She couldn't call her parents. Or Wendell. And certainly not Owen, who'd gotten her into this in the first place.

8

Owen took a seat at the long, empty table as he listened to their fading footsteps. He wasn't sure hatred was a strong enough word for the vibe Addy was giving off. There was an open bottle of Cabernet Sauvignon on the table. He filled his glass, then just stared at the blood-red liquid. Kelan probably had the perfect word for it, but it wouldn't be in English.

How long did wounds of the heart live in the blood? Forever?

A server came in with a tray of plates, followed by the butler.

"Oh, my apologies, sir. I thought I heard Ms. Jacobs come down," Spencer said.

"She did. And then she went back upstairs. I believe she would like their supper served up there."

"Very good. I'll see to it, then," he said as he served the first course.

Owen looked down at his plate of succulent filet mignon. Everything here was far more formal than anything he'd become used to. The ceremonies were the same as they'd been at Senator Jacobs' house. Nothing like the noisy, chaotic, familial meals of the team and their women and children. He missed them. He lifted his glass and swallowed an inelegant mouthful.

Visits to the Jacobs' or to Val's had been welcome breaks in his childhood. After his dad and Val's had had some sort of falling out, he would have gone crazy if it hadn't been for the time he'd spent with Jax and Addy.

He'd been a little surprised to learn that after his father's death, his wishes had been for Owen to go live with Val. He didn't think their fathers had talked in years. It had been even more shocking when he'd gotten the word in a postmortem letter that his father expected him to protect Val.

From what? Or whom?

Shit. He straightened in his chair. Everything mattered. Every action. Every word. Every outcome. All of it had meaning. The letter his dad wrote hadn't been one he'd drafted years before his death, when setting up his estate. No, it had likely been written after he'd faked his death. He'd sent Owen to Val's on purpose. But why?

Owen picked up his silverware and cut into his steak, eating absent-mindedly while he pondered things he should have long ago considered. When the meal was over, he thought about going up to check on Addy, remembering what happened with her toe.

How had it healed so quickly? The sink was full of blood. She'd dripped blood all the way back to the house from the playground. It was not a surface scratch but a deep cut. And now it was almost gone.

When he finished his meal, he went outside and found himself walking they way they'd taken back to the house. It was dark outside but the moon was bright. Someone had rinsed it off. He shoved his hands in the pockets of his jeans.

The November evening was cold, though not nearly as icy as it was inside Addy's home.

He stood in the shadows, watching the lights slowly switch off around the upper floors of the house even as they came on in the servant quarters. He couldn't help but remember different times, when he still had hope for the future.

Ten Years Ago
Fairfax, Virginia

AS FAR AS OWEN KNEW, this party wasn't going to be a huge party. Not all of Addy's friends were still in the area. Since she'd graduated a year early, many of her circle were still away at school. He was glad for a quieter celebration, though he knew the senator would likely monetize the event as an opportunity to fete supporters and connect powerful lobbyists with other players in the political game.

Damn, Owen was glad he wasn't a politician. Having to cater to bullshit from people he neither knew nor liked was not his flavor of candy.

He looked at Jax as they parked. His friend's tension had grown the whole trip in, mirroring Owen's feelings, ones he couldn't account for, except to acknowledge that this wasn't only a graduation celebration. It was also Addy's birthday party. Specifically, her twenty-first birthday, which happened last week. He and Jax had promised to take her for the obligatory tour of bars in Georgetown, now that she was legal. They'd be her bodyguards and designated drivers. Truth was, neither of them was looking forward to the party. Owen didn't want to share Addy with anyone else in the short amount of time he had with her this weekend. And Jax, hell, Jax was a bundle of nerves. Hopefully on the trip home, Owen would find a way to make him spill. The tense vibe Jax was giving off was out of proportion to the risks involved in a tour of bars.

Maybe he knew Owen and Addy's relationship was turning a corner this weekend. She was fully an adult. Not only that, but she'd graduated college. She was ready to take her place in the world and in his heart.

That had to be it. Owen supposed he'd feel the same way if he had a sister and knew what his friend was planning for her. It had to be hard letting go of

Jax's vision of her as a baby sister, switching it out for one of an adult.

For his part, Owen had been dreaming of this night since before her eighteenth birthday. Long years of torturous denial. His chest tightened as they walked into the house. She was there. He couldn't see her, but he heard her voice, felt her joy filling the big place. His lungs stopped then jumped, shocking him as she stepped from the family room into the foyer. She only had eyes for him. And she was glowing, fucking alive with light.

He didn't seem to have control of his faculties; he was just glad that Jax moved deeper into the house, leaving them alone. All he could do was drop his bag and open his arms. She ran into them, filling them, completing him. He lifted her off her feet as he straightened, his face buried in the crook of her shoulder.

"Now, Addy." He leaned back to look at her. "From this moment forward, we are together, my Laidy."

Laughter rippled throughout her body. Her eyes were shining. "I love you."

A shiver passed through him. How long had he yearned to hear those words? And she said them now, here, at her family's house, where he could do nothing about it but whisper, "I love you. Always have, always will."

She caught his face as he set her on her feet. She pulled him close so they could kiss. She was his. All his. Only his. His mouth crushed hers. Her lips parted, opening for him.

He smiled as he leaned back to look at her. "My sweet Laidy, I'm so proud of you, graduating a year early." It was as if she couldn't wait to tackle the world and wrestle it into the beautiful vision she had for it. Seeing life through her eyes always gave him hope. "What are you going to do now?"

Her smile was slow and dirty and meant only for him. His eyes widened as he took her meaning even before she leaned forward to whisper against his lips, "You."

His body surged to life, turning his dick to stone and robbing him of words. He grinned as he leaned forward to kiss her. "Soon."

"When?" she asked.

"As soon as we can get through all the festivities."

"There's only one thing I want."

His forehead was against hers. She had to be standing on tiptoes. "Then let's go. Damn everything else."

Jax cleared his throat, giving warning before leading his parents into the foyer.

Owen looked up, regretting his seconds with Addy were over already. Owen straightened and smiled at her, catching her hand, trying to play it cool by starting over. "Hi. I've missed you."

Her laugh was like bells shivering. "I missed you, too."

She separated from him to give her brother a hug. "Hi, Wendelly. I missed you, too."

Jax returned the hug, giving Owen a black look over her shoulder. "Sure you did."

"We aren't going out tonight," she said.

"No?" Jax frowned.

She reached for Owen's hand. "No, I just want a quiet night here at home."

Owen grinned at Jax, figuring he knew what that was code for.

Her dad didn't look any happier than Jax when he shook hands with Owen. The senator wrapped an arm around Addy's shoulders and led her back to the family room. She looked back at Owen, smiling, catching him checking out her ass and slim legs in her skintight jeans. Their eyes met for a flash, tightening the bond between them.

He was left in the huge foyer with Addy's fuming older brother. Owen grinned, feeling like he was standing on top of the world.

Jax stepped into his path. "Maybe you need a cold shower before you go in there?"

Owen gave a quick shake of his head. "Nope. That's not it. More like an entire night with your sister. I'm going to marry her, Jax. She's my heart and holds my soul. And she *loves* me. Did you hear her?"

Jax didn't look happy for them. What was his deal? Owen's joy slowly dimmed. As it did, Jax turned and went into the family room ahead of him. Fuck the bastard. Owen had waited years for this day. So had Addy. They were going to be together tonight, her family be damned.

ADDY HAD JUST TURNED off her light when she heard a small knock on her door. She never locked it because she wanted Troy to be able to come in if he had a bad dream. That was happening less and less often, which she hoped meant his spirit was healing from their time with Cecil. He'd seen the beatings she'd endured, though he was very young at the time. She'd tried to shield him from everything, but some stuff still got through. Like her illness. Like losing his older brother.

Troy would not have knocked. Wendell was gone. The butler would have announced himself directly after his knock. No. There was only one person on the other side of her double doors.

Owen.

Her heart jumped, and not in a good way. She fisted the covers she'd just pulled up over herself.

"Addy? Are you awake?" Owen quietly called through the door.

"No."

"Come talk to me."

"No."

"Laidy. Please. We have so much to talk about."

How she wished things, lots of things, were different. Most of all, she wished Owen was just Owen, the boy she'd grown up with, the man she'd fallen in love with. She knew that no matter what evidence she presented to the contrary, he would stick with his false persona, insisting he was just the boy who was so familiar to her.

But she knew differently...knew him for the monster he was, despite what Jax now claimed. The fact that Wendell had brought him here even made her doubt her brother's innocence. It was hard to know where one evil ended and another began. Maybe it didn't matter. She'd been working on a plan for her own disappearance—but that was something she couldn't execute until she had Augie back.

"May I come in?" Owen asked from the hallway.

"No."

"Then come out and talk to me. Answer my questions. Tell me what's going on. After that, I'll leave you alone."

How she'd ached for Owen in the beginning, before learning what she did. Knowing he was out there was the only thing that helped her through the early years. She'd dreamed he'd find her. Then she'd dreamed he'd never find her. And finally, she'd learned everything that had happened to her had been at his command.

Even knowing that, some part of her still wanted him, wanted to pretend his truth had never been revealed to her.

She went over to her door, dragging the coverlet from the foot of her bed. She heard a sound against the door, as if Owen had slid down it to sit on the floor. She knelt on her side of the double door and held her hands to the wooden panels. All he had to do to invade her sanctuary was turn the knob and come in. That he didn't just meant he was playing some game with her.

"I'm sorry I didn't come for you," he said. "Jesus, Laidy, I never even looked for you."

Addy leaned her face against the same wooden panel as Owen. She closed her eyes, wishing she didn't know what she did about him. You couldn't walk back that kind of knowledge. For someone who was all-knowing, Owen should have accepted the fact that she knew who he was. They were well beyond innocence...so why did he keep pretending things were pretty much as they'd left them ten years ago? Did he think her a fool?

"I went to my grave," she said. She didn't bother speaking up, as she really didn't care whether he heard her.

"God. I can't imagine what that must have been like."

"It was like I didn't exist. Like I'd never existed." It was laughable that she thought to make him feel guilt. Him, of all people.

"Addy, tell me about your toe. How is it that it could heal so quickly?"

Of course that was what he was most interested in...the experiments his people did on her. Had they sent anyone else from the Omni world, she would have had them physically removed without delay. "I have no idea."

"Please come out and talk to me."

She considered it. They would wake Troy if they continued talking through the closed door. She wrapped the blanket around her shoulders and opened the half of the door that Owen wasn't leaning against. She closed it behind her. He was not welcome in her room. He moved aside to lean against the far doorjamb, making room for her. Her feet and legs were covered by the blanket. She was glad it was too dark for him to see her very well, though the darkness wasn't an issue for her. That was another of the changes she'd noticed about herself. Her vision was changing.

She tucked her knees up close to her body, then waited for him to make the next move.

"I hope that, one day, you'll tell me everything that happened to you when we were apart."

And that didn't surprise her in the least. Of course, he'd had his minions report back to him on everything at the time. They probably still did. He'd been there for her initiation, coward that he was, dressed head to toe in a robe and hood. How arrogant was he to want to hear all of that again? Addy began to shake. She'd been wrong when she thought she could be his equal in manipulation. She never had been and she never would be. She wasn't a psychopath.

"But until that time," Owen continued, "perhaps

we should focus on getting Augie back. What can you tell me about the circumstances surrounding his abduction?"

Addy tightened her hold on the blanket. Augie had been gone three years now. Three long years. It was her own fault they'd taken him. Her husband had used him as an incentive for her good behavior…and participation. But when she'd gotten pregnant a second time, she started to fight back. That had only made things worse.

Thinking of those dark days made her physically ill. "It's my fault they took him. I wasn't a fit mother."

"What happened?"

"I can't—I can't talk about it."

"I haven't known you long as a mother, but the little I've seen tells me you're a wonderful parent." He paused. "It isn't because you were unfit that they took our son away."

"Yes, it is."

Her fear, her fight, her resistance, her tears, her screaming, her bruises…all of those things had fed her bastard husband's sick appetites. Even her threats against him had had their own reward for him. But her complete cessation of any sort of participation, no matter what, had cost her Augie.

At her continued silence, Owen reached for her hand, twining his fingers with hers. She should feel revulsion at his touch, but she didn't. It felt like sunlight filling her, a warmth that seeped into her cold body from their joined hands. She pulled free. She knew who he was. What he was. He was no friend to her, nor had he ever been.

Her seven years of hell at the hands of her husband had brought other surprises. Allies she'd never expected to make. They'd tried to help her, though it was her own fear that kept her from accepting their assistance. They were enemies of her husband, incentivized by different objectives than he, but even they had confirmed what Cecil had been telling her: *Tremaine is King.*

That was why she'd never reached out to her brother. He and Owen were friends. Brothers, really. And since she already suspected her father was in collusion with the Omnis for the way he let them take her and keep her, having her husband's jeers confirmed by his enemies reinforced her need to stay separate from her family.

It wasn't until her husband had begun threatening Troy that she had reconnected with her brother. He said their father sent him. She doubted that, but better the enemy you know... Her brother had helped her. He'd negotiated her divorce and settlement. He'd gotten the bastard she'd married out of her life, but that didn't mean he'd gotten her out of the Omni world.

Owen shifted, bringing her back to the present. "It wasn't your fault."

No, it wasn't. It was his, but she wasn't going to antagonize him by stating that. She had to play the game. She had to keep her emotions calm. "Where did they take him?" she asked, switching his focus from reliving her son's abduction to what happened to him.

"They put him with a group of watchers that lived not far from my team's headquarters. That group went missing, so I don't know where they are now."

Addy studied him. She doubted he'd had the same testing done on him that she had. Why would he? It was risky. She wasn't yet certain she would survive it. Many of those in the clinical trials died. Her brother had told her that was why he was already looking for the prides; he didn't want them to be Omni lab rats. He'd negotiated her ownership of this property because he wanted a location where he could build the barracks for the watchers and give them a safe place to be…and where he could observe them in case they had been subjected to the same experiments she'd undergone.

She'd survived what they'd done to her. So far. Though sometimes she wondered if hers would just be a slow death. For now, those tests meant some significant changes were occurring in her physiology. Some of the changes she appreciated. For instance, not only did she heal quickly, but her night vision was enhanced. That heightened capability now let her see Owen's face clearly, even in the dark hallway where they sat. And what she saw was infuriating. He was so thorough in his acting, that even in the dark, when nothing was clear to normal eyes, the concern on his face looked genuine. It was all part of his act. He couldn't sound genuinely concerned without his face reflecting the same emotion.

"You mentioned your team…what team is this?" she asked. She'd learned the hard way to tuck away little kernels of info for future use.

"Guys who were in my same unit in the Army. Some from my group, some from later groups."

"The same unit that Wendell was in with you?"

"The same. That unit is shutting down. I've opened a private security company, and I'm hiring many of them as they separate from active duty. I've mentioned my cousin, Val Parker? He's working for me now. As are a few dozen others."

"I see. And what is it that your security company does?"

"A lot of things, most of which I can't discuss. However, our main objective at the moment is to uncover—and destroy—the Omni infrastructure."

Addy huffed a disbelieving laugh. "Why would you do that?"

"Because the Omnis are involved in international and domestic terrorism. We're working with the FBI. We're afraid they're perfecting some sort of biological weapon. We've recovered one group of people on whom they were testing a new variant of smallpox."

Addy lowered her gaze and held her silence. Did he think she was stupid? Or just so gullible that she would feast on his every word, believing his act, believing he wasn't secretly leading the very group he was professing a desire to destroy?

"Do you remember a girl named Ace?" Owen asked.

Ace? Yes, she did. How could she forget her? Addy had heard they'd forced her to do terrible things too. She always wondered what had become of her.

"She works for me now."

"I don't remember her."

"Don't you? She shot a video of her preparing you for your initiation."

Addy shut her eyes and swallowed hard. God. She'd said she turned it off. Had Owen seen that tape? She remembered begging Ace to help her get out. All she could think of at the time was finding her way back to Owen.

"Your brother was in the tunnels looking for you at that same time. He kept all of this from me until just recently. Ace was giving him the videos of the women she helped prepare, of other people and places she saw. He was collecting it all as evidence. He never got your video. Ace didn't give it to him."

"I asked her not to record me."

"I saw that. For some reason, she didn't turn it off. Jax said he never got the video." Owen paused. "Addy —what happened that day?"

"You know what happened."

"I know some of the ceremony. I'm not asking you to rehash that. Troy said you were married to Edwards."

"Do you know him?"

"Yes." Owen pointed to the bruises on his face.

"He's who did this to me and Jax." He went silent for a bit. "How did you survive him?"

"I don't know what that means, Owen. I don't think I did survive him. I just lived longer than the hell he put me through. Shall we talk about it now? Do you want to hear all the terrible ways he tortured me? Do you enjoy that sort of thing? Is this some sort of an exit interview? Do you interrogate all the women who get out like I did?"

"Addy, I don't understand. You behave as if I'm in charge of the Omnis."

"Don't act like you aren't. I know the truth."

"The truth according to whom?"

"The truth as corroborated by friends as well as enemies."

As soon as those words were out of her mouth, she wished she could yank them back. She'd just revealed that she had secret allies. God, he was good at this fishing game. She was way out of her league. She should leave. Now, before even more of her secrets spilled out.

She stood. So did Owen. She reached for the door, but he grabbed her wrist. "Addy, are you safe here?"

"Safe? In what way?" Locked in this house through the invisible threads of fear? How could she go anywhere without both of her sons with her?

"You're scared to death."

"Of course I am. They took one of my sons. My other son is still at risk."

He nodded. "This is a very large and very porous property. I'm not sure it's adequately secured."

If he didn't know, she wasn't going to tell him. They weren't on the same sides in this conflict. "If you have questions about our security here, you should ask Wendell."

"I have. I want to bring my own team in."

Fear sliced through her then, waves of it, cold chasing hot. "No. You can't. This is my sanctuary. I will not tolerate them coming here."

"They won't do anything to interfere with you or your retreat. They're the only ones I trust at the moment. My job is to get our son back and end the Omnis once and for all."

She folded her arms over her waist, hiding them under the blanket. If they came here, she and Troy would have to leave. Owen was King. He could do anything he wanted, wherever he wanted to do it, whatever it was, with whomever he wanted. Her puny protestations mattered not at all. Still, she had to try one more time.

"This is my house. It was agreed upon in my settlement. You have no say here."

"Then I can have them stay off property. But they don't come alone. They bring their wives or girlfriends. And their children. I'd rather have them here, close and safe, than outside the wire."

Wives and children? Who were these people? Not the groupies Cecil brought to watch her ritual humiliation. What game was Owen playing? If she had them stay in town, their presence might gain unwanted attention. But was that a valid concern when she had the head of the Omnis standing right in front of her?

"It would only be temporary, Addy."

So were the visits her husband arranged. Temporary as in one night. One night was all it took to break her for weeks.

She lifted her chin. "Do what you're going to do, but know that I'll do what I'm going to do. Just remember that this is not your home. You have no authority here. In truth, neither does my brother."

Owen nodded. "Several of the women with my team have been harmed by the OWO, directly and indirectly. They've gotten themselves out of that world, and they've survived on the other side. I hope you might get a chance to talk to them. Hearing their stories, sharing yours, all of it might help you—and them—heal."

If his team and their families really weren't part of the Omni world, as Jax now believed, then why was he doing this? To further his cover? "What are you up to, Owen? Why are you doing this?"

"Why am I helping you? I owe it to you."

"It sounds as if you're going to put an end to the Omnis."

"I am."

"Why? They're your world."

He frowned, seemingly confused. "You think I like having an enemy like the Omnis? I don't. Maybe a while ago they were a force for good, but now they've morphed into an ugly and destructive group of thugs. Fighting them is what your brother and I were training for since we were kids."

It was a pretty speech, but the Omnis were *his* thugs. It was his world he wanted to end. Was he moving on to some other terrible new plan? She slipped into her bedroom, but paused just inside the closed door. If he was tearing apart the empire he built, a narcissist like him would only do it because he had plans for something even bigger and more horrific.

Maybe it was the reason her brother had brought him here: he needed her to find out what Owen was up to.

This was worse, far worse, than she could even imagine.

9

O wen was stiff when he went to his room the next morning. He'd spent the whole night outside Addy's room. The cold floor hadn't been easy on his injuries. He thought about going down for breakfast, but knew his reception would be as cold as it was yesterday.

He texted Jax to get the combo and location to his gun safe. Owen suspected he had a small armory here somewhere. Owen had the gun that Jax had given him from his stash house, but Addy needed one too. He thought it might make her feel a little more comfortable about protecting herself and her son.

He had every intention of sleeping outside Addy's door again that night, so instead of chasing food, he chased some Zs. His dreams were painful and raw.

Ten Years Ago
Fairfax, Virginia

OWEN SHOWERED AND SHAVED. He'd eased himself in the shower, worried his hunger for Addy would drive the night instead of following her pleasure. He wanted their first time to be one she'd never forget, though he hoped to give her many such nights in their lives together. He was just wiping his face off when her text came in.

Just got free. See you in 30. My room.

Make it 10, he texted back.

30. Love you.

He grinned. The next thirty minutes were going to be the longest of his life. He could hear the celebration still going downstairs. For once, he was glad the Jacobs were quintessential political creatures. Their power party would keep them busy and distracted. Not that he really cared. If needed, he'd take Addy to a hotel for the weekend, where they wouldn't be disturbed.

He pulled on one of his tailored dress shirts. It was a little overkill with his jeans, but one of his fantasies was to see Addy wearing it and nothing else. He walked out of the closet as Jax walked in.

His buddy's gaze swept over him. As usual, he didn't look happy—never did when it came to Owen spending time with his sister. Jax sighed. The shadows were deep in his eyes. Owen frowned. Jax grabbed a fistful of his shirt and twisted, closing the distance between them.

"Take her and go," Jax said. "Go far away."

"I thought about it so we could have privacy, but your folks are busy. They won't notice us."

"You aren't the one they have in mind for her."

Owen stared into his friend's eyes. He gripped Jax's hand at a pressure point, forcing him to release his shirt. "I *am* the only one for her."

Jax shook his head. "It's not going to happen. She was born into a political dynasty. She has a job to do for the family. We all do."

"You knew I intended to marry her."

"I thought you'd be over her long before this."

"I have no intention of taking her from her family. She can still do her duty to your family after we're married."

Jax clamped his mouth shut and stepped back. His face became shuttered, blocking Owen from reading anything in his expression. "I can't stop this train."

Owen jumped as his phone buzzed with an incoming text from Addy. *Where ru?* He looked at Jax. "Gotta go. We'll finish this discussion tomorrow." Owen paused at the door. "But you better believe you can't stop this train. It's on tracks I've been laying down for years."

OWEN JERKED AWAKE. He sat up, panting, sweating.

Had he dreamed what happened that night correctly? He'd forgotten all about that convo with Jax in the panic that came the next day. After that, his mind had locked everything down, only letting the wonderment of his time with Addy and the terror of losing her get through to his memories.

What had Jax been trying to tell him that night? What if Owen had taken Addy to a hotel for the weekend? Would that have changed her fate...and his? Or would it only have delayed the terrible plan her family had made for her?

Owen's heart was racing. Addy's fate had been set already, before she'd graduated college, before they were intimate.

And Jax had known about it.

Jesus. If Owen still needed proof his friend was on the rotten side of things, then he was an idiot. He shoved a hand through his hair as he paced around his room. The horror of what happened after his and Addy's first night together had done a number on Owen. Jax had been a rock to him...in the beginning. But once Owen went back to work, Jax began to distance himself. He took on separate missions. He was given his own team in the unit. It wasn't long until the work Owen was doing and the work Jax was doing never crossed paths.

He'd missed his old friend, but thought it was for the best, since neither of them could see the other without crashing into painful memories.

Then Kelan saw Jax in the tunnels. Jax had helped

him, helped Fiona. He'd said he was Ace's handler, that he'd been helping all along, that he was who sent Hope to Max.

So what was he? A double agent, working both sides of the war?

Owen definitely needed to get Addy geared up. And…he had to get her out of there, though he couldn't until he knew what kind of illness she had. He couldn't expose his team to an unknown pathogen. And for all he knew, this whole shitshow was a setup to gut him and his team. If he was right, and he was being watched, then the danger to them was real.

Either way, he had to get Addy to open up to him. Maybe providing her with a weapon would make her question her distrust of him.

Then again, maybe nothing would.

ADDY HEARD a knock on her door. She knew who it was. She didn't want to answer it, but feared dragging Troy away from his classwork if she let it go unanswered. She went out to the hallway from her office and walked toward Owen so they could talk quietly. "Did you want something?"

"I want to give you a gun."

Her brows lifted. "You want to give me a gun. What if I use it on you?"

"I already told you I'd be happy to stand in your firing line…once you and the boys are safe."

"I don't know how to use a gun."

"I'll show you. Can we go down to Jax's room?"

Jax had guns in his room? Why hadn't he told her about them? She knew about the ones in her panic room. Did he have his own panic room? They went down the staircase near her room, then walked the long way to her brother's room in the other wing.

"Why are you doing this? Why give me a weapon?" she asked.

"Because I share your fear about the Omnis coming here. I want you to be able to protect yourself. If it comes to it, you need to be able to take out as many of those bastards as you can. It's only you and me defending this place."

In Jax's room, Owen checked his phone, probably for a passcode of some sort. He went to the huge oak bookcase that covered an entire wall of her brother's room. Reaching under the lip of a shelf, he pushed a hidden button, and the middle section separated in half.

Addy gasped, shocked that this was here and she'd never known about it. What other secrets did her brother have? It felt a bit like betrayal. She couldn't hide the hurt in her eyes when she looked at Owen. He didn't say anything. He just closed the shelves, then took her hand and showed her where the button was. With his finger on hers, they pushed it, popping the spring that opened the doors.

"Now you know."

"Yeah."

The room was a good size—ten by fifteen feet of wall-to-wall weapons. There were long guns, pistols, knives, magazines, holsters, spare parts, cleaning supplies. And a huge amount of ammo. The cases were backlit with blue light, making the whole thing look cold and deadly.

Addy shivered and folded her arms. Her brother had never said anything about this to her. She walked around the room, awed by what she saw. "How long has this been here?"

"I don't know. Probably Jax put it in after your… settlement. Have you ever shot a weapon?"

"No."

"Okay, we'll start with the basics. Let's pick a pistol for you. I'll teach you how to use every single one of these, if you want, but let's start at the beginning."

"None of these will help if you're chained down." She glanced away from him, unnerved by the tightness that came over his features.

"The goal is for you to have the skill and tools you need before being chained down. But even shackles can be their own weapon. You must learn—and so must Troy—to use every tool available to you, from words and strategy, to weapons, and even your own body."

He was silent a minute, which was good, because her blood had heated and expanded, and now pumped noisily through her veins. "You think they're coming here."

"I can't know anything with certainty, especially not when it comes to the Omnis, but they've attacked our headquarters multiple times. And you're a gem they will not willingly let go."

"I have a settlement from them."

"Which is only as good as the heart of the man who signed it."

And that was the crux of it, wasn't it? Cecil Edwards had no heart. No soul. No morals. He was a monster in the skin of a man.

"Let's select a pistol. We'll begin your training now."

"Which do you suggest?"

Owen took two pistols from their racks and checked their chambers. "These two. The SIG Sauer P938 because it has a recoil that won't knock you out of your aim if you should need to fire rapidly. The Kimber Pro Carry II because I think you'll like the way it feels in your grip. They're both 9mm."

"Aren't you afraid I'll kill you?"

"No. If you shoot me, then I guess I needed to be put down."

"What happens to the Omnis when you die?"

"Nothing. I'm not part of their organization."

"We're all part of the Omnis, all of us who are in it, have left it, or who fight it. We never really separate from it."

He looked at her as if considering how to

respond. "I don't know how much you know. There's division happening inside the Omnis—it'll continue, with or without me. And the resistance movement that my team is with will continue to fight them. My death would change nothing."

"You're King. Why would you dismantle the organization you built?"

"Addy, I'm not King. Not by a fucking long shot. Your brother thinks there might several kings, all hacking away at each other. He said my dad's still alive and might be a king, maybe for the resistance. I guess your dad might be one, too."

She watched him closely, trying to sort out if he was lying. He didn't appear to be, but he could be acting. Acting played a funny game on a person's psyche. He could be lying through his teeth, but if his mind believed the role he was playing, the lie would never show.

She considered the possibility that her father was King. Was that the reason for everything that had happened? Was that why he never tried to help her and the boys?

Over the next hour, Owen gave her a crash course on gun safety, loading, unloading, and firing the gun. He filled a duffel bag with a couple boxes of ammo, two pairs of earmuffs and safety glasses, and led her outside.

They went to a field far away from the house. Owen had set up a makeshift shooting range, complete with a table for their stuff and a chair in case she got tired. She was excited about what they were doing. It felt proactive—more so than anything she'd done to prep for her and Troy's safety so far.

Again, Owen went over how each gun worked, how she should hold it, what her stance should be, how to sight in a target. He was no-nonsense but extremely patient with any of her questions. It was so very different from the time she'd spent with Cecil. He'd complained about everything—how she did her hair, what clothes she wore, how she kept the house, the menus she'd selected, how uninteresting her conversation was.

At last, they got to the actual shooting part. She found she did favor the SIG Sauer. When her magazine was empty, she hadn't hit her mark once, though she had hit the target—she would have clipped an adversary, at the very least.

When their range time was over, Owen taught her to unload the gun and empty the chamber. When she was finished, he checked it himself.

"Can I keep one of these with me?"

"Do you have a safe in your room?"

She nodded.

"Then yes, after a few lessons. When I can, I'll get you a biometric safe you can keep beside your bed. With Troy going in and out of your room, we have to be safe."

"We'll practice again tomorrow?"

"You bet. We have a lot to go over." He gave her a

worried look. "This wasn't too much for you today, was it?"

"No. Not at all. I think doing nothing, waiting for what I feel is coming, is so much harder on me."

They were a long way from the house. The sun was low but still bright. She looked up at Owen as they walked back. He was still the most handsome man she'd ever met, with his pale eyes and pale hair... the cleft in his chin.

"You know, you were never like a brother to me."

Owen met her eyes, and his face went still. "I've known you almost your whole life."

"Did you hold me when I was a baby?"

"No. I was only seven when you were born. And your father felt infants were the province of women. We didn't get to see much of your family until you were about two." He grinned, that flirty, lopsided smile. "I did change your diaper once."

She looked away so that she wouldn't fall prey to his charm. "I don't remember those days."

"I do. I know what you mean when you said I was never a brother to you. I feel the same way about you, even though we grew up together. I always thought you were a gift to me. I was in love with you forever."

At times like this, she could almost believe him. They'd talked about this a while back—a lifetime ago. Before hell had taken over their lives. Back then, she'd thought being the one who'd caught Owen's heart had made her extraordinary, as if the sun just told her that it shone for her alone. She'd adored him, in those days. It figured that so much love came at a high price —losing their lives to this war.

"And that's not weird at all." She laughed a little nervously, trying to lighten things up.

"It is what it is. Just like if I die before you, I'll wait for you to come home. I came alive before you and waited for you to become an adult. Your brother hated me for that, tried to beat it out of me. What we have is bigger than us, bigger than your family, bigger than this lifetime. Your death—or rather, your faked death—damn near killed me."

"What if…what if I don't want to be with you?" Freedom. It was what she craved more than anything. Freedom to be alone, to make her own way…to not have her choices prescribed by a man.

He squinted as he looked into the distance, then looked at her. "We were created for each other. My heart is empty without you in it. You may well choose not to be with me, and should you do so, I'll have to accept your decision. I'll never make you go against your own will. Never. In anything. Just know that I'm always here for you. As I always have been. Now, more than ever, you have to know you are free to choose the life you want. With me in it or not."

Addy felt miserable. Avoiding him all these years had been like avoiding the sun. She began and ended with him, from her first memory to now. Life without him had been terrifying. She wondered what things might have been like if she'd reached out to him right away. Or as soon as she could have. She still remembered his old cell phone number. There were times, torturous, dark seconds, when she'd chanted those digits to herself.

"Cecil knew about you," she said, almost choking on the whispered words.

Owen's whole body tightened like a fist. "I didn't know about him until recently. The girlfriend of one of my team members was bred to be an initiate. He probably oversaw her ceremony. He ran everything in the tunnels."

Addy was horrified. "Have you lost her in the system? They disappear, you know, the initiates."

"We got her out before the ceremony was completed. We killed a major participant." He watched her closely as he said this next bit of news. "The man was called a War Bringer. His job was her initiation. He's dead, too."

Addy gripped her throat. The War Bringer was dead. "Did you get Cecil?"

"No. He slipped away before we could."

OWEN DIDN'T REMIND her Edwards was responsible for his bruises—that would only scare her. "How long do I have with you?" he asked.

"I don't know."

"The doctors must have given you some prognosis."

"The doctors have no idea what's happening to me."

"Is it months? Weeks? Years?" Her answer mattered—it would decide whether he should stay here and be with her, or if he had time to go find her son. That, at least, should be his priority. She should get to see Augie again before she died. If he could give her only that, it would be the most important thing he'd ever done.

"Owen, we're all dying. As soon as we're born, we begin dying."

"You know that's not what I'm talking about."

"I don't have an answer for you. I don't believe the doctors. I refuse to believe them."

"Even if it's only minutes, Laidy, I'll take it. Tell me what they told you."

"They said my immune system was attacking my organs, that at best I had six months. That was five months ago."

The air left Owen's lungs in a rush. "How do you feel? Better or worse, now than then?"

"I'm often tired. But things are happening to me that I don't understand, things that I haven't mentioned to my brother."

"Like what?"

"Like how fast I heal. If I can heal a cut that fast, then how can my body be attacking itself? Or my hair. They said the chemo would make it so that it was months growing back. It's only been weeks. And my vision…it's changing."

"How so?"

"I can see in the dark. Not colors, of course. But

if there's any ambient light at all, I can see quite clearly."

"Do you remember when it started? What triggered it?"

They'd reached her brother's hidden armory, which Owen opened. "It started about six months ago," she said. "I don't know what happened. I can't think of anything unusual. I wasn't sick. I didn't get any shots of any sort. I don't even remember having visitors around then, so it wasn't something I caught from anyone." She looked at him. "I don't think I'm contagious. Wendell hasn't gotten sick like this."

"And Troy isn't feeling any symptoms?"

"No. Nor are any of the staff. It's just me. I don't have cancer, but they don't know what I do have."

Cancer had been his biggest fear for her. "Addy, we feel certain the Omnis are working on a biological weapon of some sort. They have no morals about who they test things on. Is it possible you're one of their test subjects?"

"I don't know. I don't remember anything unusual. I was stung by a bee, but that's not a big deal for me. I'm not allergic to them."

"Did you see the bee?"

"Briefly, before I swatted it away."

"And it looked like a regular bee?"

"Yeah. I had a bump for a little bit." She frowned at him. "How could that have done this to me?"

"Did you tell the doctors who examined you about the sting?"

"No."

They walked out of the armory and Owen locked it back up. "Would you consider leaving here, coming back with me to my team? We could run some more tests on you."

"I don't think so, Owen. I need to talk to Jax first. And I can't leave before getting Augie back."

While that wasn't an immediate no, Owen didn't like the fact that she hid behind Jax. He didn't tell her the doubts he was having about which side her brother was on—or that he might be playing both sides. No point tainting their relationship until he had proof.

They'd made progress today. He felt he was beginning to connect with her. It was a start.

10

Three Years Ago
Saddle Notch Ridge, Wyoming

Bonnie set the breakfast tray on the table by the window. She pulled the heavy damask drapes open. "You've been in your room for a week. The doctor said you should get up and about soon. Why not come over here and have breakfast?"

And then what? Heal so the cycle could start all over again? Addy didn't have much left in her. If it weren't for the boys, she would have ended things a long time ago.

"I understand that your parents are coming for a visit today."

No. She didn't want to see them. Their visits always made Cecil suspicious. "I'm sick. I can't see them."

Bonnie looked her over. "There are no bruises they can see. Just your arm brace."

Addy had called her father as soon as Cecil had left the other day. She shouldn't have. She'd had no composure to maintain at the time, should have known they'd come out. She'd cried over the phone. She'd done that once before. She knew better than to call him again, but she was desperate.

Augie was six now. He was beginning to understand what was happening between her and his father. And he didn't like it one bit, no matter what kind of brave face she put on. Cecil mostly ignored the boys, but soon he wouldn't miss Augie's changing attitude. She ignored her cooling breakfast. Food turned her stomach when her body hurt this much. She'd barely nibbled on anything for most of the last week. Most of what Bonnie brought got flushed down the toilet.

Augie brought Troy into the room. When they saw she was up, they ran to the bed. She forced herself not to wince as they jostled her. Her wrist and elbow were in a soft brace to support them while she slept, which she didn't do much of. It took a long time for her to do more than doze after her husband spent any time with her.

Augie must have seen her wince, for he grabbed Troy and kept him from wiggling around. She pushed herself up and smiled at them. So different, her boys. Augie was blond with pale blue eyes, Troy dark with rich brown hair and soft brown eyes. Not a surprise, really. They had different fathers.

"Sorry, Mama," Augie said. "I know it hurts. I was thinking we should move your room so you don't keep falling down the stairs. I'm sure Father won't mind."

Addy swept some of Augie's hair from his brow. He needed a haircut soon. "Maybe I should, but I don't want to be far from you two."

"I can take care of Troy."

"I know. And you do. But I would miss you both if I slept downstairs."

Augie nodded. "Okay. Just promise you won't do the stairs without me or Bonnie or someone."

"I promise. Grandpa's coming out to see you today." She didn't mention Roberta, her stepmother. She wasn't well-liked in the house. Addy hoped she didn't come this time.

An idea took root. Today could be the day for them all to get out of there. Cecil wasn't home, and her parents would be flying in with their helicopter. The house was too remote to easily visit any other way.

"Bonnie, why not take the boys outside? I'm going to take a shower."

Bonnie helped her out of bed. "What about your breakfast?"

"I'll eat it in a bit. When did you say to expect my dad?"

"About an hour."

Addy kissed both of her boys. "I love you."

Augie grinned. "We know…more than the sun and the moon and all the stars."

Addy blinked. "And then some."

"Bye, Mommy," Troy said as Bonnie led them away.

Addy rushed through her shower, dressed without doing any makeup, then packed a bag for each of her sons. She was still in the boys' room when her stepmother came in. Ice spilled through Addy's bones. She'd hoped Roberta wouldn't come.

"Roberta." Addy straightened. "Where's my father?"

"He's saying hello to our grandsons."

Addy didn't respond to that overtly, but covertly, she wanted to shout that nothing of hers was Roberta's, except maybe her hate and fear. She kept herself from saying anything at the moment. She needed Roberta on board for her plan to work.

Addy checked outside. The helicopter they'd flown in on was still parked on the helipad. That was a relief. Sometimes it only dropped her parents off, then left for a while before picking them back up.

She grabbed her sons' bags with her good hand and started for the door, but her stepmother stopped her. "What's this?"

"The boys and I are leaving for a visit with you and Dad."

Roberta shook her head. "No. We've discussed this before."

"Move aside."

"When will you learn some self-control? If he's hurt you again, you know who's to blame."

It was true. Addy was the one who always set Cecil off. But that wasn't going to stop her from setting him off one last time; she had to get her boys to safety. She moved into her stepmother's space. "I've learned a lot from Cecil. All his dirty fighting tactics. I know how to leave bruises that no one ever sees that hurt enough to send you to a hospital. You really need to step aside."

Roberta stepped back.

Addy took the bags and hurried downstairs. Her father was bringing the boys up to the house. Bonnie was following behind them.

"Hello, sweetheart." Her father kissed her cheek. "The boys were happy to see us." He smiled.

"You have to leave, Dad."

"We just got here. Thought we'd have a nice conversation. Catch up…on everything."

"No." She started toward the helicopter. Her dad, the boys, Roberta, and Bonnie followed her.

"Addy, stop," her dad said. She didn't. She couldn't. If the boys didn't leave right then, there'd be no other chance. She should go too. It would leave her staff to face Cecil's anger, but there was no choice —her life was in danger; theirs weren't.

"Are we riding in Grandpa's helicopter?" Augie asked.

"Yes." Addy set the bags down and opened the door.

Her dad shut it. "No." He pulled her around to

face him, grabbing her bruised arm. She winced. So did her dad.

"I can't do this anymore," she told him, tears flooding her eyes.

"Oh, you can. You married him," Roberta said.

"And I can divorce him." Addy looked at her father. "Please, Daddy. You have to get us out of here." She knew better than to beg, but she did it anyway. She had a flash that this was one of those watershed moments. Everything before…then everything after.

"Get who out of here?" came a smooth, terrible voice.

Addy slowly turned to face her husband. What was he doing back here?

"Hello, my dear." Cecil kissed her cold cheek.

She pulled the boys behind her, keeping them between her and the helicopter. She had to get them aboard. "The boys are going to visit Grandma and Grandpa."

"Are they? We haven't talked about that."

"Yes. It was a surprise invitation. I think it's a great idea."

"Do you? Well, let's go in the house and talk about it."

"They were just leaving."

"Oh, but you just got here." He kissed Roberta's cheek. "Thank you for the call. I'm always happy when you visit." He reached out a hand to shake with Addy's dad.

Addy blinked. *Thank you for the call.* Roberta had sold her out. Again. And now Cecil was making it seem as if everything was normal—except for his crazy wife.

Cecil wrapped his hand around her arm and pulled her away from the helicopter. His fingertips dug in, pinching her already bruised flesh against bone. She looked back at her kids, then her dad, silently pleading with him to take them.

He didn't.

ADDY TURNED into her pillows and cried. Why did the one memory she wanted to keep—her last sight of Augie—have to be tainted with the brutality that came next?

She rolled onto her side. Out of habit, she looked over to her door, checking for the faint blue light that filtered through the outer bank of windows from the conservatory between this wing and the other. No light came in the thin line under the door.

Owen was there again, as he had been night after night since he got there.

She slipped on her silken robe and stepped into the hall from the door in her dressing room. He was lying on the cold marble floor, stretched across her door. She went over to him and slipped down the opposite wall. Her feet were cold. She wrapped her arms around her knees and watched him.

Was he or wasn't he King?

It didn't take long for him to startle awake. He saw her then lay back down, his head on an accent pillow he'd taken from one of the chairs downstairs.

"Why do you sleep there?" Addy asked, keeping her voice to a whisper, since Troy's room was just down the hall and his door was open.

"I have to."

"Why? You have a room downstairs."

"I don't feel that you're safe here. And someone sneaking onto the property could get to you before I could from that room."

Would King sleep on a floor for a woman he used to love? Did King love anyone besides himself? No, an Omni king would not give up his creature comforts for any reason.

"Go back to bed, Laidy. You need to heal."

She didn't move. Nor did he. Minutes passed. She was wondering if he'd fallen back asleep, when his voice startled her.

"I wrote to you."

"When? When you thought I was dead? Or did you know I really wasn't?"

"I didn't know you were alive."

"Then why write to me?"

"Because we swore we would. It was the only promise I could keep of the ones I made you. I thought somehow, wherever you were, you might look down on me and see that my heart was still true."

Tears flooded Addy's eyes. She blinked them away.

"Where are they, these letters?"

"Hidden away someplace safe."

"I want to see them." She doubted he could produce them, but damn, he knew just exactly what her heart wanted to hear.

"I'll give them to you one day."

A wave of homesickness washed over her. How she longed for the halcyon days of her life before. A tear slipped down her cheek as she stared at Owen. He'd been her sunshine. Life was always better in his glow. And here they were now, in a cold, gray hallway. Neither of them was shining very much.

He sat up and leaned against her door, watching her. She swiped at her tears. What was done was done. She had to move forward, one foot in front of the other until this dark time was far, far behind her.

She got up and went over to reach a hand down to Owen. He took it without hesitation. "What are you doing?" he asked.

"Taking you to find a bed."

They walked hand in hand down her hall to the wide landing that led over to the guest hall. Tall windows admitted the faint blue light that came from the conservatory between the wings. There were four bedrooms in each of the upstairs halls. And another four in the rooms below.

She led Owen down to the last room in the hallway—the tower room. Their hands were still joined. His was big and warm around hers. She regretted having to let go of him to open the door. She flipped on the lights, illuminating the floral wallpaper that had been reproduced to match the original in here.

"Flowers? Really, Addy?"

She pressed her lips together as she sent him a frown. They went to the next room. And, of course, he had an objection. "I don't like silk. Gives me hives."

"I've never heard of a silk allergy."

"It isn't pretty."

She went to the next room.

"Can't do pink." He scrunched his face up and covered his eyes as if the room was too bright. "Jesus, Addy, it's blinding."

She bit her lip to keep from laughing at him. She was sure the final room in the hall would work. It was blue, after all, but he nixed it as well.

"It's too far from you." He started back toward her room.

She followed him. "It's the closest one in this hall."

"I'm good where I was."

"You can't sleep on the floor."

"I was doing just fine before you woke me for this impromptu tour."

"You need a bed."

"Then put me in yours."

A gasp broke from her before she could stop it.

"I'd give my soul to hold you in my arms through the night," he said. "I can't, though, because you already own it."

"It's not going to happen, Owen."

"Don't be so sure, Laidy." He dropped to the ground and resettled his pillow.

Addy took that invitation to leave, and hurried into her room.

SOMETIME LATER IN THE NIGHT, Owen was roused from his light sleep by footsteps shuffling down the hall. The dim light showed a still-sleeping Troy stumbling toward his mother's door. Owen sat up, which woke the boy. He stood there, blinking and frowning at Owen.

"Mr. Tremaine."

"Troy."

"Did you have a bad dream, too?"

"Yes." A decade-long nightmare.

"Why don't you go get my mom? She fixes nightmares."

"I didn't want to disturb her."

Troy crawled into Owen's lap and pulled his blanket with him. "Okay. I'll stay with you."

Owen stiffened, uncertain how to behave. The boy folded himself completely in Owen's lap, resting his head on Owen's shoulder as if that was the most natural thing to do, as if Owen was a safe haven.

Crazy thing was that it felt good, like he'd found his home.

At last, someone didn't see Owen as a monster.

He sighed and shoved his pillow behind his back, then wrapped his arms around Troy and settled against Addy's door. He had to accept that nothing would ever be as he expected it. He'd spent his whole life trying to be the architect of his own fate, but he'd failed miserably.

Worry for his son, for Addy, for his team, for what the Omnis were about to unleash on the world...all of it ate at him. How much had he missed in life because he was always somewhere other than in the here and now?

Right now, with this boy curled up on his lap, he felt like he was enough.

A SCANT FEW HOURS LATER—FAR too few, in fact—Owen felt Addy's presence near him. Troy didn't stir. Owen gave himself a delicious few seconds to breathe her sweet scent, a faint floral fragrance, like moon flowers that only bloomed in the night. He opened his bleary eyes to meet her angry gaze.

"What are you doing with my son?" Her question had the carrying volume of a stage whisper.

He stared into her eyes, struck by her vibrant passion. To see her defending her son, you would never know she was dying. "I love you," he whispered.

Something about her shredded his defenses. Maybe it was his lack of sleep. Maybe it was their lack of time.

"No, you don't."

"I do. I always have and always will. I was born for you. And you for me."

"No."

Owen tore his eyes from her vehement denial, looking down at her son instead. "Troy had a nightmare. I asked him not to wake you, so he climbed on me and dropped back off to sleep. As far as I could tell, there were no more bad dreams."

Addy's face softened as she knelt next to him. She reached over and stroked Troy's back.

"Shall I put him back in his room?" Owen asked.

"That would be good. He'll sleep for a few more hours."

Owen adjusted his hold on Troy as he stood up. His body hurt from another night stretched out on a hard, cold floor. He hid that from Addy, however. He refused to let her see his discomfort; he'd be damned if she would force him into a bedroom an entire wing away from her at night.

He put Troy down on the bed then stepped back as Addy covered him up and kissed his cheek. Troy didn't look anything like his mom with his dark features. He didn't look anything like Edwards, either. So who was his bio dad?

Owen walked out to the hall, tucking that question away for a future discussion.

She closed the door behind her, then stared up at

him. It took every ounce of resolve he could summon not to touch her soft skin. He looked away from her but didn't leave. Every second he could spend in her company was a gift. He wasn't willing to surrender any of them.

"What are you going to do now?" she asked.

He shrugged.

"You look ready to drop."

"I'm fine."

"You should have taken the bedroom I offered."

His gaze swiveled toward her. "There's only one bedroom I want to be in."

She opened the door to her room and took his hand. Shivers coursed along his skin. "Get in my bed and try to sleep."

It took his body a few seconds to calm the buzz that started when she touched him. "Where are you going to be?"

"In the next room. My office. I have some emails to answer. I do have some friends, you know."

"They are not friends. True friends would have gotten you out of this terrible situation."

She scoffed at that. "Bringing in anyone who isn't already in this mess is just asking for their death. And turning to anyone who is inside already…well, that's complicated. It's nearly impossible to discern where anyone's loyalty lies. I didn't know whom I could truly trust."

This was the closest they'd come to actually talking about what had happened to her. He didn't ask more questions, though he wanted to. There were so many answers he needed if he was to untangle her future and get her free. Instead, he walked over to her bed and sat down to take off his boots.

She watched him.

He held her gaze as he leaned back and stretched out on her big bed. The covers were rumpled, her pillows stacked in the odd ways that had made her comfortable while she slept. He kept eye contact with her until she looked away from him. Turning on her heel, she walked into her dressing room. From the sounds of it, she went through to one more room. He listened for a long moment, trying to decide if sleep really was a good idea.

He pulled one of the pillows out from under his head and pressed it to his face. Her scent was all over it. Sweet. Some flower he knew but couldn't identify. He pulled the pillow that was by his side and sniffed it. It was still warm. She'd probably snuggled it up against her body. He breathed against the soft Egyptian cotton, filling his lungs with her, imagining his face pressed against her breasts, as this pillow had been.

He closed his eyes and was instantly asleep.

11

_____

Over the next several days, Owen and Addy progressed through many of the weapons in Jax's armory. He watched her growing confidence. She was becoming a little more comfortable around him. She smiled more easily and even laughed a little. Every moment he spent with her, the love he'd always felt for her deepened.

He craved time with her, though he knew it was stolen—from his team, his mission, his son. He was going to have to go back soon. He couldn't leave without her, but he wasn't confident he could get her to go with him. She was tied to this beautiful place with its fiendish history. Why? Was it because she thought this was where Augie would find her again?

Owen was sitting against the wall opposite Addy's room once again. He'd grabbed a pillow from the sofa downstairs. Jax had sleeping bags—he could have snagged one of those, but the truth was that he didn't want to be comfortable. He needed to be aware and semi-alert the whole night. Comfort wasn't conducive to that goal.

He was just dozing off when Addy's door opened. Her room was dark behind her, but light from the conservatory behind him cast her in a silvery glow. She was exquisite, like a ghost version of herself, soft, fierce, strong in a way that was unique to female civilians living with warriors.

"Have you come to keep me company?" he asked.

"No."

"But you're here, so you are company."

"Why don't you sleep in your room?"

"I told you why."

"Then hire someone to guard me so you can get some rest."

"No one can guard you the way I can."

"You aren't superhuman."

"Pretty damned near when it comes to you. And yours."

"This is foolishness."

"It's reality. Deal with it."

"Owen, I'm tired. You've been out here every night."

"I know. Go to sleep."

"I can't with you out here not sleeping."

"It's a matter of self-discipline. Nothing more. Close your eyes and sleep. I'll keep you safe."

Her sigh was dramatic. She slipped back inside

her room but left the door open. "Come with me," came her whispered voice from inside the shadows.

Owen's whole body quickened. *She didn't mean it that way, you idiot. Get a grip.* He followed her. His eyes were already used to the dark, so he saw her move into the dressing room where an air mattress had been made up on the floor.

"Sleep here instead," she said, indicating the temporary bed.

"This is kind of you."

"It's not kindness. It's survival."

Owen smiled. Sometimes her voice reminded him of her child self, the kid he'd played imaginary games with. He gave a slight bow. "Goodnight, my Laidy."

She held absolutely still for a moment, then placed her hand on the center of his chest. Owen went on alert.

"Sometimes, you remind me of the Owen I once knew."

He smiled when he realized they'd both been thinking the same thing. "I am that Owen."

"Are you?"

He closed his eyes, so briefly, but when he opened them, she was gone. The doors to the dressing room were still open, but the light they admitted was meager. Owen walked around the space, which was smaller than the bedrooms in this house but bigger than several regular-sized walk-in closets. He wondered if there wasn't a hidden room in here like there was in Jax's bedroom. It would have been easy to carve out a little space between this dressing room and the bathroom behind it. Ten feet was all that was needed for a panic room.

He wondered if Addy and Troy did drills in preparation for a fast bug-out. Maybe that was something he should work on with them.

He went over to the air mattress, but his gut rebelled at the setup. It would be easy to be blocked in here, away from Addy, if the home was invaded. He didn't like it. He turned the mattress on its side and dragged it into her room, setting it near the foot of her bed then adjusting the covers.

"What are you doing?" she hissed.

"Fixing the layout." He went back for the pillows.

"You can't do that. I want it where I put it."

"No can do, princess."

"You won't get any sleep here."

"Why not?"

"I snore."

Owen laughed, then sobered. "I never knew that. We only had one night together…and we didn't spend much of it sleeping."

"Right. So now you know. Put it back in the other room."

Owen sat on the low mattress and removed his boots. "I've been bunking with men the better part of the last decade. A few of your snores will be nothing in comparison." While he hated air mattresses, he was actually looking forward to a little sleep. He slipped under the covers and folded his hands beneath his head. "Goodnight, Laidy. Don't let the bed bugs bite."

"Owen. Tremaine."

He smiled at the frustration in her voice and the way she'd used his full name as if he were a child she was fed up with. "Adelaide. Jacobs."

"Fine."

"Yes. Fine." He stared at her ceiling, though he couldn't see much of it in her dark room. It was gaudy as hell with its elaborate Victorian scrolling woodwork that had been covered in silver leaf. He listened for a long time for her promised snores, which never came.

"It's a game, you know." Her whisper startled him.

"What is?"

"What the Omnis are doing. I don't understand it. How can stealing children, torturing women, killing people indiscriminately, and all the other crimes the Omnis commit be a game? But to them, it is."

Torturing women? Had she been tortured? "Who told you it was a game?"

"Wendell."

Owen sat up and looked at Addy. Though he couldn't see her eyes, he knew she was looking at him. She moved to the edge of the bed and settled on her belly, her legs folded at the knees. She propped herself up by her elbows.

"What exactly did Jax tell you?" he asked.

"He said that I didn't see the whole picture, which is true. But given what happened to me, and even supposing I was just one of many whose lives were hijacked, I still can't see it as a game. A club where demented men get their jollies satisfied, maybe."

"Not sure any of us sees the whole picture. I'll tell you what I know, if you're interested."

"I am."

Owen spent the next hour telling her about the history of the Omnis, the apparent schism the secret org had suffered. He told her about the documentation they got from Blade's mom and Val's dad that talked about drastically reducing the world population. They talked about the dark faction's fascination with genetics and seeding a perfect race. They covered the fact that the unit he was in was formed by her dad and Greer's granddad as a response to the international threat caused by Omni allies. Jax's belief that Owen's dad was alive, and how that wasn't exactly far-fetched, given the fact that Blade's dad wasn't dead and Addy obviously wasn't dead.

"I can't honestly see how it's a game," he said. "It's more a bunch of organized anarchists who want to tear the world apart." Something he and Jax had had many a debate about in their early days in the Army. Another checkmark against him. "They've infiltrated governments. Absorbed various anti-government groups. Bought secrets and paid off officials in exchange for lucrative info. The Omnis are organized, powerful, and far-reaching. They seem too intent to have done all they've done since the middle of the last century just for whimsy."

"I almost rather your view of the Omnis than mine," she said.

"How so?"

"I can understand the logic of an organization—even an evil one—that wants to change the world. Whether I agree with it or not, it makes sense. But to be destroying people's lives just for fun? I can't grasp that." She reached over to him. He hooked his thumb around hers. "I've missed talking to you, Owen. You're the only one in my entire life who talks *to* me, not *at* me. Ever."

"Your brother just wants to protect you. Where were your parents in all of this?"

"My dad can go to hell. He visited me here. I told him what was happening, that I had to get out. I told him what Cecil did to me. I begged him for help. But Roberta was the worst. She kept telling me to quit doing things that upset Cecil, that I had to try harder to make him happy."

That news went through Owen like ice, quickly chased with fire. "Your dad was here. He knew where you were all along? I spoke to him, several times over the years. He not only set up the Red Team, but he talked me into getting my own business off the ground. He's one of my silent partners."

Son of a bitch. He was in on everything. As a silent partner, they reported their activities to him, much as they had on the Red Team. His whole fucking team was in danger. Jesus. Was Jax working for his dad? Had he been in on this from the very beginning? He'd known about his parents' plan for Addy—he had to have, to give him the warning to take her away.

There was no way of contacting his team without further exposing himself, Addy, and Troy. Nor could he contact them without the risk of bringing them into whatever danger was here...whatever trap Jax had set.

Owen let go of her hand as he leaned his head back against the edge of her bed. He'd spent part of each of his days there searching the property, checking what security Jax had set up. He hadn't found any cameras or sensors inside or outside, but that didn't mean they weren't there; it was hard to find them without the proper equipment. The only perimeter precautions in place were the men in the guardhouse, whom he'd spoken with a few times. They had eyes like fighters. Troy's tutor and nanny had the same look. He wondered again if Addy's staff were secretly Omni soldiers.

He'd found it curious that Addy stayed here, where her hell had taken place. It was also interesting that, as unprotected as it was, the Omnis had never hit this place. What kind of agreement had Jax put together? And what, exactly, did he get out of it?

The Omnis played a long game. Maybe they knew they could use Addy as bait, drawing him here, then his whole team, when he needed a pick-up. It really was the perfect trap.

After a minute, Addy moved over to wrap her

arms around his neck and lean her head against his. It felt so wonderful that he barely suppressed a shiver and couldn't hold back a sigh. For now, he had to put those worries aside. Tomorrow, he'd make a plan.

"I wish I knew if you're the Owen I knew before," she whispered.

"I'm only one-sided, Addy. What you see is what you get." He lifted her clasped hands to kiss her fingers. "There are two things I'm absolutely convinced are true. You and I are going to work through this. And the Omnis are going to fail. The when of either situation, I don't know. But I'm a patient man."

She sniffled. He shut his eyes, wishing he could talk to her without hurting her. He reached up and wrapped his arm around her shoulders then flipped her down to the mattress. She fought him, but his grip on her shoulders immobilized her.

"Stop."

"I don't want to stop," she snapped.

"Shhh."

"Don't shush me."

"Then scream," he said. "I don't care. But I'd rather you could pretend, just for tonight, that I'm still your friend, and I've come to play, not do harm." She calmed as he spoke. "Remember when I slew your dragons? Remember when I was your knight and did your bidding? Remember when I fought off your enemies and your loneliness?"

She closed her eyes and whispered, "They said you were King. They taught me to hate you."

"Remember when you didn't? Your eyes would sparkle with fun. Laughter spilled from you in giggles so infectious that even I laughed."

A tear spilled from the corner of her eye.

"Let's be who we were again tonight," he said.

"We were children, foolishly believing there'd be good in our future."

"I'm only asking for pretend. Pretend you asked me to hold you through tonight. Pretend you still adore me. God, I loved that about you. You always made me feel superhuman."

"And there is the crux of the issue, isn't it? It wasn't just my adoration you craved, but adoration in general. It's why you became King."

"I'm not King. And I don't think it's a crime to want the one you adore to adore you back. Addy, my life has forever been forfeit to you, even when I thought you were long gone. Just...give us tonight. One night to hold each other. One simple night to heal."

"Owen..."

"Please, my Laidy." He stroked the side of her face with the tips of his fingers.

"One night. No sex." She pressed her lips in a thin line.

He smiled and sighed in relief, so damned grateful that he had to clamp down on his emotions. He moved to the outside edge of the mattress and settled on his side. He'd put his SIG under the mattress there. She got under the covers and gave him her back. He pulled her close, putting an arm under her head and one around her waist. She put a hand on his where it spanned her side. His face was against the back of her head, pressed against her soft hair. He felt her uneven breathing.

When it didn't settle out, he whispered, "Imagine if you turned over and put your heart against mine? Our hearts can never lie. Never. They'll talk to each other while we sleep and settle all the discord between us."

Addy did just that, rolling over so that she was pressed up against his chest. Her skinny knee forked his. "You have to stop being so kind, Owen. It's killing me."

"I can't. Not where you're concerned. And it's not killing you; it's killing your resistance."

"I've been my resistance for the past decade. It's the only thing that kept me alive."

"Maybe it's time to surrender, then."

She pulled herself a little closer, settling her face against his neck. "I can't. Not yet. But I'll let my heart listen to yours while we sleep."

Owen gave a little laugh. "I'll tell you now what it'll say."

"What?"

"I love you."

"You can't."

"Go to sleep and listen. We can argue in the morning."

~

Three Years Ago
Saddle Notch Ridge, Wyoming

ADDY STOOD in the big foyer, listening to the sounds the front door made as it closed behind her parents. The boys were watching her. She licked her lips, but her tongue was dry. She knew what was coming, and her fear of it was paralyzing. One of Cecil's monumental rages. She gave her boys a weak smile, then asked Bonnie to take them upstairs.

"Where are you going, boys?" Cecil asked.

"Upstairs to work on their studies," Addy answered for them.

"Are you hiding them from me? My own sons?"

"They don't need to be here for this."

He smiled. "It's good for them to know that decisions have consequences. And they are part of the consequences."

"No. Cecil, don't. They had nothing to do with this."

He shouted his rage and tossed his glass across the way, shattering it against the front door. The smell of vodka filled the air. He took out his phone and texted something. Addy moved a few steps back. Slowly. She sent Bonnie a look. If things broke loose, Addy wanted the boys rushed out of the room. Bonnie gave a slight nod.

"Bring them down here," Cecil said.

Addy faced him. "Your issue is with me, not them."

"Ah, but they are the consequences for your actions."

"No."

"Yes. I said, bring them here!" he shouted at Bonnie.

She jumped, then complied.

Cecil smiled at the terrified boys as he walked over to them. He reached out and gently gripped Troy's chin. "So pretty, aren't they? Bred carefully for the roles they'll play."

Augie reached down and took Troy's hand when her toddler sniffled.

Cecil looked over their heads to her. "Pick one."

Those two words stole the breath from her chest. This couldn't be happening. "Cecil—"

"Pick one!" he bellowed.

"Why?"

"Do it, or I will." His voice was once again quiet.

"You can't take my children."

"I'm only taking one. You knew there would be consequences for calling your parents. Apparently, that's a hard lesson for your stupid brain to grasp." He caught Augie's chin in a brutal hold. "Will it be this one? He's a little older. Maybe has a better chance of surviving without you." He fisted a bunch of Troy's hair, then turned both boys to face her. "Or will it be this one? Surely, he'll die if I take him away. Look at him. He still wets his pants."

"That's enough. You've made your point." Addy went over to retrieve her boys, but Cecil backhanded her, swatting her away.

"Choose. One you can have. One you will never see again. Which can you do without?"

Addy held a shaking hand to her cheek. "Let's just take some time to cool down. You want to punish me, do it. But leave the boys out of this."

Cecil gave her one of his cruel smiles. "I am punishing you."

"Not through my boys."

"*My* boys." He looked past her. His men had come into the foyer. "She is so stupid. Clearly she can't make up her mind. I'll make it easy on you." He shoved Augie toward his men. "Take that one. This one will never amount to anything, I'm afraid."

Addy screamed. She lunged after Augie. He grabbed for her. "Mom! Mom! Moooommmmm!"

She rushed after the man who was holding Augie up off the ground. She hit the guy and grabbed at his clothes and hair until she was pulled back. She spun around to fight, but a fist connected with her jaw. She hit the ground hard, and her world went black.

ADDY'S SCREAMS WOKE OWEN. She was lying beside

him, thrashing around, wailing, and when her hands touched him, she clawed at him. He pulled her closer, but that just made things worse. When he let her go, she scrambled free and stumbled away. He went over to her nightstand and put the light on.

Addy stood in the center of her bedroom, looking dazed and disoriented. Her eyes were wildly shooting around the room. He walked over to her and gently pulled her close, not entirely certain she was awake. She melted into him, sobbing. And not the pretty, feminine kind of crying. No, this broke from her in ragged gusts that robbed her breath and her strength. When she started to collapse, he caught her and carried her over to the bed. He lay down with her, holding her, wondering what hellish memory had triggered this violent reaction.

When his T-shirt was soaked and she was cried out, she was limp in his arms, still racked by broken gasps for air. He wiped her face then pulled the blanket up over them. "Talk to me."

She shook her head.

"Laidy. You are my heart, and right now it's fucking breaking. Please. Talk to me."

"He took Augie."

"Who?"

"Cecil. He tried to make me choose which boy to lose."

"God damn."

"I wouldn't. He decided for me. He took our son."

Our son.

"When I tried to fight back, he broke my jaw. I spent a month in the hospital recovering."

Owen wrapped his arms around her and leaned over her. Her arms hooked around his back. He cried, too. For his son. For her pain. For the years they lost. For everything that had been done to him and his family.

After a while, she caught his face in her hands. Her eyes searched his. "Do you think Augie's still alive?"

Owen drew back and looked down at her. Tomorrow, he had to make a plan to get them to safety. "I do. If for no other reason than for leverage."

Despite what he'd said, he wasn't so certain. He'd tipped Edwards off that the boy was actually Owen's.

"It isn't because I snore that I didn't want you in here. It's the dreams...they come every night."

Owen nodded. "Okay." He didn't know what else to say. Her pain was so brutally intense. Dreams were probably a relief of sorts. A pressure valve. "I got you. I'm never going to let him hurt you again."

Her eyes showed she didn't believe him. And truth be told, he wasn't certain it was a promise he could keep, but he'd die trying.

12

───────

The first thing Owen became aware of the next morning was the odd sensation of being both fully rested and emotionally depleted.

The second was that he was alone in bed.

The third was that someone was staring at him.

Owen sat straight up. Troy was leaning on Addy's bed, his head propped in his hands. Owen looked around. "Where's your mom?"

"Talking to the cook."

"What time is it?"

"I don't know. We had lunch a while ago. Mom said not to bother you, so I was being real quiet."

Owen ran a hand through his hair. How the fuck had he slept so late? He'd wanted to wake up with her. Some protection he was. The room was still dark—all the drapes were drawn. The house had been so quiet. And truthfully, he'd needed to crash.

"Why are you sleeping in my mom's room?"

"She didn't want me to sleep in the hallway."

"Oh. I thought it was because of the monsters."

"There are no monsters, Troy. Only my own devils." It was a lie, but it was best to hide the truth from kids, no?

Troy's eyes got big and he straightened. "You have devils?"

Owen reached over and ruffled his hair. "I'm working on taming them. Don't you think your tutor's going to miss you by now?" he asked, trying to preemptively redirect the boy's attention.

"She was in the bathroom, but I bet she's out now." Troy climbed on the bed and crawled over to hug Owen's neck. "Bye, Mr. Tremaine."

Owen caught himself before he could say, "Bye, *son*." The kid didn't need that kind of confusion.

Owen collected his pistol, which he'd moved to Addy's nightstand, then went to his room for a shower and a shave. He let the water run over his face, washing away the salt and tears of the night.

He needed to make a plan. He couldn't use any of the phones to reach out, because every one of them had to be tapped. Jax or the Omnis could get there long before his team could. Certainly, if the staff were Omni, it could be a bloodbath. He couldn't use any computers in the house, because he was sure they were being watched. He could take one of the staff cars, but cops would pull them over once they got to the town below. They couldn't walk out. It was winter in the Rockies. And he didn't know what kind of endurance Addy was capable of. Besides, out in the woods, they'd be exposed to multiple threats—human, animal, weather. At least at the house, they could take cover in Jax's armory. Or Addy's panic room, if she had one.

Owen went in search of Addy. It was already midafternoon. The staff said she was in her study. It was the third door on the right in her hallway. It was open, so he walked right in. She was sitting at a double-sided barrister's desk, working on a laptop. He walked over to one of the tall windows that over-looked the gorgeous grounds around the home. There wasn't a lot of landscaping. The area was left wild, with huge rock outcroppings that jutted up from the ground. Gravel paths wove their way around the rocks. Here and there were beds of xeriscape plants. Nothing was in bloom at the moment. Pockets of snow still lingered in north-facing crevices of the jagged boulders.

He turned around and faced her, leaning on the window frame. Addy didn't tell him to leave. She didn't give him any attention at all. He'd told her last night that he was a patient man—maybe that had been a lie.

"Thank you," he said, breaking into her wall of silence.

A frown tightened her brow. "For what?"

"For last night."

Maybe that got through. She gave a long and quiet sigh, then nodded.

"You feeling okay today?" he asked, worried the effects of her nightmare lingered. They did with him.

"I'm all right."

Fuck that. She was frosty as hell.

"Jax just came through the gate," she said. "He's on his way up to the house."

"That a fact. Addy, I'd like you to stay up here. I'll go talk to him."

"Not without me. I have too many questions now to leave them unanswered."

"Did you call him?"

"Yes."

"Let's take him out to the firing range. He can be a target if he doesn't have the right answers." Owen grinned.

"I agree," Jax said as he came into Addy's study. "It would be a lot easier to clean up out there than in here, should you decide to shoot me."

Owen gave him a cool smile. "Don't tempt me."

Spencer came into the room with a coffee tray and some small pastries. Jax fixed a cup. Owen reheated his.

Addy shut her laptop as the butler left, then just gave her brother a sad stare. "So many lies, Wendelly. I don't know what's true."

Jax dropped down into an overstuffed armchair. "I agree. It's time. I wanted you two to reconnect first. Looks like you have. Owen's no more mangled looking now than when I brought him here, so I guess that's good." He looked from Addy to Owen. "Where do you want to start?"

Owen reached a hand out to Addy. When she took it, he led her over to the small sofa in the sitting area where Jax was. "Why did you go rogue?"

"Who said I went rogue?"

"Your dad."

"Guess you can't believe everything you're told. I separated at the end of my tour months ago."

"Why would he lie?"

"It would be easier to tell you the reasons why he wouldn't lie. I guess both answers would be the same —because it served him to do so."

"Wendell, let's start at the beginning," Addy said. "Did you know the Omnis had taken me?"

"I wondered, when I saw the corpse of the woman they said was you."

"How did you know it wasn't Addy?" Owen asked.

"There wasn't much to go on…wasn't much of her left," Jax said. "Her hands. Her feet. Bits of hair. But something about her nails caught my attention. My sister and I have the same nails, broad and flat. They're distinctive." Addy looked at her nails. "The corpse's nails were different. Curved in the middle."

Jax sipped his coffee. "I told my dad that that body wasn't Adelaide's. He showed me a note from somebody named King who said he'd taken Addy in retribution for my dad's involvement in getting the

Red Team started six years earlier. Guess it took them a while to figure out his role in all of that. Dad sent me to a contact of his—a guy named Santo who lived in the tunnels." He looked at Addy. "The same place where your hell began. He hadn't seen you. Nor had anyone in his network."

"You met Ace there," Owen said.

Jax nodded. "Yeah. I learned she was involved with prepping women for their secret induction. I gave her a camera and asked her to record everyone who came through."

"She had that camera when she was with me. I asked her to stop recording," Addy said.

"But she didn't," Owen said. "She felt guilty about not turning it off when you asked her to, so she didn't turn that one in to Jax."

Jax shut his eyes.

"You act like this is all a shock, but you knew about your parents' plans," Owen said. "You told me to take Addy and go, that they had someone else in mind for her."

"I knew they didn't want her to pick you," Jax said. "I didn't know who they had in mind. And I certainly never thought it would be what it was." He leaned forward and scrubbed his hands over his eyes. "You told me that night you'd been laying down the tracks of your plans for Addy for years."

"You knew I was crazy about her forever."

"Yeah, but then it was a train that took her from us," Jax said. He sent Owen a sad look. "I overheard

Roberta talking to someone on the phone a short while after the accident. She said you were King. Then when I talked to my dad, and showed me that note…I don't know. I just fixated on you being King."

"Why would I seek retribution for the founding of the unit I served in?" Owen asked.

"I thought you were a plant. Of course you would deny it if I confronted you."

"That's why we went our separate ways," Owen said. "I thought it was because we were both so broken up over losing Addy that even our friendship was painful. Little did I know we weren't even friends at that point."

"Yeah. I kept looking for Addy. Dad would send me on assignments that only he knew about. I thought the secrecy had to do with keeping it from the Omnis, but now I see it was for his own personal reasons that I did what I did. I was his spy, ferreting out what the Omnis knew, what they were up to, who their players were.

"You know," Jax continued, "you went to live with Val after your dad passed—or at least we thought he passed. I learned in those years while I was dad's errand boy that Jason Parker was bad. I figured that's when you'd turned. Santo said Tremaine was King. Since I thought your dad was dead, I assumed he meant you."

"Shit, Jax. That's fucked up. You never once came to me. You never gave me the benefit of the doubt."

"Nope. I bought the propaganda. I spent four

years looking for Addy. Then Ace told Santo she was leaving the system. I got her set up in the outside world. She wanted revenge on those who'd abused her. I wanted answers. I let her go for it. I took all the info she sent my way, always asking about the women she encountered. She took photos of everything.

"I didn't know Dad was an Omni until I reconnected with Addy. And then I learned he'd known where she was all along. That he'd left her there with Edwards and only reached out to me for help once her son had been taken. That kind of betrayal cuts hard. Seemed a confirmation of what I believed you'd done. That Addy had heard that Tremaine was King as well just cinched it." Jax looked at Owen. "I lied when I told you Addy stayed in to protect you. I was too much of a coward to admit I hadn't been able to figure out all the pieces. And I didn't want you to hate her for my failing."

Owen felt sick. "I wonder how much Jason and Santo knew. Even your dad. And mine."

"Roberta was there. The day I was taken. She was there." Addy looked at Owen. "I remembered that last night. I guess the nightmare I had shook it loose."

"What do you remember?" Owen asked.

"I saw her. The girl who took my place. The one who died that day."

"What did you see?" Jax asked.

"She was in my room, wearing my favorite bra and panty set. She smiled at me and pointed to my dress, said she needed that too. Her hair was cut just like mine. Her nails were my favorite shade of pink. She was my doppelgänger."

The terror in her eyes sliced into Owen. He took her hand.

"I never remembered that before. Roberta said, 'It's time, princess.' She put something against my face and I blacked out."

Owen put his arm around Addy as he began to envision all the different ways he could end her wicked stepmother. He wasn't one who favored slow kills, like Greer had done with Whiddon. No, Owen just liked to get the deed over with. Slow sex and fast death were his preferences for the major things in life. The choice was just of weapons. A bullet, a knife, or his bare fucking hands. Whatever way he chose, she was a dead wicked stepmother.

"Okay. Good. I'm glad you remembered that," Owen said.

"Dad had the girl cremated, but I'd already taken a sample of her tissue. I had that girl's DNA tested," Jax said. "I recently gave those results to my FBI contact. He's looking for the family of the girl who was murdered."

Addy looked at her brother. "She was happy that day, like she was part of some fun skit. I don't think she knew what was coming."

Owen kissed her forehead. "I doubt she did. And for the record—you are the only one of you that exists in the whole universe."

Took a bit to digest that news, but Owen still had

so many questions. "So after Ace's rampage through the Omni bastards who'd hurt her, you switched her to finding Augie."

"Yeah. I don't know what Dad did or said to Edwards to get him to back off of Addy, but I guess Augie was Dad's last straw. He confessed to me he'd married Addy off to Edwards and that she needed to get away from him. I'd been in and out of the tunnels for years. Addy wasn't the only extra wife Edwards had. Guess he felt he alone had the right genes to seed an empire."

"Except...he couldn't," Addy said quietly. "He couldn't get an erection without medical intervention. And he couldn't ejaculate without...a lot of effort. That's why he used other men, ones he approved of, men like his War Bringer. It's why he had rape parties...my panic excited him."

The horror of that quiet statement, and the visual it brought, stole Owen's breath. One more reason to ensure Edwards would meet a painful end.

"So there's that," Addy said, breaking up their shocked silence.

Jax looked at his sister. "You told me about some of what had happened over the years, ending with Edwards forcing her to choose between her boys. But not that." He shook his head. "I didn't know any of that was going on, but once I did, I set Ace on the trail of my nephew."

"How did you get a settlement from Edwards?" Owen asked.

"I blackmailed him with the video evidence Ace had been collecting," Jax said. "Made it clear that Addy was no longer his to abuse and that if he didn't sign away the castle and its contents and also provide a monetary amount equal to her suffering, that I'd blow his world wide open. He caved."

"When did you discover that my dad was still alive?"

"After Addy got sick. I'd known for a while that the Omnis were developing biological weapons. When none of her tests pointed to a known disease, I dug deeper into what they were doing. That's when I discovered the schism in the Omni World Order. I learned your dad was part of the group who still represented the original mandate of the Omnis and that he was leading the resistance against the neo-faction that came up after World War II. He was gathering up all the scientists he could to keep them safe. But that tipped Neo-Omnis off that their game was up. They started cleaning house, killing them off. That's when I figured out what everyone meant when they said Tremaine was King. It wasn't you…it was your dad."

"So you got involved in what my team was doing. Throwing us bones. Reeling us in."

"I hoped I was helping," Jax said. "I didn't come to you directly because I thought at that point, you'd never believe me."

"I probably wouldn't have, since I thought you'd

gone rogue. You know no former Red Teamers are allowed to go off grid," Owen said.

Jax nodded. "Which was the inciting event, getting you all to come out to Wyoming."

"Why didn't you join my company?" Owen asked. "I offered you a spot."

"Because more than year ago when you were putting it all together, I still thought you were dirty. I knew my dad was. And knowing he was a silent partner and that he'd helped you get set up with some lucrative contracts, I was convinced you were in bed with him. And you had Val with you, whose dad thought he was running some maniac game. From my perspective, it didn't look good."

"How is your dad in contact with the Omnis?" Owen asked.

"I think Roberta is an Omni." Jax looked at Owen, then Addy. "I can't prove this yet, but I believe she was involved with our mothers' deaths. I don't know how or why, but think about it. She murders my mom, then sets herself up to take her place. Then she has dad—the senator—vouch for her in that community…and just like that, she owns Dad. He can't expose her without ruining himself."

"But why take out my mom?" Owen asked.

Jax shrugged. "Maybe Roberta tried to work your dad over first. Maybe Jason did it to get your dad into the game. I don't know. Just think about it. Your cousin Val's mom died the same way Lion and Hope's mom was murdered. Roberta got a foothold in my family after my mom's death. Why wouldn't your mom be in that same mix?"

God. Owen hadn't seen that pattern. "Did you talk to my dad about this?"

"No. Not yet."

"So your dad sold his daughter to the devil instead of owning his own crimes?" Owen asked.

"Yeah. Something like that."

"I hope this can be proven, Wendell," Addy said. "I'd like to have some justice."

Jax nodded. "That's what I'm working on."

"You know, Dad told me he paid you to go away." She said to Owen. "He said you were happily settled down with a wife and kids of your own. I didn't believe it until he showed me a newspaper clipping of your wedding announcement. It was dated only a few months after I was taken."

Owen shook his head. "Never happened. Never could happen." Her eyes filled with tears. She nodded. He pulled her close again and looked at Jax. "So are you ready to bring our teams together to end this once and for all?"

"I don't think it can be ended. The Neo-Omni network is too pervasive. But yes, I am ready for our teams to work together. First, though, I need to track your father down so I can get Addy some help."

"Do you know who King is? Is it Val's dad?"

Jax shrugged. "He could have been. Maybe he is. But instead of being the lead dog, he diversified. He let others in, forced others in, distributing the infrastructure…and the blame. He went a little crazy. He calls this a game. Sometimes it feels like it is, like we're all just pieces on a game board, some evil Omni game of Life. Not sure he can ever be caught—or ended. He'll just morph into another persona, making someone else take the fall. Plenty of fools on hand to do that.

"But while he's been busy working his corner of hell, Edwards and others were building an empire. They're the ones with the true power. They have the international connections. They're behind the biological weapons. I've wondered sometimes if Edwards is King."

Owen thought about that, thinking about its impact on the whole team. He'd never pegged Jason for such a wily kinda guy. Didn't think he had the smarts. Or focus. Edwards, on the other hand, did. But if he was King, then that meant that Addy had been married to their worst enemy.

"How long has this been going on?" Owen asked.

"Decades. Jason was brought up in the inner sanctum of the Omni World Order. He liked the power his grandfather and father built after the end of the Second World War. By the time they bequeathed it to him, it was already a living, breathing fiend in need of a psychopath to run it. The Edwards have been in the Neo-Omni world for generations, too. From what I can tell, the Parkers and Edwards have been at odds for most of that time, fighting for power. Your dad is pushing back, forcing them to take some drastic measures to erase their foot-prints. And his search for the scientists behind the biological weapons is causing the Omnis to kill off their researchers...the only ones who could develop antidotes for the weapons they created." He met Owen's eyes. "I took you to draw your dad out."

Owen grunted. "Finally, some honesty. Where is my dad?"

"I don't know. I don't communicate with him directly. Which is why I needed you."

"How do you communicate with him?"

"Through Santo."

Owen sat back in his seat. "Santo's a piece of work."

"We all are. We're all fucking pawns in this game."

"Santo was helping me," Addy said.

"How?" Owen asked.

"My first nanny, Bonnie, was friends with him. Through him, she had a house and funds set aside for her retirement from the Omni world. She offered it to me, but I was too afraid to go. And because I was, they took Augie."

Owen shook his head. "Santo's in deep with the Omnis. Leaving with Bonnie would not have saved Augie. They would have still found him through Santo. I'm glad you didn't go with her." He looked at Jax. "I'm taking Addy and Troy out of here," Owen said.

"I think that's a good idea."

"I can't go," Addy said.

"Why?" Owen asked.

"Because this is where Augie spent his first six years. This is where he'll come back, when he can."

"I will find him and bring him to you," Owen said. "But to do that, to focus on our son, I need to know you and Troy are safe—which you aren't here. This place is open to any type of attack. You can start packing this afternoon. I'll call my team in the morning."

Addy's face was pale, accentuating the shadows that were deepening under her eyes. "Where are you taking us?"

"To my team's headquarters here in Wyoming, a short ride by helicopter."

13

Addy slept fitfully that night. Was it the right thing that they'd decided to do? How would Augie find her if Owen didn't find him first? Wendell had finally explained his new position regarding Owen and why he'd believed for so long that Owen was King, but it was hard for Addy to shift her thinking, especially when it came to Owen, whom she'd blamed for everything for so very long. Her world was one of changing loyalties and shadow truths.

She wanted so badly to believe he was the honorable man he'd always been, but time would tell who was right and who was wrong.

The door to her bedroom opened. She looked over to see her son come in the room. She was about to lift her covers so he could come and snuggle with her, but he went straight to the air mattress where Owen was sleeping.

"Mr. Tremaine," her son said in a hoarse whisper. She held still, curious as to how Owen would react. "I didn't see you outside."

"That's because I'm here."

"Should I wake Mommy?"

"Why? More bad dreams?"

"I got scared. Will you cover me up?"

"What scared you?" Troy shook his head fast, as if to say the words would bring the monster into the room. Owen sighed. There was a scuffing noise as her son got settled on the air mattress. "Do you know what I am?"

"No, what are you?"

"I'm a monster slayer."

"You kill them?"

"I eviscerate them."

"What's 'eviscerate'?"

"I turn monsters to dust. None of them can exist where I am."

"I like that." Silence took over that area of her room, quiet and thick like a shadow, then her son started talking again. "Mommy usually only lets me in her room. You're here a lot."

"I have to be here."

"Why?"

"Because it's never good to be far from your heart."

"You can't be away from your heart. No one can. You can't live without it, Mr. Tremaine."

"My point exactly. Now, if you're going to keep

talking, you'll have to go back to your own bed."

"I can't go back. The monster's tapping at my window. I think it's a banshee."

"Ah. A banshee. Now there's a sad creature if ever there was one. Can you imagine screaming for all eternity?"

Troy said nothing.

Addy could imagine that; she'd lived that eternity in the years before her settlement.

"How about if I go check out your room?"

"Do you kill banshees?"

"I kill all monsters. You wait here."

Owen took his pistol and climbed over Troy. A quick check of Addy's bed showed she was still fast asleep. He was glad they hadn't awakened her. He walked barefoot into the hallway. Troy's room was after his classroom. The light coming in from the big conservatory was an eerie gray. If he hadn't learned to appreciate low-light conditions in the long years of his military service, he could see how it alone would make someone—especially a child—feel like things were waiting in the shadows.

In Troy's room, it was even darker. The heavy floor to ceiling drapes were pulled over the window. He switched on the flashlight utility on his phone, then did a quick pass around the room. He knelt down and checked under the boy's bed. It was at this point that he heard something at the door to the hallway. Heavy breathing. A small, white shape stood there.

Troy.

"I told you to stay in your mom's room," Owen said.

"But I wanted to see the banshee die."

Owen gave the kid a half-smile. "There's no banshee here."

"You didn't look in the closet."

"Banshees are famous for floating outside windows. They don't usually come inside. As long as you don't open your window…"

"Mr. Tremaine," Troy interrupted. "My closet."

"Right." Owen crossed the room and opened the closet, which was nearly half again as large as the boy's room. Shelves of dormant toys, well worn and much loved, sat in creepy silence. Owen shined his light over them, wondering if any of those were toys that his own son had played with.

"See anything?" Troy called from outside the closet.

"No." Owen poked around any likely hiding spot, opening cabinets, shoving aside lower racks of clothes. Stepping back into the main room, he shook his head. "No monsters there."

And then a sound that made the hairs lift across Owen's neck slipped into the room—a quiet tick-tick-tick sound tapping on the window—the *second story* window.

Troy gasped. "See?"

"Probably just something hanging loose outside." He walked over to the window. Pulling the drapes open in a fast motion, he came face to face with a floating black shape.

A drone…with a machine gun suspended in the center of it.

"Shit." He ran toward the middle of the room where Troy stood exposed. He dove on top of him just as bullets began to pepper the room, shattering glass, sending debris everywhere. He commando-crawled out into the hallway, dragging Troy with him. He wanted to get to Addy's room, terrified she was going to run into the gunfire. She almost did just that as she hurried into the hall.

"Get down, Addy," Owen shouted and waved her down. "Get down now!" He dragged Troy with him, like a tiny soldier he was pulling from a battlefield. She slumped down against the wall, reaching her hands out for her son. Owen shoved the boy at her, then gripped the side of her face and pressed her all the way down.

"Do you have a panic room?" he asked, shouting to be heard.

She nodded.

"We need to get to get into it."

The blaze of gunfire had stopped. He'd noticed it had followed them a short way down the hall. Either the drone operators knew who was in which room, or they were tracking their heat signatures, which meant it was only seconds until they came over the roof and started blasting through the glass conservatory ceiling into the corridor where they were.

"Let's go." He took Troy and pulled Addy to her feet, rushing them into her room. They slipped into her dressing room. Addy used a biometric panel to open the door just as gunfire resumed in the hallway, causing an explosion of shattered glass. Owen shoved them inside and closed the door behind them.

Her panic room was right where Owen thought it would be, accessed from inside her dressing room. It had a biometric lock, one only Addy could release, which she did by looking into what appeared to be a standard mirror. A blue light came on inside a glass armory—a smaller version of the one in Jax's room. Owen shook his head. Typical Jax to be over-prepared. Just who was he prepping to fight?

The small room was fully stocked with water, MREs, and medical supplies. There were two sofas and a bathroom in there as well.

"Wendell changes out supplies from time to time. Oh, my God! *Wendell*." She turned panicked eyes on Owen.

"He's probably fine, sheltering in his own panic room. I'll find him."

He opened the case and took out a Mossberg tactical pump-action shotgun. He loaded the magazine, then filled his pockets with several more rounds. He pumped it once to chamber a round.

"I hate banshees," Troy said, watching him solemnly.

Owen put a hand on his shoulder. "That wasn't a

banshee, son. It's a drone—a machine run by bad guys somewhere. Nothing mystical about it."

He took his phone out of his pocket, turned off its security, and left it on a shelf. "If I don't come back, call Kit Bolanger." He wrote Kit's number down.

Addy's eyes went wide. She hurried over to him. "Owen—"

He caught her face and bent close to say, "I love you, Addy. Never forget that. No matter what happens. No matter who says what."

"Don't go out there." She grabbed his forearms. "We just have to wait them out. They'll be gone by daylight."

Owen shook his head. "No one comes to a place where I am and shoots at women and children. Besides, I have to find Jax and check on the staff." He looked at Troy. "This time, I expect you to follow my order and stay here with your mom."

"Yes, sir."

Before he could leave the safe room, the door opened. Jax stood there. "Anyone hurt?"

"No," Owen said.

"What the fuck was that?" Jax asked.

"A drone. Did it fire at you?" Owen asked.

"No."

Owen stepped out of the panic room into Addy's dressing room. "Close it, Addy." He looked back at her as she shut the door. When he heard the bolt click, he said to Jax, "Let's find that drone and destroy it. The staff safe?"

Jax gave him a little grin and looked over to Spencer, who was standing with a pistol pointed at the floor. Troy's nanny was only a few steps behind the butler. "The staff are all part of my crew."

"Great." He'd suspected as much. "Don't know how many drones are out there or the current position of the one that shot at us. It could be inside. Be prepared."

Jax took Addy's room. Spencer took her office. Before Owen and the nanny moved down the hall to the other rooms, they checked to make sure the drone wasn't in the conservatory waiting for them. In the poor light, it was hard to tell. Someone downstairs flipped lights on in there. Owen saw a couple more staff members move into that space.

He and the nanny went down the hall—she took the classroom, and he took Troy's room. The heavy drapes were peppered now with holes from the assault. They billowed as the breeze came in. For all Owen knew, that fucking drone had cut an opening in the window big enough for it to come through. He listened for a moment, then peeked around the door-jamb. Seeing and hearing nothing, he stepped inside the room. Still nothing. He went up to the window and looked out, and just as he did, he heard the drone start up again, lifting off a dormer above the window. As soon as it was in sight, Owen blasted it with two shots from the shotgun. It tumbled out of flight, crashing on the ground below.

Owen sighed and slumped against the wall. How

many more were out there? Who had sent it? He went into the hallway. The beautiful antique conservatory ceiling was destroyed. Jax and his staff joined him in the hallway. "We're clear in this wing." He ordered Spencer and the nanny to finish checking the upstairs. "The rest of my team are clearing the lower levels and the grounds."

Owen nodded. "Roger that." He and Jax went back to the panic room, which Jax opened.

Addy hugged her brother, then caught herself before hugging Owen. Yeah, that didn't hurt.

"Stay with Addy," Jax said. "I'll update you when we're clear."

Owen looked her when they were alone. Why was it that the drone had only fired on them, not on Jax or his staff? One more little thing that made him think twice about Jax's loyalties. He still felt like he was being played.

Owen walked out into Addy's dressing room, leaving the door to the panic room open. He paced around a bit, listening to Jax's staff call out to each other. When he came back to Addy, she was sitting on the sofa, holding Troy, who was anxiously watching everything.

"Owen," she said quietly, "thank you for saving Troy. If you hadn't been here, we would have died."

"Maybe. Maybe had I not been here, it wouldn't have happened. Who knows?"

"Are we still leaving tomorrow?"

"Yes. Why don't you lie down? Try to get some

sleep." He grabbed a blanket from a nearby shelf and handed it to her.

An hour later, Jax came back with an all clear. Owen stared at him, trying to read him, searching for some proof that would put his fears to rest. He didn't find it.

JAX'S CREW had made another sweep of the area early the next morning. It was clear, but Owen was still worried about his team coming in to a trap. Maybe the drone attack last night had been staged to force him to draw in his team. It hadn't done any lethal damage, after all. And neither Jax nor his staff were targeted in the hit, which Owen found interesting.

He dialed in to his company's hotline. Using a password to access a restricted directory, he selected Kit's number. The phone he was using was one Jax had given him; he was very aware of the fact that Jax's team was capturing everything he did. As soon as he got through, his password would be deactivated. It was standard protocol. The call wasn't patched through, but he knew all the data about his location and phone number were being sent to Max. All he had to do was wait for a call back.

It came in less than a minute.

"Go," Owen said to the caller, wanting to make sure it was someone from his team.

"*No, you fucking go,*" Val snapped. "*You called us. Jesus Christ, O. Where the fuck are you?*"

Owen grinned. It had been a long while since he'd been so happy to hear someone bitch him out. "Hey, Val. Kit there?"

"*We're all fucking here,*" Kit said, a little farther from the phone than Val was. "*What's your situation?*"

"I need a pickup. You've got my coordinates. You'll need to bring the helicopter. I've got Addy and her son."

"*You found them? Augie too?*" Val asked.

"No. Not Augie. Her other son, Troy. He's six. Use extreme caution and expect unfriendlies. Our location here was hit by a drone last night. There's a helipad you can land on near the house."

"*I need two gunners,*" Kit said.

"*I'm in,*" Val said.

"*Max, you're up, too,*" Kit said. "*We'll get a room set up for Addy and her son, Owen.*"

"In my wing," Owen said.

"*Copy that.*"

"*Helo's on its way to us,*" Max said. "*We'll be there in under two hours. You secure until then?*"

"Affirmative."

"*Copy that.*"

There was some shuffling on the phone as Val and Max left the room.

"*A lot's happened since you were gone, Owen,*" Kit said.

"This line isn't secure."

"*Roger that. We'll catch up when you get here.*"

14

Owen went outside to greet Max and Val, who were jogging across the field. Val shook Owen's hand and gave him a man hug. Max's greeting was much more reserved—a brief handshake and a hard glare. Owen led them into the blue salon where Addy's brother was.

"Thanks for the quick pick-up," Owen said. "This is Jax, Wendell Jacobs. Jax—Val Parker and Max Cameron." The men shook hands.

"You guys hungry?" Jax asked. "Want some food or coffee before you head back out?"

"I'd kill for some coffee," Val said.

"Nothing for me." Max was always wired, always ready for a fight. Owen had hired him for that…and for his staunch sense of honor. His moral compass was sometimes something only he understood, but it always led him to the right place.

"Addy's finishing getting her things and Troy's packed up," Owen said. "She'll be down shortly."

Max walked around the large salon like a caged panther badly in need of a run. "Why'd you take off?"

"It's complicated," Owen said.

"I'm a bright guy. Lay it out for me."

"Jax was my only link to Addy. I wasn't about to lose the chance to see her." Owen looked at Jax, who was propped against a side table, arms and legs crossed, looking on with calm interest. "And at the time, I didn't know which side Jax was on. I was anticipating a trap. I couldn't risk leading you guys into it."

Val nodded toward Owen's face with its fading bruises. "Looks like you were right."

"Yeah, but that wasn't Jax's doing," Owen said.

Max wasn't convinced. He paused in front of Jax and glared at him. "No?"

"Edwards and his guys broadsided us," Owen said.

Max looked over at Owen. "And you think that was a coincidence?"

Owen gritted his teeth. He and Max were on the same wave length. "I think we weren't careful and didn't watch our tail when we left Winchester's. He took us to an abandoned sanitarium way out east and worked us over. He wanted to know who was funding me." Owen looked at Val. "I didn't tell him, but I did ask about my son, which made him take off."

Val nodded. "We found Lion and his pride. All the cubs are safe...except for Beetle. Your son. Edwards took him from the pride. We didn't know why he'd singled Beetle out. I guess we do now."

Owen went quiet as he thought that over. "Any news where he's holding Augie?"

"No," Max said.

"Has he made any demands?"

"No," Val said.

"There a reason you couldn't have let us know what the fuck was up?" Max asked. "Looks like you and Jax are real cosy now."

"We only got cosy yesterday." Jax grinned.

"Addy's sick. I didn't know with what or if it was contagious. Took a while for me to feel it was safe to bring you in. And the truth is, once I was here and had Addy again, I wanted the time I took." Owen shook his head. "Screw that. I wanted to drop off the face of the earth so I could be alone with her. I still want that."

Max blinked then nodded. "Well, I'm gonna need time to trust you again."

"You never trusted me."

"True, that."

"We do what we have to do," Owen said. "Some-times that means doing it on our own."

"And yet you want us to be a team."

"I'm not wedded to a team paradigm. I am only about ending the Omnis. I believe we're stronger together, whether we move in lockstep as a team or as lone operators."

"You don't get it—"

Owen cut Max off. "Oh, I do. I like your anger; it keeps you edgy and aware. And I trust you whether you trust me or not. The rest"—he waved a hand between them—"you'll have to fucking deal with."

Max moved closer, up into his face. "I lost everything, Owen—my entire goddamned family—only to find we're being played like game pieces."

"You want to talk about losses? How about losing the woman you loved your entire life to Edwards? How about learning he tortured her for years? That she had a son you never knew about, and he was ripped away from her in a brutal attack? Talk about lost trust—her parents did this to her. We've all been played. We're about to turn this game on its head. You in or out?"

"In. Fucking in. How about you?"

Owen bared his teeth. "Oh, I'm in."

Max glared at him a while longer, then nodded. "First, we get your boy back. Then we start cutting throats. I'm done giving them a chance to be human. They can tell God their bullshit stories."

Owen stood in silence after Max moved away to resume his edgy pacing around the room. He was a hard guy to deal with. Rangy and impatient, but loyal to a fault. Owen was lucky to have him on the team—lucky to have every one of his team members.

Fuck knew he was going to need them.

Spencer brought a coffee tray into the salon and set it on a table. He fixed a cup for everyone except Max. Addy came to the door. She looked pale. Even her makeup couldn't cover the shadows that were big around her eyes. Owen was glad she hadn't put her wig on. She wore a cream-colored blouse that hung loose over tight jean leggings that were tucked into brown, knee-hi high-heeled boots. A yellow, cable knit sweater covered her from shoulders to thighs. Her nervous gaze made the rounds of the room, then settled on him.

Owen set his coffee down and went over to her. He wanted to pull her into his arms, but knew that might not be welcomed yet. "Addy, this my friend, Max Cameron, and my cousin, Val Parker. They're on my team. You're safe with them. So is Troy."

She didn't look convinced, but she did nod at both of them.

"Are you packed?" Owen asked.

"Yes. I couldn't get everything into only one suitcase each. I have five between me and Troy."

Owen smiled. "That's fine. Where is he?"

"I haven't gotten him up yet. If we're ready, I'll go do that."

"Do you need help?" Owen asked.

"No."

When she left, Owen turned to Jax. "What are you going to do now?"

"Get this house fixed," Jax said. "Now that Addy's out of here, I'll put another call in to the FBI's art crime division. They can come take out any of the pieces here that are hot. Better that than having them used as target practice."

"Good," Owen said. "There was a lot of stolen artwork in King's Warren. I wondered if the art here was as well."

Jax nodded. "Then I have to track your dad down."

Owen shook hands with him. "I want to know when you do. You know where to find us."

Jax grinned. "That I do."

Addy came downstairs a few minutes later with a sleepy Troy in tow. Owen and the guys met her in the foyer. Troy came over and leaned against Owen's leg, then looked up at Max and Val nervously. Owen stroked his head. "These are my friends Val and Max. Ready to ride in the helicopter?"

Troy glanced at his mom. She nodded and gave him a smile, so he nodded up at Owen.

"It'll be fun," Owen said. "And when we land, you'll be at my home. There are kids there."

Again he nodded, still too sleepy to do much talking.

"Bye, sis," Jax said as he hugged Addy. "I'm here if you need me." He kissed her cheek, then stepped back. Owen read the worry in his face. He nodded at his friend.

Spencer opened the front door. "Do you need help with the luggage, sir?"

"No, we've got it." Owen and Val picked up two suitcases. Max picked one up and grabbed Troy.

"Noooo!" Addy screamed, lunging for her son.

Instantly, Owen realized what was happening, but

neither of his guys did. Owen set her suitcases down and took Troy from Max, then pulled Addy close. Her eyes were wild, her face pale. "Easy," he whispered. "Everyone's safe. It's okay. Max is one of us. I've got Troy. Let's get out to the helipad."

Owen caught the look Val and Max exchanged, but there wasn't time for an explanation. He kept his arm around Addy and led her outside. Max took the lead, carrying the suitcases Owen had set down. Jax carried the last suitcase as he and Val brought up the rear. In short order, they were loaded up and heading out.

Owen reached over and took Addy's hand. She looked ready to jump out of her skin. He should have warned the guys not to go near her son. Panic had let her devils out—he could only imagine the similarities between seeing Max lift Troy and what had happened with Augie. He couldn't wait to get back to Blade's. She would be able to find a new normal there, in a place far less isolated. She'd have company if she wanted it. Troy would have Zavi and Casey to play with—and the pride boys as well.

Troy, meanwhile, had none of Addy's angst. He was leaning as close to the window as he could get, excitedly pointing stuff out. The helicopter was too loud for Owen to hear what the boy was saying, but he smiled at everything Troy pointed out.

～

OWEN HELPED Addy and Troy out of the helicopter at Blade's. The guys took their bags. The helipad was in the back of the house in a clearing over by Eddie's kennels. Apparently the entire household had been waiting, for when they neared the house, everyone spilled outside.

Owen picked Troy up and pulled Addy close. He didn't want her overwhelmed, but it was already too late for that. Most of the team, their women, the children, and three dogs swarmed them. He made the introductions, though he knew it probably wouldn't stick.

"Greer, go through our stuff downstairs, especially my phone and her devices," Owen said. "Make sure we aren't bringing something unexpected into the house."

"You bet, boss." Greer grinned as he took their bags. "Glad you're back. Addy—welcome to our chaos." Max went with him.

Owen set Troy down so he could meet the kids. They wanted to run off and play, but Addy wasn't letting him out of her sight. "Not yet, Troy. We'll get settled first."

"But Mom—"

The mom glare she gave him would have put Owen in his place.

"Jim has your room all ready for you," Eddie said. She looked at Owen. "It's the one next to yours."

The excitement over, everyone returned to what they were doing. Owen led Addy to her room. Troy and Zavi followed behind, moving slower because Rocco's boy had to point out everything interesting along the way, like the movie room.

ADDY'S ROOM wasn't as big as her old one, though it was nicely furnished in the decor of a western guest lodge. There was a short hallway between the closet and bathroom, then the room opened up to a spacious area with two double beds, a dresser, a desk, and a round table with four chairs in the corner. By the window, two leather armchairs sat facing the room, with a lamp table between them. It was a nice retreat, but without any of the gilded extravagance of the castle she'd just left. Earthy was the best adjective. And very masculine.

"My room is right next door," Owen said.

She faced him, then immediately had a flash of the way the female fighter on their team looked at him. Almost possessively. Now that he'd brought her into his world, she realized she hadn't spared a thought for his situation. Ten years was a long time to be gone from someone's life. Though he'd denied being married, he certainly could have found someone to be with. He should have done that; she wouldn't have wanted him to be alone all that time.

Addy could hear Troy coming down the hall. She put aside those thoughts for further mulling.

Her son ran through the sitting room outside this wing of bedrooms and plowed into their room.

"Mom! This house is huge. I'm going to get lost." His smile was wide and his eyes were bright. She hadn't seen him look so genuinely happy in a very long time—not since before they lost his brother.

The other little boy—Zavi—was close on his heels. "You won't get lost. I'll show you around." He turned to Owen. "Can we go see the puppies, Uncle Owen?"

Owen checked with her, but she didn't know anything about where the puppies were or if it was safe to do that, so she deferred back to him. He nodded and said, "But only if Eddie says it's okay and one of the team goes with you."

"Yes!" Zavi took Troy's arm and pushed him to the door.

"Mr. Tremaine's your uncle?" Troy asked.

"Yeah. They're all my uncles. And one aunt. They can be yours, too! Uncle Owen's the chief, so…" The rest of Zavi's words faded away as they rushed off to find the puppies.

Addy felt alone and off-kilter. She'd selfishly wanted Troy to stay with her so she had some grounding, but he needed to be a little boy. She was a stranger in a crowd that was its own community. Children and animals. Wives and husbands—or at least committed couples. She was an outsider. An untrusted interloper.

"If there's anything you need, just ask for it. Jim's our housekeeper. He does our shopping, so let him know any regular supplies you'll need. Russ is our cook. Both of them came from the same unit I was in. They're not active warriors, but they've been read in and stand ready to fight. You're welcome to use any public room in the house. And we have a gym wing. We also have a private meeting space in a bunker below the house. That's off-limits unless one of us is with you. I'll be happy to show you around, but I need to check in with my team first."

Addy nodded. She was a little afraid that, like Troy, she'd get terribly lost until she figured the place out. "Thank you."

"Our numbers are all on the list there." He nodded toward her nightstand. "Max or Greer will bring security necklaces for you and Troy. Everyone is required to wear one so we can know where you are and so that you have a way—besides your phone—to send out an emergency call for help to the team."

"When will I get my things back?"

"Greer will bring them up in a bit. We usually eat around seven; I'm sure he'll have them back before then." He looked at her, pausing as if there was something else he wanted to say. "You're safe here, but I would recommend you don't leave the grounds. At least, not until we put Edwards down and figure out who King is."

She nodded. A few minutes after he left, there was a knock on her door. It was Selena, the fighter she'd seen in the crowd that had greeted them.

"Hi," the woman said.

Addy nodded. "Selena, right?"

"That's me. I came to see if you would like to take a tour. This place is big and spread out—you might feel more at home if you know where everything is."

"That would be great. Thank you."

There was a big shadow between them. Addy didn't like it. Maybe it was just that she'd been isolated for so long that her social skills had evaporated. It couldn't be jealousy, could it? She hadn't felt that in a long time. What an ugly emotion it was.

Selena frowned at her. "Are you bringing trouble to us?"

Addy was surprised by the frank question. Maybe Selena was feeling the same thing she was. She considered her answer before nodding. "Probably. I was deep in the Omni world for ten years. I thought I'd gotten out, but Owen thinks I'm still in. I don't know. The Omnis don't let go of their own. I have to get my oldest son back from them. Then I want freedom for my boys and me. I want to live a quiet life in total obscurity."

"That's too bad. I get the feeling that Owen was hoping for a different outcome."

That made Addy's heart jump. "Do you think the Omnis can be ended?"

"Not sure. I think it might be like trying to end a country."

"Can I ask you something?"

"You can *ask*," Selena said, implying she might not answer.

"Is Owen King? My husband said he was. My

brother believed it at one time." Jax had amended his view, but Addy wasn't quite there yet.

Selena didn't blink. "Owen isn't your enemy." Selena folded her arms then leaned against the door-jamb. "Owen may not know this yet, but we have another group of watchers here—it's the one your son was in."

"*Was* in?" Addy's jaw dropped as her breath caught in her chest. "Is Augie here?"

"No. But you might like to talk to the pride's leader."

Tears filled Addy's eyes. "Yes. I do. Can we go now?" She hurried over to stand near her guard then paused. "I need to get Troy back, first."

"He's fine with Zavi."

"I'm sure he is, but we're new here. I have to see him."

"Follow me."

They walked out of the sitting room connecting all the rooms in that wing to another long hallway then up a back stairway. Owen's base of operations was bigger than the place where she'd been living, though it was nowhere near as elegant.

At the far end of the hall, they entered what had to be another bedroom wing, for it had a sitting room just like hers. She could hear boys laughing. For a jarring moment, it was almost like hearing Augie and Troy playing together. God, was her boy safe? Why had Augie left the watchers? Where was he?

Selena sent her an odd look. Addy stopped that

line of thinking. She'd have answers soon enough…she hoped.

In the room with Troy and Zavi, were two women, one young and a little heavyset, the other pregnant and with copper-red hair. Both looked up and smiled.

"Hi, I'm Mandy," the redhead said as she came over to greet her. "You must be Addy. I'm Rocco's wife and—"

"And my mom," Zavi said as he came over to lean against Mandy.

"I made a friend, Mom," Troy said.

Addy smiled. "I see that."

The other woman stood and shook hands with Addy. "I'm Wynn, Zavi's nanny and tutor…and teacher to a whole bunch of watcher boys, too."

"I was just about to go see them."

"It's Saturday, so no classes," Wynn said. "No telling where they might be. Selena, maybe give Lion a shout to see if he can come talk to Addy when he's free? He may be busy with Owen."

"We were just on our way to go see him. I'll give him a buzz." Selena took out her cell and stepped into the sitting room.

"How about we go with Selena to give Troy and his mom the tour, Zavi?" Mandy asked.

"Okay. Can we show them Aunt Eden's puppies first?" Zavi asked.

Wynn smiled. "How about we do the house tour first."

"Lion's free," Selena said as she came back into the room. "We can head out that way after the house tour, if you're okay with that," she said to Addy, who nodded.

"Thank you." She wanted to rush through everything so she could get right out to talk to the leader of the watchers her son had been with.

Mandy caught her arm and held her back as the others moved out of the sitting room. "I can't imagine what you must be going through with your son. Zavi isn't my biological son—he's Rocco's from his first marriage. Even so, if something happened to him…"

Addy blinked. "It's been almost three years."

"God. I know we've only just met, but believe me, we're all here for you. And now that Owen knows he has a son, there'll be hell to pay if he can't get him back for you quickly. Nothing stops Owen."

15

ddy was feeling overwhelmed by the size of the team's headquarters. Her castle had been a simple V. This one was an X with a long middle. She learned that the compound supported the careers of at least two of the wives here —Mandy's horse therapy center and Eden's dog-training business.

Addy hated that she was suspicious of everything. It was something she was going to have to heal from now that she was out of the Omni world, but in it, no one did anything for another when there wasn't something to be gained. She mistrusted kindness most of all, and everyone here seemed kind.

It didn't surprise her that two of the women were given space for their work. Anything for the appearance of independence. It fit that these men, consumed by this secret war, would want to keep their women happy...and quiet. Fiona and Hope

189

worked for the team in their capacities as an assistant and mechanic. Wynn worked and lived here.

What did surprise her was that two other women worked outside the home—Ivy at her diner and Remi at the university. And Ace was, apparently, part of the team, like Selena.

Addy hadn't met everyone, but her mind absorbed all their pertinent details, tucking them away as if her life depended on it—because it did. Everything—on the surface, at least—seemed normal…as normal as could be for the circumstances, and that was something Addy knew nothing about.

She didn't have enough facts yet to determine if one, some, or all of them were Omnis…or if they were truly fighting them, as they claimed. It was hard to know who was in and who was out. The Omnis had people everywhere—governments, royal families, society's glitterati, all the way to the working classes. Many of the world's powerbrokers were owned by Omnis. It would be naive to think some of those here weren't also owned.

She'd thought her brother was fighting them, but after talking to Owen, she wasn't so sure. She was in over her head, trying to stay afloat, keeping very, very calm and still so the sharks wouldn't eat her.

She went with the women and boys to do the outside portion of the tour. She was interested in what they were showing her. Everything she learned about the lay of the land and its people might come in handy sometime. Owen had said there was a bunker underground. She wanted to get a tour of that as well.

Outside, the yard was as beautiful as the rest of the estate. Manicured and well maintained, she could tell, even though winter had browned and desiccated everything. The wide lawn was broken into two areas, an upper portion close to the house and a lower portion farther away, which was now occupied by a noisy bunch of young boys who were engaged in some sort of guided sparring lesson. They were laughing, grunting, yelling.

Troy looked up at her. She knew that lonely look in his eyes. She smiled and ran a hand over his head. "Are those watchers?" she asked her tour group.

"They are," Selena said.

"They're the group my son was with?"

"Yep."

She stopped to observe them, her heart in her throat. One of the young men in the group separated from the others and jogged over to them. He was tall and lanky. His dark blond hair was just a little curly and a tad too long. Tawny brows covered some sort of tattoos, not fully obscuring them. His eyes could tell stories, but right now, they seemed happy. Addy sent a look at Mandy, trying to quell the odd mix of panic and gratitude she was feeling.

"Hi," he said to the group, then held out his hand. "You must be Addy. We were told you'd be moving in. I'm Lion."

Addy went cold at the touch of his hand. This

young man had seen her son—recently. He'd worked with him, fed him, kept him safe. "I'm Augie's mom," Addy said. What an odd name Lion was.

He looked a question at her, one Selena resolved for him. "Beetle's mom."

Lion's distinctive brows lifted. "He said you were dead."

Addy pressed her lips together. "I'm not." She forced herself to breathe. "How long was he with you? Was he okay?"

Lion's face went blank. Why? Was he trying to hide something from her? Did he have bad news? She reached out to touch him, which seemed to startle him.

"Please. I need to know."

"He came to our group this summer. He wasn't with us very long, but he was a loyal member of the pride."

"Why did he leave? How did he leave?"

Lion looked sick. "There was a fight. He was taken from us."

"By whom?"

"Mr. Edwards."

Addy gasped. A cold, clammy sense of panic took over her gut. She grabbed Troy's hand and started back toward the house. Troy was struggling to keep up, but she couldn't slow down.

Selena came even with her. "What's the rush? Where are you headed?"

"I have to see Owen."

"Owen's busy."

Addy stopped. She wiped a tear from her face, unaware she'd been crying. "Does he know Cecil took him?"

"Maybe not. He just got back."

"Then I need to see him." Addy continued toward the house.

Selena tapped her ear, then said, "Boss, Addy needs you. We'll be in the den."

The others caught up with them, their faces filled with concern. "What's going on?" Mandy asked.

"We're going to talk to Owen," Selena said. Mandy looked shocked.

Wynn gave Addy a calming smile. "Why don't you leave Troy with us? He can play with Zavi while you meet with Owen."

Addy grabbed Troy and pulled him close. "No! He stays with me." She sent a panicked look around at the group. Lion was there. A leader of watchers. The kind of group Troy would disappear into.

Wynn put her hands up slowly. "All right. We'll all go back. We'll wait with you in the living room."

Addy gave Selena and Lion both a narrow-eyed look as she picked up Troy and started toward the house at a fast pace. They would not have both of her sons. Even if it killed her...which the coming confrontation very well might. Her hold on Troy tightened, as his did around her neck. Did he remember when his brother had been taken? He'd only been a toddler. God, she hoped he didn't.

The den. Where was the den? Selena touched her elbow and pointed down a hall. Addy followed, painfully aware that a leader of watchers was close behind. By the time they reached the den, all of her swirling emotions had coalesced into anger. Troy's weight no longer seemed significant. Heat coursed throughout her body.

She closed her eyes, fearing she was starting to hyperventilate. Warm hands pulled her close to a body of steel. Owen. She knew his scent. His arms went around both her and Troy.

"Breathe, Laidy. Sloooowly. I got you."

She did, through her nose so she could take in the hint of cloves from his skin. Her eyes felt a little less like they were burning.

She leaned back and looked at him. "I know where Augie is. Cecil took him."

"I know."

That took her aback. She stepped out of his arms so she could get a better look at his face. Of course he knew. He was King, wasn't he?

"Honey, I think you should sit down." He tried to lead her over to the leather sofa that was next to French doors leading out to the patio, but she shrugged him off.

"You knew."

He frowned at her, tilting his head a little as he stared into her eyes. "I just learned when the guys came to pick us up."

Nice recovery. She didn't buy it. Her simmering

anger built into a boiling rage. Her mouth was dry. Her eyes burned. She had to be breathing too fast, for she felt a little lightheaded. She didn't resist when Owen again tried to draw her over to the sofa.

His team members were coming into the room… from a closet. They took one look at her and froze in horror. Troy looked up at her, then gasped. He caught her face in his hands, his eyes and mouth opened wide. "Mommy. Your eyes."

Owen knelt in front of them. Worry covered his face. What was wrong with her eyes? She rubbed at them until he caught her chin and turned her face to one side, then the other.

"What are you doing?"

He took out his phone, set it to front camera, then showed her as he took a pic. *Oh my God.* Her eyes were…glowing. They looked like animal eyes reflecting light, but the light was *coming from her eyes*. She set Troy on the sofa and made a beeline for the bathroom she'd seen next to the closet.

OWEN LOOKED at the picture he'd taken of her. He frowned at Kit as he handed his team lead his phone, then followed her into the bathroom.

"What is this? What kind of trick is this?" she hissed, turning to glare at him.

He held her face so he could better examine her

eyes. "I don't know. I've never seen anything like this. Has it happened before?"

She blinked, then looked at him sideways. "Am I hallucinating?" She shut her eyes and covered them with her hands. "Tell me this isn't a dream. Tell me I got out of that house."

"You're out. Good and out, and never going back."

"My eyes are burning." She looked up at him.

He nodded. "We all see what you're seeing. Does it hurt?"

"A little." She drew a ragged breath. "Make it stop, Owen." She put her hands over her eyes again. "Make it all stop. All the changes in me. The time we lost. The hell with Cecil. Losing Augie. I want to go back. I want a do-over."

"I can't set the clock back," he whispered, touching his forehead to hers. "Our do-over is now and forward."

"What changes is she talkin' about?" Max asked. The whole group had turned to face the bathroom. He was the closest to it.

"I don't know all of them. Something is different, changing her."

"No shit," Blade said.

Owen gave him a quelling look. "She heals strangely fast." He faced his team, blocking her from view.

Addy rested her head on his back. How did he know just when she most needed his big shoulders? "I can see in the dark like it's daylight," she said. "I can remember things with high precision. Words. Things I hear and see. I can smell…more. I can distinguish faint scents from heavier ones. Now this. I'm a freak."

The room was silent, but she knew they heard her.

"Hey, cuz," Val said, breaking the silence. "We don't discriminate against aliens here." Air whooshed from his lungs as Ace elbowed him. "Ooof!" He winced and, protecting his ribs, he said. "As long as she's on our side… She is on our side, right?"

Owen didn't laugh. "She's not an alien. The Omnis did this to her."

"Did what, exactly?" Selena asked.

"Changed her," Owen said. "It isn't anything the doctors who examined her can identify. They tried treating it with chemo, but that only made her sicker."

"Then we better find docs who know what they're doing," Angel said.

"Sure. Like who?" Owen asked.

"Like Wynn's parents. I believe they're still alive. They were researchers for the Omnis. Jafaar has them now."

Owen checked Addy, who met his glance with just a little glimmer of hope. "What makes you think they have a clue as to what to do to reverse this?" he asked Angel.

"They were groundbreakers in nanotechnology research. Her dad was a chemical engineer, and her mom was a molecular biologist. They both died in a suspicious lab fire. While you were gone, Jafaar had

Wynn kidnapped. She was stung with a tiny bumblebee drone that injected her with something that knocked her out. Later, when she had a chance to get away from Jafaar, she saw a couple who might have been her parents. I think I saw her mom at her house just after it was hit by some Omnis."

"Addy was stung by a bee a few months ago," Owen said.

"You said Jax told you that your dad was looking for all of Omni's scientists and because of that, King was killing them," Ty said. "Maybe that's why Wynn's parents made a run for it? It was run or die."

Owen nodded. "We'd only just started our meeting downstairs, but I can see it involves more than just our team. I want everyone there. Let's convene in the living room in a half-hour." He looked back at Addy and Troy, who was leaning against his mom, watching him with big eyes. "It's not a talk for children."

"Then I'll sit it out," Addy said.

"No. We need you. We need all the women there. And Russ and Jim."

"Casey can sit the boys," Kit said. "I'll set up a movie for them—a couple of movies. But let's hold the meeting after dinner. We need time to go through Addy's things."

Owen accepted that. "After dinner, then. We can meet in the dining room instead of the living room."

Max frowned and exchanged glances with Greer.

"Spit it out, Max," Owen said.

"Can we trust her?" He thrust his chin toward Addy. "We don't know anything about her."

"Yes."

"No," Addy whispered from behind his shoulder.

"No?" Owen lifted a brow.

She shook her head as she looked at what she could see of his team. "What if Cecil and others can hear through me? What if I'm broadcasting?"

"Who's Cecil?" Greer asked.

"Cecil Edwards. My demon. Her hell," Ace answered.

"How would that work?" Kelan asked.

"No idea," Addy said. She was still slightly behind Owen, shamefully glad he stood between her and his team. "But then, my eyes shouldn't change when I'm angry. And all of the other weird stuff that's going on shouldn't be happening either. I don't know how any of this works."

"Right," Kit sighed. "Best we can do is have Kelan wand you to see if you're sending off signals." He shook his head. "That's the weirdest thing I never thought I'd hear myself say. Greer, Max, finish going through her devices. The rest of you—go through her bags and clothes. Not sure what we're looking for, but since we know the Omnis can weaponize insect drones, I don't want to be too careful."

"Agreed," Owen said. "I want Lion at the meeting. And Blade's dad, too."

"Roger that," Kit said.

.   .   .

THE ROOM EMPTIED OUT, leaving Owen alone with Addy and Troy. Her boy seemed terrified. Owen smiled and set a hand on his head, then looked at Addy. "I'd like to say everything is going to work out, but we both know that's not a given. And I want to ask you to trust me, but I know that resource has been depleted for a long time. So I'm just going to say that you have me and my entire team behind you. They're bright, capable warriors. Every one of them has been harmed by the Omnis; they have skin in the game. I trust them with our lives. You and Troy are safe here. Most of all, you aren't alone—you've got all of us with you."

Addy almost wavered. She'd heard similar heart-felt offerings from her brother two years ago and had fallen for them. Completely. She'd believed Wendell, and look where she was for it...an Omni science experiment, still under Cecil's thumb, not a step closer to having her son back.

"Do you think Wendell was ever even looking for Augie?"

Owen stroked her cheek, pushing a lock of hair behind her ear. "I think so, at least until he learned which pride he was with. Lion is a natural leader. Augie would have been safe with him. I think Jax felt finding my dad and stopping the slaughter of the Omni scientists was a higher priority. He thought you were dying, you know. He needed them to save you. We still do." He shook his head. "All I know for a fact is that I love you."

Troy moved between them to hug Owen. "I love you, too, Mr. Tremaine."

Owen smiled at her. He knelt and set a hand on Troy's shoulder. "Thanks, bud. We're going to get through this."

"I know. We'll keep Mom safe, like Augie would have done."

"Just like that." Owen nodded. "We'll make your brother proud. You know, everyone here calls me Owen. You think, if it's all right with your mom, that you could do that too?"

Troy looked up at her and smiled when she nodded. "I guess that's okay. Owen."

"Do your men need my help getting into my devices?" Addy asked.

Owen stood, then handed her his phone with a text screen open. "Enter your passwords. They'll take it from there."

16

Addy went to her room after the meeting in the den. Troy had gone off with Zavi again. Those two were going to be a handful, having the run of a place the size of this one. She splashed her face with cool water, then got a wash-cloth and ran it under the cold tap. She wrung it out, then put it over her eyes, trying to get them to go back to being normal. Was that even possible?

After a few minutes, she checked the clock on her nightstand. It was almost time to meet for dinner. Her purse had been delivered to her room, along with all her other things. Her sunglasses were in there. She put them on, then left her room. She ran into Owen's cousin by the backstairs.

"Hi, Addy," Val said.

"Val." Addy stopped in the hallway. Of all Owen's team, Val felt the safest to her, maybe because he was Owen's cousin.

"I guess you aren't broadcasting all of our secrets, since you aren't in isolation." He grinned.

"No. But the eye thing has gotten worse."

"Do they hurt? Does light bother them?" he asked.

"No. I just don't like being different."

Val shrugged. "We all have our issues. Rocco, for instance, is recovering from severe PTSD. Blade's dad was one of King's henchmen. Kit's mom was an alcoholic and an escapee from an Omni isolationist group. Greer sees ghosts. My dad is some evil kingpin. Max was a felon who almost killed Owen——"

"Why did he do that?"

"He was angry for the trickery that dragged him into this mess," Val said. "For a while, he blamed Owen, but we know now it was the Omnis who brought him in."

"What issue does Owen have?"

"Owen? Hmmm. His is the worst of all. For a decade, he's just been a tin man, hollow and aching for his heart, which he lost when he lost you."

She sighed and took off her glasses. Val's eyes widened. "Goddamn." He lifted her chin, bringing her face more into the light of the hallway. "They're purple now."

"Are they?" She pivoted on her heel and hurried into the hall restroom. "Oh my God. What am I going to do?"

"Nothing. They're gorgeous," Val said, leaning against the doorjamb. "I just told you we all have our issues. Yours happens to be eyes that light up like mood rings. Let's enjoy that."

"I'll freak everyone out."

"Yeah, but in a good way."

"Addy?" a woman asked from the doorway.

Addy turned around to find Ace standing there. She knew those eyes, that beautiful, angular face—she'd remembered them as soon as she'd seen her in Owen's den. Her arm was in a cast. "Ace? Is that really you?"

"I'm sorry I didn't come to say hello before this. I wasn't ready to face you."

"Why?"

"Because of what I did to you."

Addy reached over and took Ace's good hand. "You didn't do anything to me."

"I failed you. In so many ways. You asked me to stop taping you. I didn't. Then when I gave my tapes over to your brother, I didn't give him the one of you because I felt guilty for taping when you'd asked me to stop."

"Ace, honey, you were a kid. I don't blame you for anything. How could you have known what to do in that situation?"

"I could have gotten you out. I knew the ways."

"You aren't to blame for what the Omnis did. They are." Addy felt fierce and angry suddenly. It probably showed in her eyes, magnified by the big tears pooling there. "We survived. They don't get to have us. Not any part of us." She hugged Ace, and felt relieved when Ace hugged her back.

"I'm sorry," Ace said.

"I'm glad you're here, out of that world."

Ace nodded then caught Addy's shoulder as she studied her eyes. "Your eyes are beautiful. Do they just change randomly? Like on a timer? Like LED Christmas lights?" She smiled.

Addy chuckled. "I don't know. This just started happening. It's crazy."

Ace shook her head. "It's not crazy. It's biology. Lots of animals change color, like chameleons and octopuses." Ace hugged her again. "I can't wait to catch up with you, share our stories. I'm so glad you were strong."

Addy returned the hug, not entirely sure she had survived…at least not yet. "I want to hear your story, too. It can't have been easy for you."

"It wasn't. I'm getting back on my feet." Ace released Addy so she could put an arm around Val's waist. "I have Val and the team now—a home and a purpose."

"I'm happy for you," Addy said.

Val led them out into the hall. "So go ahead and wear your glasses, Addy. Or put out your crazy shingle. No one will judge you here."

"Yeah, no one cares about my hair anymore," Ace said. "At first, they were a little weirded out." She looked up at Val. "God, can you imagine if I could get my hair to change color on its own?"

"I love it when you call me God." Val laughed when she punched his side. "Maybe the good doctors Ratcliff can get to work on that. As soon as we find them, that is." They moved down the hall toward the huge living room that was at the heart of this mansion.

Addy followed a little more slowly, bracing herself to join Owen's people. Her son and Zavi ran toward her down the long hallway. Troy's face was alight with childish joy, mirroring Zavi's mood.

"Mom! Zavi eats with the watchers. Can I do that?"

"No. You'll eat with me." He was fearless here, happy just being a boy. She loved that this place had brought it out in him, but everything was still so new, and she wasn't as trusting as he was. She knew too much to be naive.

"Mom, pleeease."

"Troy—" Before she could finish her response, Owen joined them.

"I understand the watchers eat dinner first, Addy," he said. "They weren't here when I left, so some changes have been made to our routine, since the table isn't big enough to accommodate everyone. Casey, Kit's daughter, and Zavi, Rocco's son, have been joining them. Sort of a segregation of children and adults. Troy's welcome to join them."

"I don't know these watchers or why they're here…" Her voice trailed off. Maybe they'd come for Troy.

"You will after our meeting tonight. I was surprised to learn they were here, but they're safe, and I'm glad for it. You're welcome to stay with Troy, but I'd like you to eat with me. They'll just be in the dining room. We'll be next to them in the living room."

"So can I, Mom?" Troy asked.

Addy sent Owen a quick look, then nodded.

The boys laughed and jumped up and down. "Zavi said I can have a sleepover after dinner. Can I do that, too?"

"No. We don't want to impose. It's our first night here."

Once again, Owen stepped in. "They'll be near Rocco and Mandy, in their suite of rooms. No one's leaving the house. It'll help with our meeting, since I expect it will run long."

"The meeting Mandy and Rocco will be at too. No?"

"Yes, they'll be there. And while they are, Casey will babysit the boys. It's just a sleepover, Addy. Remember when I'd come for the weekend?"

"And you and my brother would pick on me?"

Owen looked shocked. "Never. Really, we strive for normalcy here. There's so little of it in what we do," Owen said. "Let the boys have a sleepover."

"Please, Mom!" Troy said.

"I'll talk to Mr. and Mrs. Silas," Addy replied. "If it's all right with them, it's all right with me."

"Yes!" Troy shouted, then both boys ran off down the hall.

She looked at Owen, thinking she should put her sunglasses back on just to block him from getting in. They started toward the big living room. She stepped closer to him and said quietly, "I very clearly remember an October night that you were over. You dangled a life-sized scarecrow outside my window, making it dance and move."

Owen chuckled.

"It made this horrible moaning noise."

"Scared you, huh?" Owen laughed.

"Scared me?" she said, like that was the under-statement of the year. "You then spent the whole weekend popping out of hiding places, shouting 'boo!'"

Owen squeezed his eyes shut as he laughed. "And every time you were startled. Every damned time."

"I'm so glad I could be the source of your jollies."

"I never knew screams could hit the octave you did when you saw that scarecrow." He laughed. "Oh, your face…"

"Are you laughing at me?"

"Not at you. With you." He shook his head, still laughing. "No. No, I am laughing at you."

She leaned near him. "Well, I do believe I wet the bed as well. Roberta was not happy."

Owen looked at her in shock, then laughed. The more he thought about it, the more he laughed, until he bent over and held his knees, he was laughing so hard. He lifted a hand. "No. Wait. I can't take any more. It hurts."

She couldn't quite keep a smile from her face. Owen used to laugh so easily when they were children...before...everything. She used to laugh, too.

He straightened, sobering as the last ripples of laughter faded away. His pale blue eyes held hers. She fought a shiver. How many nights and days had she conjured up the image of them like this, standing close as they were now, just him and her, their eyes dancing, saying things they didn't openly acknowledge?

"I had to sleep with Wendell for days after you left. I couldn't go to my parents. They never liked their sleep interrupted. You know how they were. But Wendell let me stay with him when I got scared. He was there for me when it counted. In those days. I thought he still was, but now I don't know."

He gave her a slight bow, and, to his credit, kept a straight face. "My deepest apologies, my Laidy. I'll find a way to atone for that terrible weekend. I have a lifetime of sins to make up to you. It's a debt I take seriously."

Addy felt heat rise from her neck to her face. She wondered if her eyes were changing to yet another color.

"And we'll figure out where Jax stands," he said. "I have my doubts, too, but that doesn't mean they're real."

She turned from him to see everyone who was

gathered in the living room watching their exchange in stunned silence. They all seemed in awe of Owen, just as she was.

She whispered, "We have an audience."

As Owen looked into the room, everyone quickly returned to what they were doing. Except Val. He gave her a wink and lifted his beer. As they stepped down from the foyer into the living room, he went behind the bar and poured a glass of Balcones for Owen.

"Addy, what's your pleasure?" Val asked.

She blinked, taken aback by his question. Memories so horrible that they needed to be burned jumped to the front of her mind.

"To drink," Val clarified, yanking her back to the present. "What can I pour for you?"

Addy lowered her gaze and forced herself to slow her breathing. "Um. Wine. I guess." She flashed a glance around the bar. "Whatever's open."

"Pinot Noir it is."

He poured the glass. She grabbed it and quickly lifted it for a sip, just catching the tail end of the confused look Val shared with Owen. "I'm glad you're being brave," Val said in a quiet voice not meant for the whole room.

Again, she missed his meaning. He pointed to her sunglasses, which were perched on her head. "Smart to keep them near. Wear them when you feel uncomfortable. Or don't wear them at all. Either way, be at case with us. You and Troy are safe here. Soon Augie will be, too."

His words of kindness left her feeling raw and exposed. Kindness had been so scarce in her world that it actually hurt to feel it. She looked over at Owen, who was watching her. Val stepped away from the bar and went to the oversized armchair Ace was sitting in. Lifting her like she was a mere pillow, he sat down and settled her on his lap. She leaned against him, entirely comfortable with his open affection in front of all these people.

"There's something I've been curious about for a while," Val said, looking at Ty. "As far as you know, was Jax ever here at the house?"

"Not when I lived here," Ty answered.

Val looked around at the group. "And we're pretty sure Jax was Ace's handler, right?"

"We got his fingerprints everywhere at Ace's stash house," Greer said.

"Plus he admitted to it," Owen said. "Why?"

"Ace saw blueprints of the bunker and the tunnel leading into it," Val said. "Those were never publicly available. The original bunker and the modifications Bladen made weren't submitted for county permits. Those plans don't exist anywhere Angel has been able to find. So how did Jax have them to show to Ace?"

"He could have been here when I was in Afghanistan," Blade said.

"Yeah. With Amir and your daddy dearest," Val said.

Max sipped his beer as he looked at Owen. "You said, months ago, that Jax had gone rogue."

"So…is he an Omni?" Kelan asked.

"I don't know," Owen said. "He may just be under so deep he's lost who he really is. It's interesting, however, to consider that his dad was instrumental in getting the Red Team formed and funded. They pulled all of us who had a reason to hate the Omnis together, then sent us overseas to fight terrorism—"

"Conveniently keeping tabs on us while they kept us worlds away from the real action," Ty said.

"Right," Owen agreed. "I had a couple of partners help me get it off the ground. Val's one. The senator's the other. If he's bad, he's bad all the way through. And he knows everything we're doing."

"And he's who sent us here to Wyoming," Kit said.

Owen's nostrils flared. "Max, we need to put up a wall between the senator and us."

"We can't lock him out without him knowing we're on to him."

"Delay sending stuff to him," Owen said. "Send him incorrect info."

Max nodded. "Copy that."

"Jax said he was on a special assignment for his dad," Owen said. "I'd actually invited him to join Tremaine Industries. He declined. I learned yesterday that it was because he knew the senator was dirty…so I was guilty by association. He also said he had his own crew. In some ways, it seems he's working with us, and in others, against us."

"We figured out some other pieces while you were gone," Greer said. "We knew my grandfather had been part of organizing the Red Team. Guess who Santo is?"

"Henry Myers." Owen's voice was flat.

Addy gasped. "He was my lifeline."

"I told you he was bad. But even I didn't know how bad," Owen said.

Ace nodded. "I'll be killing him."

"There'll be no need to, once I'm done with him, sis," Greer said.

Sis? Were Greer and Ace siblings?

Greer answered Addy's unspoken question. "Ace is my baby sister. We thought she was murdered in our house when she was a baby. Santo either took Ace from her crib—when she was only two—or facilitated that happening so no alarms went off in the house. They sliced her up in a bloodletting that left us convinced she was dead. Santo handed her over to the Omnis to be raised in hell."

"Oh, Ace—" The thought of that racked Addy with grief.

Ace shrugged. "I survived. And I killed most of those who used me." Her eyes hardened. "Except Edwards. He's next."

Kelan shook his head. "You don't get to end all of them, Ace. Don't be selfish."

"She can have him. I get Jafaar," Angel said.

213

Max shook his head. "First come, first served, bro. Get in line."

"Pick who you want, but leave my dad to me," Val said.

Owen looked around the room. "Addy's parents are mine." His eyes met Greer's, then Ace's. "And Edwards is mine."

Addy shivered, then folded her arms. This Owen was terrifying. His eyes were cold, his face hard. No one in the room countered him.

"What did you mean about Santo being a lifeline, Addy?" Ty asked.

"I didn't know how to get out," Addy replied. "I didn't know who to trust or how to go about getting away. The house where I lived was surrounded by miles of national forest, so remote we couldn't get internet for many years...or so I was told. The telephones were monitored. And any time I tried to stand up for myself or my children...there were consequences. Brutal consequences, not only for me, but increasingly for my sons. Cecil told me Owen was King. I believed him. I had no reason not to."

"Do you still?" Ty asked.

Addy stared at Ty, trying to avoid the pull of seeing Owen's reaction. "I've learned that Omnis have perfected the art of living double—triple—lives. I've learned nothing is what it seems on face value."

"Not an answer," Ty persisted.

Owen bent his head and sipped his whiskey, then

stared into his glass. "Leave her alone. I said she was safe here. They beat those beliefs into her, Blade. She believed what she had to in order to survive. Leave it at that. She has to heal in her own time, like we all do or have."

"Finish what you were saying about Santo," Rocco urged her.

"My parents came and visited me." A wave of anguish washed over Addy. "I thought…I thought my nightmare was over. But it wasn't. Be a good wife, they said. Make Cecil happy so he has no need to punish you…" Her voice trailed off. The room was silent, except for the boys having dinner in the next room. "My nanny at the time was friends with Santo. They offered me a way out—or what I thought was one. I always thought of him as a lifeline…until today."

The room was quiet after she finished talking. There was so much more to say, so much more to try to understand. So many of the pieces didn't fit, but all of that would have to wait for their after-dinner meeting, since the kids' meal was breaking up. They were clearing the table. When it was reset for the adults, Zavi brought his parents over to talk to her about the sleepover.

"Zavi would love it if Troy could stay with him tonight," Mandy said. She pointed toward the far end of the house, opposite from Addy's room. "You were in our wing earlier, just before we started our tour. We'll have our door open at night. If he gets scared, he can come in. Or we can always bring him back to your room."

"If you're sure it won't be an imposition—"

"Not at all," Rocco said.

"Well, then," Addy said. "I guess it's okay with me, too."

The boys shouted and ran upstairs. A young girl stopped in front of her—Casey. "I know moms worry. Mine sure does. But I'll be with the boys until Uncle Rocco and Aunt Mandy are finished with the meeting. If you like, I can come get you when it's time to kiss him goodnight."

Addy nodded. "I'd like that."

"Great." Casey smiled and waved as she hurried after the boys. "See you later, Ms. Jacobs!"

Jacobs. How Addy hated that name suddenly, with all the privilege and horror it brought. She resolved to find a new name for herself and her boys.

The living room began to thin out as everyone moved into the dining room. Owen set his glass down on the bar. Instead of following the crowd, he caught her arm, turning her to face him. He pulled her close, then kissed her forehead. "I love you. I promise to never scare you again," he said, but the smile he gave her was haunting.

Before she could respond, the moment passed. He led her into the dining room. There was an empty seat at the head of the table and one just to the right of it. Ivy, Casey's mom, sat across from Addy. She owned the diner in town, Addy reminded herself.

They hadn't had a chance to chat yet, but the wife of Owen's team lead looked nice. They exchanged smiles.

ADDY DIDN'T OFFER much to any of the discussions at the long dinner table that night. Sometimes there was only one conversation going at a time that everyone participated in, other times, sections of the table—or even just couples—would break into separate conversations. The mood was upbeat. Several of the guys would glance toward Owen with a look of relief. How long had he been gone?

Addy surreptitiously studied everyone around the table. Seeing them together let her connect who was with whom. Strange how easy it was for her to remember details. She wondered if that was another part of healing after the extreme stress she'd been in during her marriage.

The surprising thing that caught her attention was how familial the group was with each other, teasing and laughing in friendly ways. It felt genuine. These people, whatever side of her fight they were on, didn't fear each other. Geniality like this was hard to fake. She looked at Owen, and he met her eyes. If he wasn't King, if he really was just Owen, what had his life been like during her hell?

Hopefully, she'd learn more in the meeting that was coming after. Dinner finished a little while later.

Everyone picked up their plates and helped clear the table. She did the same, wanting to blend in.

"Can I help in here?" she asked. "Maybe put food away?"

Ivy smiled and shook her head. "We've got this. Russ and Jim do the cleanup, but we try to give a hand where we can. Owen, what time are we meeting?"

"In a half-hour or whenever everyone's ready."

Addy hadn't realized he was right behind her.

"You have a minute?" he asked. "I want to take you to see Troy."

"I was just going to go looking for him."

Owen took her hand and led her into the hallway. It felt better than she liked to admit, having that connection to him. She should have pulled free, but she didn't. They turned away from the living room stairs to a back flight like the one by her bedroom wing.

He let go of her hand as they went up the stairs. She could hear a TV on. The kids were laughing and arguing as they played a game. At the top of the steps, Owen smiled at her as they went into the sitting room that connected the three bedrooms in this wing.

Her son was sitting at a round table, playing a board game. Zavi was on his knees on the chair, leaning on his elbows to look over the game. Casey calmly reminded them of the game's rules. She noticed them and waved. "Hi, Uncle Owen, Ms. Jacobs. Everything okay?"

"It is." Addy walked over to them. She ran her hand over Troy's head. "I think we're about to have our meeting. You have everything you need for the night? Your toothbrush and pajamas?"

"Yep. We got everything. I brought some toys, too." He pulled a chain from around his neck and showed Addy. It was a security necklace just like the one she'd been given. "Look, Mom, what they gave me. If you press this, it's like a shout for help."

Addy didn't hear anything from the necklace, but suddenly there was a stampede from downstairs. Rocco and Kit flew up the stairs, followed by several others on the team. "Troy!" Rocco shouted as he cleared the stairs. "Troy!"

Owen caught them before they charged into the little living room. "Just a test. Sorry. Everything's cool."

Kit sighed and shoved a hand through his spiky hair.

"Wow. It really works!" Troy said.

"It's not a toy," Owen said. "Remember, it's only to be used when there's a big problem and no one is near to help you."

"Yes, sir. I'll remember."

Rocco chuckled and came over to see what the kids were playing. "Well, that's the sort of crisis I like —one that's easily resolved." He looked over to Kit with a grin.

"Sorry, Dad," Casey said. "Couldn't catch him before he squeezed it."

"No worries, Case," Kit said. "Was a good trial run. So, we'll be downstairs. You good up here?"

"Yup. We got it," Casey answered. "I'll put them to bed at nine."

"Aww. Can't we have a little longer?" Zavi asked. "It's a weekend. No class tomorrow."

"How about I put you to bed at nine, but then you and Troy can have another half-hour in your room if you don't get too wild?"

Zavi sent Troy a grin. "That works."

Addy kissed her son's head. "All right, then. Since that's decided, I guess we'll leave you to your fun. Troy, be good for Casey."

"I will. Night, Mom. See you in the morning."

"Wait until you see breakfast, Troy…" Zavi began to fill Troy in on the feast they always had in the morning.

The guys who'd run upstairs with Kit and Rocco had all disappeared, but Owen waited for her. "Feel better?"

"I feel okay about this."

Owen nodded. "It's a start."

VAL CAME into the living room to wait for the meeting to start. He'd just gotten there when Kit shut off Troy's emergency summons. Selena was standing by the French doors.

"You okay?" he asked Selena.

"It was only a test run," she said.

"Wasn't talking about that."

She shrugged and smiled at him. "Yeah. I learned a while ago blondes weren't my thing."

Val's grin was a little sad. "Smart call. You comfortable guarding Addy?"

"It's the job."

"You trust her?"

"Not yet. She's very reserved and thinks Owen may be King. Not sure if she's hiding something or just holding back. Time will tell."

"She did surrendered her devices for a check without argument."

"True. What's your take on her?" Selena asked.

"It's been years since I've seen Owen laugh like he was earlier. I hope she's what he needs."

"Me, too."

Ace joined them. Val opened his arm for her to come close. "Talking about Addy?" she asked.

Val nodded. "Any thoughts?"

"I think the Omnis have cornered the market on head fucks. It's going to take a while to unwind everything they've twisted around her. I hope Owen will give her that time. I know I'm a long way from being untwisted."

Val drew her close and kissed her forehead. "I kinda like you twisted. Keeps me guessing."

17

A ddy and Owen returned to the dining room. She was still shaken from what had happened upstairs. Those necklaces were good to have if Owen and his team were truly allies. Owen held out a chair at the long dining room table —the same one she'd sat at for supper. He seemed tense, which didn't calm her nerves. When Cecil had been uptight, she was his relief valve, suffering some twisted abuse of his that appeased his nerves.

She hoped Owen didn't do the same.

The others all returned to the table. Russ and Jim were the last ones to join them. The tablecloth had been changed out for a fresh one. Fiona was going around the room, setting small notepads and pens down. The convivial attitude of supper was replaced now with the team's somber attention.

Owen stood behind his chair and looked the group over. Twenty-two in all sat at the table. "We have a lot to catch up on. I missed quite a bit while I was away. And I learned a few things that I need to share. Usually, these meetings are held in the bunker and kept among the team. But everything from here out may affect not just those of us in the fight, but everyone near us. None of this is to leave this room. We're still not to openly discuss our business. Children have big ears. So do staff—Carla or the guys in the construction crew working on the basement. Things they might overhear could be used against them, so we have to remember to keep this compartmentalized. Let's get started. Kit, bring me up to speed."

Kit told him about recovering Lion and most of his cubs, with the exception of Beetle. Addy couldn't be silent. She leaned forward and looked down the table to Lion. "Can you tell me anything about him? Was he well?"

"He was when Edwards took him. He's learned the survival skills we teach. He's a competent trapper and tracker. He came to my pride from a different group of boys, but they'd trained him well. Edwards is a sick man. I don't like that he has my cub. I don't know why he would have taken him."

"The night Jax and I left," Owen said, "we ran into Edwards. He broadsided Jax's SUV. We tried to fight our way out of it, but they used a flashbang to stun then capture us. We spent several days in rotting cells in the basement of a mental institution out on the plains, getting worked over pretty good. Edwards wanted to know who was funding us. I didn't tell him, but I did ask him about my son. I'm afraid I'm why he took Beetle from you, Lion."

"Shit," Kit grumbled.

"I bet Edwards is seeing his house of cards about to tumble down," Ty said. "We knew they'd begun cleaning house since they're killing off their researchers."

"So what does Edwards want with Beetle?" Kit asked. "Why take him?"

"Leverage. Against Addy or Owen. Or the senator, since he's Jacobs' grandson," Ty said.

"My parents and Cecil are friends," Addy said. "They visited us several times, knew what was happening to me, to my sons, but refused to go against my husband. It wasn't until Augie was taken and I spent time in a hospital with a broken jaw that things began to change. Wendell had been estranged from us for years. Somehow, my dad got him to help me. Wendell worked out a divorce agreement. Or, I guess, just a settlement, since I was never legally married to Cecil."

"So does that mean your dad and brother had a falling out?" Ty asked.

She nodded. "When we finally spoke, Wendell told me he'd been searching for me for years. My parents knew where I was, so why didn't he? I tried his number a couple of times, but it never went through. Owen's, too. I didn't have internet at the house until after the settlement. I learned early on that any attempt to reach the outside world had severe consequences, so for the most part, I quit trying. I couldn't put my sons in jeopardy. When my parents wouldn't help me, I thought Jax wouldn't either. And Cecil had me convinced that Owen was King. My parents said what was happening to me was Owen's choice. Even Jax, when he did come back into my life, said Owen wasn't to be trusted."

Addy knew her words hit Owen hard. So much pain could have been avoided if she'd somehow found him. How she could have done that when everyone surrounding her was owned by Cecil, she didn't know. She should have tried harder.

She, not Owen, was to blame for Augie's fate.

"That explains a lot about Jax," Owen said. "After the train wreck, he became distant, and we went our separate ways in the Red Team. I thought it was just how we both reacted to our grief over losing you. But after talking to him yesterday, I can see how it's possible he thought I made all of this happen." Owen sighed. "He said he'd collected a DNA sample from the girl who was killed in the crash and that he was working with the FBI to identify her."

"That's something we can corroborate with Lobo," Kit said.

"Do it. Jax has a safe house northwest of Denver. He wouldn't have taken me there if he still doubted my loyalty." Owen looked around at the group. "You know, my mom and Addy's died the same year. Jax thinks their deaths weren't accidents. He said he thought Roberta killed his and Addy's mom so she could take her place in the senator's household."

Addy shivered. "I never liked her."

"None of us did," Owen said. "Greer, Max, see what you can find out about her. Who was she before marrying the senator? Also, on the phone I gave you are dozens of pictures I took at Addy's of her art collection. Given all the stolen pieces found in the tunnels, I'm curious to know if those pieces are also hot. Jax said he was working with the FBI on that, but pass those on to Lobo. It's another way we can confirm info from Jax."

"Copy that," Greer said.

"What's next?" Owen asked.

"We're reconfiguring the basement to house Lion's pride and any others we recover," Kit said.

Owen looked at Ty. "That okay with you?"

Ty grinned. "Not really. You know how I hate that basement, but I don't have a logical argument. Kelan's gonna bring in his shaman to bless it. So, I guess it'll work out. It's a big space; we could house several prides down there."

"Did Jax tell you what he did with the watchers Ace handed over?" Val asked.

"No. But he acknowledged having them," Owen said.

"Sheriff Tate's on our asses to turn the boys over to their parents," Kit said. "We're working on identifying surviving family members, but the boys haven't only been sourced from the Friends. They've come from some of the other Omni isolationist groups around the country. Reuniting them is not going to be a fast exercise. And we can't send them back into the same conditions that put them in danger. So we're stuck for a while having them in our custody."

"Hopefully, we can change that around soon," Owen said.

"Only if it's in the best interest of the boys," Remi said. "Some of them identify with their pride as their family, so ripping them away and returning them to strangers may cause more damage than help."

"Hmmm," Owen grunted.

"Moving on," Kit said. "Angel discovered that Wynn's grandmother's body had been exhumed. Not sure who has it, but we're leaning toward it being Jafaar. Angel mentioned Jafaar kidnapped Wynn. He used a drone made to look like a bumblebee to deliver a sedative, then hijacked the ambulance she was in. While she was a prisoner, she saw him talking to a couple that may have been her parents. She overheard them discussing setting up a lab for Jafaar so that they could replicate the genetic modifications they produced for the Omnis. He's angry that he was left out of the equation and wants a piece of the pie for al Jahni."

"Yes," Wynn added, "but I'm not positive they were my parents. They died thirteen years ago. The people I saw were too young. They didn't look middle-aged. But it was dark and I didn't get a good look at them."

"I saw a woman outside Wynn's house in Cheyenne," Angel said. "I also didn't get a good look at her, but she looked like Wynn's mom in an old photo she had. The Omnis attacked us there. The guys I fought were hyped up on something. They burned Wynn's home down."

"So Jafaar has her parents?" Owen asked. At Angel's nod, he looked at Addy. She knew he was thinking they might have the antidote to whatever had been done to her.

"We put a tracker on Jafaar's car," Ace said, "but it hasn't moved from the motel. He was with Wynn's parents in some warehouses east of Cheyenne, so he's got the use of multiple vehicles."

"How did Jafaar get Wynn's parents?" Owen asked. The room went silent. "You said you saw a woman who might have been Wynn's mom," he said to Angel. "And then Wynn saw them with Jafaar after she was kidnapped. How did he get them?"

"That's something we don't have an answer for," Kit said.

"Grams said she saw them while she was at Jafaar's," Wynn said. "I just thought it was a dream her meds had tricked her into thinking."

"They must have gotten away from the Omnis at some point," Rocco said. "Jafaar wanted me to turn Wynn in—I guess as bait for your parents, so he didn't have them at that time."

"After Grams' funeral, I left," Wynn said, sending Angel a regretful look. "A man began following me

228

around. He said my parents sent him to find me before the Omnis did. Maybe he gave them to Jafaar. He also said that you all would kill them before giving them a chance to be heard."

"That guy was an Omni operative," Angel said. "He was fishing for info on your parents, which means the Omnis also didn't have them at that point." He looked at Owen. "So if the Omnis didn't have them and Jafaar didn't, then they were loose when I saw your mom at your house, only I didn't know it was your mom at that point."

"If it even was," Wynn said to Angel. "The people I saw at the warehouse weren't old enough. Maybe they were just made to look like them."

"And maybe they were them," Owen said. "We know the Omnis fake the deaths of people who go into their world. They did it with Blade's dad, maybe my dad, with Addy."

"Either way, he's got them now," Ty said. "It's unlikely Jafaar would go to the WKB for the lab he wants, being on the outs with them like he is."

"The tracker didn't show him moving when he had Wynn at the warehouse in Cheyenne," Kit said. "Rocco, get with Yusef and see why. See if Wynn's parents have been at the motel, too."

"Roger that," Rocco said. "Jafaar told Yusef, my CI, that I was a Fed. That may be something we have to deal with down the road."

"How did Jafaar know that about you?" Owen asked.

"That's unclear," Rocco said.

"In other news," Val said, "my father popped in for a visit. He brought the library from his secret room…and dumped a bombshell on us." Val looked at Kit, then Kelan and Lion. "Not only did he kill my mom, but he fathered both Fiona and Lion. And he was responsible for their mothers' deaths. Fiona and Lion are my half-siblings."

"We checked their DNA—" Owen started.

"And we retested our DNA. Daddy dearest said he fucked with the CODIS database."

"Where's Jason now?" Owen asked.

"In the wind," Kit said. "We tried to hold him here until Lobo could take him, but his lawyer made a visit to the sheriff, and we were forced to hand him over. Of course, the lawyer got him out of jail. Lobo's looking for him now."

"He also said this whole thing was a game," Val said. "No idea what that means to him or to us. Don't think it's a game to everyone involved. The bastard did say that he'd called everyone to come in, that it was all over."

Addy looked at Owen. They'd talked about this whole mess being a game. It still didn't make sense to her.

"Shit. I was only gone a couple of weeks," Owen said.

"Yeah, two critical weeks," Kit said.

The emotions Addy saw on the faces of the men and women around the table seemed genuine. A group this large couldn't all be acting, could they? Owen started pacing at his end of the room. She tensed every time he walked behind her. He stopped once, stepping up to his chair, his gaze sweeping both sides of the table. Instead of speaking, however, he resumed his pacing. No one spoke, though she doubted any conversation would have disturbed his concentration. At last, he broke his silence.

"It's all connected," Owen said. "Someone knows everything that's going on. We don't know who that is, but it's likely that it's Jason, the Jacobs, Jax, or Edwards. Maybe even my dad."

"My dad told us the game was over and people were being recalled," Val said.

"To where?" Owen asked.

"That's the sixty-four-million-dollar question," Ty said.

"It's likely the site we found in Colorado isn't the only headquarters the Omnis have here in the U.S.," Owen said. "I think they have several around the country and internationally. Someone inside is helping us…maybe Jax. We were sent here for a reason. Either to get us as far away from their core site, or to bring us closer to it, depending on who really sent us. Given what we found in Colorado, and also where Edwards was keeping Addy, and the fact that Jason came out here to disappear, I think we're very close to their home base."

"Maybe there's a section of the tunnels that the Feds didn't open or see," Ace said.

"Or another tunnel complex. Fuck knows there's a ton of abandoned silos in the area," Val said. "Maybe each kingpin in the game has one himself."

"Taking the show underground is strategic," Ty said. "Keeps drones from hitting them and satellites from observing them. Lets them operate invisibly from the rest of the world."

"There was a section in the WKB silo complex I wasn't allowed to investigate," Max said.

"The WKB?" Addy asked.

Owen looked at her and explained, "The WKB is the White Kingdom Brotherhood, a prison gang cum biker gang acting as enforcers for the Omnis. They're based about an hour west of here."

She nodded, taken aback by all the info shared so freely here. It had taken her years to unravel a fraction of what they were divulging at the table.

"And the Omnis showed up to the place where Wynn was being held just before we got there," Max said. "We've tracked those vehicles to the WKB compound. They haven't left it since."

"Pete's in your confidence, isn't he?" Owen asked Max.

"So far, the info he's given me hasn't been wrong."

"See what he knows."

"Copy that."

"Owen, back to Jafaar," Wynn said. Addy noticed her voice wasn't as confident as the men's. She wasn't a team member, but a tutor and nanny—this had to be way out of her comfort zone. "While I was locked away, I overheard the couple with him, who may or may not have been my parents, offer to replicate the genetic modifications in return for my freedom."

Owen crossed his arms. "That's not technology that we want turned over to an Afghan warlord. We have several data points for the WKB compound. Let's refresh our eyes out there. I want to know who's going into that silo, changes in the general population. If Jason and the others involved in this are thinking to make a last stand, they'll be calling in reinforcements. I'll give Lobo an update. Kit—I want Wynn's parents, or whoever they are, captured alive. They may be able to help us with Addy's situation. I don't want to leapfrog them in priority, but they're important. If we can get them out of this mess quickly, do it."

"We'll make it happen," Kit said.

Owen sent another glance around the table. "My priority is my son. He's not the team's priority. I want to be clear on that."

"Fuck that, O," Val said. "Nothing on the table's more important than your boy. Except the doctors Ratcliff, so they can help Addy."

"No. This is coming to an end. Fast. We can't blow the opportunity we have to make it end our way, not theirs," Owen said.

"The guys have been searching for Omni real estate holdings," Kit said. "They've hidden them well inside stacks of dummy corporations. Greer's working an algorithm to crawl through the data and unravel the connections. No matter how this ends, that forensic work will be useful to the FBI. We'll dig back into that and see how far we can get. I don't want us to be spread too thin. You may need to bring in additional guys."

"I can't," Owen said. "Senator Jacobs will know we're staffing up."

"Then we're gonna have to be lean and mean," Kit said.

"So...back to Jax," Kelan said. "Which side does your gut say he's on?"

Owen shrugged. "He got Addy out of her marriage, but kept her at the same house where Edwards had held her. He claims to be the one who sent Hope to the WKB to find Lion. And he was who told her to search out Max. He was in the tunnels when Kelan and Fiona were taken. He helped Kelan get out so he'd live to save Fee. But...he perpetuated the lie that I was King, keeping Addy and me apart. He sent Ace out to find prides to save them from being lab rats...but what did he do with them? I don't know. I keep seeing him on both sides."

"Maybe he did those things so he wouldn't blow his cover," Ty said. "Maybe he's in so deep he doesn't have a side anymore."

"King stopped Holbrook's abuse of my cubs," Lion said. "And he gave me permission to stay as their leader. Both dispensations I would not have expected from the bastard. Is Jax King?"

"Maybe he's leading the resistance?" Angel suggested.

"He told me my father was head of the opposition," Owen said. "I don't know. We need to find my dad. Jax said his hunt for the scientists behind the human modifications was leading to their deaths."

"Your dad's killing them?" Rocco asked.

"No. The Neo-Omnis are, to cover their tracks. Or so Jax says."

"I overheard my fake parents say something about that," Wynn said. "They feared for their lives if they were turned back over to Syadne. Jafaar offered them safety in exchange for the formulas they had."

Owen shook his head.

"Let's stop there," Kit said. "We've got our next steps figured out."

Lion leaned forward. "Kit…regarding the WKB, my cubs are trained to watch without being seen. Let me take them back into the woods."

"No," Hope said. "It's winter already."

Lion looked at his sister. "My cubs have survived many winters without the comforts they now have."

Hope gave him a frosty glare. "Sure, but then they had the barracks at the WKB as a home base. They don't have that luxury now. We have them—and you —safe here. Please, Lion, don't do this."

"One of my cubs is missing. Nothing else matters to me and my pride until he's recovered." He looked at Addy, then Owen. "And it isn't because he's your son. It's because he's my cub. It would be the same with any of them."

"I can't, in good conscience, send you and your boys into this," Owen said.

"You don't have a choice. We are like the wind. You neither own us nor can you hold us, but you can —and should—use us."

Owen sighed. He closed his eyes and rubbed his forehead. "Kit, I need a rendezvous point for them supplied with food, clothes, blankets, medical supplies, and comms. Work it out with Lion."

"Copy that," Kit said.

Owen looked at Lion. "I want regular check-ins. You—and all your cubs—will return here when this is done."

Lion just nodded.

Addy was surprised that Owen would use the kids as irregulars in this fight, but if they could do what Lion said they could do, she'd be grateful as hell. Augie was lucky to have gotten in with such fierce, capable boys. She had no idea if the Omni World Order was about to go down in flames, or if it would persist like a coal fire, burning underground forever. Either way, the skills her son had learned and the friends he'd made were ones he could fall back on the rest of his life.

"There anything else we need to cover?" Owen asked. Everyone shook their heads. "Kit, organize what you have to. You need something, let me know. I have resources the company doesn't know about."

~

It was midnight. Owen had waited until the house was silent, debating all the while if he was doing the right thing. If Addy didn't believe him by now, then it was unlikely his sappy love letters, written when he was out of his mind with grief—or later, when he'd come to terms with her ghost—were going to make any difference.

He could retrieve the letters and decide later what to do with them. He turned off the security in the hall, the elevator bedroom, the elevator, and the weapons room. Maybe the time for fear had passed. Maybe it was time to lay everything on the table and let her make of it what she would.

In the weapons room, he opened the cabinet with the false back where he'd stashed his locked boxes. Retrieving them, he stood and came face to face with Max—the stone-cold fighter version.

"What are you doing?" Max asked.

"Not something that concerns you."

"I might have bought that before you went AWOL. Now, not so much. There's too many odd pieces in flight, and I gotta tell you I'm not a fan of mysteries. What's in the boxes?"

"None of your goddamned business."

Kit walked in behind Max. Both of them stood shoulder to shoulder, arms folded. "Let's just say we're making it our business." The smile he gave Owen was full of teeth and empty of humor.

Owen looked down at the steel boxes, feeling an unwelcome warmth flush his neck and face. He set them on the big counter in the middle of the room, then fished the keys out of his pocket and tossed them near the boxes.

Kit and Max opened the boxes, then, seeing the contents, looked in question at each other. Inside were bundles of letters, grouped by year.

"Open them," Owen ordered. Some of the letters had been postmarked to and from him. Others simply had dates on the sealed envelopes.

Max used his pocket knife to unseal a random letter from a packet dated five years ago. Owen felt raw and exposed as he watched his men, like a schoolboy caught passing a love note to his girl being made to stand in front of the class and read it aloud.

Max pulled another letter out from a different bundle and scanned it. "Shit." Kit did the same. "These are love letters."

Owen said nothing.

"To Addy," Kit said. "You wrote these when you thought she was dead."

"Fuck. Me." Max folded the letters he'd been reading and stuffed them back into their envelopes. "I'm sorry, man. Don't know what I was expecting, but it wasn't this."

"Yeah." Owen forced that answer past his throat.

Kit handed the keys back to Owen. "What can we do?"

"Nothing. Unless you know how to un-brainwash someone?" Owen picked up the lockboxes. Both men flanked him as he got into the elevator.

"Remi might have some ideas," Max said.

"I'll talk to her," Owen said, though he knew he probably wouldn't. Just thinking about his lost Addy years felt like chewing razor blades. Discussing it with anyone would be even worse.

The guys went their separate ways when the elevator reached the main floor. Owen took his boxes into his room, but just stood there, still debating what to do with them. After a long while, he knocked on Addy's door. Maybe he'd be spared further shame tonight if she just ignored him. But she didn't.

Her door opened. He stared down at her. Her features looked pale, backed by the shadows in her room. "What is it?"

"May I come in? Just for a moment?"

She stepped back, opening the door wider for him. She turned on a lamp. He walked to the small table in her room and set the boxes down, along with their keys. "These are for you."

"What's in them?" she whispered.

He unlocked one and showed her. "The letters I promised to write you."

Her eyes filled with tears that sparkled in the dim light.

"Make of them what you will. Burn them, if you want."

She picked up a bundle and held it close to her. "Owen—"

"Night, Addy." He was just out of arm's reach—

and glad for the distance, because once she came to him, he'd not be able to step away again.

ADDY SAT at the table and stared at the boxes, shocked that Owen had actually written to her. Inside each were several bundles of envelopes, grouped by year. There were more letters in the earlier years of their separation than the later ones. Some of the envelopes were sealed, some opened. She could see how aged some of them were.

She took out the earliest bundle. It was dated to the year she was taken. He'd started writing to her six months after her faked death. She opened the first envelope, then set it and the letter down, too overwhelmed with emotion to read it. She ran her hand over the neat, small script Owen used. His words were in all caps. So precise. So like him.

He hadn't lied about writing to her. She'd wondered again what his life had been like without her. She'd know as soon as she could gather the courage to read them.

My Laidy,

I went out to get you flowers, but when I came back, you were gone. I never expected that. I'm not quite sure how to live without you. I don't want to, but I just keep breathing, like even my own body won't release me to come be with you.

A shrink I talked to said if I wrote you, then it would

be a way for my soul to talk to yours, wherever yours is now. Heaven, I hope. In fields of flowers. There were lilies and daisies in the bouquet I brought you. I know how you loved them. Maybe they have those in heaven?

Ever your knight,

Owen

18

"Hey, Rocco," Max said as he came into the bunker room the morning after. "Before you call Yusef, there's something you should know. A request for bids for a lab being developed in Denver went out over the dark web. I think it might be the one Jafaar is working on. Kelan knows the address." He called it out.

"That's the warehouse where I first saw them holding Fiona, before we were transported to the fight club," Kelan said.

"Who's funding the lab?" Kit asked.

"A new company, one that isn't as expertly stacked inside dummy corporations as the Omnis' stuff," Greer said. "It sifts out to one of al Jahni's fake businesses here in the U.S."

"Kelan, Angel, get down there and stake it out. Get some eyes up so we can see what's happening," Kit ordered. "We want Wynn's parents alive, whether or not they're actually her parents, feel me?"

"That's nonnegotiable," Owen said. "They may have information about what's happening to Addy. No telling how many are left who could help her. They're golden fucking unicorns and we need to get them before the Omnis track Jafaar down."

Angel stood up. "I don't have a beef with the researchers. I do have an issue with Jafaar. Do we have permission to use lethal force?" he asked Kit.

Kit said to Owen, "Thing is, boss, we don't know how dirty the whole system is. I'm pretty sure Lobo's solid, but how clean the levels above him are...who the fuck knows anymore. Letting him live may be as good as setting him free."

Owen looked at Angel, Kelan, then Kit. "I want him alive. He's our connection to al Jahni. We need to know what he knows, like what he intended to do with the human modifications he's setting up a lab to produce. And where Grams' body is."

Angel didn't look happy. "Roger that." He and Kelan left to gear up.

Rocco called Yusef, but his call wasn't picked up. "If I don't hear back from him, I'll head out there. Right now, I'm going to have breakfast with my family." The room emptied out.

"I'm going with Angel and Kelan," Owen said.

"You don't trust them?" Kit asked.

"I do...I just need something to do."

"Did you give Addy the letters?" Kit asked.

"Yeah."

Kit grinned. "So what you're really doing is running away?"

Owen gave him a cool glare. "Maybe."

Kit laughed as Owen went into the weapons room to gear up.

"Keep digging into the real estate angle," Owen told Max and Greer. "King's hanging out somewhere, probably with Edwards. If there's any word of Augie, I want to know right away."

"Roger that, boss," Max said. "We're on it."

ADDY TOOK A QUICK SHOWER. Troy wasn't back from his sleepover yet. She'd read Owen's letters during the night, getting through about a third of them. They were filled with his loneliness, all of them, but his sorrow had slowly given way to quiet rage. He'd known no peace in their years apart. He'd confessed to her the times he'd been with other women. There hadn't been many, and none that he'd truly enjoyed.

She was nervous about seeing him this morning. Nervous and excited. She dried her hair and put her makeup on, a ritual she wanted to do for him, so different from how she'd hated doing it for Cecil. She was tired, but she hoped Owen would look beyond that and see her...see that she knew how wrong she'd been about him.

There was a knock on her door. She opened it, thinking it was Mandy bringing Troy back before breakfast. It was Owen. He was dressed in beige cargo pants, beige everything, even Kevlar vest. She stepped back into her room. He followed her. The door shut behind him.

He looked over her head to what he could see of the bedroom. She'd put all of his letters away—she hadn't wanted Troy getting into them. When Owen's gaze returned to hers, he seemed uncertain.

"I read them. Some of them. The bouquet you got me after our night, when…when—"

He kissed her before she could finish, a hard, possessive kiss. He pulled her up against his body, crushing her against his vest. It hurt. And it felt wonderful. She tightened her arms around his neck and bent her head, giving him more of what he wanted. His hand forked her hair, holding her head so he could devour her mouth. Heat shot through her body, making her want more, making her whimper.

He eased up, hearing the sound she made. He still held her off the ground. They were face to face. He was breathing hard. "I have to go."

"Okay."

"Don't leave the house without Selena or one of the guys. Promise?"

"Yes."

"You'll be here when I get back?"

She huffed a little breath with her smile. "Try to get rid of me."

"Never."

He set her back on her feet, then turned at her door for a last look. She tried to smile, she really did —she just hated the thought of him going away.

"Be safe, Owen."

"I will."

She stared at the door for a long minute, fighting the urge to chase him down the hall and give him another kiss goodbye. Her whole body was tingling. She kept still, savoring that feeling, one she'd only had from him.

After a few minutes, she made her way to the dining room. Troy was already there, sitting next to Rocco, Mandy, and Zavi. Wynn was there too. Kit and Ivy and their daughter came in from the kitchen. The big table was filling up again.

"Mom! Zavi was right. Look at all the food. I ate pancakes and sausages and some fruit. I want one of the pastries, too. Can I?"

Addy smiled. "No. If you've eaten all of that, you don't need any more. Let's save some for everyone else. There are a lot of people to feed here." She made herself a plate, though she had little appetite. "Thank you, Mandy, for letting him sleep over last night."

"He was good as gold," Mandy said. "The boys really get along."

"They do."

"Did you get some rest last night? I know it has to

be a shock coming here. It was for all of us," Mandy said.

"I didn't get much sleep, but it's my own fault, I was up reading." Addy sipped her coffee. Troy and Zavi did a lot of talking and laughing. Those two had become friends instantly.

"Why don't you come to class with me tomorrow, Troy?" Zavi asked.

Classes…school…she'd forgotten about all of that in their evacuation. He could miss a few days, but keeping him out of school for too long would not be good.

"That's a great idea," Wynn said. "Would you mind if he joined us?"

"I-I haven't given it any thought," Addy said. "He had a tutor at our house. I don't know where he's at with his studies in relation to where Zavi might be."

"No worries there. I can do an assessment over the next few days."

"I'd like that, Wynn. Um, I just don't know how I'll pay. I don't have any money."

Mandy reached over and touched her hand. "Don't worry about it. We can figure that out later. Let's just get him started with his studies so he doesn't lose ground."

"Then yes, if you're certain it won't be too much of an imposition."

"None at all. We've been studying with the watchers in the gym, but they've"—Wynn paused

—"ah, gone on a field trip for a bit, so let's use the classroom in Mandy's wing, okay?"

"They're gone?" Casey said, interrupting the conversation. She looked crushed. "When are they coming back? They *are* coming back, right?"

"Case, don't worry about them. They're doing one of their exercises," Kit said.

Casey looked from her dad to her mom. "They'll be back before you know it," Ivy said.

Addy wondered at Casey's concern for the boys. "Sure," she said, answering Wynn's question. "What about supplies for Troy? I don't have anything. I should have packed that, but didn't even think about it."

"We've got that covered," Mandy said. "We brought in a ton of stuff for Lion's pride. I'm sure we have what we need."

"Then that's settled." Addy looked at her son. "I want you to be respectful of Miss Wynn, Troy."

"Yes, Mom. She's not going to make me read, is she?"

"Reading's very important," Wynn said.

"It's hard. And it doesn't make sense."

Addy smiled. "Maybe Miss Wynn can help you with that."

"I bet we can figure out a way for you to read that's not so hard," Wynn said.

"Miss Wynn's nice. I never get in trouble. You won't either," Zavi said. "Want to go up there now?"

"Sure," Troy said.

"Is that all right?" Addy asked Mandy and Wynn.

Mandy smiled. "Absolutely, as long as they don't make a mess. Wynn is also our nanny, but she has weekends off, so the boys are welcome to tag along with me today. Zavi usually helps me clean out stalls on the weekends. I could use another pair of hands if you can spare Troy."

Addy looked at Troy, who was thrilled to have an excuse to be with his new friend. He nodded vigorously. "That sounds great," Addy said. "If you need me, I'll be in my room." With the promise of a couple of hours to herself, she couldn't wait to get back to Owen's letters.

"Rocco, I got Yusef on the line," Max said over comms. *"He's not calling from his usual number."*

"Copy," Rocco said. "Put him through."

His phone rang. Rocco took the call. *"Khalid,"* Yusef said.

"Good morning, Yusef."

"I missed your call. I'm calling from a friend's phone. I think I'm being followed. I don't know if Jafaar can listen to my calls. It is getting very bad."

"What's happening?"

"After your meeting with Jafaar, he got nervous. He went to some store in Denver and bought counter-spyware tools. He found the bugs in his room and in my living room. He also

checked his car and found one. He thinks I planted them. He is threatening my sons and my wife. He's desperate."

"Desperate for what?"

"I don't know."

"Yusef, is he still staying there?"

"Yes, but he comes and goes."

"Does he ever have another couple with him? Dark hair, mid-thirties to mid-fifties?"

"I saw them one time. They aren't here now."

"If you ever see them again, I need you to call me immediately."

"I will. What am I going to do about Jafaar? My family's in grave danger."

"He won't be a problem much longer," Rocco said. "Just keep working with me. We're closing in on him."

WHEN NIGHT FELL, Max went to Hope's old digs on the WKB compound, where Feral had been crashing. He punched the kid's shoulder. "Wake up."

The kid came up off the mat he'd been sleeping on, ready to fight. Max caught his fist midair. "Chill. It's just me."

"Mads." Feral relaxed slightly. "What are you doing here?"

"Some shit's gonna break loose soon, probably here. When it does, I don't want you in the middle of it."

"Sure. Sure. When's it gonna happen?"

"I don't know. But you won't miss it when it does. You catch anything odd happening lately?"

"I was watching the workers going into the silo. There's twice the staff coming and going now."

"You guys moving more dope than usual?"

"No," Feral said. "They're going into that section no one goes into."

"Huh. Okay. Look, when this is over, you're coming with me."

"Where?"

"I want you to join the group of watchers who used to live here," Max said.

"Those freaks? No, thank you."

"It's three squares, a roof, clothes, and a purpose. You got a better option?"

Feral licked his lips. "No."

Max got up. "You got my number. Call me when things shake loose. In the meantime, I need you to watch my back. I have to refresh some eyes I put out."

Feral got out of bed. He was fully dressed, still wearing his coat. "You been watching us?"

Max grinned. "You have so much shit to learn."

He went around and swapped out old cameras for new. Greer was monitoring their field of view. In less than an hour, it was done. He and Feral bumped fists. "Thanks. Now get outta here. Keep your head down and your eyes open."

Max went across the compound to Pete's digs above the clubhouse. The place was trashed, as usual.

A sweet cinnamon scent came from a bunch of candles that were lit on the table with their drug paraphernalia. Three women were in bed with the club president, naked and riding a heroin high, like Pete.

Max took a Narcan syringe out of his pocket. He bit off the cap, then punched that sucker into Pete's thigh. He pocketed the capped syringe, then hoisted Pete's naked ass over his shoulder and carried him into the bathroom. No telling what his reaction to the anti-opioid was going to be. If he barfed on his bed, it would likely still be there the next time Max was over.

If there was a next time.

Max propped him by the tub, then sat on the toilet and waited. He could see Pete's body beginning to react, twitching, then he jerked awake. He looked around the room, panting hard, his eyes frantic and dilated. Max grinned at him.

"What the fuck, Mad Dog?" Pete leaned his head against the broken tile behind him. "You ruined a perfectly good high."

"Yeah? Well, you better park that horse. I gotta talk to you."

"No, fuck you." Pete tried to rise, but his legs weren't cooperating.

Max kicked him back against the wall. "Hey, I was being nice, putting you in here. I coulda strung you up over a cliff."

"What do you want?"

"I'm hearing rumors a war's coming here. It ain't your war; it ain't your fight. Tell your boys to clear out. King's going down. Nothing they can do about it."

Pete sighed. "It ain't my men you gotta worry about. King's bringing his own fighters in. Some of them were our guys; most I don't know. It's like they don't know us anymore. They're different."

"And you didn't see fit to tell me about this?" Max snarled.

"I'm telling you now."

"So get your guys out. Quietly. A couple at a time. Don't tell the newcomers what's happening. Tell your crew to stay far, far away for like a month. After we take King down, Feds are going to be all over this place for a long while. Leave King's dope. The Feds are going to find it—let that fall on King's head, not yours."

"Doesn't sound good."

"It ain't...for King. Won't be here or there for you and your boys if you do what I say."

"It's cool," Pete said. "You did us good with the smallpox. Heard how it went through the Friends. That coulda been us. So we'll do it." Pete narrowed his eyes. "We do still have a deal, right?"

"Yeah, we do." Their deal was for Max to take Pete out fast, or at least give him enough heads-up that he could OD before the Feds—or King—took him. The WKB club prez was deathly afraid of dying in an acid bath. Max grinned. Maybe that would be a fitting end for King. He hoped Owen gave him the chance to make it happen.

19

———

Addy called Selena the next morning, after breakfast and getting Troy started with Zavi in class.

"Hi, Selena? I need to go out today."

"Where are you going? I'll need to clear it with Kit."

"I have a doctor's appointment."

"Are you sick?"

"No." Addy felt embarrassed saying it. Best just spit it out. "I want to be checked for STDs. In all the testing that was done on me, I don't think they ever tested me for those."

"Oh. Sure. What time and where?"

"It's this afternoon. Two o'clock. At the clinic in town. I already made the appointment."

"Copy that. I'll make it happen."

"I'd rather no one else knew why I'm going to the doctor's."

"No worries. That's need to know only."

254

When the time came to head to the doctor's, Addy was glad that Selena didn't ask any questions. Addy filled out the extensive paperwork, feeling more and more freakish as she did. She didn't know anything about her family history. Those were the sorts of things she might have learned had she had a normal relationship with her parents.

A few minutes later, the nurse called her back. She stood. Selena didn't.

"Want me to go with you?" Selena asked.

Addy nodded, but the nurse said. "Just the patient at this time."

Selena stood. "I'm her bodyguard. If I don't go with her, she doesn't go."

The nurse asked, "That okay with you, Ms. Jacobs?"

"Yes," Addy replied.

After the standard check-in, Addy and Selena were taken to a small exam room. Selena waited outside until the doctor came in. She gave Addy a quick glance, introduced herself, then sat on a stool by a computer. "Ms. Jacobs, I understand you're here for an STD exam."

"Yes."

"All right. I have some questions that I need to ask." She flashed a glance at Selena. "They're of a personal nature. Maybe your friend would like to step outside?"

"I'm not shy. And there's nothing I have to hide," Addy said.

"Okay. Let me just take a moment to read over your questionnaire."

Addy felt her nerves tightening up. Selena was going to learn things Addy hadn't even told Owen.

"All righty then. I have a standard list of questions I ask of all my patients prior to doing STD tests. I want you to be comfortable and as forthcoming as possible. If you're ready, we'll get started."

Addy nodded. Her hands were clasped tightly together. She drew a couple of long, slow breaths.

"These are standard questions. There are no right or wrong answers. No one's judging you. I just need to make an assessment of what type of tests we'll be doing. Are you in a relationship now?"

"No. Maybe. I don't know."

"Are you sexually active currently?"

"No."

"When were you last active?"

"A few years ago."

"Have you ever had multiple partners?"

"Yes."

"Did you ever have unprotected sex?"

"Yes."

"Were your partners male or female?"

"Male."

"Which of the following sexual practices did you engage in? Oral? Anal? Vaginal?"

"All of them."

"Are you having any symptoms? Discomfort? Discharge?"

"No."

"When we're finished here, would you like to discuss birth-control options?"

"No." Addy didn't want a hormonal treatment—that might really mess her body up with everything else she was going through. She and Owen would have to stick with condoms for the time being...if they decided to move to the next step.

"Are there any questions you have for me? Any other topics you want to cover?"

"No."

The doctor began her physical examination. Selena stood near Addy's head. During the pelvic exam, the doctor looked up at Addy, shock on her face. Addy met her gaze unflinchingly. She knew what the doctor had seen. Scars. From the day she hemorrhaged after one of Cecil's punishments that included being gang-raped.

Addy wiped away a tear. Selena was watching her. Her eyes went wide. She whipped her sunglasses off her head and handed them to Addy. "I think the lights are bothering your eyes again. Put these on."

Damn it! Addy had forgotten all about her eyes doing their thing. She quickly threw the sunglasses on. The doctor finished her exam, removed her gloves and washed her hands. She came back over to Addy, who was sitting up on the exam table.

"Your eyes are bothering you?"

"Oh. No. I'm trying out a set of fad contacts. They change colors like a mood ring." She tried to laugh it off. "I should have taken them out before I came here."

The doctor nodded. "Never heard of that." She sent Selena quick look, then put her hands in her lab coat pockets. "Addy, I saw signs of sexual trauma when I examined you. They appear fully healed." The doctor sighed. "Are you still in the same situation that led to those injuries?"

"No. That's over."

"I would be happy to recommend a counselor. There are resources available to help you—"

"Thank you. Really. But that situation is over."

The doctor nodded, not looking convinced.

"Will I… Will the scars affect my ability to have more kids?"

"I don't know. They may. I would need to do a more complete exam before I can answer that question. Are you thinking of becoming pregnant?"

"No. I just wondered about the future."

"When you're ready to tackle that, I'll be available. In the meantime, I'm going to have my nurse come in to draw your blood and take these swabs down to the lab. We'll have the results in a few days."

"Thanks, doctor."

"Good day, ladies." The door closed behind her.

Addy handed Selena back her glasses.

"Good cover with the mood contacts," Selena said. "They should really make such a thing."

Addy nodded.

"Does Owen know?" Selena asked.

"No. I'm not sure I'm going to tell him. I'm not sure he needs to know."

Selena leaned back against the counter. "Some burdens are lighter when they're shared."

"He's already carrying more than his share. He doesn't need mine added."

"Okay. Your call."

The nurse came in and was startled to see Addy's eyes. Addy threw out the mood contacts excuse again, which sparked an entire discussion about pop culture and fads. Addy had to promise to send her the link to the site where the nurse could buy her own. When she left, Selena stepped outside again so Addy could get dressed.

She heard a man Selena greeted as Doc Beck stop by. The convo was almost finished when Addy stepped out of the exam room. "Doc—this is Addy. Addy, Doc Beck. He's seen almost all of us at one time or another."

Addy was about to shake his hand when he gasped. He caught her chin and tilted her face this way and that. "How are you feeling?"

"Fine." She pulled free. "It's just fad contacts. I shouldn't have worn them today. Sorry to startle you."

"Mood contacts. That's good. You sure you're feeling well?"

"I feel great." Which was true.

"We'll be seeing you, doc. Take care." Selena grabbed Addy's arm and drew her out of the clinic.

They didn't talk until they got to the SUV. "Doc was weird today."

"How so?"

"Not sure. Can't explain it."

"I guess the eyes set him off."

"Maybe." She looked at Addy. "Any other errands you need to do before we go back?"

"No, that was it. Thanks for coming with me today. I felt safer having you with me. I didn't want to be alone with people I don't know."

Selena grinned. "Sure."

SELENA WENT STRAIGHT DOWN to the bunker when she got back from Addy's appointment. She came out of the elevator and crossed through the weapons room to the ops room. Only Max and Greer were in there.

Greer looked up. "Hiya."

Selena nodded at them. "Yeah. Got a question."

He grinned. "We got answers. So I guess that works out okay."

"You checked out Doc Beck, right?"

Max exchanged looks with Greer, who answered. "Yeah. He was on a list of potential dates that Ivy was going on before she and Kit hooked back up—'bout the time you started with us. He had us check him out. No red flags."

"Before they got together?" She smiled, thinking

that drama would have been something to see. "I was busy with Casey then. When I started, there was none of this Omni shit. We were tracking foreign and domestic terrorists. Did you recheck Beck after that all started?"

"Why do you have a sudden issue with the doc?" Max asked.

"I just took Addy in for her lady checkup. Ran into him. He acted funny when I mentioned her name…like he knew about her."

Max shrugged. "Well, Owen's big news in this town. His girl would cause a stir."

"I never mentioned Owen. None of us talk about him with civilians. Addy's never left the house. How would he know she was his girlfriend? Unless…"

"Unless?" Greer prompted.

"Unless he's Omni. When he saw her eyes, he was all over her, examining them, asking her how she felt. Addy said they were fashion contacts, but he immediately knew they changed with her mood. How would he have known that? Maybe from the GYN who examined Addy, but I doubt they'd had a chance to chat so soon after her exam."

"Fuck. Me," Max snapped.

"Yeah, we'll dig into him more," Greer said, turning back to his computer and clearing the screen.

OWEN HAD BEEN GONE FOREVER, Addy thought,

though she knew it had just been a few days. She and Troy had settled into a nice routine with his classes. She'd been reading and rereading Owen's letters. They were both sword and panacea. It hurt her to read how much he hurt after losing her. As recently as a few weeks ago, in his most recent letter, his emptiness was as great as it had ever been.

One of his letters had mentioned Selena. He'd kissed her, then set her free. His words had seemed sad to acknowledge that after Addy, no woman could quite measure up.

Part of her wished he'd found comfort, somewhere, anywhere. Mostly, she was glad he hadn't—and how unfair to him was that?

She thought about how he'd behaved at her house, kind despite her standoffishness. Patient, too. The exact opposition of Cecil. Addy packed the last of his letters away and left her room, wandering absentmindedly into Owen's. She didn't have an open invitation to go there, but it wasn't locked, and she needed very much to be near him just then.

It was the first time she'd been in his room. His space didn't look like the rest of the household. Its furnishings weren't Western influenced at all. More like Eastern. His bed was a simple platform style. Single floating bamboo shelves flanked either side of it. Both had lamps. One had a Bonsai tree. Instead of the dresser, armchairs, and table set that her room had, the only other furniture in his room were a pair of mid-century teak chairs that were angled for a person sink into the upholstered cushions.

The walls were painted in a soothing shade of pale green. There was no carpet in his room. The floor was oak. A large, white rug of woven cotton was on this side of his bed. On the wall above the bed was a large piece of art that looked to have been made from shells and stones and other media, giving it a three-dimensional appearance.

Addy had had no idea that Owen liked the clean lines of Asian decor. Truthfully, she knew very little about him at all.

She needed to get some air. There was a set of doors near the stairs. One led into the gym, the other to a portico that ran alongside the gym building.

She went outside. The morning was bright, and though it was cold, the sun was warm. She saw Eden and Angel come from the corner of the gym building and go across the lawn. They waved to her. Looked like they'd just come from a run. At the end of the portico, she stopped. Leaning against one of the support pillars, she crossed her arms, admitting how wretched she felt. How long had it been since she'd known any joy at all? Any not shadowed by fear.

Maybe it was her recent visit to the doctor that had stirred things up in her. She knew she'd sustained scars from her time with Cecil. It was like a bit of him would always be with her.

"Hey!" Rocco said, startling her as he came around the corner of the gym.

"Hi. Sorry. I didn't see you there."

He waved that off. "We just finished our run. I was doing some cooldown exercises." He frowned. Maybe her eyes were some weird new color. "You okay?"

She nodded, then shook her head. God, she didn't know Rocco at all—she didn't want to break down in front of him. "Just thinking about things."

"You know, sometimes it helps to talk about stuff." He gave her a sheepish grin. "I learned that the hard way."

"How?" She'd much rather hear his story than tell her own.

"Stuff happened in Afghanistan, over a lot of years. I lost a wife and an unborn baby. I wasn't dealing with it very well."

"What did you do?"

"I gave my son to Mandy, then I took a gun out to the field to kill myself...and her horse."

"Oh, God. Rocco, I'm so sorry."

"For real."

"What happened?"

"Mandy's horse had been through traumatic times too. I felt sorry for him. He was just like me. I think he knew why I'd come out to the field. The horse screamed at me. Then I screamed. And it felt so good that I kept screaming. I fired those bullets I'd brought up into the air. Then something broke loose in me. I cried. The horse kept everyone away for a while. We both mourned. That night, I decided to live the rest of my life. I'll tell you it's not without sorrow. But I've learned to appreciate the fact that my sorrow shows I have a soul, shows I'm human and alive. I thank God every morning for the new day I have and the chance to know good things that balance out the bad. I'm a miracle, Addy."

Addy tried to blink away her tears.

"I think you could be one too, if you choose to be. Owen sure could use one."

She nodded. "He wrote me letters. All the years he thought I was dead, he wrote to me."

"That what he was doing?" Rocco smiled. "We all saw him writing his mysterious notes. I'm glad he was writing to you. So you're out here trying to figure out how you're going to leave the past behind and move on?"

She nodded. "I don't know if I can."

"Haven't you given Edwards enough?" Rocco asked.

"I haven't given him anything," Addy said.

"That's right. He took from you. He took everything."

"I didn't even give him hell."

"Continuing to punish yourself means you're still letting him steal your power. End it. Cut off the feed."

"How?"

"By being present," he said. "Right here, right now…it's not a bad place to be. Don't live in the past. Don't live in the future. Live this very moment. Here, where people love you. Where you and your son are safe. Owen is going to find Augie."

"What if he doesn't?"

"Lion's pride and the other groups he's been in taught Augie to be resourceful. Don't underestimate your son's strength—or Owen's determination." Rocco straightened. He squeezed her shoulder and smiled at her. "Let a little hope in. I learned that one, too."

20

Addy heard the commotion in the foyer later that afternoon. Her heart jumped, hammering out a beat that was too big to hold inside her chest. She pulled a deep breath as she stepped out into the sitting room connecting the suite of rooms near hers. Had Owen come back with the group? Or, at the very least, was there news from him?

She started down the long hall, afraid but hopeful. Her son and Zavi joined the group, followed by Zavi's tutor.

Oh, God. Owen was there. With his friends, but *alone*. He saw her. She stopped. He went still.

The others turned to see what he was looking at. Seeing her, they parted, leaving her a direct path to him. He didn't turn from her. No. He faced her, leaving himself open and vulnerable. She saw in his face everything she was feeling. Everything.

She'd read his letters, listened to his heart, learned he'd suffered every bit as much as she had. Her heart had died early on in her hell, but his had died again and again.

A tear slipped down her cheek. So much time had passed. So very much time. She wasn't going to waste another second of it. Her pace quickened. She ran the last few steps before throwing herself at him. He caught her up in the tightest hug she'd ever known, tight enough that it warmed her heart.

Her arms were wrapped around his neck. She lost all awareness of the world around them. She didn't know where she ended and he began. She filled her lungs with his scent.

"I'm sorry," she whispered. "I'm so sorry."

He bent and lifted her legs, draping them over his arm. He tightened his hold until she was face to face with him. "Not as much as I am."

She caught his head in her hands, looking into his eyes as she said, "I love you."

"I love you." His mouth came down on hers.

She lost herself in his kiss, only becoming aware that they were moving when the light dimmed in the hallway.

ANGEL LOOKED AROUND at the group clustered in the foyer, and slowly grinned. "About freaking time." Troy was frowning as the two went down the hall. Angel tousled his hair. "Don't worry about your mom. She's in good hands."

Rocco called down the hall, "Troy's with us, so have a good...talk."

Zavi snorted. "My parents always have a talk after my mom kisses Papa."

Rocco laughed and tightened his hold on Mandy, whose cheeks had turned pink.

"Want to go see the puppies?" Zavi asked Troy, who nodded, giving the long hallway a last look.

"We'll go with you," Blade said, holding his hand out for Eddie.

Angel checked Selena's reaction to what had just happened. "You okay?"

She nodded. "Why wouldn't I be? Why do you guys keep asking me that?"

Angel shrugged. "Greer was taking bets on which cousin you'd hook up with."

Val laughed.

"Assholes," Selena muttered. "I'm gonna cause Greer some pain." She looked around for him, but he'd slipped away from the group.

Ace came forward. "Good idea, Sel. My brother's an idiot. Let's go make a plan for that pain."

"Shit," Val said as they walked away. "That can't be good."

"You weren't in on that bet, were you?" Wynn asked Angel.

He started to nod, then shook his head, making a full circle. "No. No, that would have been inappropriate." Wynn's brows lifted. He looked over Wynn's head and mouthed, "Help me," to Val.

Val grinned and tucked his hands up under his armpits as he looked around at the group, his expression soft. "I love my family." He nodded toward the two women who went outside. "Even the vicious ones."

Mandy gave him a hug. "We love you too."

"So, did you find my fake parents?" Wynn asked Angel.

"We did," Angel said. "They seem legit. Max is processing them in the bunker. We were going to give them some time to get settled, maybe let them eat in their room. They're anxious to talk to you."

"Yeah, me too. But I don't want to do it alone."

"I'll be there," Angel said.

"Can everyone be there? I don't trust them. And I don't trust myself to hear them properly, if they really are my parents."

Val nodded. "We got your back. How about after dinner, we bring them down to the living room? I'm sure Greer's got a thumb press somewhere." He looked at Angel. "You got the water board?"

Angel laughed.

"Torture isn't necessary. Just don't leave me alone with them," Wynn said.

Angel put his arm around her shoulders. "Never. How about we go see those puppies? They make everyone's day better."

"You sure it's okay to leave Troy with them?" Addy asked.

"Absolutely," Owen said. "Mandy's as fierce a mother as you are. If she needs us, she'll come get us."

He opened the door, then kicked it closed behind him, setting her on her feet outside the bathroom.

"I'm not fierce."

"Aw, sweetheart. You are the very definition of fierce. It's an honor to have you in my heart."

She pressed her hand to his chest.

He caught her fingers and lifted them for a kiss. "Addy, I know that things between you and others haven't been good. I need you to know I'm not like them. I will never shame you or hurt you."

Her eyes lowered to his chest. He bent a little to get her to look at him.

"So much hate. So much time lost," she whispered.

He nodded. "And so much time still to come. We can begin again. Now. Here."

"Shut the door on the past?"

"Yeah."

"I can't until I get Augie back."

"Just our past. Augie's our future."

"Your letters were beautiful."

"Did you read them?"

"All of them. I've been crying for days."

Owen sucked in a sharp breath. He smoothed his thumb over her cheek. "That was never my intention."

"I wish I'd gotten them when you wrote them." She looked up at him. "Did you get the man you were after? And the doctors?"

"We got the doctors. They're a little traumatized, but safe now. Jafaar got away." He kissed her forehead. "Addy, I desperately need a shower."

She nodded. "I could use one too."

He smiled as he stared into her eyes, framing the sides of her face with his hands. She'd always been smaller than him, but now he realized how much smaller. Something about her big personality always made her seem larger than life. Her hands moved from his forearms to his shoulders. He looked at her as he started to unbutton her shirt. He hoped she didn't notice his hands shaking. Shadows still filled her eyes.

He leaned close to whisper, "There is only us now, my Laidy."

She shook her head, sorrow in her eyes. "There's never only us when there's everything else in between us."

He knew what she was talking about. All those years. All the others they'd been with—through choice and force. He took hold of her waist and pulled her close. "Let's let it all go, all of it, even if it's just for this moment. I accept your past. I hate it. I would undo it if I could. But we're here, safe, together

—just where I always wanted us. I'll make you forget the others."

Panic flashed in her eyes. "I don't want you to make me do anything."

He reached over and locked his door. "Can I at least make you scream with pleasure?"

She shook her head. "Especially that. No sex that makes me scream." Tears filled her eyes.

Owen brushed them away with his thumbs as he leaned his forehead to hers. He just wanted her to know that she was safe with him, that'd he'd never hurt her, that they could stop whenever she wanted. But all this talking was digging a hole for them fast.

"Laidy," he said as he caught her face between his hands and brought her focus to him. "There's so much I want to say, but I don't think words matter now. Only time does, and that's not something we can have instantly, so I'm just going to ask for your trust."

She wrapped her hands around his wrists, smiling sadly as her gaze lowered to his lips. "I guess we begin over now."

"I'd like that." He grinned. "Damn, I'm as nervous as a kid."

Her arms went around his neck. "Show me, Owen. Show me what your love feels like."

He kissed her mouth, then stepped back and tore the Velcro straps of his Kevlar free and set it next to the wall. He took off his tan pullover and tossed it and his tee on the floor. Sitting on the bed, he untied his boots and kicked them off.

He put his pistol in the drawer of his nightstand and was about to drop his cargos but stopped, distracted by the sight of her undressing. He watched as she unbuttoned the rest of her blouse, pulling it from her waistband. Her hair was still short, but had grown out another inch since he first saw her. It was darker than the white blond it had been when they were kids, but its current color was much richer with its streaks of browns and light blonds.

He reached over and fingered a few locks. She looked up at him, then let her gaze roam freely over his chest. He wasn't a hairy man—just had a little golden furring over his pecs. He wondered if that was to her liking. Not much he could do about it either way; he wasn't about to suffer through what Val did in the name of manscaping.

He needn't have worried. Her eyes darkened as she looked him over. He knew he'd changed in the decade they'd been apart. Bulked up quite a bit. Working out was his refuge. Then tears filled her eyes when her gaze hit the fading bruises that lingered from his time with Edwards.

"Owen. God." Her cold hands touched his hot skin. His body contracted at the gentle contact. He didn't stop her hands from touching his blotchy patches. It was like she was putting him back together. When she met his eyes again, he bent over and kissed her, long and deeply, wanting to distract her.

Her hands began to fuss at something near his crotch. He looked down to see her unfastening her jeans. She pushed them down her hips, revealing a pair of light pink panties. So goddamned feminine. Her legs were lean and soft. He pushed his cargos down, exposing his black boxer briefs and the hard-on they barely contained.

Her lips parted as she saw how ready he was for her. He stepped closer to her, studying her as he pushed her blouse off her shoulders. Gooseflesh rose across her skin as he helped her take off her tank top. Her bra matched her panties. Its silk cups held generous breasts. She was bigger there than he remembered. He smiled as he rubbed his hands over her upper arms.

"You're beautiful," he said, then took her hand and led her toward the bathroom.

He put a couple of towels on the warming rack, set some washcloths in the shower, then started the water to warm it up before they got in. He took out a box of condoms and removed one. When he looked up, he caught the sight of her in the big mirror over the sink. She was completely nude. His mouth went dry.

Turning, he pushed his boxer briefs off, then pulled her against his body, feeling her soft skin from his chest all the way down his thighs. Though slim, she was curvy in all the right places, the complete opposite of him. He kissed her as he held her close.

Steam was filling the bathroom. He opened the stall door and set the condom where he could reach it. After adjusting the temperature of the water, he let her get in first. Standing with her in the hot stream of water, he ran his hand down the side of her face, over her chin, down her neck, down her chest, ending at her navel. It was a shame her scars were all on the inside. They were harder to heal because they couldn't be seen, and she was the only one who could feel them.

He moved his head into the stream of water, hiding his tears. He pulled her against his body, letting the water wash over both of them. Her arms were folded between their bodies at first. He held her until she slipped her arms under his to wrap them around his back. The roar of the water was loud in his ears. He felt her body shake as her tears came. He held her as she wept. Such quiet rage. She should scream and pound him. He kissed her temple, holding her until the storm broke.

"Addy, my Laidy, wash me. I'll wash you. We'll purge the pain."

She pulled free. Taking up the soap, she lathered a cloth then began stroking it over him. "Your bruises hurt me."

He nodded. "I know. It's how I feel about your scars, the ones I know are there but I can't see. I'll give you my pain if you give me yours."

"How will that help?"

He lifted his shoulders. "It's how it works. We carry each other's burdens. In time, they won't wear so heavily on us."

She sighed. Her hand went still. "He was never kind to me. Even his polite words sliced like knives."

Owen nodded. The ugliness was coming out. He hoped that meant light was getting in. Her stories were going to randomly come out. He had to be man enough to listen to them. It was part of carrying her burdens. Each one she let out would be one fewer weighing her down.

He lifted her chin and kissed her lips. They were soft under his. Her hands ran down his chest to his abdomen, then lower still. She wrapped her fingers around his dick. He felt himself jump in her hands. He deepened their kiss as he reached for the packet and covered himself.

"Put your arms around me. Let me in, Laidy. Please."

She stood on her tiptoes and wrapped her arms around his neck. He caught her waist and lifted her so she could lock her legs over his hips. He moved to lean her against the wall of the shower, then slowly lowered her over his stiff cock. She pulled his face to hers and kissed him as he joined their bodies. The sensation was exquisite. With the hot water pounding down on his back, it was almost too much to feel. He began to move in her, slowly, gently, showing her with each stroke all the love and patience she'd never known.

The heat grew. He shivered. The feel of her in his arms, her body, her pleasure offered up to him, was too much to hold back. He lifted her up and down, faster and faster. "Addy, I can't——"

She tightened her arms around his neck, lifting herself up to whisper in his ear, "It's okay, Owen. Let go."

He bent his head into the nook of her neck and did just that, letting his body pump into hers, taking his release. It was beautiful. It was lonely. It was everything and nothing and nowhere near enough.

21

Addy's panic set in as soon as they'd separated in the shower. She should have faked an orgasm. She knew to do that. She'd had years of training. How was Owen going to react to her failure? With fists? Or cutting words? Or threats against her boys?

It was hard to breathe. The air was damp, but her mouth was dry.

Owen got out of the shower first. He dropped the spent condom in the trash, then wrapped a towel around his waist. The other he brought back to drape over her. She ventured a fast look at him. His eyes were sad, as if she'd taken something from him. She looked away, uncertain what to do with that information. He'd be angry in a moment, when he realized it was her fault.

Fear cooled the shower's heat from Addy's skin.

She tried to calm her rising panic by remembering

this was a new place, new rules, new people…new places to hide. Standing before her was the good Owen from her memories, but the bad Owen from all the lies she'd been told made her question her safety. A punch from him would hurt so much more than any of Cecil's.

He frowned at her, worry in his eyes. It was coming, the anger. It was getting even harder to breathe. Was this the real Owen, or was he playing a part? Was he really the bad Owen?

"Do you need a moment?" he asked.

She nodded, trying not to show the relief that stormed through her.

"Take all the time you need. I'll be waiting for you."

He closed the bathroom door behind him. The room's steamy warmth was quickly evaporating. She stared at the door, wondering how much time he'd give her before he slammed back in. In a panic, she slipped out of the bathroom and out of his room, rushing into hers. She didn't lock the door because that would only enrage him if he thought she was trying to avoid him.

Instead, she dressed quickly, choosing a pair of beige slacks, a tank top, and a black V-neck sweater. She picked a pair of black stilettos that Cecil always favored. She'd just finished blow-drying her hair when she saw Owen leaning against the doorjamb of her bathroom, his arms and legs crossed, anger in his eyes. She jumped, then dropped her blow-dryer on the counter, the noise loud in the suddenly quiet room as the fall shut it off.

"I'm sorry. I'm almost done." She brushed out her hair, then scrambled to collect her makeup so she could apply it quickly—hard to do when her hands were shaking.

"Done…doing what?"

"Done cleaning up so I don't look like a lowlife."

His brows lifted. Good and bad Owen tangled in her panicked mind, mixing with similar experiences with Cecil. Her husband's wants changed on a dime. She could never make him happy enough to avoid his fists.

"Who said you could ever look like a lowlife?"

She lowered her gaze to the counter. Shame. She'd always let Cecil down, no matter how she tried not to. No matter how important it was to do the right thing for herself and the boys, she'd always failed. "He did."

"I'm not him."

She nodded quickly, trying to keep up with the issue at hand, her mind racing to see where it would fall out. "I'm sorry."

"Sorry for what?"

She licked her lips but didn't look at him. "For taking so long. I'll just be a minute more."

"Laidy…I thought we were going back to bed. For at least a little bit, until they call us to talk to the doctors."

She looked at him, searching for the anger that

preceded the fists. She nodded. "I just want to look right for you."

He frowned. "Do you always put makeup and clothes on before going to bed?"

"H-he always liked it that way. Do you not?"

Owen lifted a shoulder. "It's not about what I like —it's what you like that matters."

She looked away, trying to unravel that comment.

"Baby, look at me."

She did. He was getting angrier. Her gaze darted around the bathroom for someplace she could take cover, but there was no place, and he didn't move from the doorjamb.

"Answer truthfully. Do you wear makeup to bed when you're alone?"

She shook her head.

"Do you want to wear it to bed when you're with me?"

What was the right answer? What was it? "No."

"Then don't. I'm not the boss of you. There are only two places in our lives where we aren't equal: your security and your children. I'm in charge of the former; you're in charge of the latter. Do you understand?"

She nodded, but she didn't understand. "I don't like these clothes." She looked at him quickly, surprised that popped out, wishing she could unsay it.

"Then wear what you want to wear."

"I don't have anything I like." She quickly added,

"It isn't that I don't like what I have. It's just that sometimes I want to wear other things."

He smiled. "What do you want to wear?"

"Slouchy clothes. Stretchy knits. Cheap jeans. Chucks. Nothing designer or couture." She tossed the eyeshadow case across the counter. Did he know she was testing him? Pushing to see where he'd break and what her boundaries were? "And no makeup."

"Then we'll get you those clothes. And you're beautiful with or without makeup."

She looked at him. It was freeing being honest. He didn't seem to be reacting negatively. "I don't have any money. I've never had any of my own money. I can't buy them."

"Would you accept a gift from me? A *gift*, Laidy. Something offered for no reason other than the giving."

Her eyes watered. She folded her lips together and bit them. She took a few breaths, calming herself at last. This was the good Owen. He'd met her crazed behavior without getting too upset with her. "I don't know who I am, Owen. I don't know if I can accept."

He came into the bathroom. She tensed when he lifted his arms, but he only wrapped them around her. "We'll find you, Addy. I promise. It's really a lot simpler than you're thinking. There is no right or wrong when it comes to me or us. Listen to your heart. Listen to mine. Pick joy. All the time. That's all there is to this."

She released a shaky breath, then leaned into him,

really leaned. He took her weight without complaint. He was definitely the good Owen. There was no bad Owen. "I don't know anything. I don't know what end's up, what's real, what's a nightmare. I want you, but I keep fearing evil Owen."

He rubbed her back. "Evil Owen. Don't tell my team about him. They'll believe you." He chuckled. He looked down at her, brushing a stray curl from her face. "I do know what end's up. So until we unscramble you, maybe you could rely on me?"

She nodded.

"And also, I'm just putting this out there, there's a psychologist in town who's a solid guy. He did great with Rocco—he's still going to him. If you ever want to see him, I can take you there or bring him here."

She leaned back and looked up at Owen. Her eyes had to be some crazy color, for he looked shocked seeing them. This was all still too raw for her. She was dealing with her very soul here. It was too soon—and she was too fragile—to trust it with someone else. "Can we just start with you for a while?"

"You bet." He pulled on the black T-shirt he'd been holding. "Hey, I was thinking you must be starving. Why don't we go say goodnight to Troy, then snag something from the kitchen? We've already used up our cuddle time, and we'll have to meet with the Ratcliffs soon."

She smiled, relieved he understood how much seeing her son would reset her. Addy nodded then looked at herself in the mirror and realized she hadn't started her makeup, then remembered she didn't have to. She gave Owen a little smile and left the bathroom. He followed her into the hallway. His feet were bare. She had the feeling he was completely at home just as he was.

She could learn from that.

He reached for her hand as they went up the backstairs in their wing. Neither of them spoke as they made the long trek through the core of the house to the far bedroom wing where Rocco and Mandy had their suite of rooms. The couple was on the sofa in their sitting room, watching TV.

Mandy smiled as they approached. "Hey, you two." She and Rocco got up to greet them.

"We wanted to say goodnight to Troy," Owen said.

"Great timing. We just put them to bed," Mandy replied.

"I hope Troy hasn't been any trouble for you," Addy said.

"No trouble at all. He never is."

Mandy and Addy started toward Zavi's room, but Owen stopped Mandy. "Can I have a quick word?"

"Sure," Mandy said. "Addy, go on in. I'm sure they're still awake."

When Addy left, Owen looked at Mandy.

"How are things going?" she asked quietly.

He looked from her to Rocco, then shoved his

hands in his pockets. "Fine. Look, do you remember bringing in clothes for the ladies? Seemed like for a bit we kept needing extra things."

"I do."

"Any chance there's a pair of pajamas or something casual that might fit Addy?"

"Oh, I'm sure there is. What does she need?"

Owen shrugged. "Something slouchy."

"Yeah, we've got that somewhere. I'll dig it up and take it to your room...her room?"

"Her room. We're going to get some late dinner."

"Wynn said she wanted us all there when she met with her parents...or whoever they are," Rocco said. "Russ just took a meal tray to them, so you've got a little time."

"I intended for us all to be there anyway," Owen said. "The time's over for hiding this shit, now that we're all targets."

"Casey's coming up to hang with the boys when we meet," Mandy said. "Hey, do you think Addy might enjoy some riding lessons? Could be a good distraction."

Owen blinked as he stared at her. Rocco's woman was spot-on. "Yeah. I think that may just be exactly what she needs."

Addy came back in the room. "What do I need?"

"Riding lessons," Mandy said. "There's something about spending time on a horse that puts the world into perspective. Do you know how to ride?"

"I did ages ago, when I was a kid. I haven't gone riding in forever. Do you do English or Western?"

"Western."

"I never learned that."

"Same principles, just a little different practice. Want to try?"

"Yes. That would be fun, actually."

"Yay! I have some free spots tomorrow. I'll come get you."

"Can Troy join us?"

"Of course," Mandy said. "But in the beginning, let's work on each of you separately. We'll work up toward a trail ride with a whole bunch of us."

Addy smiled. A real smile, Owen noticed, not one of the placating fake ones she'd cultivated, which he fucking hated.

"I can't wait," she said. "Thanks, Mandy."

They went down the stairs in Rocco's wing, then headed for the kitchen. The lights had been dimmed, as it had been shut down for the night. Owen turned them up, then went searching in the fridge for something for them to eat. "Looks like stroganoff was dinner tonight. Sound good? Or do you want me to make some sandwiches."

"Stroganoff, please," Addy said.

"Works for me." He took some out and heated it up, then dished it out for both of them, making sure their portions were equal. He took a bite, then moaned. Russ was a helluva cook. They sat on tall stools at the counter that overlooked the sink.

"There's no way I can eat all of this. I'll get fat."

He shrugged. "Eat what you want." He took another bite, watching her eat. "You know, I don't care if you're fat. I don't care what you wear. I don't care if you have makeup on or not. I care about the real you. I care that your soul's near mine and neither of us is alone."

"I'm not sure I still have a soul."

He smiled. "You do. It's in there. I'm glad you're going riding with Mandy."

"I'm looking forward to that."

They ate in silence for bit. Owen went around the counter to get them both some water. "Can I ask you something?" He ran the tap.

"Sure."

"Who's Troy's father? It's not Edwards."

"I don't know."

Owen frowned. "How can you not know?"

"He was conceived at one of Cecil's rape parties."

"Fuck." All kinds of questions jumped to Owen's mind, but he thought he'd peeled off enough of her layers for one night. Or maybe he wasn't ready to hear the story.

"Yeah." She pushed some noodles around on her plate. "I think it may have been a guy Cecil called his War Bringer."

He looked at her. "That guy's dead. He tried to initiate Fiona and Kelan killed him."

Addy looked at him. Her beautiful and changing eyes went from glowing blue to orange. "Good."

"You don't seem to hold any resentment toward Troy for his origins."

"I don't. I love my boys. Even when I thought Augie was Cecil's, I loved him. They're so innocent, Owen." She sighed, then looked at her plate for a minute. "Do you think blood runs true?"

"How so?"

"Do you think Troy will be like his father?"

Owen shook his head. "Not possible. You got him away from Edwards early enough. And you've taught him kindness. He may well grow up to be a warrior, but I can't see him fighting on the same side as his bio dad."

Owen's phone buzzed. He looked at the text. "The people claiming to be Wynn's parents are coming down to meet with us. If you're okay with it, I'd like you there. They might know something that could help you."

"Yes, I'd like that. Maybe they can explain what's happening. Guess it's good I dressed after all."

"You could have met with them in jammies. Wouldn't have been good for my concentration, but you'd have been comfortable." He smiled when she laughed, glad he'd talked her down from her panic earlier. That had been a terrifying thing to watch.

22

Angel let himself in to Wynn's apartment. When she saw him, she grabbed him in a big hug. He held her tight, wondering how he'd ever lived without her. After a minute, he pulled back. She knew it was time for the meeting. She ran her hands over her hair, then straightened her sweater and smoothed her jeans.

"My God," she said. "I'm so nervous. Are you sure it's them?"

"No. Not at all. They look like they're my age. Nowhere near old enough to be your parents."

"How is that possible? Do they think we'd be easily fooled by imposters?"

"We'll have their DNA results back in a couple of days. We'll compare it to yours." He gave her a half-grin. "You know, fuck Owen. You don't have to meet them if you don't want to. I'll keep them locked up in the bunker while we get this sorted out."

She lowered her gaze to the fleece pullover he wore. "If I hadn't seen what happened to Addy, I wouldn't believe any of this was possible." She met his eyes. "I'm ready to talk to them."

"I'll let Kit know we're ready." Angel sent a text.

Wynn's nerves tightened as they went into the living room. Selena was the first to join them, then the others came in. Max and Greer were the last, bringing the couple who said they were her parents. Wynn studied them, bombarded by so many thoughts simultaneously. The pain of losing them, the shock of moving in with Grams, sorrow that Grams had passed just weeks before seeing them again, worry about how they'd survived the Omnis, anger that they'd chosen their jobs over her. Fear that it might not be real. Everything. It all locked her up. She couldn't speak. Didn't reach for their hands to return their offered handshakes when introductions were made. Joyce and Nathan Ratcliff. They used her parents' names; they looked exactly as they had in the photo of them she had...but they weren't her parents.

They were talking to her, but the words slipped away. She tried to recall what their eyes looked like in her memories. But what they'd seemed like to an eleven-year-old was nothing like what they seemed to her as an adult. She saw sorrow and guilt in theirs. Was that acting? Had Jafaar picked random people to have cosmetic surgery so that they looked like the old pictures of her parents? Why? Why had they left her? Why had they come back?

She looked at Angel, afraid she wasn't ready after all. He put his arm around her. "Why don't we all sit down?" he suggested. "This isn't something easily understood. I'm sure it's overwhelming to everyone."

Wynn and Angel sat on the sofa, across from the people posing as her parents. Angel kissed her temple and squeezed her hand, then whispered, "Breathe, baby. We'll sort this out."

"Start at the beginning," Wynn ordered. She rubbed her thumb over the butterfly that Mr. Edwards had carved into her palm.

The couple exchanged glances, then Joyce focused on Wynn as she started their story. "Your father and I were doing groundbreaking work in the field of gene therapy using bio-nanotechnology. We presented our work at a conference and were approached by a venture capitalist that wanted to hire us. He had deep pockets. We were tempted by his offer. His financing could take our work light years beyond where it was."

The man continued. "We didn't take his offer, however. There was just something off about him. His company was new. The man himself, and the principals he listed, had no history in our field or any other scientific venture. Sometimes, if something's too good to be true, it is. We sent him packing."

"Or we thought we did," the woman said. "When we turned him down, things got ugly. He gave us two choices. Go to work for him, and he would spare you and Grams. Or resist and he would kill you both and still take us."

Wynn listened intently. All of it made sense with what she now knew of the Omni world, but that didn't mean any of it was true. She refused to be duped simply because she desperately wanted their story to be true…wanted her parents back in her life…wanted the world to be not quite so evil.

"There were so many times we tried to leave," the woman said. "Every one of them was met with renewed threats against you and Grams. They bought a house near you. Let us see you from a distance. We went to your high school graduation. We visited your college, saw you walking around campus. Went to that graduation ceremony, too. Never were we allowed to speak to you, though there were times we walked right past you. It was hell, but it was wonderful getting to at least keep tabs on you."

"Thirteen years," Wynn said. "That's how long you were gone. Thirteen years. In all that time, you couldn't have reached out?"

"We made sure Grams had money for you," the man said.

"Did she know?" Wynn asked.

"I wonder about that. She was presented with the trust fund for your and her support shortly after our deaths," he said.

"That fire in the lab that 'killed' you," Wynn said, using air quotes, "killed a lot more than you. It destroyed careers and ended the reputation of the business you worked for."

The woman nodded. "It would have taken many

more lives had we not cooperated. The people who had us meant business."

"And you couldn't get word out to the cops or the FBI or someone that you were being held against your will?"

The woman sighed. She looked at the man. "We tried. Several times. Each time, something bad happened to you or Grams. Remember Grams' car accident? Remember the flu that sent you to the hospital? Remember Grams' stroke?"

Wynn shut her eyes, chilled by the near-death experiences these people knew about. Still, someone doing background research on her would have turned them up. Nothing in her life had been hidden.

"So you were responsible for Grams' stroke?" Angel asked. Wynn was glad he did, because she couldn't have voiced that question.

"Not directly. But indirectly, yes," the woman said.

"Explain yourself," Owen said.

"We heard there were fighters here who are taking a stand against the Omnis," the woman said. "We thought we had a chance to get out if we could contact you."

"The chemical they gave to Grams was meant only to induce a coma," the man said. "But that coma caused a blood clot that triggered the stroke. When that happened, we went on strike. We refused to continue working, and we shut down our lab at a critical point. In order to get us back online with their program, we negotiated for the ability to treat

Grams. They moved Grams out of the palliative care center and into a private residence under their control."

Wynn gasped. "Grams said she saw you there. I thought it was just a dream she had. Of course, she couldn't have known you were imposters."

"We aren't imposters, Wynn," the woman said. "We are your parents."

Wynn let that slide. She didn't have enough information yet to argue the point. For now, she was going with the imposter theory. "So you did something to her. You're why she recovered so completely."

"And we're why she died," the man said.

"How so?" Owen asked.

"They kept her sedated for your visits," the woman said, "but we were seeing remarkable recovery from her. Her cells were regenerating. The man holding her, Jafaar Majid, saw the power of the work we'd been doing. He wanted it for his employer. He tried to negotiate with a man named Mr. Edwards for the franchise. Apparently it was denied him. He ordered Grams to be murdered for two reasons. He wanted to strike back against the Omnis, weakening their hold on us. And, we think, he wanted a corpse so that he could begin reverse-engineering what we'd done to Grams."

"You gave Grams the same regenerative modifications that you gave yourself, which is why you look so young," Owen said. The couple nodded. "But you aren't immortal."

Wynn looked at him. Where was he headed with this?

"No. We can be killed, just like any other living organism," the man said.

"But it can take more to kill us," the woman added. "If we sustain a mortal injury, and receive life support quickly enough, our bodies can regenerate and heal."

Owen looked at Addy, then back at the couple. "One of our own has been modified. Can you tell me if the modifications you developed were the ones given to her?"

The woman nodded. "We'll need a blood sample, but yes."

"Our lab wasn't the only one at work on these modifications," the man said. "The Omnis had dozens of labs going. Some of their work was successful, some not. Didn't stop them from testing it on human subjects…often without proper protocols."

"What was their objective with these human modifications?" Ty asked.

The woman pressed her lips together and sighed. "They wanted to engineer the perfect human. But they had several ideals they wanted configured. The perfect warrior. The perfect servant. The perfect mother. And, just in general, the perfect life—long, healthy."

"And they wanted it done in a way that could be commoditized," the man said.

"What does that mean?" Wynn asked.

"They wanted a corner on the market," Ty said. "They wanted to control the market. Can you imagine the value of these human modifications? To live forever? To live forever in good health? To be able to decide who gets to live forever?"

The man nodded. "That's the franchise Jafaar wanted for his employers. He's willing to kill for it, and so are the Omnis."

"We were told the Omnis are cleaning house and eliminating their researchers," Owen said.

"It's true," the woman said. "They don't want to risk these formulas slipping out into the wider population. They won't even file a patent on them for risk of exposing their secrets."

"So are these modifications truly epigenetic?" Angel asked. "Can they be passed down from parents to children?"

"In some cases," the man said. "They can be passed from mother to child. It's complicated. The ability to procreate is severely limited in those who've been modified. Once the shots are started, they have to be continually renewed, as the nanotechnology wears down inside the human body. Once started, especially on older patients, if the nanos are not renewed, the body begins aging at a rapid rate, one that sends it into shock and shuts it down. One lab has discovered how to trigger this rapid demise even on young patients." He looked around at the group, then stopped at Owen. "This has the potential to be an extinction event if it's not stopped...or if the antidote isn't widely available at every hospital and clinic and remote medical outpost in the world."

"How do these triggers operate?" Owen asked.

The man looked disgusted with himself. He squeezed his eyes shut and shook his head. "It depends on the type of nanos that were injected."

"Another aspect that could more slowly affect world population is that unless certain modifications are made to the formula, it's nearly impossible to conceive," the woman said. "That was one of the pieces we were working on in our lab. On the one hand, it makes sense if people are going to be living longer and longer lives. But it wasn't done for altruistic reasons. It was done so that only a handful of world leaders could decide who gets to procreate."

"These modifications automatically give huge power to a small set of individuals, then," Ty said. "Talk about an evil empire."

"So we find the formulas—and the labs making them—and eliminate them," Rocco said.

"We thought that at first," the man said, "but we're now hearing reports about spontaneous mutations occurring among the affected population. It's like the human organism is being retrained by the behaviors of the nanos. Like nature is taking back over, healing and improving itself."

"So that's a good thing," Greer said, frowning.

"In theory, perhaps," the woman said. "We don't know the full extent of these mutations. We don't know what they're doing, not doing, what they're changing in the human genome. We opened Pandora's box."

"The formulas for the human modifications are still in the control of the Omnis," the man said. "If they act quickly, they can situate themselves in a power position. And that's what they're attempting to do."

"I'm sorry about Grams' house," the woman said to Wynn. "We were there that night. We'd been hiding in her house until you came."

"I saw you," Angel said.

The woman nodded. "We were trying to make contact with Wynn, but the Omnis followed us to you. We brought them to you. I'm so sorry."

"We narrowly escaped," the man said. "We talked to the fire department and the sheriff, told them we were neighbors of yours. We wanted to find out how to reach you. They gave us Kit's information."

"We didn't know which side of the Omni war Kit and the rest of you were on," the woman said. "We came up here and stayed in a hotel, checking the pulse of the townspeople to see if you were safe or not. Finally, we got up the courage to talk to the police. We gave a statement to the deputy. It sounded so crazy, what we had to say. I mean, what sane person would believe us? But it was such a relief to finally reach out for help. And then Jafaar showed up and our freedom was lost. Again. He took us. He took you." She looked at Wynn. "We had no choice but to go with him in exchange for his releasing you. Which he did. He kept his word."

"Only because he figured it would be easy to take her again, if and when he wanted," Angel said.

"So the deputy's dirty," Ty said, looking at Kit. "Is the sheriff?"

Kit's jaw clenched. "We'll find out."

"Angel, escort the Ratcliffs to their room," Owen said. "I would suggest you don't leave the house," he said to the couple. "For your own protection."

"Don't worry about us. If we're safe here, we won't cause any problems," the woman said as she stood. "Besides, we'd like to get to know our daughter again."

Wynn got to her feet. "We don't know that you're my parents yet."

"The DNA doesn't lie," the man said.

"Maybe not naturally, but it's your creative playground. You could make it lie. Goodnight." Wynn left the room, heading down the hall toward the backstairs to her apartment, in the opposite direction that Angel was taking the couple.

"WE GOT INCOMING," Max said before anyone else could leave the room. Angel was halfway up the stairs with Wynn's parents. He paused, looking over the banister to Kit.

"Who is it?" Kit asked.

"Doc Beck." Max looked around the room. "Anyone expecting a house call?"

Silence met his question. The doorbell rang. Kit opened it. "Doc. Weren't expecting you."

"Yeah. Sorry for the late visit." Beck looked into the living room and saw everyone standing there. "I need to talk to you and Owen…and Ms. Jacobs."

Addy tensed. Owen moved to stand in front of her. "What's this about?"

"I'd like a private word with Ms. Jacobs, then we can talk."

Addy gripped Owen's shirt, then tiptoed to whisper, "I don't want to be alone with him."

He nodded. "Doctor, let's go to the den."

Beck moved deeper into the foyer, catching sight of the couple claiming to be Wynn's parents. "Doctors Ratcliff?" he asked.

"Dr. Beck?" the man answered. Owen saw the look Wynn's dad exchanged with her mom.

Beck seemed to relax a little. "Glad you're here. You might want to join us."

"It's cool, Angel. Bring 'em back down," Kit said. "We'll be here when you're finished with Addy."

Owen led the way down the hall to the den. When the three of them were inside, he closed the door.

"This is a confidential matter concerning Ms. Jacobs only," Beck said, staring at Owen.

"She's asked me to stay with her."

Beck made a face, then handed an envelope to Addy. "Your tests came back clear."

"What tests?" Owen asked.

Addy's face reddened. "I saw the GYN at the clinic a couple of days ago. I wanted to be sure I was clear of STDs."

"Oh." Owen folded his arms. "Okay." He blinked, unable to keep the hint of a smile off his face until he looked back at Beck. "And what is it you wanted to say to my team?"

"I ran into Ms. Jacobs at the clinic. I saw her eyes. It was a clever cover she gave, saying it was from 'mood' contacts. The staff fell for it...and have been looking for them ever since." He chuckled. "But I knew that wasn't the case. Owen, I'm working with your father. He sent me here in part to patch you guys up like I have been, but also to watch for the mutations to show up. With you guys in the thick of things, we surmised you would be among the early recipients. And I'm glad to see you found the Ratcliffs. They've been missing for a couple of months. We weren't sure they'd survived the Omni purge that's been going on."

"Shit," Owen said. "Why didn't you come to me sooner?"

"Orders."

"So my dad really is still alive. Where is he?"

"He moves around a lot, but he's on his way out here. I'm sure you'll see him soon."

So many damned secrets. Owen was sick of them. "Let's take this to the team. They're waiting in the living room."

The doctor left first. Owen caught Addy by the

hand and brought her to face him. Holding both of her hands, he smiled. "That is good news about your tests."

Shadows crowded her eyes. "It's a miracle."

"How long since you were with anyone?"

"A long while. But you know, some of that stuff doesn't go away."

Owen kissed her forehead. "Well, you're clear. I'm clear. We're good."

She sighed and nodded. "Yeah. We're good."

23

Kit was sitting on Sheriff Tate's front stoop early the next morning when he came out. Tate went down the stairs, then turned around and faced Kit. "What is it now?"

Kit stared at him, wondering if he could see in the sheriff's eyes the slow rot of Omni influence. He couldn't. Didn't mean it wasn't there. "Are you dirty, Tate?"

"What the fuck does that mean? You been drinkin', Kit?"

"I wish. Wouldn't feel so disgusted then."

"Look, I had one cup of coffee this morning, not nearly enough caffeine to help me make sense of your cryptic comments. You got something to say, say it."

"Have you ever heard of the Ratcliffs?"

"No."

"Never got a report from them about a potential human extinction event?"

"Jesus, boy. You high?"

"They talked to Deputy Jerry. Begged him for protection. They've been through hell. They needed help. You didn't bring them to us."

"Because this is the first I'm hearing about it." Tate rubbed his hand over his head. "When did this happen?"

"A couple of weeks ago."

"Where?"

"At the station."

"We record everything. They'd be on the video."

"Where's Deputy Jerry?"

"He's off today."

"Then let's go take a look at the tapes." Kit came down the steps.

"Not so fast. What's this human extinction event you're talking about?"

"Just what it sounds like. Total and complete Armageddon. That's all I can say."

At the police station, they pulled up the security footage from the same date as the videos Kit had taken from Ivy's diner across the street. When nothing showed on the station's recordings other than an ordinary day of normal activity, Kit played his videos, one taken from street level, one from the third floor of Ivy's building. Both showed the Ratcliffs going into the police station.

"That them?" Tate asked. "That the doctors you're talking about?"

"Yeah. Who was on shift that day?"

"Just Jerry and me."

"And yet Jerry's nowhere on these tapes." Kit straightened, putting his hands on his hips. He hung his head, then looked at the sheriff. "If you're in on this, sheriff..."

"In on what, Kit? What's going on? Ain't it about time you read me in?"

"No can do. Not now."

The sheriff stood. "You got a fucking extinction-level event, whatever the hell that is, coming to my town. You better rearrange your thinking, fast."

"It's not just your town it's gonna hit, though this may be ground zero. Your hysteria is not going to help us. Evacuating the town is not going to help us. The only way we can shut it down is to catch who's behind it. At the very minimum, your deputy's in it up to his neck."

"So let's bring him in."

"No. Let's leave him loose and stupid. See where the rat runs. I want access to his comms, his phone, his vehicle GPS." Kit pointed at the sheriff. "And you keep your fucking mouth shut. Act normal. We'll take this from here."

Tate slammed his desk chair into his desk. "Whatever you need. Just don't let my town go down in history, read me?"

Kit didn't answer. He opened the sheriff's door and calmly walked out of the station. "Max," he said into his comms, "you heard the convo. The sheriff's gonna patch you in."

JAFAAR'S PHONE RANG.

"I hear you have something I want," Edwards said over the phone.

Jafaar stared at the small window on his phone, surprised it was Edwards on the other end of King's line. He knew Edwards was King's right-hand man, but usually, calls from that number were digitally modified. Did that mean that Jafaar had pestered King enough to bring him to the table?

He knew Edwards knew about the Ratcliffs because he'd put the word out himself…hoping for just this call. The damned Feds had taken his bargaining chips, but Edwards didn't need to know that. "I do," Jafaar replied. "You know what I want."

"You can't bargain with something that already belongs to me."

"I can if I have them and you want them." Jafaar sighed, playing his hand carefully. If Edwards learned the Feds had the Ratcliffs, all bets were off. "I'm not your enemy, Mr. Edwards. I want a franchise, not full ownership. I want to extend your power, not eclipse it. You can't run the world without trustworthy partners, correct?"

"Bring them to me. We'll talk terms then."

"No. Let's hammer out our agreement first. I want it in al Jahni's hands before I bring you the scientists."

"Very well. I'll have my lawyers draft an agreement. Then I'll send coordinates for our transfer."

"It's a pleasure doing business with you," Jafaar said, but the line was dead before he finished.

Jafaar took a moment to savor his win. He had only to give Deputy Jerry the app that would trigger Owen's woman's termination sequence. Once she was on death's door, Jafaar had no doubt Owen would hand over the doctors in exchange for hope of a cure. Of course, Jafaar didn't have it; only the doctors could figure that out. And by then, it would be too late.

Selena brought Addy, Troy, and Zavi out to the arena. It was a beautiful, crisp autumn day. The sky was a deep, cloudless blue. The sun was warm. It felt wonderful to be outside. Addy smiled at the boys. How strange to be doing something normal. Selena would protect them. This activity wasn't a power play, wasn't an act of survival, wasn't anything necessary at all. Addy hadn't had many of these days in the last decade.

"I'm so excited for our ride today, aren't you boys?" she asked.

"I get to ride a lot," Zavi said, tilting his head. "I have my own pony."

"Is that her?" Troy asked, pointing to a dark brown Shetland pony tied up near a corral.

"Yeah, that's Betty. Isn't she beautiful? Mom likes me to groom her before I ride her. Want to help me with that?"

"Sure!"

"Okay. Come up easy so we don't scare her. I'll tell you everything I do. Let her sniff you. That's how she says hello."

Mandy came over and said to Addy, "Betty is the kindest old pony I've ever met. She's very patient with kids, like she knows they're colts and that they don't always behave correctly. She's been a great asset to me here."

"So you give lessons?" Addy asked. "Is that what you do here?"

"That, and much more. This is a hippotherapy center. My background's in physical therapy. I opened this center as a way of helping clients with their physical, mental, and emotional needs. Sometimes, we work with injured people to help them regain strength and balance. Sometimes counselors and psychologists bring their patients here to work on their specific needs. It's absolutely amazing the ways horses can help humans. Sometimes, it's like they just know better than we do what our patients need."

Addy smiled. "That's impressive. I'm so glad you invited us out here."

"I think the boys will be busy with Betty for a little bit. Want to start with you?"

"Sure. I warn you, though, riding isn't something

I've done much of. And when I did, it was English style."

"No worries. We'll start at the beginning."

OWEN CAME down to the corral, wanting to see how Addy and Troy took to riding. He hoped they loved it. Addy needed something to get her out of her head and into the world. And this was a beautiful day to do it. The boys were running in and out of the stables, chasing each other. Something about all the noise and laughter made him feel a little like the world was going to be okay. Changed, maybe, but okay.

Selena smiled when he stopped next to her at the corral fence. Addy was getting instructions on her posture, using her legs as guides for the horse, how to hold the reins.

"She's good people, Owen. Tough as hell."

"And fragile as hell."

"I dunno. I think tough wins over fragile any day."

"Thanks, Sel. I hope so."

The boys saw him and ran over. "Owen, are you going to ride today?" Troy asked.

"I don't think so. I just came to see how you and your mom were doing."

"That's Zavi's pony, Betty."

"I know. She looks beautiful."

"We groomed her," Zavi said. "Now we're just waiting for our turn."

Owen didn't see Addy dismount, but when she came out of the fence, he couldn't look at anything else. Mandy came over and got the boys, lifting Zavi onto Betty's back and Troy onto the horse she had in the corral. He was vaguely aware of the fact that Selena had pulled back, into the shadows of the stable.

He smiled at Addy. Her eyes were a soft blue, bright like the sky. If she ever got contacts to cover her changing eyes, he'd miss them. They told him so much more about her mindset than her words ever let on. He lifted a hand and brushed her hair off one cheek, then bent over and kissed her temple.

"You look happy."

"I am." Her arms went around his waist. He pulled her close. They both watched the boys in the corral. "Thank you. For today. For everything. Mostly, for not giving up on me."

"I will never give up on you, Laidy."

"Today's the best gift of my life. The only thing better would be getting Augie back."

"Soon. Let's just have this moment a little longer. Things are coming to a head, Addy."

She looked up at him. He didn't try to hide the concern he felt. "I'll help however I can."

Owen smiled. "I know. I just need you to be strong a little longer."

She leaned her cheek against his chest. Holding her in his arms like this, for real, not just in his imagination, was a miracle. Maybe, just maybe, he'd done something right in his life to earn this second chance with her.

WYNN FOUND she had a little time to herself. Angel was busy with the team, and the boys were out riding horses. Casey was doing some quiet study. Wynn went to her apartment over the garage to make a cup of tea. The kettle's screech almost covered the knock on her door, which she'd left open in case Casey or the boys needed her. She peeked around the corner of the little galley kitchen and saw her parents—or her fake parents, since the jury was still out—standing in her living room.

She removed the kettle from the heat, then went into her living room to greet them. The wall of distrust was still firmly in place. She folded her arms, keeping her hands to herself.

"Hi," she said.

"Wynnie," the man said.

"Don't call me that."

Her snapped retort hit a nerve. She wasn't sorry, either. Her mind scrambled to find some test, some proof that they were who they said they were. "Did you test your research on yourselves? Or did someone infect you?"

The couple exchanged a look. "We tested on ourselves," the woman said. "We didn't want to test it on other humans if we weren't willing to test it on ourselves."

"And, honestly," the man added, "if it had had a terminal effect, it would have been our ticket out."

A test question popped into Wynn's head. "What was the color of Grams' and Gramps' living room before Grams did her renovation?" Her mom grew up in that house. She should remember that fact.

"It was green," the woman said. "Army green. My mom missed Dad terribly after he passed, but she was sure glad to get a chance to redo the house according to her tastes."

That was true. "When did the step break in her basement stairs at Grams?"

"I don't know," the woman said. "It wasn't broken before we left."

True. "What was my best girlfriend's name before I moved in with Grams?"

"Page."

True. "What was her hair color?"

"Beautiful, deep auburn."

True. "What kind of sandwiches did her mom make us when we had sleepovers?"

"Grilled peanut butter and jelly. I never let you have those because they were messy."

True. "What did we always do with the candy after I went trick-or-treating?"

"We checked it all for razor blades. It was a thing back then. And then I'd sneak the Krackel bars out for your father."

True. All true. They knew everything. Wynn covered her mouth, trying to find a way to keep debunking them, but her gut was telling her they were the real deal. They looked only a little older than she was, but they were her parents. She closed her eyes and started to cry. Suddenly, her parents were there, both of them, holding her, crying with her.

God. It was real. Her parents were alive. How she wished Grams was there to see it.

"We love you, baby girl," her dad said. "So damn much."

LATER THAT NIGHT, when the house was quiet and Troy had been put to bed, Addy was lying next to Owen when the house phone rang. He answered it. "Tremaine."

"Hi, Owen."

Owen smiled a little as he put it on speaker. "Hi, Troy."

"Is my mom there?"

"Yes, she is. Do you want to talk to her?"

"No. I just was practicing with the phone."

"Okay."

"I'm not scared."

"I'm here for you, boy, if you need me."

"Have a nice sleepover."

Owen grinned. "Thanks. Night, Troy."

"Goodnight, Owen."

Owen hung up, then released a long sigh. "God, I feel so guilty for taking you away from him."

"He'll be asleep in a few minutes."

"So you told him you were sleeping over?"

She nodded. "I don't have to, if you don't want me to."

"Oh, I do want you here. I want you in my arms every moment I can have you. I'm just surprised you broke it to him."

"I didn't want him to wake up in the middle of the night and not know where I was. I told him sometimes grownups need grownup time."

"That what this is?"

"I hope so."

He caught her and pulled her over on top of him. "I hope so too." He decided to go slow, let her choose what happened between them and when. He caught the back of her head and drew her down for a kiss. It was a leisurely exploration of her lips and her mouth and his self-control. She set her elbows on his chest and dug her hands into his hair. He was glad the light was on; he wanted to see her eyes change color as her body warmed up. It was magical, like making love to a fairy. She was a one-of-a-kind woman, and she was his.

He rolled her over and settled between her legs. Her arms were around his neck. For a long moment, he just stared into her eyes. "Do you know how lucky we are?"

Her eyes widened. "You can't mean that. If we

were lucky, we'd never have been torn apart to begin with."

"We found each other again. We get this do-over. How many people do you know who've survived a tragedy and gotten a second chance?"

"Owen?"

"Hmmm?"

"How am I going to make a life for myself?"

He wasn't sure how to answer that. Did she want a life away from him? "Any way you want to."

"I'm dead to the world."

"We'll fix that."

"I haven't paid taxes my entire adult life. I haven't had a job and can't get one without any work history. I have no credit. I'm an invisible woman."

"All of that can be repaired, reversed, fixed. That's the easy stuff. Being without you was the hard stuff. I'll help you."

"My boys need vaccinations. I have no idea how ready Augie is for school. Even Troy, for that matter."

Owen smiled at her, feeling a little thrill that she was talking to him like a valued friend. "Wynn can do those assessments. Doc Beck can administer the vaccines." He kissed her. "The real world is very demanding and very real, but it isn't an issue at this exact moment. Right now, it's just you and me. The rest will take care of itself…and you can be sure we'll face it together."

Those assurances didn't ease the tension in her face. "Without a job, I can't pay for any of that."

"Your job has been surviving. You're a rock star at that. For the rest, I have money. What I have, all of it, it's yours, you know."

"I want my own," she said. "I need my own."

"Okay. When it's safe for you to go out in the world, you can take any job you want. And what your job doesn't cover, I will. I don't want you stressing over something I have plenty of, you understand? Stress and you aren't friends right now."

She frowned. "I need to be on equal footing with you."

He shook his head. "Won't ever happen. I will never be equal to you. You are so much more than me. Smarter, kinder, stronger."

"But money is power."

"Maybe, to an asshole like Edwards. But to me, money is just money. A means to an end. A tool. Nothing more or less." He sighed. Running his thumb over her jaw, he asked, "If I promise that we'll work it out so that you're satisfied, even happy, can we let this go for now? Will you trust me?"

"I'm trying to trust. It isn't something I've had much experience with."

Owen smiled. "I'll take it." He kissed her. "Ready to sleep?"

"Sleep?"

"Yeah. You know. We turn out the lights, close our eyes, quit worrying. You start to snore."

She punched his shoulder. "You don't want sex?"

"I do. Desperately. But you've spent a lifetime

having it taken from you. I don't want that between us. I want you to come to me when you're ready. Until then, I can take all the cold showers I need to."

"Can I still sleep here?"

"I don't want you sleeping anywhere else. Is Troy okay?"

"He slept in his own room before we came here. He'll be fine. He's even closer to me in this room than he was at the other house."

MUCH LATER, in dark of the night, Owen heard his door open. He rolled over, tensing. The guys always knocked if they needed him in the middle of the night. No alarms were going off; no dogs were barking. Still, the hairs lifted on his neck when a little shadow walked over to the bed...dragging his blanket.

Troy.

The boy looked at him, then went around the bed to Addy. Owen rolled back over to watch them.

"Mom, I had a bad dream," he whispered.

Addy lifted the covers to let him in. She tried to keep him next to her, but that didn't work. "No. I want to be in the middle." He climbed over her and got between them.

Owen tried not to grin.

"We can't disturb Owen," Addy whispered, easing her hand over the side of Troy's face. "Be still. Go to sleep."

Troy held himself as still as he could, but it wasn't for very long. "Mom, I got to say something." She didn't answer him. Owen wondered if she'd gone back to sleep. "Mom. Mom. Mom."

Owen grinned. If this was normal, how the fuck did any parent ever get any sleep?

"Shhh," Addy said. "Honey, we'll talk in the morning."

"It can't wait."

"Then what is it?"

"I think we should keep Owen."

Owen wrapped his arm around Troy and pulled him close. "I agree. Now be quiet." He looked over at Addy and smiled, knowing she could see him in the dark.

24

Owen leaned against the corner of the bathroom in Addy's room, watching her tuck her son in. It had been another long day spent trying to find Augie, Edwards, and Jafaar. Greer and Max had been monitoring Deputy Jerry's communications. Owen knew something was going to break loose shortly...he just hoped they were ready for it.

Addy finished the story she'd been reading to Troy. She set it aside, then kissed her son. Seeing them together always made him feel as if the world wasn't all bad. He wondered what his own son was like and how he'd fit into Addy and Troy's family dynamic.

Probably like he'd never left.

Addy gave her son a final hug and kiss. Troy reached out to Owen for one as well, which took him by surprise. He hugged Troy, then got a kiss on his check. Owen looked up at Addy, feeling a little lost. She just smiled that happy mom kind of smile.

"Are you having a sleepover with my mom again, Owen?"

"I am. She and I both sleep better that way."

"She's nice to sleep with. Can I come over if I have a bad dream?"

"You can. And if the door's locked, you could call us like you did last night. Maybe call us first so we're sure to unlock the door."

"Why do you lock it?"

"Because sometimes we're talking and having that grownup time," Owen said. "Often, it's best if that isn't interrupted. It's a concentration thing."

"Oh. Like reading."

Owen chuckled. "Yeah. Like that. Night, Troy."

"Night, Owen. Night, Mom."

"Night, honey. Sleep tight. Your water's on the nightstand."

He rolled over to his side. "Have fun grownup time."

Owen grinned at Addy. No sooner did he get her into his room than he locked the door and started helping her remove her slouchy pajamas. When she was naked, he let himself feast on the sight of her. He touched his fingers to her ribs. What he had in mind for them wasn't going to be easy to do.

"Grownup time sounds terrible," she said, laughing against his mouth.

"It does, doesn't it?" He took off his clothes,

stacking them on one of his teak chairs. "Tonight, though, I have something else in mind."

"What?"

"Do you remember the picture I left in your room the day I came to your house?"

"The one of the dead person?"

Owen laughed. "That wasn't meant to be a dead person. It was me, when you drew on me when we had chickenpox."

"I don't really remember that time. I was a lot younger than you."

"Well, it gave me an idea. Have you heard of *wabi-sabi*?" Owen asked.

"No."

He took her hand and led her to his bed. "It's a Japanese aesthetic philosophy. It's been described differently by many people, but at its heart, it's a principle that sees beauty in the acceptance of melancholy and longing. It's the understanding that nothing lasts, nothing's finished, and nothing's perfect. Not things. Not people. Not societies. And not souls. What's most magical about it is that the *wabi-sabi* of something can be seen and therefore appreciated. For instance, the Japanese who honor this principle sometimes do so by fixing broken things so that the breaks can be seen. They'll take a broken vase and glue the pieces back together with thin veins of gold so that the break is shown and accepted."

"I like that."

"Sometimes, when we have soul injuries, they

can't be seen. They live in the darkness inside of us, festering there, growing, expanding until all we believe we are is darkness and broken and unheard."

Tears filled her eyes. "I feel that way."

He nodded. "I know."

"I'm trying not to. I try to find things every day that are beautiful."

"I felt broken and empty after I lost you. I couldn't breathe. I couldn't think. I could only get angrier. And now, to find I could have helped you, but didn't—it's another break in my soul. All this time I was fighting ghosts, not the real enemy. My life was a waste, for all the hard effort I gave the right thing, it was still the wrong thing. I am *wabi-sabi.*"

"I am, too."

He nodded. "Do you trust me?"

Her answer wasn't fast in coming. She nodded, but somehow, without the words being said, her trust wasn't fully given.

He showed her the metallic pen he'd taken from Zavi's classroom. "I'd like to use this pen to draw the breaks that live inside you. The gold will let light in and let the scars out. I can't heal you. I can't undo what was done. But I can accept you as you are now, the beauty of your strength and all you've withstood. I'd like to show you that beauty too. We are all becoming…something, even you. You aren't any longer the woman I abandoned."

She caught his hands. "You didn't abandon me.

Your life was taken from you too. You can draw the *wabi-sabi* on me if I can on you."

He nodded. "I'd like to let the light in."

"How does it work?"

"I listen to your body, hear where it says it hides a scar. And I draw where it shows me." He smiled at her. "There's no actual cutting and breaking. It's an energetic thing."

ADDY NODDED, but felt trepidation about what was to happen. He lit several candles around the room, then switched off the lights. The flames flickered with the slightest shift in air current. He selected a song on his phone that was a mixture of instruments and a background of rain.

He had her lie down on the bed. He stood next to it, silently, observing but not focused on her body. It wasn't anything like the other times she was stretched out naked in front of a man. She wasn't bound. It was only the two of them in his room, and there was no malice in his eyes.

"This makes me nervous," she whispered.

Owen met her eyes.

"You're studying me."

"Addy, what you're thinking right now, does it give you pleasure?"

"No."

"Then don't think about it. Switch it out for what we're doing."

"This isn't about pleasure."

"It's not. It's about relief and healing."

"I'm going to close my eyes."

"Okay."

He sat on the side of the bed. Lifting her hand, he began to draw on her wrist. The lines went around and around her wrist like the restraints that had often bound her. He smoothed his hand over her forearm, on both sides, then drew a spidery web. So many times, Cecil or one of the others had grabbed her there. The thin lines went up and around her elbow. She thought of how often they'd held her arms behind her, bent up in a painful hold, giving them leverage. The lines continued to her upper arms, circling around her arm. He drew lines on her neck, so tender compared to the violent hands that had squeezed her there.

The pen went up to her face. She could feel him draw a ragged circle, like a fist mark in broken glass. It went over her eye, her nose, the other side of her chin. He repeated similar marks on her left arm as he had her right. And then he started on her body, his hand skimming over her skin like a Braille reader.

He drew lines over and around her breasts. He crisscrossed her heart with his pen. Her ribs, too. His hand paused on her lower abdomen. She held her breath, bracing herself for his questions, but they never came. He continued his exploration over her hips and down her legs, circling her ankles as he had her wrists. It was like he'd seen all of her wounds when they were fresh.

She opened her eyes when she no longer felt the pen moving over her skin. He was staring at her, like all the dark inside her had crawled from her to him. She was too raw, too exposed to look away or shield herself, so she just let him in.

"How did you survive?" he asked in a broken whisper.

"I wasn't brave enough to end it in the beginning. By the time I was, I had my boys and couldn't."

He was kneeling between her ankles. She'd told Selena she wasn't going to tell Owen all that had happened, that his burdens were enough for him to carry. But it was clear to her now that his *wabi-sabi* exercise had reached inside her and pulled them out anyway. She felt a thousand pounds lighter...and he looked that much heavier.

She knelt in front of him. "It's my turn."

He handed her the marker, then lay down where she'd been. Addy wasn't at all certain she could do what he did, but she was curious to know what his body might tell her. "How do I do this?"

"Quiet your mind. Push everything out of it. When it's empty, let me in. Draw what you hear."

"Through my hands..."

"Right. Use them like metal detectors, only they're not sensing metal but soul wounds."

She closed her eyes and waited for her mind to go

quiet. It took effort. She always had a constant stream of fear running through it.

Once her mind was quiet, she ran her hand over his right hand. Was it only her imagination, or could she truly sense the past injuries there? Soul wounds, he'd said. Were these soul wounds? Or just…injuries? Her eyes met his. He offered no guidance.

She ran her hand up his arm to his shoulder. It was hard to explain what she was sensing. She hesitated to believe it was real. She had to be doing it wrong—she hadn't drawn a single line.

Her hand eased over the golden hair on his chest. It wasn't super thick, just enough for a manly fur. When her hand moved over his heart, she gasped. A jagged shard of emotion slammed into her hand on its way to her heart. She looked closer at his chest, looking for signs of a surgery or a scar from a knife or bullet. There was nothing. But the pain there was real.

"Owen, what happened to your heart?"

"You."

Val had said he was a tin man after she was taken, empty and searching for his heart.

"Do you have it back…your heart?"

His big hand settled over hers on his chest. "Almost."

"It's your only soul wound, isn't it?"

"Yeah."

She huffed a choked breath. "Do you suppose, between us, there's a whole person?"

He sat up. His eyes held hers as he measured his words. "I sincerely hope so."

She settled between his legs, letting hers drape over his thighs. His cock was long and heavy between them, but she didn't care. She had to draw the pain out of his heart with that magical ink of his.

She flattened the hairs over his left chest, then emptied her mind again and gave it over to the pen, drawing as she felt moved to. The design looked like a messy explosion, like someone had ripped his heart out, dropped it on a sidewalk, and stomped a heel into it.

Radiating out from his wrecked heart was a line that went up to his neck, paused just below his ear, then swiped up to a line crossing out his eyes. Another went down his chest, over his lean stomach to his groin. Two more reached up to his shoulders. His broken heart made him deaf and blind, burdened his shoulders, and stole all of his joy. The *wabi-sabi* let her see his story.

His soul injury was so different from hers but no less debilitating.

"Your *wabi-sabi* isn't as pretty as mine. I'm sorry."

He smiled. "Scars are what they are."

She looked into his eyes. "Do you feel lighter?"

"I do."

"I do too."

He sat up and brushed a bit of hair behind her ear. "I love you."

She nodded. "I know." She couldn't say it back.

He'd only just let the dark out of her, and the light he'd let in was overwhelming. The connection they had at that moment made her aware that her inability to say it back hurt him. She felt his pain as keenly as he did. She rose up on her knees and settled over him, joining their bodies.

He hissed a sharp inhalation. His thighs tightened under hers. He caught her waist and looked up at her. He'd given her the grace of coming to him in her own way and time. She didn't want to love him. She didn't want to be so vulnerable. But trying not to was just living a lie. She did love him. She always had...even when she hated him.

She caught his face and leaned down so their noses touched. Her body moved over his. He was hot and hard inside her. "I can't say I love you, Owen, as if it's something new...because I never didn't love you. Always. From the very beginning, when you would visit us. You were light in a world I instinctively knew was very dark. You are golden to me, like the light you let in with your *wabi-sabi*." Holding his face, she kissed him. "I love you. But those words don't even begin to cover what I feel for you."

He smiled up at her. "I know."

She touched her palm to the center of the gold lines she'd made, right over his heart. Owen was the only man who'd ever made love to her. The others had abused her body. It wasn't even sex she'd had with them. It was something else, something dark and twisted and cruel.

Owen took over their lovemaking. He wrapped a hand around her hips, holding her as he pumped into her. With his other, he caught the back of her neck, bringing her face to his for a kiss so deep and endless that she lost herself in him. She wrapped her arms around his neck and gave herself over to the feeling of being part of him, no longer two separate beings but the one complete person they made together. All the years lost between them slipped away, replaced by something deeper and richer than any human who'd ever lived had ever known, or so it seemed to her.

An unfamiliar warmth spread through her, fanning out from where Owen entered her, deep inside her, reaching her heart and stopping there. She cried out as a wave of energy took her over, something she hadn't felt since the last time she was with him. Her arms tightened around his neck, holding on for fear she would float away, out of his control, out of hers.

And then the very thing she feared happened. Waves of feeling took her over. Distantly, she could hear herself mewling, hungry for more of the infinity she glimpsed. She writhed against Owen, her body demanding something from his. More. Everything. All of him for all of her.

She wasn't certain how long her orgasm lasted. Seconds or minutes. It took everything from her. She cried when it was over, weeping into his neck. "I don't know who I am, Owen."

His arms were tight around her. He wasn't letting

go, and that made her feel safe. "Laidy, we can find out together."

"Don't let me go."

"Never. I got you," he said.

"I wish I was brave like you."

"I wish I was resilient like you."

She pulled back and looked down at him. Everything he was, everything she was to him, was laid out in his eyes. More beautiful than any gemstone, what she saw was truth.

THE NEXT MORNING, Addy stood in Owen's bathroom, staring at herself. The night before had been like a rebirth of sorts. She still felt lighter inside than she had in years. Probably since the first night she and Owen were together ten years ago.

Owen came into the bathroom. "What are you doing?"

She looked at his reflection. They were both nude. The gold metallic lines on both of them were still bold. She studied the two different patterns on them, seeing two different stories of survival. "Look at us."

He did. His face was somber. "How do you feel this morning?"

"Phenomenal."

He smiled. "Really?"

"I do. You let the light inside me. There can't be dark where there's light. And it's all over my face."

She laughed. "Cecil would hate this. He was always careful to keep from marring my face. Or when he did, he kept me hidden. I can't hide this. And I don't want to hide it. I was going to shower, but I don't want to wash it off yet."

Owen stepped closer and pulled her into his arms. "You aren't upset that I did this?"

"No. Your *wabi-sabi* worked wonders for me."

He smiled, then kissed her forehead.

"I need to go wake Troy up for school."

"Okay. Will I see you for breakfast?"

She nodded. "You will." She kissed his mouth, then threw on her robe and left his room. In her room, she dressed in her new casual clothes and put on a soft pair of moccasin flats. She washed her face and hands carefully so that she didn't disturb the ink, then brushed her teeth, brushed her hair, then went over to wake up her son. She pulled the drapes wide, letting in the morning light. She felt as bright as that light.

She sat on the edge of Troy's bed as he woke. He was always super cuddly in the morning. As usual, he climbed into her lap and snuggled in. She smiled as she held him, grateful for him and the morning and the new life she'd been given. As he woke, he slowly focused on her arm…and its marks.

"Mom, you've been drawing on yourself." He ran his hand over the gold lines, then gasped when he looked up and saw her face. "You're going to get in trouble." How scared he looked.

She hugged him. "No, I'm not. We don't get in trouble here like we used to at the old house."

He ran his hands over her cheeks. "It's every-where. Why did you do this?"

"I didn't. Owen did. Isn't it beautiful?"

"Why did he do that?"

"Because he thought there was something hurtful I was keeping inside that needed to come out. So he gave me places for it to come out."

"It worked. The problem's gone from your face."

She laughed and hugged him again. "It is, isn't it?"

"Do you love Owen? 'Cause I do. I think he should be my new dad."

She chuckled. "That's moving a little fast."

"He's not like my old dad."

"Very true. Owen's pretty wonderful." She set Troy back on the bed then picked an outfit for him. "We're going to be late for breakfast if we don't get a move on."

A few minutes later, they walked into the living room. Wynn and Angel were there, along with Rocco and Mandy and their son. When Zavi saw Troy, he stood on his chair and called him over. He'd been saving a seat for him.

"Zavi, we don't stand on chairs," Mandy reminded him. Too excited to see his friend, he just switched to kneeling instead. Zavi stared at Addy—first at her eyes, then at her whole face. He pointed his finger at his face and swirled it around. "Ms. Jacobs, you got stuff on your face."

"I do. Isn't it beautiful?" She smiled at his confusion. He nodded, unconvinced.

"Owen drew on her," Troy said. Even that made her happy.

"Why?" Zavi asked.

"I don't know. To fix her, I think. Or something like that."

After the boys ate their breakfast, Wynn took them up to class. Addy poured a second cup of coffee, then went into the living room to wait for Owen. Greer and Remi came in, followed by Val and Ace.

Greer helpfully pointed out the markings, too. "That coming from your skin?"

Addy laughed. "No. It's *wabi-sabi*."

Greer tilted his head. "It's what now?"

Max and Hope came in. She was collecting an audience.

"*Wabi-sabi*."

"It's the Japanese art of accepting melancholy," Kelan said as he and Fiona joined them. "It's knowing the truth that nothing's permanent, perfect, or complete."

"Oh."

"Owen drew the lines," Addy said. "He used the gold to let the dark out and the light in and put the broken pieces back together. Isn't it beautiful?" There were some nods, but she knew they didn't get why it made her so happy. "You don't get it, do you?"

"Get what?" Max asked.

"I'm broken. The Omnis don't keep broken things. I let the broken out. I'm broken all over. Cecil can't touch me now."

"Damned right about that," Max said. "He'd have to fucking go through all of us to get to you."

"But even if he were a ghost and got through you, I'm protected from him, you see?"

Silence was her answer. Ace came over to her. She took off her T-shirt and showed Addy her back. "I get it. I did the same thing."

A huge blue swallowtail butterfly covered her back. Part of the beautiful design was covered by her bra strap. The tail points of the wings slipped below her jeans. It was exquisite.

Addy ran her hands over the complex design. "You are protected." And then she wrapped her arms around Ace's shoulders and hugged her. "Oh, Ace. We survived them."

Ace turned to face her and returned the hug. After a moment, Addy realized everyone had gotten quiet. Val was standing between Ace and the room, facing everyone else with his arms on his hips, blocking them from curious eyes. Ace pulled free and wiped her eyes, then pulled her T-shirt back on. Addy heard a sniffle and saw Fiona in Kelan's arms.

So much harm had come to these people. How had Addy ever thought them complicit with the Omnis?

She looked over and saw Owen standing at the

living room entrance. How much had he heard or seen? He hadn't washed off his lines either. His team observed him in stunned silence as he came down the steps and walked up to her. He ignored them, watching her cautiously until she smiled and stepped into his arms.

He hugged her, then kissed her temple. "You eat yet?"

"No. I was waiting for you."

"I'm starving." He kept an arm around her shoulders as he led her into the dining room. "Doing *wabi-sabi* makes me hungry." He grinned as he walked them into the dining room.

25

Selena was already sitting at the bar in the billiards room, an amber beer bottle in her hand when Val came in. Ace was still getting dressed upstairs. Kelan was right behind him. It had been a tough couple of days, waiting for the other shoe to drop. Val was glad to see some of the team were gathering for a nightcap.

Kelan opened a bottle of Shiraz, while Val set about making a ginger mojito for Ace. Selena looked at them, but didn't greet them. Val had asked her before how she was doing and had the door slammed in his face. He knew she knew he was there for her— no point forcing someone to talk when they weren't ready. This time, Selena surprised him.

"It isn't that I'm jealous," she said to no one in particular.

Val met her eyes.

"'Cause I'm not. I'm happy for you and Ace, you and Fee, Owen and Addy. I'm happy for all of you."

Val stopped what he was doing and leaned against the wall of the bar. Kelan did the same.

"I've learned, watching you guys, that you know it when it's the right one. But what if that muscle or skill is broken in me? What if I never know?"

"You knew when it was the wrong one," Val said. "Same skill."

"But they've all been wrong. All of them."

"Nothing happens that isn't supposed to," Kelan said. "Those guys taught you something you needed to learn. Even this delay you're feeling, which isn't much of a delay because you aren't even thirty yet, is part of your plan."

She sighed and sipped the last of her beer. Val opened another and set it in front of her. "Fuck the plan. I miss him," she said.

"Who?" Val asked.

"I don't know. That's the thing. I feel him in my heart and I don't know who he is. I haven't even met him yet."

"Tell me about him," Kelan said, intensely watching her.

She shrugged. "I have to be making this all up. Some psychosis because I want what you all have. I'm pretending there's someone for me."

Kelan shook his head. "Your intuition has always been phenomenal. Tell us about him."

She looked at Kelan, trying to read him. "He's dark. And hollow. And aches for me."

"Wow." Val's brows lifted. "See, that's gonna be some explosive sex, when you two get together." Kelan gave him a quelling look.

"You think he's real?" she asked them.

"Dunno," Val said.

"I do. Your energy is calling his," Kelan said. "I felt that way about Fiona. It was very real."

"Do we know him, Sel?" Val asked.

She shook her head. "Don't think so. There's something…different about him."

"I look forward to meeting him," Kelan said.

Selena pressed her lips into a thin line and shook her head. "I have to be making him up."

"I don't think so."

"Well, one thing's for sure," Val said. "When and if he comes into your life, if he doesn't treat you like gold, we'll kick his ass."

She chuckled. "Really, Val? If he doesn't treat me like he should, I'll kick his ass."

"With us standing behind you," Val said.

"Hiding?" Kelan asked, raising a brow.

"Maybe," Val said, laughing.

JAX WALKED around the formal living room of the house he'd grown up in. At some point, Roberta had redecorated. He remembered hearing about that. The antique cherry escritoire that his mother had loved was gone, and so was everything else he remembered from his childhood. It could have been a stranger's home.

It was, really, just that. He had no sense of who his father was and why he'd done what he'd done. Jax hoped it wasn't for something as simple and arrogant as keeping up his public persona.

The butler had told him his stepmother wasn't at home but that his father was, which was good. He wanted to talk to his dad without her interference. His father came into the living room. They faced each other coldly, like strangers. Or enemies.

"Son."

"Dad."

"Would you like to join me in the den?"

Jax nodded. His dad had aged significantly in the five years since he last saw him. He'd lost weight. His hair was more salt than pepper. His steps were slower. Jax refused to feel sorry for him. An old monster was still a monster, especially when he remained in the thick of things.

"What brings you to town, son?" Dean asked as he shut the door.

"Questions."

Dean took a seat behind his desk and gestured for his son to take one of the leather club chairs in front of it. "I knew this day would come."

Jax stared into his father's eyes. "I'm sure you did. I know who Roberta is, and I know what she's done."

Dean nodded. "It was only a matter of time, I suppose. I raised you to ferret out the facts."

Jax smiled inwardly. His dad said that with such dignity. Like a monster could raise anything but a monster. "What I don't know is...why? Why you let her into our lives. Why you let her soil Mom's memory. Why you let her near your children."

"I didn't know, at first," Dean said. "After Mom's death, I was just a ghost of a man, facing an uphill battle in my campaign, with two motherless children at home. I had no will to continue the fight. Then she came along. She was my rock. She ran things for me, helped me keep on top of what was happening at home while I was away. Eventually, we became lovers. She was just so rock solid."

"Did she tell you she'd killed Mom? That her role in your life was premeditated?"

"Not until years later. Things had not been good between us for a while. I wanted to divorce her. That's when she told me." His face tensed. "By then, I'd brought her fully into my world. Not just with you kids, but my friends, my peers, Washington influencers. I was how she got in, got access to everyone."

"That was when you started aggressively training Owen and me. What tipped you off?"

"I started to come out of my fog. Roberta had a lot of power...power I'd given her. I began to question things. Owen's mom had died the same year as Mom. Nick Tremaine always questioned his wife's death. The coroner said she died of anaphylactic shock from a bee sting. Nick said she wasn't allergic to bees." Dean leaned back in his seat, his gaze lost in memories.

"Nick warned me about Roberta, about how coincidental her appearance in my life was, coming just when it did. We even had a falling out over it. Roberta made me feel alive again. I didn't think she could have done anything wrong." He looked at Jax. "So when I began to be suspicious, I confronted her. She denied it. That gave me plausible reason to doubt my fears, but they never went away.

"When she invited the Whiddons over for dinner, I was concerned again. Everyone knew Senator Whiddon was dirty. I didn't want him in my home. Nor did I want anyone thinking I had an association with him. Roberta brokered a deal on some legislation I'd been wanting to bring to the floor. After that deal, there were others. When I told her it had to stop, she fought back, saying if I exposed her now, not only would my career be over, but all the legislation I'd fought so hard for would become suspect. Everything in my life would be undone. And it wasn't like we could dig Mom's body up and redo an autopsy. She'd been cremated." Dean sighed. "I had a circle of close friends, ones I trusted with my life and had since Vietnam. Nick Tremaine and Henry Myers."

Jax knew this part of the story. Those two men had been frequent visitors to their house when he was a kid. It was through Nick that Jax met Owen. Even then the adults had been prepping him and Owen for a fight against an enemy neither of them fully understood.

Only one of his dad's trio had turned out to have any kind of conscience at all. But his dad didn't know that he knew, so Jax let him spill. There were ears listening. He'd told his FBI contact about this meeting. They were out there now, in a moving van across the street, waiting to make a run on the house when Jax gave the go-ahead.

First, though, Jax wanted everything on record. All of it. The lies. The justifications. The connections.

"I asked Nick and Henry for help," Dean continued. "We couldn't find anything connecting Roberta to the Omnis, but we knew Whiddon was under their influence. We agreed that I'd become compromised. They thought we could use it in our favor, that I could be an agent for the fight against the Omnis. I could use her as she used me. That's when Nick faked his death. Henry, too, developed a secret identity that he used in the tunnels where the Omnis were building a fortress hidden from the world above."

"You sent me to Henry when Addy was taken."

Dean nodded. "He decided to make his part-time gig in the tunnels a full-time thing. He thought he could break the Omnis from within if he taught the tunnel residents to fight. Men and women, even kids."

"Did you know that Henry's granddaughter was in the tunnels?"

"I knew the Omnis took her."

"The Omnis didn't take her. He did. He stuck her

343

like a pig. She bled out so profusely, it's a wonder that she, a toddler at the time, lived. He gave her over to the monsters."

"The Omnis sent an assassin to his house. They fought. It wasn't Henry who hurt Ace. It was the assassin."

"He let it happen."

Dean sighed. "Nothing is black and white in this. Henry had to choose between losing his entire family or making a tithe of one member. It was the lesser of two evils. He couldn't get her out without putting the rest of his family in jeopardy. He went in after her, developed his Santo persona so he could watch over her."

"Bullshit. The Omnis forced her into prostitution and he did nothing."

"Women are made for sex."

Jax felt sick. "She was fourteen."

Dean waved that away. "He taught her to fight. She's the warrior she is today because of him."

Jax had to take a breath. This meeting wasn't about him...he had to remember his goals, had to keep his dad talking. If he didn't get it on tape, who would believe such a crazy story? Besides, he didn't want to say anything that would get Ace into trouble.

"So, go on," Jax prompted. "You figured out Roberta was an Omni plant, that she'd killed Mom. The three of you decided to fight back, leaving her in place."

"Yes. While you and Owen were at West Point, we

laid the groundwork for the Red Team. It was supposed to be completely dark, but Roberta found out about it."

"How'd that happen?"

"I don't know. We suspected Whiddon. He was chair of the subcommittee responsible for the funds. Anyway, he redirected the original intent of the Red Team to focus on terror threats outside the U.S. I went along with it, because at the time, we didn't yet know if the Omnis were being organized by foreign interests."

"Whiddon knew everything we did."

"Yeah. Which was why I got with Owen to organize Tremaine Industries."

"And still Roberta was along for the ride, watching everything."

"I tried to break free of her when your sister graduated college. Addy was an adult. She was ready to stand on her own, even if my career imploded. It was time to cut myself loose. But she acted first."

"She took Addy."

"Yeah. She gave Addy to the Omnis. I couldn't come clean then, because I knew I'd never see her again if I did."

"You left Addy with them for almost eight years," Jax said.

"Seven. I told Edwards to back off. I finally got the balls to make him do it when I saw how desperate Addy was to get away. They took Augie from her because of me. I didn't do anything on her behalf for months out of fear. That's when I called you."

"You told me Owen was King."

"You knew so much by then, but not everything. I wanted to keep you off-kilter." Dean sighed and looked down at his desk. "This isn't a conversation I ever wanted to have with you."

"Why didn't you call on your friends, Nick and Henry?"

"I'd already sent Henry to her, through her nanny. He set up a safe house for her, provided her a means of escaping, but she was too broken then to chance it. She didn't want to risk losing Troy. That's when I got you involved."

"Henry knew where she was after she was first taken." His dad had no comment to offer him. As chatty as he'd been to this point, Jax found that curious. He took his silence for confirmation, the fucking bastard. "You had me chasing my tail for years. I believed you when you said Owen was King. There were times on missions where I almost set him up to die. I thought he was behind what happened to Addy."

"I had to do that."

"Why?"

"Because I couldn't let you get too close to the truth. I couldn't risk losing you like I'd lost your mom and Addy."

"You couldn't because you were a coward."

Dean nodded.

"Where's Roberta?"

"I don't know. She didn't tell me where she was going."

Jax set a document on his dad's desk. It was a marriage certificate from almost forty years ago. "Did you know you were a bigamist? Roberta was already married when she married you."

Dean stared at the document a long time. Jax had the names on it memorized. Cecil Edwards King and Annie Roberts. "She married King. You gave your daughter in marriage to the very devil I've been chasing. You married her off to your wife's lawful husband. How fucked up is that? I'm gonna ask you again, where's Roberta?"

Dean sat back in his chair and stared at Jax. "She didn't tell me. For the last three years, we've lived separate lives. I let her stay in the guest house, but we never do anything together in public or private. I don't know where she is."

"Did you know that we identified the girl Roberta had killed in the train wreck?"

"How? She was cremated, too."

"I took a sample of her blood while she was still in the morgue. Your silence about her death and Mom's makes you an accessory to both murders."

"I wish that was all I was guilty of."

Jax wanted to unscramble that cryptic statement, but he sensed his dad was at an end of his confessions. The FBI could try to get more out of him. There was just one more thing Jax wanted to know. "Tell me where Augie is."

Dean shook his head. "I can't. I don't know."

"Goddammit, Dad. Do one good thing. One. Where is my nephew?"

"King took him. That's all I know."

"I'm done. I'm out." After those words, mere seconds passed before the house was overtaken by the FBI. Jax never saw his dad reach for a gun, but he suddenly had it in his hand. The FBI agents were shouting at him, shouting for him to put his weapon down. He didn't.

He put it up to his head and pulled the trigger.

Owen was with the team in the billiards room when Jax's call came through. Max motioned everyone to silence, then fed the call through the speaker system.

"Owen."

"Jax."

"I know who King is."

"Who's fucking King?" Owen asked quietly.

"It's Edwards. They fed Addy to King. Roberta is Edwards' legal wife. That's why she kept telling Addy to shut up and put up and keep Edwards happy."

Owen sat down. He didn't talk. He was glad Addy was upstairs. He'd been just about to go get her when Jax's call had come in.

"My dad's dead, O. But I got a lengthy confession from

him before he shot himself. The FBI was listening in. They came in to take him, but he took himself out first."

"Tell me, did you know your dad was dirty all this time?"

"Not until I got Addy out. She told me my dad and Roberta had visited her several times. She said the same day that Augie was taken, our parents visited. She begged them to take her and the boys away, but they didn't. That's when I knew. My dad played me. He played everybody. My dad confirmed that Roberta had murdered my mom, then wiggled her way into my dad's life. By the time he figured it out, he was in too deep. I think he did start the Red Team for the right reasons, but he couldn't toe the line for us. When you told me you were starting your own gig, and that my dad was a silent partner, I thought again that you were on the side of the Omnis. It didn't help that Val was also a silent partner, given who his dad was. I couldn't come to you, Owen, because I didn't trust you any longer. That's the real reason I sent Ace your way. She was always an excellent judge of character."

"Santo kidnapped her, his own granddaughter," Owen said.

"He had a choice to surrender her as a tithe or have his entire family slaughtered. He and the Omni assassin they sent fought. It was that guy who cut her up. The threat hung over the Dawsons the entire time Ace was inside. It's why he eventually went in full-time himself. He could only teach her to fight; he couldn't change her path. I don't know if the threat still exists, but she and Greer seemed to have backed them off. And now that the tide is turning against the Omnis, their focus has moved elsewhere."

The line went silent, but Owen knew Jax hadn't hung up.

"I told Addy you were bad. I kept her from you." There was a pause on the line. *"I just wanted to tell you that I'm sorry. I know it doesn't mean jack shit, but I needed to say it."*

Owen held his cell phone to his forehead briefly, then said. "I'm just glad you finally got her out. Let's just focus on that."

"The FBI found the girl's family. Addy's doppelgänger. They found her family."

"Good. So where is Roberta now that she doesn't have the senator to manipulate?"

"Not here. My dad said he didn't know where she was, but your dad said everyone's heading to Wyoming, including him. Everyone's heading to the WKB compound. I gotta tell you they aren't coming in to negotiate a peace plan with you guys. They're going so they can draw you there and take you out. The game's over."

"No, it's not. We have the Ratcliffs. The human modifications the Omnis were developing have multiple uses and have been widely distributed. We didn't figure it out or shut it down in time. It has the potential to change the world order and even become a mass-extinction event."

"Like the Georgia Guidestones talk about."

"Yeah. That and a hundred other conspiracy theories about the end of modern civilization. We found reference to their desires for a mass kill-off of the human population in some of the papers we've uncovered. This technology makes that possible. Did your dad say where my son was?"

"No. I don't think he knew. I'm on my way out there."

"Right. Then we'll see you in hell." Owen dropped the connection. The room was quiet. At last, they knew who King was.

"We can't make the mistake of thinking we're only dealing with meathead gang-bangers," Kit said. "Angel has already encountered their altered warriors."

"They're strong and certainly focused, but they seem separated from their instincts," Angel said. "It's like they're hopped up on crack. We fight smarter than they do. I'm not worried about them."

"Why converge on the WKB compound?" Blade asked.

"Because they've been cultivating the bikers as their soldiers," Max said. "It's remote. It's defensible. And there are multiple ways out if a retreat becomes necessary."

"We've been monitoring the compound since I refreshed our eyes out there," Max said. "Nothing's been going on other than it's slowly emptying out. I warned Pete to get his guys outta there. The fewer there are, the fewer we'll have to kill. Lion's been out there with the boys. He's checked in, but hasn't had anything to report."

"Are we sure what's going to happen is going down there?" Rocco asked. "You certain we can trust Jax?"

"No, I'm not," Owen said.

"We need a battle plan," Blade said. "We have to get ourselves in position before this shit goes down."

"And we need coverage here," Kit said.

Owen agreed. "Let's take this discussion to the bunker. Blade, get your dad over here. I want him brought up to speed."

26

Owen took a detour to his wing before heading down to the bunker. He hoped Addy was still awake. He wasn't sure how she would take the news—about her dad or about Edwards being King.

A light was on in the sitting room. She was on the couch, reading. When she saw him, she smiled. He didn't return it.

"What is it?" she asked.

He knelt in front of her. "I have some news. About your dad. And about King."

"Okay. What about my dad?"

"Jax went to question him about a few things. Turns out Roberta did in fact murder your mother so she could take her place."

"Oh, my God. Did my dad know?"

"Not at first, but he did eventually. He knew before you were married. Your brother told us he'd been working with the FBI to identify the girl who was killed in the train wreck. They found her family."

"Those poor people. At least they have closure now. They must have always wondered."

"It appears Roberta was a bigamist. She was already married when she married your father."

Addy's eyes got big. Owen wished there was an easy way to say what he had to, but there wasn't. "Honey, she was married to Edwards."

"The whole time?"

Owen nodded. "Only her name wasn't Roberta, it was Annie Roberts. And her husband's name is Cecil Edwards *King*."

Addy gasped, then covered her mouth. "Cecil's King?"

"Yeah. It's a motherfucking miracle you survived those two."

She reached out and hugged him. He stood, bringing her to her feet so he could hold her.

"So what's going to happen to my dad?"

"Jax had coordinated his meeting with your dad with the FBI. When they came in to arrest him— honey, your dad killed himself."

Addy buried her face in his chest. She didn't cry, though—she had no tears for her dad. She just leaned on him. Owen rubbed her back. "I know it's no excuse for his behavior, but they completely owned him. His only choice, most of your life, was to do their bidding."

She looked up at him, her eyes shifting from blue

to orange. "So I was in the Omni world my whole life, wasn't I?"

"I'm afraid so."

"And Jax? Do you know more about which side he was on?"

"I'm leaning toward him being on our side now. We think this whole thing is going to break loose really soon. I need to go talk to the guys."

"I understand."

"I hope I'll find you in my bed when I get back."

She smiled. "That's where I'll be."

Owen's room was dark when he returned a few hours later. He hoped Addy was where he'd asked her to be. Tonight of all nights, he needed to be with her. The curtains were open. Moonlight filtered in through the sheers, spilling over her slight form in his big bed.

Owen stripped and slipped under the covers, already hard for her. He rolled to his side behind her, but stopped himself from reaching for her. He didn't want to spook her.

"Laidy. Wake up."

She smiled but didn't stir.

He put his hand on her hip and kissed her shoulder, the nape of her neck, her cheek.

She rolled onto her back. His hand settled on her

soft—naked—belly. She touched his face. "Are you all right?"

"I'm the one who should be asking you that question, given what happened earlier."

"I'm glad it wasn't you or Jax who had to take my father out."

Owen didn't share that sentiment, but didn't feel the need to point that out. He moved over her, settling himself between her legs, holding himself up on his elbows. The silver moonlight made her look magical. The feel of her soft body under his was divine. He kissed her again, letting his tongue stroke hers. He kissed the side of her mouth, then let his lips explore hers, the upper, the lower, then both together as his tongue stroked the seam they made.

He arched his back to kiss her neck, her chest. Her hands were on his shoulders as he put his face between her breasts and pressed them to his cheeks. He nuzzled the underside of one breast, then let his thumb flick her tightened nipple while he kissed and nibbled and sucked the other breast.

He looked up at her, a breast in each hand, and grinned. "I love these." They were more than a handful, such generous bounty. He held one, pointing its erect nipple upward. Taking her hand, he rubbed her nipple around her own hand. She looked from his eyes to what their hands were doing.

He sucked her middle finger into his mouth, then pulled it out and rubbed her damp finger over her nipple. When he moved it away, he blew cool air over her skin. He could feel her body tighten.

Holding the sides of her chest, he bent his face to the valley between her breasts, kissing and licking as he moved down the center of her ribs to her soft belly. He caught her navel in his mouth, biting gently, then swirling his tongue there. He made his way, ever so slowly, over to her hip, grazing it with his teeth.

He slid down her body so that his shoulders were between her thighs, leaving her wide open. She was neatly groomed there, a tight triangle of soft curls. He rubbed his cheek over her mound. She gasped as she propped herself up on her elbows.

He was hungry to taste her. He looked up at her, then had to pause to watch the storms he saw her in eyes, wishing he could see what colors they took on. The room was too dark for that. He lifted her legs over his shoulders as he lay between them. Reaching a hand up to her breast, he kept a forearm pointed downward on her belly and used his fingers to separate her, then bent his face to her core.

She gasped when his tongue first touched her. Her thighs tightened against his face. He took his time exploring her with his tongue, his lips, his fingers, finding all the places and ways of touching her that made her breath hitch. When he felt the first reflexive jerk of her hips, he knew he'd found a way into her dormant soul.

He adjusted his hold, using one arm to steady her hips, freeing the other so he could penetrate her as he sucked her clit. She gasped. He knew she was close to an orgasm—he could feel the tension in her thighs. She was so wet. He tapped his fingers against her g-spot as his tongue stroked her clit.

Addy cried out as an orgasm took her over. She braced her feet on the bed and thrust against his face. Owen held her in place, keeping his fingers working her from the inside as his mouth did its magic outside. One orgasm slipped into another and another. He knew she was barely aware of him shifting positions so he could enter her. He felt the last little tremors slip away as he moved inside her.

She cried out when he seated himself, filling her. He knew it was from hunger, not fear, because her legs locked around him, keeping his hips against hers. She reached for his face. He lowered himself fully against her body, then arched down so he could kiss her, wondering if she tasted herself on his lips. Such sweet nectar. He fucked her mouth with his tongue as his body took hers. Her hands were everywhere over him—his back, his chest, his face. She dug her fingers into the back of his head. They were both breathing hard.

When he felt his release was imminent, he slipped a hand between their bodies to gently rub her clit. He wanted her to come with him. He waited, waited, waited...then crashed through with her, pounding into her, egged on by the way her inner muscles clamped and tugged at him. She was pushing up against him, thrusting into his thrusts, making little whimpers until he slammed deep in and spilled himself.

When it was over, and the last tremors were easing from her body, he lifted himself up to his elbows to look down at her. Her eyes were dark. He imagined them turning purple. He touched her soft cheek. "I love you."

"I love you too." A tear slipped from her eye. "It was never like that. Not once."

"Of course not. What you had before was torture. This is love. Big difference." He eased himself from her, then rolled to his side and straightened the covers over them. "You're staying with me tonight, yeah?"

"Yeah."

He drew her close. "I want you in my bed every night, in my arms the rest of our lives, Laidy."

Addy sighed and sat up. Owen pushed himself up on his pillows, hoping like hell she wasn't about to kill his dreams. He shouldn't have said anything.

"Owen, what if this is all true, everything the Ratcliffs said. What becomes of us?"

"Nothing changes."

"But I am. I've been modified in ways we don't fully understand yet. What if…I live forever…"

"…And I don't."

Addy nodded.

"We don't yet know what we're dealing with. Let's figure that out first. Maybe it can be reversed."

"What if it can't? What if I'm one of those people

whose body takes over the work the nanos were doing?"

Owen turned on the light. This was too serious a discussion to be having without his being able to see her face.

"Would you take the modifications, too?" she asked.

"I would."

"I don't know if I want you to. It's dangerous. Your body might not survive the changes the nanos trigger."

He lift her hand and kissed her knuckles. "It's an easy decision for me to make, Addy, though I know it's not a simple one. We lived without each other. It wasn't a good time. Whatever happens, we'll go through it together."

27

——————

Jafaar watched Deputy Sheriff Jerry Whitcomb pull into the lot. He moved a little deeper into the small park, away from the few people who were there so that their conversation wouldn't be overhead. This time, he hadn't brought any food for the ducks in the pond. Didn't matter. He wouldn't be there long. He knew the perfect way to grab the Ratcliffs—or at least get them to the place he wanted them.

The deputy caught up to him. Jafaar kept walking. "Good afternoon, deputy. I'm glad you were able to make our meeting."

"Did I have a choice?"

"It is only a simple task I need from you, at the moment."

"No. I have to lay low. I think the sheriff's onto me."

"Perhaps. But this task won't cause you any bother. I need you to run an app for me."

"I left my phone in the cruiser."

"I have the app on this phone. All you need to do is go to the house where the Feds are. Get within twenty feet of a certain woman there, and run the app."

"That's *all?* That place is lousy with Feds. It's locked down seven ways to Sunday."

"You were friends once with Mrs. Silas, no? She gives lessons to Ms. Jacobs every afternoon. Visit them during one of their lessons. Be near Ms. Jacobs when you click the app."

"What does it do?"

"It changes the lineup of power in my favor. More power for me, means more power for you. Do it this afternoon."

Jerry drove back to Wolf Creek Bend. Jafaar's request seemed innocuous enough. He didn't know who Ms. Jacobs was, but he should be able to figure it out by getting close to Mandy. He had a bone to pick with Mandy anyway. She could have chosen him. He would have kept her safe. He and Amir's other guy were the ones harassing her—he could have reassured her that she wouldn't actually be harmed. As long as she cooperated.

All he had to do for today's exercise was drive out

onto BLM land, then come back into the group's compound from the rear. An evergreen forest backed to the corrals where they'd be. He couldn't drive in at that point, but it wasn't a long hike. He could get in, run the app, and get out before anyone even saw him. Or so he thought before the sheriff started pestering him on the radio. He shut it off. He was almost to BLM land. He'd be out of cell phone range too very shortly.

His phone rang. Jerry ignored it. When it rang a third time, he picked up.

"Sheriff."

"Jerry. What are you doing?"

"Got a call from a rancher about a dead cow. Out on BLM land."

"That ain't our jurisdiction."

"True, but didn't think it hurt to check it out. Rancher's a friend of mine."

"The call didn't come over dispatch."

"Nah. Like I said, it was a friend of mine, so he called me direct. I won't be long. I'm just about out of cell phone range, sheriff. I'll be back to the station shortly." Right on cue, the line cut out. Jerry smiled and dumped his phone on the passenger seat.

He drove a good ways onto BLM land, then came back toward the Fed's place on a little-used dirt road that dead-ended in the woods, then had to go the rest of the way on foot.

~

OWEN WAS WATCHING ADDY, Rocco, Mandy, and the three kids ride around in the parking area in front of the stable. They were all having fun, doing the same simple maneuvers that Addy and Troy were learning. The parking lot gave them a bigger area to move around in. Troy was a natural, even though he looked tiny on the back of the big horse he was riding. Addy...not so much. The point of the exercise this afternoon was to get them both comfortable with communicating to their horses. Owen could tell the work was completely absorbing to them.

"Owen, Rocco," Kit's voice came over their comms. *"Deputy Jerry's gone rogue. Sheriff's on his way over. I don't know where Jerry is. Get everybody inside. Do it now."*

Shit. Owen ran toward the group. Rocco was grabbing kids off saddles. He handed Troy to Addy, swung Zavi under his arm, and was hurrying Casey and Mandy out of the parking lot. Mandy was resisting leaving the horses loose. Rocco caught her and forced her to focus on him. "We got incoming. Forget the goddamned horses. You and the kids need to get to safety. *Now.*"

That got through to her. Owen picked up Troy and grabbed Addy, then ran them up the hill and into the stable. Rocco brought up the rear. The horses followed him, so he let them into the corral. Just as well, Owen thought. Gave the deputy less opportunity to hide. A siren was wailing in the distance, coming up from town.

Owen told everyone to wait just inside the stable

door while he started clearing the stalls. The deputy wasn't in there with them, so he moved them deeper inside, getting them into the hay storage area, which was on the end of the stable nearest the house.

No sooner had he done that than the deputy stepped into the big opening. Owen drew his gun. "Deputy. We weren't expecting you." He kept his voice calm, as if drawing a weapon on a cop wasn't an illegal activity. Jerry didn't seem particularly stressed, which helped Owen relax some. He was just messing around with his phone.

"Put the phone down, deputy, and step away from the barn," he directed him.

Jerry pocketed the phone, then frowned as he looked up at Owen. "What's the big deal? Can't an old friend stop by and check in? Mandy and I are friends. You know that."

Kit was running from the house. Owen had to keep the deputy's focus. He knew Rocco was coming around the corral side of the stable. The siren had stopped, but he could see lights flashing from the parking lot, so the sheriff was there, too.

"You know, deputy, I don't want to make this anything it's not," Owen said. "Where's your vehicle? I didn't see you pull up. Feels a little bit like you were sneaking up on us. Why would you do that?"

"I wasn't sneaking. I had to check out a dead cow incident. Just over on BLM land. Saw you guys and thought I'd say hi."

The sheriff came up, his hand on his undrawn weapon. "Jerry, I'd like you to come with me."

"I can't do that, sheriff. I left my vehicle back a ways."

"Don't worry about it. I'll have one of the other guys bring it in for us."

Jerry heard Kit behind him. He whirled around. Owen lunged, body-slamming Jerry before he could draw his weapon. The sheriff cuffed him while Owen kept a knee on his neck. They disarmed him, then the sheriff hoisted Jerry to his feet.

"I'm disappointed in you, son," the sheriff said. "You were supposed to be one of the good guys. Who are you working for? What were you doing out here?"

"Check his phone," Owen said. "He was messing with it."

"The sheriff's call was the last one for a few hours," Max said over their comms.

"Sheriff, if you don't mind, we'll take that phone," Owen said. "My guys can check out what he was doing with it." The sheriff handed it to him. It wasn't passcode protected. Owen frowned. "There's only one app on it." He handed it to Kit. "Get this to Max."

"Owen," Mandy called from inside the hay room. "Something's wrong with Addy. She fainted."

Owen ran into the hay room to the women and kids. Addy was draped across Mandy's lap, out cold. Owen knelt and felt her pulse, glad it was there and strong. He wondered if it was another situation like what had happened with Wynn and the bumblebee drone.

"Did you see a bee or bumblebee or another bug? Was she stung?" Owen asked.

"I don't know. I didn't see one," Mandy said.

"She okay?" Kit asked.

"She's breathing. I need to get her up to the house," Owen said. "Max, Greer, are we clear out here?" he asked via his comms. "There any other tangos we need to know about?"

"Negative," Greer answered. *"We did a sweep of our systems. Jerry's the only one who got through."*

"Did you do something to her?" the sheriff asked Jerry.

"I wasn't near her," the deputy said.

"Let's go back to the house." Owen lifted Addy and started for the house. Rocco followed with the kids and Mandy. Kit stayed to help the sheriff.

OWEN TOOK Addy to his room and set her on the bed. He loosened her clothes, washed her hands and face, and put a cool rag on her forehead. Nothing revived her. He remembered Troy saying his mom fainted a lot and wondered if this was normal for her. She hadn't fainted in the time they'd been reunited. He had smelling salts in his first-aid kit. He grabbed them and waved the pungent capsules under her nose. They had no effect on her.

He thought about calling an ambulance, but after what had happened to Wynn, he couldn't risk that. He looked up to see the room crowded with his team. Thankfully, Troy wasn't there. "Call Doc Beck. I want him over here now. And get the Ratcliffs in here. Maybe they know something."

As soon as he said that, he remembered them mentioning something about using an app to trigger the nanos' kill-off procedures. He looked up at Greer. "Tell me the Wi-Fi jammer we're using here extends to the stable."

Greer shook his head. "It doesn't."

"Get into that app. See what it does," Owen said, then looked at Wynn's dad, who'd come into the room. "Tell me an app didn't just kill Addy. Tell me it isn't that simple."

"It can be," Nathan Ratcliff said. "A self-destruct can be triggered in a dozen different ways. The preferred was via code in the belief it could be better controlled than via hormonal delivery."

"Find out what the deputy did," Owen said.

Greer rushed out of the room, grabbing Wynn's dad on his way out. Wynn's mom came over to sit beside Addy. She took her hand. Owen was struck by how peaceful Addy was just lying there.

"If her nanos were triggered, we need to act fast. We have to figure which nanos she was given," Joyce said.

"In what ways could they be attacking her?" Owen asked.

"Again, it depends on the type she was given, but it's possible they're collecting in an artery, forming an artificial clot," Joyce said. "They could cause a heart attack, a stroke, an aneurysm. Other nanos might trigger a lethal chemical change that sends her body into anaphylactic shock. We have to know what we're dealing with. And for that, we need a specialized lab."

Doc Beck came in then. Owen cleared out the room so he could do his examination. He took her vitals. "Her blood pressure is dangerously low."

The doctors consulted each other, rattling off terms and treatments at a mind-boggling speed. They talked about an exchange transfusion, but discarded the idea almost as soon as it had been proposed—they didn't have the four hours that could take.

Four hours. Addy didn't have four hours left.

Owen jammed his fingers into his hair. The others had come back into the room. He looked at Kit. "Get my helicopter up here. We're going to need to evacuate her…as soon as we decide where. Doc Beck is finding an appropriate lab. And tell the sheriff the deputy may well have succeeded in murdering Addy."

Max came into the room as Kit left. Whatever news he was about to impart didn't look good. "Heard from Lion and Feral. A couple of helicopters just dropped off Edwards, Mrs. Jacobs, Jason, and Santo. There're all there. One of the cubs saw Beetle, too."

Owen closed his eyes. Beetle was there, just an hour away. It was no coincidence that this had happened to Addy right now. "Does Lion know where my son is?"

"No. They lost sight of him."

"Owen," Beck looked up from his cell. "I found a lab. It's near here"—he paused—"but I need you to talk to someone."

Owen grabbed the phone.

"Son?" came a long forgotten voice on the other end. Owen put the phone on speaker. The room went quiet.

"Dad?" Of all the fucking times for his past to slam into his present, now was the worst. "I can't talk now."

"Listen to me. The lab facilities you need are out at the WKB compound, in the silo. Problem is, all the bastards are gathering there as we speak. They did this on purpose to draw you out. You can't go there. You'll be ambushed. They'll fucking slaughter you and your team. You can't risk the Ratcliffs. It's no exaggeration to say that all of humanity depends on them for their survival."

Jax had said the same about the Omnis attempting to draw them out. "Understood. What is it about this lab that makes it the one we need?"

"They've been doing human testing there. On WKB bikers. They have a few dozen modified fighters there, plus more they've brought in. They do have medical support systems there, but more importantly, they have the software labs responsible for the nano termination coding. They have what you need to reverse what's been done to Addy."

Owen lowered the phone, but kept the connection live. He felt sick as he looked at the guys gathered in the room. He had two options: get Addy to a medical facility that could do an emergency exchange transfusion, and hope that the time it took to transport her, prepare the transfusion, and complete it happened fast enough to save her life. Or have his team hit the WKB compound, potentially losing several lives to save one— and there was no guarantee they could even save her.

"I can do the exchange transfusion at the clinic," Beck said, "but I don't have enough units of her blood type on hand. I would have to get those up from Cheyenne."

"We don't yet to understand what type of nano she was given, what type of termination was coded— we don't even know if an exchange transfusion would work," Joyce said.

"Owen," Val said, breaking through his thoughts. "This is our chance to end the Omnis. This is what we've been working toward. We'll get you and Addy into the labs, then we'll take out the Medusa heads running the org."

Owen shook his head. "It's a suicide mission. They know what the deputy did. They know we're coming. They're waiting for us. They have Augie there…somewhere."

"We anticipated this," Kit said. "We've stashed our weapons and ammo strategically around the compound. We've rigged explosives at key points.

We're readier than they are. Let them think we're coming in blind—it gives us another advantage."

"We have eyes out there—not just the cameras, but Lion and his cubs have been watching everything," Max said. "They know, real time, what's happening. I can get into the Omni computers and patch in Greer and Nathan so they can work it from here." He looked at Beck. "If you're game, you can be Joyce's eyes and hands onsite. The Ratcliffs can work it remotely through us."

"Agreed," Beck said, without hesitation.

"Owen," Kelan said quietly, "we're only as strong as the weakest among us. If we aren't willing to take a stand for your woman, then we don't stand for anything after all. And if that's the case, we should just cede this war to the fucking Omnis, because we are not better than them."

Owen felt the crushing weight of his decision. He looked at each man and woman who hadn't yet spoken. Each nodded at him.

Owen lifted his phone. "We're going out there, Dad."

"Be careful, son. Be damned careful." The line went dead.

"Max, you've been in the one renovated silo under the WKB compound," Owen said. "Where's the most likely place for this software lab?"

"The finished silo has ten floors underground," Max said. "The lowest is just a mechanical room. The next floor up is where I saw the one space I wasn't allowed into. The floors above were Syadne meeting rooms, offices, dorms. Other floors warehoused drugs. There's not going to be much happening in the unfinished areas of the tunnels. No light, no power, no Wi-Fi."

"We have to clear the silo space and hold it for the FBI," Kit said. "We need to split up. Owen, you take Addy, Doc Beck, Ace, Max, and Angel and go into the tunnels the back way. That should give you a little extra protection for transporting Addy while things are exploding above ground. The rest of us will clear each floor of the silo on our way down to the ninth floor. Access to each level and some of the areas inside each level are protected with biometrics. Each of you has enough explosives to blow several doors."

"We need people alive and machines intact," Owen said. "If there are lab workers inside, hold them."

"What about the key players?" Val asked. "Where's it likely we'll find them?"

Kit shook his head. "Could be anyone's guess. They might be holed up in the finished silo; they might be somewhere else entirely."

"And is lethal force authorized?" Angel asked.

"Only as a last resort," Owen said. "The more info we can get out of everyone we find, the better it's going to be for the bigger fight. Kit, tell my pilot to get up here and wait on standby. It's a short flight from here to the WKB compound if the helicopter's needed, but I don't want it flying into enemy fire unnecessarily. We're going to have to drive in—it isn't safe for the chopper and it will just expose our attempt to sneak in the back way."

"Copy that." He stepped out to give that order.

The battle plan they'd made laid out who would go and who would stay and the positions each was responsible for. It didn't need much change. They'd already agreed to take the silo while Lobo and his men took the main grounds, and Lion and his pride watched the silo tunnels.

All they had to do now was execute that plan.

Owen nodded. "Then let's gear up and get out there."

And, please God, let them all come home safe, he said silently to himself.

28

Ace and Val were in the weapons room, gearing up. Val put his M16 in its case. Ace caught him staring at it.

"What gives, Val?" she asked.

"I didn't want to take my dad out this way."

"With a bullet?"

"No. By a sniper round. I wanted to look him in the eye. I wanted him to see me do it."

"Val, this is the man who tormented you your entire childhood, the monster who calls this war a game. You are a legend in the sniper world for what you did in Afghanistan. What better way to take him out than using the very skill he mocked?"

Val closed the case, then bent over and kissed Ace. "I love you."

"I love you too."

"I wish you were staying here. Your arm's still in a cast. You don't need to break it again."

Ace stared into his eyes. "This is what I do, what I am."

Val's nostrils flared. "I know."

"Besides, Greer's stuck here. One of us has to end Henry. I think I've earned that right."

OWEN CAME BACK in the house after prepping the backseat of an Expedition for him and Addy with some blankets and a small armory. The women were saying goodbye to their men. The emotion in the room was dense. Owen saw Troy standing off by himself. He picked the boy up and carried him down the hall to Owen's room where Addy still was.

"Say goodbye to your mom, boy." That sounded so fucking final that Owen quickly added, "She'll be all better when we bring her home."

Troy got on the bed and kissed her, then settled down next to her so he could lay his head on her chest. "I love you, Mom. Augie's not home. You can't die yet. Please, Mom. Mommy."

Tears were spilling down Owen's face. He picked the boy up and hugged him. Troy wrapped his arms around Owen's neck in a choking grip. He could feel the sobs racking the boy's little body.

"Don't let her die, Owen."

Owen looked over to see Mandy at the door, wiping her own tears away. He knelt on the floor and pulled Troy free. "I'll do everything in my power to save your mom and find your brother."

The boy drew himself up to his full height and looked into Owen's eyes. "I believe you. I love you, Owen."

"I love you too, boy." Another quick hug, then Owen sent him off with Mandy.

Addy was lying there so peacefully, so pale and still. He smiled and sat next to her, then leaned over and kissed her lips. "I love you, my Laidy, but you can't leave me alone. Stay strong and fight, for your boys, for me, for us as a family."

"Ready, O?" Kit asked, standing by the short hallway into the room.

Owen nodded. He lifted Addy into his arms, holding her close, her head resting against his shoulder. He walked down the long hall and into the foyer. The women stood aside, letting him through. He heard a couple of them weeping. Troy was there, with Mandy. The boy broke from her and ran to hug his hips. Mandy came right after him and pulled him away. Owen walked outside, hoping to hell and back that he'd be returning with her alive.

He set her in the backseat, then came around the other side, lifting her head and shoulders to his lap. He tucked the blanket around her as Kit and Doc Beck settled into the front seats.

"There's been a slight change to the plan, boss," Kit said. "Yusef called Rocco and told him Jafaar had taken his boys as his personal bodyguards and was headed toward the WKB. Rocco's meeting up with Lobo to head him off. Yusef's boys are not in any way part of this, and Yusef's been a good ally. If they can get him before he gets to the compound, it's one fewer bad guy to fight, and Rocco might be able to keep the boys out of trouble."

"Copy that."

HIGHWAY I-80 WEST was a complete standstill. Fortunately, Rocco was coming from the opposite direction —heading away from where he most needed to be. It was worth it to put Jafaar down. He had to drive on the wayside to get around the stopped traffic. When he got to the front of the traffic jam, he parked and got out. Jafaar held one of Yusef's sons in front of him, a gun to his head. The boy had tears running down his cheeks. Lobo shouted over to Rocco to hold his position. Rocco nodded and stood still.

"Jafaar," Rocco called out in Pashto, "let the boys go. You aren't authorized to kill them. Abdul Baseer al Jahni still needs them. If he loses you and them, it is too dear a price to pay. I can provide what you wanted. I can send al Jahni the formulas."

"You trick me," Jafaar said, stepping back to swing his focus toward Rocco.

"No. I'm speaking Pashto. The Feds can't understand me. Let the boys go, turn yourself in, minimize al Jahni's loss. If you do that, I will send him the formulas you needed so that he can have his own corner on the human modification market. You will have achieved your goal and also will remain honorable."

"You don't have it. You're lying."

"I'm not. We have the scientists. They will give al Jahni the formula as a means of mitigating the power King has. It's all a power play, no?"

"If I give up the boys, the Feds will shoot me."

"Not if you toss your weapon down," Rocco said.

Jafaar looked from him to Lobo. He shoved the kid toward the car and went to his knees. He tossed his weapon off into the wayside. As Lobo charged toward him, he grabbed another weapon from his jacket, which he aimed at Lobo. Yusef's son kicked his hand, dislodging the weapon as it discharged, sending the round harmlessly into the field.

Lobo's crew swarmed him. Rocco walked over to the boys. One was still in the car. They were younger than Lion, but not by much. Rocco had read their files. Good kids. Trying to live the lives their parents had given up so much for. He held out a hand to the one Jafaar had been holding a gun on.

"You did good," Rocco said in English.

"Are we in trouble?" the boy asked.

"No. You'll need to go with my friend Lobo here to give your statements. They'll get you back to your parents in no time. I'll let your dad know you're both okay."

"Thanks."

Lobo's guys yanked Jafaar to his feet and walked him over to one of their vehicles. "I will hold you to your promise," Jafaar said.

"Yeah, about that," Rocco grinned. "See, I'm not authorized to make deals with terrorists. You got nothing."

Lobo came over and shook hands with Rocco. "Thanks."

"Sure. Don't keep the boys too long. Their parents are beside themselves."

"My guys will take them back to the motel and get their statements there. I'm headed west. How about you?"

"Same. I'll cut over and follow you."

OWEN LIFTED Addy out of the SUV. They were parked on a Forest Service road behind the WKB. As he understood it, there were three ways of getting into the underground missile complex. One was the main entrance under the old warehouse. Another was through the grease pit in what had been Hope's garage. They were taking the third access point used by the watchers that was hidden in the woods. One of Lion's cubs came out from some trees like a little shadow.

"Fox," Max said.

"It's this way," the boy said, waving them into the woods, leading them to the tunnel entrance. Max opened the hidden gate.

"Be careful of the stairs," he said as Owen went by. Fox lit the way with a lantern. Max, Ace, and Angel shined their flashlights into the dark, making sure Owen's way was well lit. Doc Beck followed with his own flashlight. This complex was nothing like the tunnels were Fiona had been taken. It was a rough dugout cut into granite. And though it wasn't as large as the Colorado system, it still made for a good hike deep inside the underground passageway.

Fox stopped and looked at them. "King's men are everywhere. Big ones."

"Can you draw a map in the dirt showing where they are?" Owen asked.

Fox set his lantern down and drew some lines in the dirt. Owen had to turn halfway to the side to see over Addy. "Where are we now?"

"Here," Max said. "This tunnel runs into the main corridor here. The tangos are blocking our entrance into the Syadne tower here."

"On the schematics Angel showed us there was a spur tunnel just before the branch that leads to the tower. Can we get that far without them seeing us? I need a safe place to stash Addy and Doc Beck while we clear the way."

"Possibly," Max said. "If not, we'll make it safe." He grinned up at Owen.

Fox provided expert navigation. The Titan missile complex they were in had three silos. Owen knew from Max's time here a few months ago that only one of the silos had been renovated. That was where the lab was. Near it was another short tunnel that led to an equipment terminal.

Unfortunately, they couldn't get close to it. Faint light in the main tunnel alerted them to King's fighters, who were spreading out into the space. Owen's group shut off their flashlights. Max looked around the corner of the tunnel. A guard stood halfway between where they were and where they needed to go.

"I got this," Angel said. He picked up a metal shard and chucked it down the tunnel in the opposite direction. The guard's flashlight flashed in that direction. He rushed toward the sound, only slowing to check out their tunnel when he was already in the middle of the entrance. Angel charged him, knocking his flashlight to the side and moving the fighter away from them.

They hurried down the wide main tunnel, stopping at the opening to the next tunnel that led to the Syadne tower. Max checked around the edge, then held up two fingers. "Wait here."

He walked into the tunnel, moving without stealth like he was supposed to be there. He wore typical biker leather, his cuts, and a kerchief on his head in the club colors. One of the men pointed a lighted automatic rifle at him. "Identify yourself."

Max held his hands up. "Just Mad Dog. Club sergeant-at-arms. Making sure you're in position. And what is this, a fucking brew-fest? Spread out. You got a lotta ground to cover down here." He walked past the first guy and stopped next to the second one. He looked over the guy's weapon and stance. "Keep it like this." When the guy eased his grip on his AR, Max shoved the rifle's butt up into his nose, killing him instantly. Before the guy hit the ground, Max pivoted and fired at the first guy, dropping him.

Between that gunfire and Angel's fight, they'd lost their stealth advantage. Max waved them forward. They managed to get into the spur tunnel Owen had been looking for. It was near the end of the tunnel that led to the Syadne tower, so it was a good place to hole up while the rest of the way was cleared. He couldn't bring Addy and Beck into the middle of a gunfight.

"We'll stay here," Owen said. "Max, go meet up with the rest of the team. I'll send Angel when he gets back. The lab is one floor up in the tower. Clear the way, then come get us."

"Copy. Watch his back, Ace," Max said, pointing at her.

"On it," Ace answered.

Owen set Addy down behind a pile of debris. Ace used her flashlight while Beck checked Addy's vitals. He didn't look happy with her status. Owen adjusted the blankets around her. It was not as quiet in the tunnels as he thought it would be. Metal groaned in the distance, making eerie sounds that could almost be human. There was a constant drip of water somewhere near them. They all heard a slight rustling of fabric. Ace turned, her hand on her weapon.

Another little boy came out of the shadows. He whispered something to Fox, who looked at Owen. "There's man in here, a little ways farther back. He's looking for Ace. He's old. He has a long white beard."

Ace looked at Owen. "Santo."

Owen nodded. "Can we trust it's not a trap?" he asked Fox.

"We're on the same side, sir. I don't know about the man."

Owen asked Ace, "You up to dealing with him?"

"Fuck yeah. I promised Greer."

"Then go."

The second boy ran down the tunnel, leading Ace away. Owen hated sending her alone. Santo was a sneaky bastard who'd manipulated her most of her teen years, and did so again a few weeks ago. But he couldn't leave Addy unguarded.

ACE HURRIED AFTER THE BOY, trying to move as silently as he did, as silently as Santo had taught her to. The boy ducked into one of the tunnels leading to an unrenovated silo, then pointed to a small offshoot from it, like the one Owen was in at the other tower. Ace felt the hairs rise on her neck, sensing Santo before she ever saw him. She dropped her flashlight, letting it light the little stretch of tunnel indirectly.

It caught the white wool of Santo's homespun outer robe. His beard was the same color. He was an old man. And she was going to kill him. The facts were comforting to her.

"Hello, Grandpa."

"Figured you knew who I was when your brother came looking for me," Santo said.

"Did you? Why didn't you give yourself up?"

"There's only one way out of this game."

"It's no game."

"It is if one of its players decides it is."

"So because Jason Parker says it's a game, it is?"

"When you end up playing by default, yes."

"You know I'm going to kill you."

"It seems appropriate. I don't have a lot of fight left in me."

"I just want to know why," Ace said.

"Why what?"

"Why you took me from my crib. Why you left me with the monsters."

"I don't have an answer that would pass your strict sense of justice. I did it because having you in the tunnels with me gave me a cause, a reason to keep fighting."

"You did it because you didn't want to be alone?"

"You find that surprising? Jason would say you were my game piece."

"You had two pieces in the game. Me and Greer."

"Better to cover as many bases as possible. The truth is that this thing is bigger than you or me or any family. The Omnis are going to gut the world with their new technology. The only people who will survive them are the ones who know how to fight. You are a fighter. Your brother is a fighter. I feel I've done right by you."

Ace scoffed. "Are you going to surrender? Or are you going to fight?"

"Surrender."

That answer disappointed her, actually. But Owen wanted these bastards alive. So be it. "Then lie down on your stomach and put your hands behind you." He did as she requested. She took out a set of zip cuffs and knelt on his thigh. Next thing she knew, he shifted and kicked her head, knocking her over.

She rolled over and sprang to her feet. He moved like a man half his age. She ran at him, launching her knee into his chest. He stepped back, moving with her momentum, then came at her fast, his hands slicing through the air. She blocked him each time, but his energy was escalating. She could feel him leading into a kick. Before he could, she ducked and swiped her feet into his, tangling him up. Her full range of motion was hampered by her arm cast and the heavy operations gear she was wearing.

He leapt to his feet. "What happened to your arm?"

A wash of guilt flooded her. "Edwards' goons got a good hit in."

"You let them."

"I let them nothing. They got the jump on me."

"I taught you better than that."

In the seconds between his words and his next advance, Ace wondered if her love for Val and her new found comfort had softened her, stealing her edge. She didn't have time to process that thought before Santo was on her again. Maneuvering in the cluttered space of the tunnel took focus.

The moves they made were familiar. They each got in some good strikes, and they each made good blocks. It was like dancing with an old friend. Ace's heart softened toward Santo, and she realized that was not a weakness. It was honor. Val had taught her to see her own value. And because she could see it in herself, she could see it in others.

Santo had taught her hate and vengeance. Val had taught her love.

She felt her grandfather slowing his attack and tried again to get through to him. "We don't have to fight. It doesn't have end this way. You have valuable knowledge. Surrender. Please. Grandpa."

He pressed forward hard. Their encounter became less of an exercise and more of a fight. And when that shift happened, she didn't take time to consider it—he'd taught her not to. A shift like that was lethal. She didn't want either of them hurt. Her best bet was to let him wear himself out.

She executed a couple of backward flips, escaping his brutal kicks and punches. When there was a little space between them, she fought for her breath. "Love doesn't weaken, Grandpa. Did you never learn that?"

"I learned there are things bigger than oneself."

"Things worth abandoning your honor for?"

"We all make sacrifices for a greater good."

"What about me? Was I nothing to you?"

"You were my sacrifice. Of course you had meaning."

"But what kind of meaning?"

Thankfully, their conversation gave them both a moment to regroup. If she could keep him talking, she might be able to get through to him.

"I had a choice," he said.

Ace's heart squeezed uncomfortably in her chest. "What kind of choice?"

"Lose you, or lose your entire family."

A chill skittered along her spine. How terrible to be faced with that. She could see the Omnis doing that, too.

"It wasn't really a choice." In the faint light of the section of tunnel they were in, she could see his shoulders slump. "I watched him cut you. He'd sedated you with chloroform, then sliced you all to hell, hoping that would make everyone believe you'd been killed, not just kidnapped."

"It worked, as you know. They did think I was dead. My parents lived with that for more than two decades. Greer hates you. But I don't." Tears distorted her vision. She was glad he couldn't see them.

"All I could do was build a following in the tunnels. Teach as many as I could to fight, resist, learn. When they made you service their men, I stayed in full-time. I took every minute with you that I could get. I knew you would become a sword of vengeance. And like hardened steel, you did just that."

Ace heaved a long sigh. "Come home with me. You get to heal, too."

"No. I will never heal. I don't deserve to. I deserve to die. Here and now."

"I won't kill you, Santo."

"You will. Or you will die. One of us is not leaving this tunnel alive." He followed those words with a forceful advance that left no doubt he'd meant what he said. She tried retreating, but he cornered her between a big metal bin and the tunnel wall.

The little watcher who'd brought her to Santo carried his lantern out into the section of tunnel they were fighting in, giving her enough light to decide on her next move. She jumped on the metal box as Santo came at her, then grabbed a pipe overhead and swung forward, kicking him in the throat, hard enough to lift him off the ground. He stumbled back, then fell on a pile of jumbled metal. One of the spikes shoved all the way through his chest. Even in the weak light of the tunnel, she could see the dark stain spreading across his woolen robe.

She rushed to his side. "No! No, Santo! Dammit. Don't you dare die."

His eyes met hers. He gurgled for a minute, then went still.

"Damn you. We could have fixed this." She caught his hand and cried, weeping for all of it—what was, what wasn't, what would never be.

When she was spent, she realized he was wrong about love. Love didn't weaken a person...it only strengthened what it touched.

Ace returned to where their fight started and picked up her flashlight, then looked around for the kid. He didn't come out, but she knew he was still nearby.

"Look, kid. Get outta here. Go find Lion and stay with him. You don't need to see this stuff."

She wiped her left hand across her face, then tasted the blood from her cut lip. Her broken arm hurt like a sonofabitch. She walked back toward Owen, checking at every turn that the way was clear. Angel and Owen were fighting four men outside the spur tunnel. For every hit they got in, they took two more. Looked like the fight had been going on long enough that the guys were winded. Ace watched the fight, trying to see where she could break in. She was glad it was a hand-to-hand fight instead of a gunfight...until a knife slashed toward Owen. He snagged the guy's hand between his, then kicked his groin, grabbing the knife free as the guy doubled over. In a smooth motion that went almost too fast to see, he cut that guy's throat and stabbed his second opponent in the neck.

Ace ran to help Angel, sliding her leg between one of his opponent's feet, tripping him. When he went down, she smashed her cast into his face, knocking him out. Angel's second opponent dropped about the same time, a knife sticking out of his eye.

Gunfire came from the tunnel where Owen had been. Owen rushed to the opening in time to see a guy coming out, carrying Addy over his shoulder. Owen kicked his knees in. He screamed and fell, dropping Addy as his legs caved beneath him... bending the wrong way. While Owen hurried to Addy, Angel and Ace rushed into the tunnel where Doc Beck still was. He was standing there with Owen's SIG, staring down at a dead Omni.

"You good, Doc?" Angel asked.

"Yeah. You guys?"

"Fine," Ace said. They went back to the Syadne tunnel. Owen had just picked Addy up. "Was she hurt?"

"No. Angel, go ahead and make sure the way's still clear," Owen said. "Ace, hold your position here. I'll send more help as the team frees up. Beck, with me."

Ace watched them head to the Syadne tower. The door to the tower was blown out. They stepped inside and disappeared into a stairwell. She hoped everything would work out for Owen. He was different than she'd expected him to be. He and Addy deserved a chance.

A few minutes later, she heard a commotion coming from the tower.

Instinctively, she retreated inside the tunnel, shutting off her light. Someone was exiting the Syadne tower. Light from the broken door spilled into the bigger tunnel, backlighting a couple that was hurrying toward her. They kept looking behind them. Edwards and some blond woman whose hand he was holding. Not Edwards. King. Fucking King. Was that Roberta—or Annie Roberts—Jax and Addy's stepmom with him?

Ace stepped out in front of them, shining her flashlight into their eyes. It was Edwards, all right. "Going somewhere?" she asked.

Owen came out of the building behind the couple. They were so focused on her that they didn't hear him. Edwards fired off a gunshot into the light. The woman cried out when he pushed her back against the wall of the tunnel, out of the line of fire.

"Turn around, King," Owen called out. "Ace isn't your enemy. But I am."

Owen's flashlight was blinding as he shined it on the couple. Ace lowered hers so it wouldn't affect his vision. "How long did you think you could keep the game up?" he asked King.

"Long enough to win, which I've done," King said. "I own the world."

Owen laughed. King shot toward him, but missed. Owen's shot didn't. It hit King's ankle. Roberta screamed. King stumbled to his knees.

"I'll be sad to kill you," Owen said. "I can't tell you how many times and how many ways I thought about doing it."

Why was Owen toying with the bastard? Ace wished he'd polish him off. Prolonging it just put him at risk. What would Troy do without a mother or a father?

King shot at Owen again. Thanks to Owen's flashlight, he missed again. Owen shot King's hand, sending his gun flying out of his grip. Roberta ran for it, but Ace got to it first. She reached for one of her zip ties, but they were gone. She must have lost them in her fight with Santo.

She held her gun on Roberta, ready to take her out.

"You're not going to kill me, despite your sick dreams," King said to Owen.

"Why's that?"

"Because I'm the only one who knows where Augie is."

Ace couldn't see King's smile, but she could hear it in his voice.

"Okay," Owen said. "So I guess we'll do it the hard way. Which works for me, since it's one of my sick dreams. I'll tell you how it's going to go. I have six more bullets in this mag. I'm going to blow out parts of you that aren't strictly necessary. We'll see how long you last. The sooner you tell me, the less pain you'll have to feel."

Owen fired into the thigh of King's uninjured leg. He screamed.

"Want to talk?" No answer.

Now Owen really did need to move faster, Ace knew. Shock was going to set in and they'd lose King.

Owen fired into his other thigh. King lay back, twisted in an odd way, and laughed. He used his uninjured arm to try to drag himself away. "Oh, poor, poor Owen. The love of his life is dying. His boy is dying. Such a sad, sad life, Owen has. Annie told me how much you loved dear Addy. It was fun taking her from you."

Owen fired into King's shoulder, immobilizing him. "Where's my son?"

"I'm sure my men have heard the gunshots. They had explicit instructions to carry out. If I didn't make it to them in a timely way, they were to drop your boy into the acid pools. I'm so sorry I can't be there to see that."

"Fox!" Owen bellowed for the cub.

The boy ran toward Owen from the Syadne tower. "Sir?"

"Where are the acid vats?"

"This way." Fox took Owen's flashlight and ran around the bleeding King, who was too broken to grab for him.

Owen stooped and lifted King's body, carrying him over his shoulders. Roberta screamed and leaped after them, grabbing at King until he shouted for her to stop. Ace followed them. She'd heard about the acid vats when she lived in the Colorado tunnels. It was a threat King liked to lord over the serving class there. She'd never been sure they were real, but she was afraid she was about to find out.

They took some turns that Ace wasn't certain she'd remember, and came to a place with a deep black pit. I-beams ran across it to some rooms on the other side. She didn't see anyone there. Were they too late?

"Fox, get out of here," Owen ordered. The boy ran ahead, disappearing from sight. Roberta was still screaming. Owen carried King's limp body. Lifting him off his shoulders, he dropped him down to the I-beam. Ace looked down into the still, dark pools, wondering if they really were full of acid.

The sizzle that came every time King's blood dripped was her answer.

Owen crouched down. "Tell me where my boy is, and I will end you with a quick bullet. Don't tell me, and I'll end you with a quick dip."

"You won't kill me. You don't have the balls."

"You know, you little bastard, my balls are like fucking boulders." Owen walked off the I-beam and headed straight toward Roberta. He grabbed her hair and shoved her forward. Despite her struggles, Owen's balance was unwavering.

"I don't need you anymore, King. I got your wife. She knows everything you know, doesn't she? She knows what it takes to be a good wife, to do everything her husband wants, even if it's letting him cohabitate with a sweet young girl who only ever wanted to be a good daughter."

"Leave my wife out of this," King said. His voice was getting weak.

"Like you left my woman alone? What about all those rape parties? What about all those months she spent in the hospital for broken bones? What about taking her little boy away from her? You want me to be kind to this bitch? You don't even know the meaning of kindness."

Fox ran back into the cave. He pulled Ace down so he could whisper in her ear. Ace looked at him, shocked. "You're sure?"

The boy nodded.

"Owen," Ace called. "Lion has your son. He has Beetle. He's bringing him down."

OWEN HUFFED A BROKEN SIGH. He looked up when Lion came in the cave, his arm on the shoulder of a young boy. Owen nodded. Tears filled his eyes.

"Lion, take the boys and Ace back up to the Syadne tower. Do it now."

When they were out of sight, Owen wrapped his arm around Roberta's neck. "Addy tried to be a good daughter. She tried to make you proud of her. You. A monster. Of course, it never worked. But you could have shown her a little decency by helping her get away from the turd you married. For your cruelty to her, you've earned your fate."

He slipped his knife between her ribs and cut upward to her heart, ending her life only seconds before he tossed her into the acid pool below.

King roused enough to scream and stretch his broken arms toward her. Owen knelt beside him. "Don't worry. You'll see her in hell shortly." He pushed King after his wife, then walked away.

29

O wen walked at first, then walked faster, then ran back toward the Syadne tower. He prayed that Addy was still alive, that she might rally enough to see her son before she passed. God, he hoped she was still alive. What were the chances that Max was able to get into the Omni system and crack the code that was killing her?

He took the stairs by twos and threes, then rushed into the room where he'd left Addy with Beck, Max, and Angel when Kit had alerted them that King was in the elevator.

Addy was still lying where he'd set her. Augie was draped over her stomach, crying. Owen looked over to Beck, who was standing behind Max. He shook his head.

"We got in, boss," Max said, without looking back at Owen. "Greer and Nathan have control of the application. They're making some adjustments."

Owen knelt next to Addy and took her hand. It was cold. How much longer could she hold on? He put his hand on his boy's back. "Beetle. Augie." The boy looked at him. "I'm your father."

His son blinked. He thought Augie might argue. Instead, he looked at Lion for confirmation. Lion nodded. Augie's chin trembled. He threw himself at Owen. Owen held him tight.

"You killed him, didn't you? You killed Edwards? He hurt my mom so much." Augie sniffled. "I thought he'd killed her when he took me. I never thought I'd see her again."

"He's done," Owen said. "He's not going to hurt anyone anymore. We're going to stay here with your mom. My men have a way to help her."

"Is she going to live?"

"Yes. Yes, she is."

"Got it!" Max shouted. He lurched out of his seat and hurried over to them. He knelt beside Addy and pushed a button on his phone. Nothing happened. "How will I know it worked, Nathan? Nothing's happening."

"The app shows the nanos received the signal," Nathan said. "Give it a minute."

Doc Beck came over and took her pulse. Owen moved to her shoulders and drew her up over his lap. Wrapping his arms around her shoulders, he put his face against hers. "C'mon, Addy. You can do this. You're stronger than this. This is the last time you'll have to fight back from anything. Augie's here. Troy's waiting for you at home. C'mon, Laidy."

The room went quiet. Doc Beck pressed his fingers against her throat. Owen looked up at him and saw him shake his head.

"No. No. Goddammit. No."

Doc Beck looked crushed as he got up and moved away.

Owen shoved his face against Addy's hair and cried. When he looked up a minute later, his team had come into the room. Lobo, too. They stood as silent witnesses to Addy's passing and the black hole of Owen's grief. He bent his head and kissed her hair. She still smelled so much like his Laidy. How was he ever going to live without her?

"Dad. Look. She opened her eyes," Augie said.

They were open. Was it just a death reflex?

Addy arched her back and gasped for breath. Beck ran to her side, but he needn't have bothered. She reached up and held Owen's arm in a weak grasp, then turned to her son.

"Mom!" Augie said. "You are alive."

She tried to lift her arm, but didn't have the strength. Augie hugged her.

Owen put his face in his hand and tried to calm the pain in his heart. His team was laughing and hugging each other.

"She's coming out of it," Nathan said. "We're getting a read on her vitals from the nanos. She's going to be okay, Owen."

"But we have to stop this from happening to anyone else," Joyce said, her voice coming from a little farther away than Nathan's.

"We do. And we will. We have control of this lab now," Lobo said.

"What now?" Owen asked the Ratcliffs. "Does she need to go to the hospital?"

"I don't think they could help her," Nathan said. "They don't have the specialized equipment of the sort she might need. But it looks like it's reversing itself. She really just needs rest and monitoring. Bring her home, Owen."

"Addy, I'm going to take you out of here. Just close your eyes. Augie and I have you," Owen said. A tear slipped from the corner of her eye. Owen scooped her up, blankets and all, and started for the elevator. "Val, bring one of the cars around. Augie, hold your mom's hand so she knows you're with us."

Half the group got in the elevator with them. Val was in the front so he could get off first. When they arrived at the warehouse floor, he opened the horizontal doors. Standing there to greet them was his dad, Jason Parker.

"Hello, son," he said, grinning.

The team shifted fast, moving in front of Owen and Augie, blocking them. Val got off the elevator and shut the doors. The elevator started to descend. Owen didn't know if Val had sent it away or if someone below had summoned it. They heard a shot, and then another.

Ace screamed Val's name. She hit the button for the warehouse floor over and over.

It took forever for the elevator to go back up. When they got to the top again, Kelan held Ace back while Angel cracked the heavy doors just a bit. First thing they saw was a pool of blood. And two bodies. One prone…one sitting.

Ace shoved the doors wide and ran out. Val was leaning against a post, holding his arm. Blood was seeping between his fingers. Jason was on his back, a bullet hole in his head. The pool of blood was coming from him.

"I got to do it my way, Ace. I got to look him in the eyes."

Ace kissed him, then kissed him a thousand times all over his face. Doc Beck cut off Val's sleeve and applied a makeshift bandage to his upper bicep.

"Get the helicopter," Owen said. "Kit, go with them. Ace—I want Beck to check your arm out, too. That cast's looking a little worse for the wear. Send the helo back in case anyone else here needs it. I'll get a car over to you when we get to Blade's."

"*Hey, O,*" Kit said via their comms a few minutes later when they were up in the helicopter.

"Go, Kit."

"*You should see this place from the air. It's lit up like a Christmas holiday.*"

Owen laughed. "Guess that'll keep them busy for a while. You get an update from Lobo?"

"Only that the site's under control. I'm sure he'll swing by when he can. What about Roberta and King?"

"Dead."

"And Santo?"

"Dead," Ace said.

"Jafaar?"

"In FBI custody," Rocco said.

"And Pete?"

"Lives to fight another day," Max said.

"Call us from the hospital when you get an update on Val," Owen said.

"Roger that," Kit said.

On the car ride home, Addy was again stretched across the backseat, her head on Owen's lap. This time, though, her feet were on her son's lap. He stared at her the whole way home, holding one of her hands. Owen grew worried when she closed her eyes. He stroked her face, easing a bit of hair from her temple. She smiled without opening her eyes.

When the SUV pulled up to the front of the house, Owen thought every light in the house was on. They were going to walk into a mob of people, all of whom had become his family. He reached over and gripped his son's shoulder. "Augie, I have to warn you, we live with a big group. They can be overwhelming. It's a lot of families. They're good people. They're our family. You'll be safe here."

"Is Lion here?" Augie asked.

"He will be soon. My team is bringing them home."

"Okay."

Owen lifted Addy out of the vehicle. Selena, who'd driven them home, opened the front door. Owen carried Addy up the stairs. He heard the noise when Sel first opened the door, then heard the silence that followed. He couldn't stop smiling as he walked inside, Addy in his arms and his boy right behind them.

As expected, they were swarmed by everyone who'd stayed behind. After a minute, they made way for him so he could set Addy down on the sofa. Augie remained standing beside her protectively. Owen put a hand on his shoulder. "Everyone, this is my son, Augie."

Owen saw movement at the top of the stairs, then three kids charged down them and into the living room.

"Augie!" Troy shouted as he launched himself at his brother.

Augie laughed and caught him. After a long hug, he held his brother's shoulders and pushed him back half a step. "You got big, Troy."

Troy laughed and swiped the moisture from his cheeks. "So did you." He looked at his mom, who was smiling. Gently, so not to jostle her, he climbed up next to her on the sofa. He touched her face. "Mom? Are you okay?"

"I will be, sweetheart. I just need a little rest."

"Okay." Troy looked at Owen for confirmation.

Owen nodded and smiled. "The Ratcliffs say she's going to be fine." He looked around at the group. The guys would have checked in already, but he wanted to give them an update and hear what happened here after they left. "Everyone here okay?"

"We are," Greer said. "It was quiet. We were never the focus."

"Val took a round in his arm," Owen said. "Kit and Ace are with him at the clinic, where Doc Beck is patching him up. The rest of the team is staying to help lock down the site. King, Roberta, Santo, and Jason are all dead. The FBI has Jafaar. It's over. For now."

Owen watched Greer's reaction to that news. Of course, he knew it already.

Greer ground his teeth. "The first phase is over. We still have to get ahead of these human modification formulas."

"Indeed," Owen said. "Greer, can you get a car over to pick everyone up from the clinic? They should be almost finished over there."

"Roger that." He kissed Remi, then left the room.

"We'll talk more tomorrow. Right now, I need to get Addy tucked in." Owen stood and lifted Addy. The boys followed them back to his room like little ducks. He loved it.

Owen set her on his bed. "Is there anything you need? Water?"

She nodded. "Please. I'm so thirsty."

Troy ran into the bathroom and came out with a cup for her. Owen helped her sit up so she could drink. When he took the cup from her, she reached her hands out to her boys. "Look at you, both here together." She shook her head. "There were times I feared never seeing this again."

"I thought you were dead, Mom. I saw my da"— he looked at Owen—"Mr. Edwards hit you so hard, you flipped over and didn't get up."

Addy rubbed Augie's hand. "That was the worst day of my life. But that and all those bad days are over now. Tomorrow, I want to hear all about your time with the watchers."

"Mom needs some rest now," Owen said. "Tomorrow's a big day for catching up." He kissed Addy's forehead. "I'm going to get them settled, then I'll come back in. I won't be long."

"I love you," she said.

"I love you too. You have no idea."

The boys each hugged Addy, then Owen led them from his room into theirs. "Augie, you'll share this room with Troy, for now." He looked at his son's clothes, seeing the homespun wool top and pants, the leather moccasins, the lambs-wool vest. "I don't have anything for you to wear. I can grab one of my tees for you—"

"I'm fine, sir. I don't need anything else."

Owen set his hand on his boy's head. He looked like a mini-Owen—same pale eyes, same white-blond hair Owen had had at that age. He really was his boy. "This is a lot of change in a short time. I know we have some things to work through. I hope you'll be patient with me. Having my son back is a big deal." He smiled. "How about you boys go brush your teeth? Then I'll tuck you in."

Owen followed them to the bathroom. Troy was already in his pajamas and ready for bed, so he showed Augie where the toothbrushes were. Augie washed his hands and face, then did his teeth. They both had to use the bathroom after that. Troy came out first. He got into the bed he always used.

"Is Mom coming back to sleep with us?" Troy asked.

Owen sat on the bed and put his hand on Troy's chest. "No, I think this will be your room with Augie. She's going to stay in mine."

Troy looked like he was about to tear up. What a hellish day the boy had had. Owen pulled him into his arms and hugged him. "It's all over, boy. Your mom's safe. Your brother's here. Edwards is dead." So were the boy's grandparents. Everything was different now. Troy settled back on his pillow. "Get some rest," Owen said. "We have a lot to do tomorrow. You have to show Augie all around."

Troy nodded. "Okay."

Owen went over and sat on Augie's bed. His son had taken on the same feral edge that all the watchers had. He was observant, quiet, and ready to bolt.

Owen gripped his shoulder. "I don't know what normal is, Augie. I've never been a dad before. I'd like for us to figure it out."

"Yes, sir."

Owen got up and walked to the short hallway, switching off the light as he went. "Night, boys."

"I'M glad you're back, Augie." Troy said. "I tried to do what you would do while you were gone. I took care of Mom."

"That's good, Troy."

"Do you think Owen'll be my dad, too?"

"Yeah, I do. Especially since I don't plan on staying here."

Troy pushed himself up to look over at Augie. "What do you mean? You just got back."

"I'm not a boy...I'm a cub. I belong with the pride. We look out for each other."

"We could look out for each other, too."

"Go to sleep, Troy."

OWEN WENT INTO HIS ROOM. Addy was sitting up. Every time he saw her, she had a little more color in her face. He smiled as he sat on the edge of his bed. He took her hand. It was still cool, so he tucked it under the covers.

"I told the boys you were sleeping in here with me from now on."

She smiled. "Okay." She stared into his eyes.

He was mesmerized by the slight shift in her eye color. He'd better warn Augie about that so he wouldn't freak out.

"Is it true that Cecil is dead?" she asked.

Owen nodded. "Yeah. And Roberta, Santo, and Jason Parker—Val's dad."

"It really is over."

"And it's just beginning. We still have to figure out about these nanos. I don't ever want someone to reprogram you like that."

She nodded. "I have faith in you."

That stole his breath.

"And our son's back." She smiled.

"He's going to have some adjusting to do."

"He'll do just fine. He's proud and strong and tough like his dad."

Owen smiled. "Are you hungry?"

"No. Just tired."

"Then I'm going to take a shower. I have to get Edwards' blood off me. After that, I need to check on my team. You go ahead and rest. Call me if you need me."

Val refused the wheelchair as they left the clinic. Ace and Greer flanked him, just in case his stubborn ass got dizzy.

"I'll go get the SUV," Greer said.

"I can walk," Val growled. "I'm fine. Besides, the pain meds haven't worn off."

They got Val into the backseat. Ace just stood there, next to the open passenger seat, trying to find the words to tell Greer about her fight with Santo. When she didn't move, Greer sent her a worried look.

"I'm sorry," she said to him.

"For what?"

"I want didn't want to kill Santo. I thought I did. I thought terminating one of Omni's Medusa heads was good, but things aren't so black and white for me anymore. He wanted me to kill him." She fought back tears. Assassins don't cry. Val reached out and took hold of the fingers sticking out of her fresh cast. "I wanted to hear his story. I wanted to make sense of what happened to us. I wanted him to face his family and tell them the truth. I wanted...I don't know...I wanted..."

"Justice," Greer said.

"Yeah."

Greer gave her a sad smile. "I think Justice is a myth, Ace. I'm not sure it really exists. I think we just take what we get and learn to live with it."

"I disappointed you."

Greer shook his head. "Oh, no. Not possible. I couldn't be more proud of you than I am right now." He pulled her into a hug. "Let's go home."

Val scooted over to make room for her next to

him. He pulled her in close and kissed the top of her head. "I'm proud of you, too."

30

Owen was bringing coffee to Addy the next morning, when he saw Troy come out of his room, rubbing his eyes. The boy came over and leaned against Owen's leg. Owen's hands were full, so he couldn't give him a hug or pick him up. It was weird and wonderful to have affection offered so openly.

"I'm taking Mom some coffee. Want to wake her up with me?"

Troy nodded and ran ahead into Owen's room. He hurried to the edge of the mattress, then slowly climbed up like a little cat prowling. Addy opened her eyes and smiled at him.

"Hi, Mom."

"Hi, baby."

Owen watched them hug. They talked about normal things, like the night's sleep and the coming day. Nothing about death or sickness or crazy murdering Omni bastards. Owen set the mugs down on his nightstand and got under the covers with them. This was what it was all about. Peace. Joy. And family.

Owen handed Addy her coffee and sipped his. "Where's Augie? Still sleeping?" he asked Troy.

"No. I don't know where he is. He wasn't in bed this morning."

Cold fear iced out all the warmth Owen had just been feeling. Addy sent him a panicked glance. Owen set his coffee down and used the team's security app on his phone to see where his son was. It indicated Augie was still in his room. Owen tossed the covers off and went to check. He wasn't there.

He sent a text out to the team, doubting they were on comms yet.

After the longest thirty seconds ever, Lion texted back. *I have him. We're out back talking.*

See me in the den when you're finished, Owen responded.

Copy.

Owen went back into his room. Addy was scrambling for a sweater to cover her pajamas. Owen caught her shoulders and gave her a reassuring smile. "He's with Lion. He's okay."

"You couldn't find him by his security necklace?" Addy asked.

"He didn't have it on."

"He can't take that off."

Owen nodded. "I'll talk to him about that." And other things.

Addy released a long sigh and leaned her head against his chest. Owen wrapped his arms around her slight body, feeling the softness of her breasts against his ribs. "Why don't we all get dressed so we can go to breakfast?" he said. He tilted his head and looked at Addy. "That is, if you're up to it."

"I am." She smiled.

Troy left the room as fast as he'd come in. Owen shook his head. "Your boy likes his breakfast."

Addy smiled. "That, and he gets to see Zavi."

Lion looked at Owen's son. His former cub. The boy had just begged him to let him stay with the pride. They walked out to the half-wall separating the two tiers of lawn.

"The thing is, Augie, you aren't one of us," Lion said. "We're orphans; you have parents—parents who are good people. Strong people. People who put you first. Every one of us in the pride would kill to have what you have, and you waste it. Pride members don't waste anything, least of all people."

Augie's shoulders slumped.

Lion put his arm around him. "I'm proud of you."

"For what?"

"For surviving."

"I was scared. I cried."

"I cry, too."

"You? When?"

"When it all gets to be too much. Then I usually round you all up, and we go do some training. Feels better to take action than to drown in fearful thoughts."

"I couldn't get out," Augie said. "I couldn't do anything. They just locked me in there. I didn't know if anyone knew where I was. *I* didn't know where I was."

"Your dad about lost his mind trying to find you. And you didn't know it at the time, but the watchers saw him put you in there. You were only there an hour or two."

Augie wiped his cheeks. "They said there were pools of acid near my room that they would drop me into. I didn't know what to do."

"You stayed calm. You stayed alive. Those were the right things to do." Lion gave Augie a sideways hug. "Go be a son. Be a brother. Be our friend. Don't be a jerk. Your parents were hurt by the Omnis, too. Not just physically, but mentally. They have wounds that need healing. Heal together. Be a family. Give us an ideal to look up to."

"Can I still train with you?"

"That's up to your parents, but I would welcome that."

Augie stood up and nodded at Lion. "Okay. I will."

OWEN STOOD at the French doors in the den, watching as Lion and Augie walked up from the lower terrace and parted ways. Augie went toward the entrance near their bedroom wing. Lion came toward him.

Owen opened the door and let Lion in. "What's going on?"

Lion shrugged. "Nothing you wouldn't expect."

"And what should I be expecting?"

Lion's smile was a little sad. "You know how we talked about keeping the pride together? That, in some cases, it might be more harmful to return boys to their families than it is leaving them with the watchers? That's the issue here."

"There's no issue. Augie belongs with his family."

"I agree. That's what I told him. But look at it from his perspective. For the last three years, he's been learning how to survive. That's a powerful way of living a boy doesn't let go of easily. There's nothing stronger any of us feels than to survive. We're how he's learned to live."

Owen leaned against the front of his desk. He'd asked Augie for patience and tolerance as they all learned to be a family. Those were luxurious emotions compared to an existential reality.

He looked at Lion. "What do I do?" Of all the adults here at Blade's, Lion knew the most about raising boys.

"Chill."

Fucking chill? Fuck that all the ways to hell and

back. He'd just gotten his son in his life. All four of them finally had a chance to come together to be a real family, and he was supposed to *fucking chill?*

He supposed his reaction to that directive showed on his face.

Lion smiled. "Boys are a lot like cats. Curious. Intelligent. Independent. If you want them to do what you want, you have to let them see it themselves. Lead him to the behavior you want. Otherwise, you're just herding cats and neither of you will ever be happy."

Owen sighed. Parenting was hard as hell. It was easier to face a bastard like Edwards while tied to a chair, getting beat up by his goons. "Okay."

Lion started for the door to the hallway, but stopped. "Augie wants to know if he can still train with us?"

Owen looked at Lion. Maybe that was the answer…the bridge to his son. A foot in both worlds, sure, but that wasn't a bad thing. "Yes, he can. Thanks, Lion."

OWEN LOOKED AROUND at the huge gathering in the team's main living room the next afternoon. A day had passed since the big fight at the WKB compound. Lion and his watchers were there, as were the entire team and their women and children and some of their parents. Max had even brought one of the biker

guys back with him. Everyone was visiting, reconnecting.

His team needed this time to regroup.

Owen had thought, when they'd first moved in to
Blade's, that it was way more space than they needed.
But if his group got any larger, he was going to have
find a bigger place. Addy sat next to him on the sofa.
Troy was on floor playing some game with Zavi.
Augie was over with Lion.

Addy had taken a shower this morning and then
attacked her breakfast like a teenaged boy. Her energy
was improving rapidly. So much had happened in
such a short amount of time, but she—and he—were
adapting well.

"Hey, guys," Jim said. "Don't know how this
passed your attention a few days ago, but we missed
Thanksgiving." He grinned. "Kinda miffed Russ. He
was looking forward to making the feast. We still have
all the fixings. It would be a shame to let them go to
waste. How about we make it happen tomorrow?"

Owen smiled at Addy. Thanksgiving. With everyone. She returned his smile and reached for his hand.
"I think that sounds like a great idea," he said.

Max frowned at his phone, then said something
that Owen didn't want to hear just then; "We got
incoming."

"Who is it?" Kit asked.

"Jax." Max looked at Owen. "He's got someone
with him."

Addy tried to get up, but Owen gave her a slight

shake of his head. He crossed the room and opened the door. He instantly knew the man with Jax. They stared at each other, not quite enemies, but not friends either.

And then the man held out his hand. "Son."

Owen looked over at Addy, then at his own son, then at Troy. Slowly, he reached out and took the offered handshake. "Dad. So it's true. You are alive." This wasn't how Owen had expected it would be. He was looking at man who was near his own age. Now he knew what Wynn had been feeling when she met her parents. His dad must have taken the same nanos that they had.

The man put his hand on Owen's shoulder. "You did it, son. You did what none of us was brave enough to do. You ended King."

Owen looked from his dad to Jax then back. "This mean you're King now?"

"Fuck no."

"So I don't have to fight you?"

"No." The man sighed. "I knew how I'd raised you, and I knew I was giving you over to my enemies to finish raising...but I didn't know which side of this war you'd end up on. I should have guessed it would be the right side."

Owen shook his head. "All those years, all that time, you were alive and in hiding. This could have been ended years ago if you'd just come forward."

"We can't always have the benefit of hindsight when we're facing the future."

"Whatever the fuck that means…"

Jax punched his shoulder. "O. Take a breath. I brought you your father. We've got work to do. The Omnis are down but not out. Now can I come in and say hello to my sister and nephews?"

Owen stepped back. "Everyone, my dad, Nick Tremaine. And Addy's brother, Wendell Jacobs."

Addy got up. She didn't yet have the steam to run forward, so she just waited for Wendell to come to her. She hugged him tight. When they parted, Jax looked shocked as he stared at her.

"Whoa. Nick said they'd started you on the nanos, but I didn't think they were a different kind than what he'd taken," Jax said.

Addy nodded. "That's why I was so sick."

"How are you feeling now?"

"Considering the Omnis just cyberhacked her nanos and almost killed her…she's doing great," Owen said as he came to stand next to her. He held a hand out to Jax. "You staying for a while? We just realized we missed Thanksgiving. You're welcome to join us."

Jax smiled at him. "I'd like that. Can't remember the last T-day I celebrated." He looked around him, "Where are my nephews?"

Troy and Augie came over to hug him.

"Boys, this is my dad, Nick," Owen said. "This is your granddad, Augie."

Augie frowned. The kids who'd had anything to do with the Omni world had a keenly developed sense of suspicion. Owen regretted that, but respected it too.

"You don't look like a granddad," Augie said.

Nick wasn't offended. "I don't. It's true. The world is changing, Augie, in unexpected ways."

"I hope you're going to be here a while, Dad," Owen said. "I'd like to catch up with you."

Nick gave Owen a long, hard look, then nodded. "I'd like that, too, son."

Owen put his arm around Addy. "Dad, you remember Addy Jacobs."

Nick took her hand and gave her a sad smile. "It's been a long time, Addy. Jax has told me a lot about you. I'm so glad Owen found you again."

"Thanks, Nick." She smiled as she leaned against Owen. "I am, too."

KIT SAT on the sheriff's doorstep, waiting for him to come home. His shift should have ended a while ago. A patrol car came around the corner and parked in front of the house.

The sheriff slammed his door shut. "Goddamn it, boy. I'm getting tired of seeing you." He walked up to his porch.

Kit grinned. "It's over."

The sheriff's gray brows lifted. "Is it?"

"For now."

"What about that human extinction event?"

"On hold. That part's not over."

"So does this mean you're clearing outta my town?"

Kit's grin widened. "Not yet. Don't know the plan, but the immediate threat has been terminated. Jerry still in your jail?"

"No. The FBI picked him up. How about that Jason Parker? You get him?"

"We did."

"And that little gal Jerry tried to kill?"

"She's back on her feet."

"So I can breathe easy, then?"

"For now. Ivy sent me over to see if you'd consider joining us for a make-up Thanksgiving dinner tomorrow. Seems with everything going on, we just passed it by. I'd like it if you'd come."

Sheriff Tate slowly smiled. "Guess I could do that. What time?"

"Around one?"

"I'll be there."

Kit got up and went down the stairs to shake hands with him. "Thanks, sheriff. For everything."

THE WIND WAS COLD. Owen thought the temperature was supposed to warm up a bit, but right now, the damp chilly air cut to the bone. He was glad he'd had Addy put her coat on, but he was too nervous to grab his. He had a hand in his jeans pocket. At least one hand was warm. The other held a carved wooden box. Her freedom. His hell. He tried not to think of what he was about to do.

When he looked over at her, she was framed by the gray clouds behind her. Her nose was already pink.

"What did you want to see me about?" she asked.

He gritted his teeth. "Your freedom." He handed her the box. It wasn't heavy, and yet the weight it placed on him felt a metric fuck ton of lonely. "Here."

She looked at the box but didn't reach for it. What kind of life did they live that a gift was a burden? He wanted to smash it, but doing that was as good as putting her in chains. "Take it."

She did, but held it as if it contained a mass of spiders. "What's in it?"

"Open it."

"I don't want to."

"I need you to."

Cautiously, she lifted the lid. Inside was a long, folded legal document. She took it out and tucked the box under one arm as she read it. She looked at him, tears pooling in her eyes. "I don't understand."

"I wish it could have been written for a human instead of a lawyer, which I'm not. The gist is that I'm giving you a million dollars to start your life. You and the boys. Anywhere. You can do anything. It specifically states that I have no say in your life. You may seek my advice if you wish, but you're under no obligation to take it. Ever."

"I still don't understand."

"It's your freedom, Addy. My Laidy. Your life is yours. Freedom isn't mine to give, but I am anyway. Someone had to. You could go back to school and get your masters. You could start a business. You can do anything with this seed money. Give it away, if you want. Of course, I'll still pay for the boys' education, up to and including college."

Tears spilled down her cheeks. He had to look away.

"You want me to leave."

"No."

"Then why do this?"

"You've never been free to make your life what you wanted it to be."

"Neither have you. We were both born into this hell."

Owen shrugged. "I feel as if I've made my choices consciously. Except for losing you. You didn't get to do that…until now. You've never been able to make choices about your own life."

"What if I don't want to go?"

He blinked, silently screaming for her to pick that choice.

"What if I choose you? Is that an option?" she asked.

"Yes."

"I can still go to school while I'm with you, no?"

"You can."

"I can still make a career while I'm with you."

"Of course."

"I can still have my freedom and have you."

Owen huffed a breath. "I would gladly beg you to stay."

She shut her eyes and shook her head. "Then why do this?"

"Because it has to be your choice."

She gave a pained sigh. "Tell me what you want, Owen. In your words. Let me see it in your eyes." She put her hand on his chest. "Let me feel it in your heart."

He covered her warm hand with his ice-cold one. "Addy, stay with me. You own my heart. If you go, I'll die." He shrugged. It was as simple as that.

Addy pulled free, then knelt on the ground and opened the beautiful box. She tore the contract into pieces and dropped them inside it. Then, standing, she slammed her heel down on it, again and again, crushing it into little slivers. Her eyes had gone orange. She looked furious, absolutely on fire, as she glared at him.

"Don't you ever put me in a box, Owen Tremaine. I won't stand for it."

She pivoted and started back toward the house at a fast pace. He frowned at the shattered box, then rushed after. "Addy, wait!" She didn't. He ran and caught her up, spinning her around.

"Put me down."

"No."

"I said put me down."

"No. Not while you're mad at me."

"I'm not *mad*. I'm furious."

A ray of sun was just peeking through the clouds. He turned her to catch the golden light. God, she was gorgeous. A thing of shifting lights and colors, a mystery caught in a prism. He would never understand her, but holding her gave him extreme joy. "Does this mean you're staying with me?"

She caught his face. He could see her struggling to find the right words. "Owen, I'm not *staying*...because I was never *leaving*. I love you. I *love* you. Don't you see?"

"Yes. I do see." He didn't see. Was she or wasn't she his?

She looped her arms around his neck. "Then put a ring on my finger and change my name. I can tell I have my work cut out for me with you."

He laughed, then tossed his head back and laughed even harder. She was his. Forever.

EPILOGUE

Casey grabbed the white cardigan that her mom had forced she wear to the dinner. She hated having to cover up her pretty dress, but Mom insisted, since they were eating outside on the patio. Heaters were set up all around the two long tables. It wasn't needed, but when she'd tried to reason with Mom, Dad had given her that look, the awful one he probably gave his men.

Her dress, a sleeveless deep pink taffeta that was fitted in the bodice but flared out from the waist, was perfect. She turned sideways, admiring the feminine curve of her bust, aided by the slightly padded bra she was wearing. She couldn't wait to see Zoe next summer at camp—she was finally getting breasts.

The day wasn't entirely ruined. Mom did let her wear a pair of black patent-leather, low-heeled pumps, probably because Uncle Val had picked them out for her, as he had her dress. They were from a shopping trip several of them had taken a while back to get the pride some clothes.

She was hurrying over to Miss Wynn's apartment. They were going to go down to the pride to make sure they were all dressed in their new outfits that they hadn't had a chance yet to wear. They'd been practicing tying ties. So had she. She hoped Lion needed help with his.

She couldn't think about that now, or she'd be all tongue-tied when she saw him.

Uncle Angel opened the door to Miss Wynn's. "Hello, Casey. You look very beautiful. Here to help Miss Wynn with the boys?"

"Yup. Is she ready?"

"I am!" Miss Wynn called from her kitchen. Casey heard the oven doors close and went to see what she was doing. The whole apartment smelled of cinnamon and apples. Wynn grinned at Casey as she set a Dutch apple pie on the counter next to another two already cooling.

"I promised Russ I'd make the pies for today. Three Dutch apple, three pumpkin pie, three pecan."

"Yum. I might skip the turkey and go right for dessert," Casey said, smiling. "Are you coming with us, Uncle Angel?"

None of Dad's men were truly uncles, except for Rocco, since he was married to Dad's sister. But Zavi called them all aunts and uncles, so she did too. It was a big family she had now, something she used to only dream about when she and Mom were alone.

"Not me," Uncle Angel said. "I'm the pie delivery boy."

Miss Wynn kissed him. "Let the apple pies cool a little first."

He caught her around the waist and drew her back to him before she could hurry off. "Hey. Happy Thanksgiving. Our first together."

Miss Wynn's eyes got teary before she hugged him. "Thank you."

Uncle Angel laughed. "No, ma'am. Thank you."

Miss Wynn smiled at her as they stepped through the door.

"Why did you thank him?" Casey asked in the hallway.

"Because I'm grateful he came into my life, brought me in to the big family we have today. That's what Thanksgiving's all about, isn't it? Being thankful?"

"Yeah. Do you think the boys figured out their ties?"

"We'll see. Some of them seemed to have it figured out. Knowing Lion, they probably practiced it a lot when we weren't there."

The boys were in the basketball court, where their classes were held. They looked different than they did wearing their wild-boy clothes. Today, they were wearing beige khaki trousers, white Oxford shirts, blue jackets, and blue striped ties.

A couple of free-standing mirrors had been set up for them to use during their tie-tying lessons. The younger boys couldn't figure it out, but had made interesting knots and seemed satisfied with that. Some of the older boys did have their ties properly done, but were having a devil of a time helping others tie theirs.

Lion wasn't one of those. Her heart stopped for a whole beat when she saw that he did need help. Miss Wynn gave her a small smile that made warmth rise on Casey's neck. She didn't hear what the teacher said, but the boys having problems crowded close for help. She fixed three of them. Then Fox was there, tugging at his shirt and jacket.

"You look very handsome, Fox," Casey told him.

"I don't care about that. I hate this. I can't move. I can't run or fight."

"But it's a party. You don't have to do those things," Casey said.

He yanked his tie out to the side and mimicked choking. "Our enemies could hang us with these."

"No one's going to hang you today," Uncle Max said as he joined them. "And if you want to look like a human, you have to dress like one. Besides, the rest of your pride—and all of us—are wearing suits."

Casey's heart fell when Uncle Max went straight toward Lion, but Miss Wynn redirected him. "Max, can you untangle Owl's tie? Somehow he's gotten it in a knot."

Oh, God. That meant that Casey really was going to get to help Lion with his. Her mouth went dry as she went up to him. Would he notice how her curves stood out so nicely in this dress? Or the lemon-scented bath wash she'd used?

"Can't do it?" she asked, trying not to smile as she looked at him.

"No." He looked disgruntled.

"Want some help?"

"You ever wear a tie before?"

"Sometimes. Girls can wear anything they want." She couldn't let him know she'd been practicing for this very moment.

He put his hands on his hips. "Do your worst. It has to be better than my worst. Which is every damned time."

She smiled. He handed her the tie. She reached up to unbutton the wings of his collar. It seemed he'd gotten taller than when she'd first met him. And she was wearing heels today. His body was hard beneath her wrists. She tried not to linger, shooting him a quick glance to see if he'd noticed her touching him. She flipped his collar up. "You have to bend closer so I can get this around your neck."

He did. She almost fainted…and then he sniffed her, making her skin tingle. "You smell good. Is that lemon?" he asked.

Casey knew she had to be blushing because her neck and face felt on fire. "Yes." She made short work of doing his tie, then drew him close so she could fold his collar over his tie and button it down again. She didn't lift her gaze above his neck the whole time. And when she finished that, she adjusted the lie of the tie, smoothing her hand over it down his chest.

"Thanks, sweet pea. Your best is a whole lot better than my worst."

"Sure." She stepped back, wishing, *wishing* that had taken a lot longer to do. The rest of the boys were all tidied up. She met Max's gaze and got a raised eyebrow from him.

Aunt Hope came in then, thankfully stealing his focus. The boys began filing out. Jim had promised all kinds of delicious-sounding appetizers to hold everyone until dinner. The feast was scheduled early, so they'd all skipped lunch.

Hope checked Lion, then kissed his cheek. "I'm so happy we're together, Lion."

He gave his sister a big hug. "Me too."

Casey followed Miss Wynn and the boys out.

MAX DREW Hope into his arms as the gym cleared. "You see Lion and Casey together? I think I need to tell that boy how to play it cool with the girls."

Hope looked shocked. "Casey's thirteen. He is not thinking about her, so you'll do no such thing, Mads."

He grinned and kissed her.

"Is that playing it cool?" she asked.

"No. That's me, hot as fuck for you. We could be late to the feast…"

"Not a chance. We're all here, all of us together.

And the war is over. Mostly. I don't want to miss a minute of today."

He kissed her forehead. "I love you."

She sighed. "I love you too."

OWEN REACHED over to take Addy's hand. Everyone was out on the wide patio, sitting at two rows of tables. Russ and Jim had made everything look amazing, with tablecloths, autumn flower arrangements, and little gourds scattered here and there.

The entire pride, who looked great in their suits, were enjoying the feast. His fighters were relaxed and happy. All down the line, the families sat together. Ty's dad was there. So was the sheriff. Even Owen's dad. Jax sat across from Addy. Troy was next to her, but Augie was with the watchers. Owen tried not to fixate on that. His son was here. Safe. The rest they could work on. It just wasn't easy seeing the sadness in Addy's eyes when she looked over at her boy, who was sitting with his back to them. Maybe it was time he had a talk with him.

A convo Val was having midway down the table caught his attention. "…So I guess Ace and I will be going to physical therapy together in a few weeks."

"And we just have to walk out to the stables for our sessions," Ace said.

Val frowned and looked from Ace to Mandy. "Don't tell me I have to ride a horse."

"Nah, Val, you don't have to ride one," Rocco said. "Mandy knows how fussy you are. You can bench press one so you can get your arm strength back."

Mandy laughed. "Look at it this way, Val. If you do start riding, you can get a whole new wardrobe…"

Val's brows went up. He smiled at Ace. "I would look good in a cowboy hat."

Blade shook his head. "Nothing like a rhinestone cowboy to put a shine on the place."

Owen felt an odd swelling in his chest. It was happiness, through and through. He looked at Addy, wondering if she felt the same. He'd never expected to have so large a family, and now he couldn't imagine life any other way.

OWEN WAS in the sitting room outside in his bedroom wing with Addy and Troy that evening. She was reading her son a bedtime story. It had been a hectic day. It was nice getting to unwind with them. There was just one thing missing: Augie.

Owen's phone buzzed. *Partners' meeting. Den. 5 min.*

"Hey. I have to go talk to Val." Owen kissed Addy. "Wait up for me, okay?"

"We will. You'll go get Augie afterwards? I think he's still with the pride. It's time for bed," Addy said.

"You bet."

Owen got to the den first. Val closed the door

behind him, then perched himself on the arm of the sofa.

"What's up?" Owen asked.

"Today was a good day."

Owen nodded, waiting for Val to get to the point.

Val read his impatience and grinned. "Just wanted to touch base, see how you're doing. I'm glad the guys know and are cool with my being a silent partner."

"Silent, right," Owen scoffed.

"So how are you doing with the dad stuff?"

Owen sighed. "I'll figure it out."

"I don't doubt it. But what's it like?"

Owen absently stared at the edge of the carpet that framed the sitting area of the den. "It makes my heart hurt. I get the feeling Augie doesn't want to be my son."

"I don't think that's true. He doesn't know you yet. When you were gone, your absence affected all of us. For a quiet guy, your not being here was sure loud. You're not a helluva lot older than I am, but you pull us all together. Like a dad. Augie will learn that about you in time."

"I hope so."

"He hasn't had a lot of experience with dads. The first one he had really fucked him over. Then three years with the watchers, which was probably the best thing that could have happened to him under the circumstances. Lion, and whoever was his leader before that, were good guys. But being a cub is his norm now. Fitting in, being needed…having something important to do. Somehow, you may need to appeal to that. Talk to him. Listen to him. He's not a fighter waiting to take orders. He's a boy who needs to know there's a spot for him in his family."

"Of course there's a spot for him."

"You know that and I know that, but does he?"

"I just don't know how any of this works." He looked over at Val. "It's not like we had normal childhoods to pull from."

"Who does? What the fuck is normal anyway?" Val laughed. "We all just survive our childhoods so we can spend a fortune on shrinks. You aren't going to go wrong with him…or not so bad the shrinks won't be able to fix, anyway."

Owen laughed. "Great."

"So what's the plan with Addy? She's not out of the woods yet, not when someone with an app can still take her out."

"We'll continue to work with the Ratcliffs and the other scientists my dad found. Thing is, they said the nanos need periodic renewal. I don't know how frequent that is, but she only had one dose—from the bee sting, I'm guessing. Unless the doctors who examined her gave her more of the modifying agent. I wonder if she's one of the people whose physiology is taking over from the nanos. On the one hand, we may be able to just let the nanos wear out and pass from her system. On the other hand, she may have to maintain a certain level of them. I don't know. But I don't like the idea that she will be forever young, while I age and die."

"You could take the modifications, too."

"Addy and I talked about that. But what's it like never getting old? Living longer than your children and friends?" He shook his head. "This is not something I ever expected to deal with."

"Talk to your dad. Ask him. He looks like your brother now. It's so fucked up that it's cool."

"And we're definitely going to need to increase or improve our technology. Anywhere Addy goes, she's going to need to be protected from another cyberattack. And I don't know what may happen to Wynn from the bumblebee that stung her. Maybe it was just a sedative that was delivered. Maybe it was the nanos."

"We need our own lab."

"We do. I'll talk to Ratcliffs, Doc Beck, and my dad. We could build one here, but there might be another place that makes more sense, like at the clinic."

"And what about Jax? We joining forces with his team?"

"Yeah. I think so. We have a lot to still figure out."

Val got up and came over to put a hand on Owen's shoulder. "Okay. Just remember, you aren't in this alone."

"Thanks, Val."

It wasn't until the next morning that Owen caught Augie by himself. He and Addy wanted to break the news to the boys that they were going to be married. His boy's security necklace placed him in the movie room. Alone.

The room was dark. A faint bluish glow came from the blank screen. Augie was sitting in the back row. Owen sat next to him. "Want me show you how it works? Might be more fun than watching nothing."

Augie shrugged.

"Want to talk?" Owen asked.

"No."

"Mind if I talk?"

Augie shrugged again. "Go ahead."

Owen suddenly didn't know what to say. How do you tell your own flesh and blood everything that's in your heart when there's no foundation to base it on? Jeez, how the hell do you talk to a kid?

Augie looked at him. "You got something to say or not?"

Owen looked at the blank screen. "I have so much to say that I don't know how to do it in a way that makes sense. I didn't know about you until a few weeks ago. When I learned your mom and I had a son, my whole life shifted. For a long time, it hadn't been about anything. And suddenly, it was. I know you're a kid and that probably doesn't make any sense at all. One day, we'll tell you what happened and how it was that I didn't know about you." He looked at his boy. "I would just like to say that I'm very glad to have you in my life. I have no idea how to be a dad, but I'll figure it out."

Augie nodded. "I don't know much about being a son. I was a good cub."

"I know you were. I'm proud of you for that. Being a cub isn't something just any boy could do."

"I thought my old dad killed Mom the day they took me." Tears were filling his son's pale blue eyes.

"She was hurt pretty bad. Spent a while in the hospital. She's one tough lady, your mom."

"What's going to happen to her with her sickness?"

"I don't know yet. It's brand new territory for all of us. I do know she's safe here. You and your brother are safe here. We have the experts on hand to help us work through this. We'll take it a day at a time and figure it out."

"What if she dies?" The tears that had been gathering splashed down Augie's cheeks.

Owen shook his head. "I can't even think about that. I'd be wrecked. You and Troy would be crushed. But the truth is, life would go on. It has a way of healing. Maybe it's just its relentless march forward that stops for no one. If something happens to your mom, you'd still have me. And if something happens to me, then one of my friends here will take you and Troy into their families. You know why?"

Augie shook his head, his eyes still swimming tears.

"Because that's what families do. And that's what

we are. It's pretty damned awesome. There is one thing I'm going to need your help with eventually."

"What's that?"

"When it's safe to do so, we may try to reconnect Lion's cubs and the boys from other prides with their families."

"Lion said the watchers were orphans."

Owen nodded. "Some of them are. But some may still have families out there who are sick with worry like your mom and I were when we didn't have you. You may need to help them make that transition."

"What if they don't want to go?"

"That's something we'll have to work through. They should never have been taken from their families in the first place. You reconnecting with us will be a help to them down the line, when and if that's something they may face. You good with that?"

"Yeah. I could do that, Dad."

Owen smiled at his son. "Thanks, son. Now let's go find your mom. She and I have some news for you boys."

They stood, but before they could walk out of the movie room, Augie had another question. "When you and Mom get married, will you be Troy's dad, too?"

"How'd you know we were getting married?"

"Your men were watching you from the living room windows the other day."

Owen shook his head. There was no frickin' privacy here. "So that's the news Mom and I wanted to break to you boys. Pretend you're surprised and delighted. And about Troy—you bet I'll be his dad, too. I love you both very much."

Augie hugged him. Owen returned the embrace, feeling happier than he'd ever been or ever even knew he could be.

OWEN HAD a hand on Augie's back when they joined Addy and Troy in the little living room in their suite. Addy studied Owen's face, terribly nervous to see how his talk with their son had gone. Looked like it went pretty well.

"So, boys, Mom and I have some news for you." Owen looked at her. "Do you want to tell them or should I?"

"You go ahead."

"Mom and I are getting married." He grinned.

Augie hugged Addy, then hugged him. "That's great."

Addy looked at Troy. He looked a little sad. "Does this mean I have to go be a cub now, since you aren't my dad?"

Owen looked shocked. He knelt in front of Troy. "I can understand that thinking, but that would break my heart. I already consider you my son. Our marriage just makes it official. I'd really like to be your dad."

Addy started to cry silent tears.

Troy looked at her then jumped into Owen's

arms. "I thought you were going to get rid of me, since you had Augie back."

Owen tried to chuckle, but it just came out like a choked sound. "What kind of father does that sort of thing?" He hugged Troy, then squeezed his head against his face and kissed his temple. "Not the kind of father I am." He reached a hand over to Addy, who took Augie's hand, too. "We're a family. We stick together."

Troy climbed off Owen's lap and onto Addy's. "Okay. Then you can get married."

Augie laughed. Owen leaned forward and hugged Addy around Troy.

"I guess it's official. We're going to be Tremaines soon," Addy said, smiling as Owen gave her a quick kiss.

"Do I get to call you Dad?" Troy asked.

Owen's brow lifted. "Try calling me anything else."

Dear Reader,

I hope you've enjoyed the Red Team series. Your emails, reviews, and enthusiasm have made it so much fun to write these stories!

You may have noticed that while so much of the storyline from this first set of books has been wrapped up, some things have not, and still other new things have been introduced toward the end of this series, leaving us no time to explore them. As you close this last page and have that sense of dread that the Red Team series is over--fear not!

I've always felt this first set of stories in the Red Team made up Season One. The adventures will continue in Season Two.

My next series is a spinoff of the Red Team featuring new heroes, new bad guys, and new couples, all in the Omni World discovered by the Red Team. In fact, Selena will be in the new series, which I'm calling "O-Men: Liege's Legion."

After I finish Season Two, I can see another series for Lion and his pride. And still another for all the secondary Red Team characters you've written to me about (Fang, Lobo, Jax, and Nick...) who need their own happily-ever-afters. The O-Men have several mini-series or seasons still to go!

The first O-Men book will be out in 2018. I hope you'll go on a new and wild ride with me as we start Season Two!

Warm hugs,
Elaine

PS - I would love it if you could take a minute and leave a review right here. A sentence or two is all that's needed. Doing so will help other readers find this series!

OTHER BOOKS BY ELAINE LEVINE

11 Freedom Code

Men of Defiance Series

(This series may be read in any order.)

ABOUT THE AUTHOR

Elaine Levine lives in the mountains of Colorado with her husband and a rescued pit bull/bull mastiff mix. In addition to writing the Red Team romantic suspense series, she's the author of several books in the historical western romance series Men of Defiance. She also has a novel in the multi-author series, Sleeper SEALs.

Be sure to sign up for her new release announcements at http://geni.us/GAlUjx.

If you enjoyed this book, please consider leaving a review at your favorite online retailer to help other readers find it.

Get social! Connect with Elaine online:
    Reader Group: http://geni.us/2w5d
    Website: https://www.ElaineLevine.com
    email: elevine@elainelevine.com